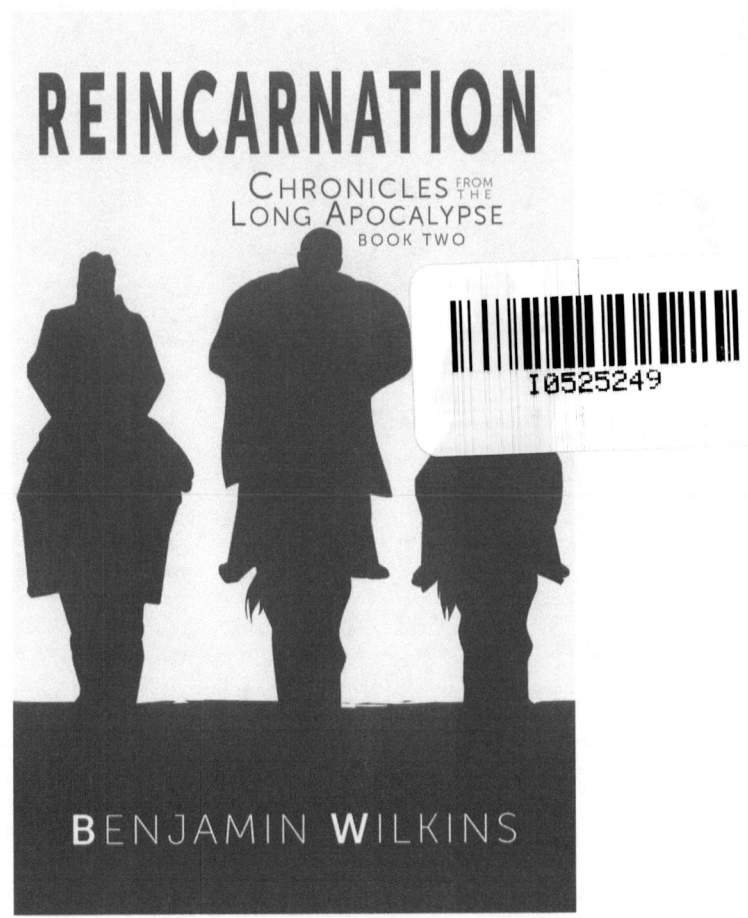

REINCARNATION

CHRONICLES FROM THE
LONG APOCALYPSE
BOOK TWO

BENJAMIN WILKINS

I0525249

Free Download

Sign up for the author's New Releases mailing list and get a free copy of the second book in the Chronicles from the Long Apocalypse series for your trouble.

Follow the link below to get started:

http://www.benjaminwilkins.com/list_signup2

TRANSCENDENCE

TRANSCENDENCE

CHRONICLES FROM THE
LONG APOCALYPSE

BOOK ONE

BENJAMIN WILKINS

WILSON
BOULEVARD
PRESS

First Edition

Printed in the United States of America

Jacket design by Benjamin Wilkins

ISBN 978-0-9979086-0-2

Wilson Boulevard Press
Sedona, Arizona

www.wilsonblvdpress.com

FOR TEDDY

May your future be forever and completely
devoid of the horrors contained herein.

AND JOSEPHINE

You are the light balancing
the scales of my stormy dark.

Prologue

The Father in New England
a Decade before This Story Begins...

N O SWITCH WAS FLIPPED or button pressed. No infection broke out and ran amok, killing the lucky ones and turning the rest of us into zombies. The end of the world as we knew it did not begin with a bang. It happened like most of the endings on our planet—in the dark, behind the scenes and in oblivion, until it reached a critical mass and an invisible countdown began ticking off the time left before every-thing we knew would blow up in our faces. And yet, for all the chaos and change to come, when it finally took shape enough for us to make it out in the darkness, the apocalypse was not really an end at all.

It was a beginning.

Not that anybody cares now.

Not that it matters anymore.

But for the record, the world ended back in the sev-enties and nobody noticed. It crept up on us while folks were disco dancing with John Travolta and watching *All in the Family* on their new high-tech twenty-inch color televisions. Mankind almost never sees the important things coming. Like Germany electing Hitler after WWI, the consequences of what we started years ago were as unintended as they were awful. If humanity had ever been any good at connecting the dots we might have stopped it, but for all the science and logic most folks swear by, as a species we are simply too swayed by the emotional nature of our own experiences to ever really see things clearly.

For generation after generation folks just kept their noses to the grindstone, clocked in and out of work, ate frozen pizza and drank light beer like nothing was happening. Emmett Kessler was no exception, though he'd moved on from light beer years ago. Even now, years after the Shibuya Incident, when the news was almost entirely made up of reports of *berserker* activity, Emmett just plodded along, going to work, drinking after, and disappointing his wife and daughters.

Folks kept repeating the party line that anybody could be one—your coworker, your neighbor, your friend, your loved one. There was no pattern, vector, or relationship that the big wigs in Washington and Atlanta had been able to figure out. Emmett knew what everybody else did: It wasn't a virus. It wasn't bacterial. It wasn't even a disease in any kind of traditional sense. He constantly heard about how the physical effects of *berserking out* built upon each other with each episode, eventually leaving those possessed looking like hulking, monstrous giants, which, as far as he was concerned, only seemed fair considering they seemed to have the strength and speed of monsters.

"*Why* should *they get to look like people?*" he remembered once saying to the bartender Jack, as the men around him were discussing the latest revelations and trading theories as to the cause. That was what people did after Shibuya. They theorized. And they drank.

In Jack's bar, where Emmett could be found most nights, it was alien DNA that was the most popular theory, though the other day he'd heard a pretty compelling idea that Wi-Fi and cell phone electromagnetic radiation may have been what was causing random folks to go crazy and kill everybody around them. Of course, the theory wasn't quite compelling enough for him to shut off either his phone or his glasses, nor seek out a Faraday cage. He'd need some actual proof before he took things to the level of being even remotely inconveniencing.

Emmett remembered the Shibuya Incident like it was yesterday. It was hard not to since every screen on the planet seemed to recast the slaughterfest at least once a day. For him, just like for everybody else, that night had instantaneously opened his eyes to the threat of berserkers, the way 9-11 had opened folks' eyes to the threat of radical Islamic terrorism decades ago. But just like radical Islamic terrorism didn't begin with 9-11, Shibuya was just the first time the phenomenon had been captured in broadcast-quality video and recast live with enough clarity to actually make out what was happening. It was not when it began.

Not that anybody cared about that.

As Emmett and the rest of the world had watched thousands die in those streets in Japan, the world's consciousness had shifted. Gone were the days when there could be unexplained episodes of extreme violence. There was no more pretending that it could have been something else at play, no more pockets of plausible deniability, no more turning of blind eyes. Violence, as of that moment, regardless of how it may have been actually propagated, could now only come from one source in most folks' minds.

Berserkers. They could be anywhere. They could be anyone.

In the days when Emmett was still drinking at Jack's, it all seemed a little too surreal to take in. Like the potential of the car you were riding in getting hacked. Yes, it happened. Yes, it was scary. But at that point it just hadn't yet happened to enough folks Emmett knew personally for him to change any of his behaviors or routines—though those days were coming fast, even if Emmett and everybody around him were in denial about it. And denial aside, it was a good time to drink yourself stupid. The fact that more people didn't just kick their meaningless obligations like family and work to the curb sooner was a testament to humanity.

Sure, it was more of a testament to how slow, complacent, and enslaved to our routines we'd all become than it was to anything else, but it certainly did say something about us as a species. How many other "intelligent" life forms out there would continue paying taxes; posting pictures on Facebook and Instagram; buying iPhones, Glass, and Rift headsets; or lining up to see the next *Star Wars* movie in the face of an apocalypse? But that was what us human folk did.

To Emmett's credit it had been the end of the world that had driven him to take up drinking at the professional level. He had always been a happy drunk. Alcohol loosened the straps on his emotional load. Sometimes it even let him put it down for a bit. Even before Shibuya, though he clung to his routine like a rabid pit bull with lockjaw, somewhere behind the curtain in Emmett's mind his own theory had been developing. It was the one good theory in the ever-growing haystack of shitty ones. Of course, he didn't know that yet. The numbers were still lining up and would continue to do so for a long time to come. But Emmett had a strong intuitive muscle, so part of him deep down knew where it was all going. And that was why he'd started drinking in earnest.

He sat on his barstool and drank like a pro, half listening to the news on the TV mounted among the liquor bottles in front of him, half smiling at his own dark thoughts, his load significantly loosened by cheap bourbon and Diet Coke.

While Emmett drank, occasionally commenting on the reports coming out of the tube, the aging bartender, Jack, who could have been Norman Rockwell's inspiration for Santa Claus minus the red suit and sunny disposition, stared at him disapprovingly as he dried a pint glass. In times like these just about any bartender could get away with being a judgmental prick, as long they kept the inebriating liquids flowing. The era of drinking therapy and barkeeps pulling double duties as reluctant counselors or unsanctioned priests started to fade away after the Shibuya Incident. And while it was a good time to start drinking, keep drinking, or drink more, the actual act of drinking itself for most folks was no longer a good time. Alcohol has always done a long list of wonderful things for those who imbibe: killed the liver, slurred the speech, turned the right foot into the left, filled the heart with confidence neither deserved nor earned, dulled the voices in the head, made bad ideas seem brilliant, and generally always caught up to folks in the end—just to cherry pick—and none of that had changed. It just sort of became less fun. It was like drinking just wasn't for amateurs anymore. It was serious business. And for some reason that fact really pissed bartenders off.

But that wasn't why Jack the bartender was giving Emmett the stink-eye. Jack had decided Emmett had had enough for one night, and while Emmett was a happy drunk most of the time, experience had taught the fat man behind the bar that under certain circumstances that fact just wasn't true anymore. And he knew those circumstances were about to walk through his front door.

Emmett looked up at the TV. A reporter stood in front of a squad of soldiers marching on some military base somewhere nearby. He didn't know or care which one. It probably wasn't in Maine anyway, since the only military institutions left there were navy and Coast Guard, and these guys looked like regular army—not that he'd be able to tell the difference. The reporter was talking about some law that was just passed—

"Giving soldiers situational immunity from any charges of brutality or abuse in their response to the berserker threat. . ."

Emmett laughed to himself at how ridiculously terrifying the world his two little girls were going to grow up in was. Where anyone could suddenly turn into some kind of superpowered raginator and rip them apart. Or, if they got really lucky, they'd just be raped and murdered by soldiers no longer bound by consequences for their actions.

"Here's to your future, girls," he mumbled, before he downed his drink and waved at Jack for another.

Jack just watched him without moving. Emmett waved louder, but still the large man ignored him. For a second Emmett considered tossing his glass at the man to get his attention, but even as blotto as he was, that seemed like it might not be as effective as it would be satisfying.

"Jack!" he said instead.

Before he could get further upset at Jack for ignoring him, something on the TV caught his eye.

"Shit. . ." he said to himself.

On the TV there was a photograph of a mother in her forties with her two young boys sitting on the front steps of a somewhat restored colonial farmhouse. He'd missed what the story was about, but all the stories were about the same thing these days, so he felt pretty confident in guessing what had happened. Somebody'd gone berserk. Family was killed. It was always the same—actually, usually it was worse. Just one family being killed was kind of like when the planes hit the World Trade Center: how both buildings didn't have anywhere close to the number of people in them that they could have had. That day could have been so much worse. Just a mother and her two boys, while tragic, sure, was actually a blessing. Usually it was a whole lot worse. Of course when 9-11 happened folks weren't feeling lucky that it wasn't worse. What could have been doesn't matter much when people are jumping from a hundred stories up to keep from burning to death.

Something about the woman in the photo on the screen was familiar to Emmett. Had they said her name yet? Probably. But he'd missed that part. A past life maybe? *Real life seems like a past life these days*, he thought and chuckled.

"Oh well," he told himself. And then it hit him, and one of the numbers that would eventually add up to his theory of what had wiped out mankind, of what had killed his own children's future—the one solid explanation in an ever-growing mountain of shit ones—one of those numbers fell into place. Suddenly Emmett didn't care about how lucky it was that only one family had been destroyed by the incident.

"Hey, I know that woman," he realized out loud. "Susan and I went to the same fertility doctor—"

"Julianne Barnes," the reporter on the TV continued.

But no, that isn't right, Emmett thought. *It was Julie Anne Barnes.*

"Discovered having taken her own life after beating to death her husband and both her young children as a berserker," the reporter summarized, before passing it off to the cops for a sound bite.

The cop in this case was a baby-faced Asian guy who thought the world might need another rundown of what folks already knew. Just in case one guy out in Iowa somewhere had missed it the first five thousand times it was reported.

"Since every time a berserker turns, their physical appearance becomes more and more muscular, it appears that Mrs. Barnes had not yet been experiencing regular episodes," he explained. "So until we get her HGF levels back from the autopsy, we can't confirm exactly how far gone Mrs. Barnes was at this time. However, even though she still"—he raised both hands in big air quotes—"*appeared* human, due to the fact that we did find what we believe to be several of her teeth at the scene, which is a common side effect of this. . . *condition*—"

"So, it's likely that Mrs. Barnes has killed before, then, Officer?" the overeager reporter cut him off.

"Well, we have no confirmation of that at this time," the cop answered flatly.

Emmett looked from the TV to Jack, who still had not brought him a fucking refill. Jesus, what is wrong with this guy! he thought to himself and banged his glass on the bar.

"Hey!" he teased drunkenly. "You gonna fuck me with your eyes all night or are you going to get me my drink, Jack? I've been empty here for like ten minutes, man."

A shake of the head, no, was all Jack responded with.

Really? One syllable is too much to give to a thirsty soul in times like these? Much less a drop of bourbon? Emmett thought—or maybe said out loud, he couldn't really tell anymore. "Come on, Jack. Don't be an asshole. Let me drink to my fucking dead, murdering almost-friend."

This time he was sure he said it out loud, because Jack actually responded.

"Last one, Emmett."

Man, some folks are pissy tonight, Emmett thought and smiled. But his glee was short-lived.

The moment Jack had been dreading had arrived. The bar door swung open and along with the cold outside blew in the redheaded, waif-thin, exhausted (but still attractive in that heroin-addict model kind of way) mother to Emmett's daughters, who, just for the record, didn't do heroin, or even drink for that matter. But the regulars in the bar still knew who she was and, likewise, knew that tonight, like almost every night, she was here to drag her drunk-ass husband home before he got into trouble. A few of the bar patrons who had witnessed the lengths Emmett would go to to continue drinking if left to his own devices, and who had more manners than empathy, actually greeted her by name.

"Hey, Susan," one said.

"My heart goes out to you," another said.

My heart goes out to you? Emmett thought, as he turned on his barstool with a squeak to face his wife. *What the fuck does that mean?*

"So I guess you're not going to pour me that drink, then, eh, Jack?" he said over his shoulder as he slid off this perch.

"I'll pour it for you tomorrow, Emmett. You're done for tonight."

Susan touched Emmett on his shoulder when she got to him. To her it was a gesture of love, a signal that she still cared for him, even though he'd been lost inside a tumbler for a while now. But drunk or sober, Emmett had been for a long time unable to take in how much she still loved him in spite of the drinking. Instead he just felt his own shame reflected back to him in everything she did and said.

When she reached the counter, Susan gave a *Thank you for your help* look to Jack, but that gesture too went misinterpreted and all Jack saw in her eyes was his own inadequacies as a friend. But what the hell was he supposed to do? God, he hated this. Why couldn't Emmett just be trusted to get his own ass home?

But he knew the answer to that already. Left to his own devices Emmett wouldn't go home. He'd just find somewhere else to drink, and when that bar, or the one after, finally closed, he'd break into the closest house and look for booze there. The man had proven himself a resourceful, if not particularly law-abiding, professional alcoholic enough times already. And in this new world, that would only end with him poking some unsuspecting berserker bear with a short, sharp stick, getting him and God knows who else killed.

So sharing in Susan's misery each night as she took him home was better than sharing in her panic the next morning when she showed up looking for him because he hadn't made it back there at all.

Besides, as he watched them leave, Jack didn't think the world was actually ending. He'd have laughed in your face if you suggested the apocalypse was already in full swing.

* * *

As they walked, or more precisely as Susan walked and Emmett stumbled, out the exit and into the cold white, snow-covered New England night, Emmett looked at his wife and said, "Fucking Julie B. berserked out and killed her whole goddamn family. Probably a bunch of other folks too. You see that?"

She had.

"And you're worried about your husband doing a little after-work drinking?" he tried to joke, but failed.

"Please don't make this worse than it is, Emmett."

The Kessler family car was an old 2018 Toyota Prius—not exactly the best car when it came to snow and ice, but Emmett had put studded tires on at the beginning of the season and the thing did okay most days. At least if the driver was sober, it did okay; drunk off your ass in a snowstorm is a recipe for disaster no matter what you're driving. Not that it would have mattered much, since severe weather was notorious for making even self-driving *smart* cars do stupid things, but a newer Prius would have had at least some kind of sophisticated auto-pilot technology standard. Emmett had long been determined to put any new-car money the family might have saved up to a much more practical use: booze. Besides, he could drive just fine unassisted, thank you very much.

Happy drunks tend to be particularly stupid ones. Somewhere in his booze-soaked cerebral circuitry, Emmett thought it might win him points to grab the keys out of Susan's hands when she took them out of her pocket and jump into the driver's seat himself. The cold night air had grounded him enough to stop the world from spinning out from under him, but at that point he didn't actually have any intention of driving. At least that's what he would tell himself when he lay awake at night playing what was about to unfold over and over in his mind. He was just trying to be funny.

"Come on, Emmett." Susan sighed heavily.

If she'd only laughed at him instead it might have all gone down differently, or so Emmett would tell himself all through the trial and sentencing. It was a bunch of bullshit, of course—nothing that happened next was Susan's fault—but Emmett wouldn't be ready to look that truth in the eye for a long time coming.

Emmett shut the door just as she got to it, grinning like a two-year-old testing a boundary for the thousandth time. His wife banged on the window, nothing about this fun or funny to her.

"You're plastered. You can't drive."

She even sounded like she was talking to a two-year-old. So, Emmett escalated things. As she reached for the door handle, he locked the car, his now victorious grin widening and widening, until the rearview mirror caught his eye and he realized his two daughters were in the backseat.

His oldest, Jennifer, who was just about to start first grade, had the reddest hair and the greenest eyes the world had ever seen—or if not the world, at least the reddest and greenest anybody in Emmett or Susan's family had ever seen, which at the time for Jennifer was the world, so it counted just the same. Her already big eyes were wide as saucers as she tried very hard not to cry in front of her father.

Emmett's youngest, Bobby-Leigh (yes, with a hyphen), was almost two years old, and like her sister she clearly took her looks from her mother—pale skin, a galaxy of freckles across her cheeks and nose, jade eyes, and Susan's signature red hair. She was one of those babies who hardly ever cried. The kind that seems to see things grown-up folks can't. The kind of kid that makes folks wonder.

Seeing his girls in the backseat could have ended it. But Emmett went the other way; if he couldn't get Susan to laugh with his joke, surely he could get Jen and Bobby-Leigh to. So he escalated, again.

"Please, Emmett. Just open the door," Susan pleaded, her breath visible in the cold and looking like dragon's fire.

Emmett shook his head gleefully. "No."

They stared each other down, the whole time Emmett truly expecting her to break out in a grin of her own and start laughing at her hilarious husband. But of course, she didn't.

"Fine. Let the girls out of the car if you're going to drive drunk," she eventually said. And again, this too should have ended it, but Emmett went the other way and managed to get offended by the idea that he would put his children in jeopardy by driving when he couldn't do so safely. Somehow he managed to skip over the fact that he was threatening to do exactly that, but logic was not part of his mental process at that moment.

"Jesus, like I'd do anything that would hurt my own children after all the bullshit and money we went through to have them? I'm fine. Just get in."

Susan crossed her arms, her dragon breath fuming, feeling totally taken hostage by this man she loved. And she did love him still. Though right now she'd gladly have hit him in the face with a fence post if it meant ending this stupidity and getting everybody home in one piece. She knew Emmett didn't really want to drive, but she didn't know it was a laugh from her that would have de-escalated the situation—a situation that from Emmett's side was quickly getting to the boiling point.

Happy drunks are great. But the cold fact is happy drunks don't always stay happy, and the reaction best trigged by alcohol, after stupidity, is anger.

"I'm fine. Get. In. The. Car," Emmett said, no longer trying to make anybody laugh.

"No."

They stared each other down as the water, or whatever it was in Emmett's pot at that point, boiled over. The girls—Jennifer frozen in fear and Bobby-Leigh seemingly tuned out altogether—watched as Emmett pressed the "Start" button on the car.

"Fine. Stay here, then," he said. "I'm sure Jack would just love to give you a ride. . . home."

From the backseat, Jennifer broke her silence and screamed.

"Mom!"

Tears poured from her eyes. Bobby-Leigh, back from la-la land it seemed, suddenly started screaming too. It was possible that until that moment, Emmett might have forgotten briefly that the girls were in the backseat. A fact that would have made happy-drunk Emmett laugh, and might even have ended this disaster before it got rolling. Unfortunately, happy-drunk Emmett had gone home for the evening and the only one left in the office was the irrational, something-to-prove drunk Emmett.

"Sit. Now. Stop crying," he commanded, immediately regretting the sharpness of his tone.

"I just want to get out, Daddy. Please. Just let me—"

"I'm fine," he said, trying to be softer this time, trying to reassure her. "I am fine."

While Emmett was distracted by the girls, Susan moved around the car and banged on the passenger-side window. The sound startled him, and out of muscle memory, or instinct, or maybe even an unconscious need for self-preservation, he unlocked the door before he realized what he was doing. Instantly, Susan ripped the door open and planted herself in the passenger seat—still fully expecting Emmett to come to his senses, which he might have done had she not said the following.

"Please, Emmett. Let me drive. You're scaring me. You're scaring the girls. Enough is enough." Her voice was calm, neutral, nonconfrontational. He should have responded positively to her plea. Hundreds of books on crisis negotiation would have told her she was doing exactly the right thing. But sometimes the right thing just isn't, and Emmett responded to her rational, even-keeled, placating tone by laughing like that was the funniest thing he'd ever heard. Ironically, if they'd switched their responses and he'd spoken in a calm, nonconfrontational manner and she'd laughed like a stoned hyena, what happened next would not have happened at all.

But it went the other way. Emmett put his foot on the gas and shot out of the parking lot, rocking the passenger-side door shut and trapping everybody inside the old Japanese hybrid for better or for worse.

When it comes to things turning out for better or for worse, folks almost always end up with the latter. The Kesslers were no exception.

Susan was stunned by the atrocity that she'd unwittingly become a part of. It was even worse in her mind, because she had instigated it somehow. She didn't speak for what felt like a long time. Instead, she noticed that snow had started falling again. She noticed how brave her girls were trying to be. She even noticed that the sane part of her husband was screaming on the inside for the insane part of him to pull the goddamn car over and let her drive—a fact she could see reflected back at her in his eyes.

She breathed in.

She breathed out.

Emmett stayed on the road.

She breathed in again, and then—

Beep! Beep! Beep!

The car's lane-departure alarm chirped as she felt the car cross over the middle divide, and her breath caught. Emmett corrected his course, but too much, and the car swerved dangerously close to a ditch at the side of the road. In the backseat, the levy of bravery holding back the cries of the girls broke, and the tears and sobs came hard against their thin frames, shaking them in little tremors that warned a massive earthquake was coming.

Emmett was really trying to drive straight, but he wasn't.

Susan, who at this point was the only one not wearing a seat belt, turned and leaned over the passenger seat to the back and tried to comfort her children.

"It's going to be okay," she lied. "It's only a couple of miles to the house. There's hardly anybody out. We'll be okay."

Jennifer didn't believe her, she could tell. And Bobby-Leigh probably didn't understand her. If ever there was a moment in her life when she wondered how the hell she got to where she was, this was it.

Another course correction from Emmett, but not as bad as the one before. Maybe they'd make it home without an accident. Maybe she'd call a divorce lawyer in the morning if they did.

Oh, Jesus, is that really where this is all heading?

"I'm totally fine. I actually drive better a little drunk."

Yep. That's where this is heading, she thought sadly as the car swerved again.

"You're not a little drunk, Daddy. You're a lot drunk," Jennifer said from the backseat with every ounce of courage she had. Susan was proud of her. And that was the last thing she felt for her daughter, because Emmett turned around in his seat to dispute the little girl's assessment. Or maybe to just remind her that she didn't know anything about being drunk, so she should keep her mouth shut. Or maybe to apologize for everything. Whatever it was that he turned to say, it never made it out of his mouth, because as his body turned right, his drunk hands on the wheel turned left into oncoming traffic.

The girls screamed. Emmett jerked the wheel back instinctively without actually understanding what was happening. Susan's body, unrestrained by a seat belt, smashed into his.

The car began to skid.

Susan's eyes suddenly dilated to the size of nickels as the headlights of an oncoming logging truck lit the inside of the old Prius like a flashbulb. Another jerk of the wheel by Emmett and the truck whipped past without contact, just an angry blare of its horn. Time ticked by slower and slower, as Susan felt her entire body start to burn from the inside out. She felt something cold and dark filling her mind like an oil spill in the ocean. Coating. Covering. Pulling her down into the heat that felt like it was boiling her blood in her veins.

"Stop. The. Car," she managed to breathe more than say, as she grabbed the wheel and pulled it hard, the intention of putting the car safely on the shoulder of the road already slipping away before her hands made contact with the hard plastic of the steering wheel. She was already gone inside when the car flipped and rolled, skidding across the road on its side, heading straight for the bank of snow as though off a launchpad. She didn't hear her girls' screaming. She didn't hear the horrible crunching of metal and snow and pavement all being ground together.

Her body was tossed like a rag doll into the air and bounced around the old hybrid like a fleshy pinball as the car spun. For an impossible moment in Emmett's mind his wife just hung there in the air. Their eyes locked—but Susan's eyes no longer belonged to her. Her body, also no longer hers, was frozen for a terrible second as her now supercharged muscles engorged and she actualized into a berserker for the first time. And then—

CRASH!

Ground.

Gravity.

The timelessness stopped.

The girls' screaming stopped.

Life as they knew it stopped.

The airbags exploded around them. But the monster that two seconds ago was Emmett's wife and the mother of his children ripped through them like cheap toilet paper, snarling and grabbing but taking nothing with her as she continued through the windshield in an explosion of safety glass, out into the snow.

Out into the cold.

Out into the dark.

Gone.

* * *

The *click-click-click* of the turn signal was the first sound Emmett heard when he opened his eyes. Or maybe it was the wind. Adrenaline had fried the alcohol in his system and may have popped a few of the regular circuit breakers in his brain as well. The circumstances that had put the car upside down against a tree off Highway 25 in the middle of a snowstorm flooded back into his memory as his system rebooted, but they came in jumbled. Or maybe the circumstances just didn't make any sense now that he'd sobered up a little.

Regardless, now wasn't the time to try to be piecing the past back together. He was upside down. A nasty scratch along his cheek was bleeding all up his face and into his hair, but other than that he didn't think he was actually hurt—banged and bruised for sure, but functional in the ways that mattered.

One of the doors must be ajar, he thought absently.

The dome light was on. The only other light was the yellow flash-pause-flash of the turn signals. The storm had picked up, and outside the car the darkness was cold and thick with falling snow. The blinkers pushed some of the blackness back, but between strokes, the night was an abyss—the kind that stares back at you gnashing its teeth if you look into it for too long. He quickly found himself looking away.

He managed to twist around and see the girls hanging in their seats behind him, both unconscious but breathing and not bleeding that he could see. He looked at the torn passenger-side airbag and jagged-glass-edged hole where the windshield used to be. A flash of memory hit him: Susan being thrown through the glass into the gaping jaws of the night. It was just a flash, not enough to remember any details, but enough to fill his heart with dread and trip an intuitive tingle for urgency. He stared out into the blackness wrapped in swirling snow and tried to make out where his wife's body had ended up, not wanting to see it but knowing it was out there somewhere. She must have been tossed pretty far because he didn't see any signs of her at all.

The animal-like whining of the wind outside the car picked up, drowning out everything but the *click-click-click* of the blinker flashing on and off.

Jesus, this car has an extraordinarily loud turn signal, a nearly subconscious part of Emmett's mind observed. It felt like it belonged on a clock more than a car, a clock attached to explosives, ticking the time down.

Click! Ten. Off.

Click! Nine. Off.

Click!

Suddenly the hairs on Emmett's neck and arms stood up. Maybe it wasn't the impending doom hidden in the sound of the flashers that was spooking him. Maybe it was what those cycling yellow lights did to the shadows as they went through the rotation of being on and then off that was giving him the willies. He could see outside the car, then could not. *Click*, able to see, then off, blackness. Able to see, then not.

The shadows must be playing tricks on my eyes, he thought, as he squinted through the cold, snow-filled night, half-convinced he'd seen something moving out there but telling himself he knew better. The only thing out there was Susan's body—which is exactly why he should have been scared, but between the booze and the accident, her berserking out just as the car struck the tree, and then crashing through the windshield was a detail momentarily lost to all but the deepest parts of his mind. Unable to identify where the sense of urgency was coming from but equally unable to fight it, he quickly popped open his seat belt and turned his attention to the girls.

Just as his eyes shifted to his daughters, the yellow flash of the blinker caught the red hair of his wife billowing in the wind.

Click.

Darkness.

Instinctively, Emmett looked over his shoulder and into the abyss, but—

Click. Flash. She was gone.

"Hey!" he called out to his daughters, as he tried to shake Jennifer awake, turning once again to the staring abyss outside the car, squinting even harder now into the freezing blackness between each turn-signal flash.

Click. Flash. Nothing was out there.

Click. Flash. Still nothing.

Click. Flash. Nothing.

But something was. Every cell in his body was screaming it.

"Susan?" he called out into the snowy night, feeling stupid the moment the sounds left his throat.

Click. Flash. No response came.

"Mommy?" Jennifer said, calling Emmett's attention back to the inside of the car while behind him, as the yellow signal light flashed, the berserker Susan darted through the snow and was caught by the light for a fraction of a second again. The monster moved so fast, it was just an angry blur of denim, pale skin, and red hair lost in the swirling snow. Emmett turned and looked over his shoulder, but missed it again. His rational mind tried to get him to focus on getting the girls out, while his lizard brain continued to sound the alarm.

"Are you okay, baby?" he asked Jennifer.

"No."

"Yes, you are. Yes, you are. Can you get out of the seat belt?"

"No."

"Yes, you can. Just try, baby. I'll catch you."

The sudden sound of something (fingernails?) being dragged across the metal of the Prius's body snagged both Emmett and Jennifer's attention.

"What was that?" Jennifer asked.

Emmett didn't know, not for sure—at least that was what he told himself with his rational mind. But his face betrayed the truth that his lizard brain had been screaming about since he woke up: They were in trouble. Big, fat, ugly, red-haired berserker trouble.

"Dad?"

Outside the car, the flash-flash-flash of the turn signal hardly pierced the veil of the shadowy night. Susan was nowhere to be seen, which was just fine because Emmett wasn't wasting any more time looking.

"Hold on to me," he said, hoping only he could hear the terror in his voice. He maneuvered himself into the backseat enough to undo Jen's seat belt. The harness snapped out of its lock and sent Jennifer tumbling clumsily into her father's arms. Emmett pulled her to him, thanking a god he didn't really believe in that she was okay.

It was a short-lived reprieve.

The door to the seat Jen was just ejected from was suddenly ripped off the car and thrown carelessly into the night. Susan's supercharged berserker body filled the space in a flurry of clawing, ripping, angry limbs, flesh, and teeth. It reached for Jennifer with a vicious hiss, just missing her, as she and Emmett launched themselves to the front of the car. Her nails shredded the back of the driver's seat instead of the flesh of her daughter. Then, as quickly as she'd appeared, she was gone.

Pieces of foam from the seat's back mixed with the snow and floated in the air like gravity was just a suggestion, not a rule of physics. Emmett tried to remember how to breathe, and his oldest daughter tried to stop screaming. Sucking in breath at last, Emmett put his finger to Jen's mouth to hush her, and by some miracle she was able to quiet herself down. Pure love dripped down off his cheeks in the form of tears as he locked eyes with her. He wanted to tell her that he was sorry, that he'd never drink again, that he'd be a better father, a better man, from now on, but he didn't. What he did do was reach into the glove box and pull out a nickel-plated Smith & Wesson .45 snub-nosed revolver.

"Get your sister," he said as he popped the cylinder and confirmed the gun was loaded. "Get your sister and stay in the car. No matter what happens. Understand? Do not leave the car."

Jennifer didn't answer. Her little brain was already working serious overtime to process what was going on. To keep her from losing her mind, there was a certain amount of mental triage happening. But Emmett didn't have time to repeat himself.

Though he'd never seen a berserker in the flesh, he knew how the rage worked, or at least how it was supposed to work. The first time a person berserked out, they'd be insanely strong and wicked fast, but they'd basically look just like they always had. Up to that first episode there was no way to tell berserkers apart from normal folk, but afterward, HGF would be present in the blood and would steadily increase over time. What exactly HGF was, however, remained a mystery to the scientific community at large. The letters stood for *hyper growth factor*, which when spelled out did nothing to clear the vagueness of how it worked.

Regardless of the biological mechanics, the results were well documented: Every time you went berserk, the massive steroid-like effect of HGF on the body would give the five- to ten-minute-long episode the equivalent results of months, if not years, of competitive bodybuilding. Berserk out too many times and you'd have the physique of the Incredible Hulk, or bigger. But as it bulked the body, HGF damaged a number of synaptic receptors in the brain, causing the berserker to slowly lose intelligence. Also, HGF, for some unfathomable reason, caused your teeth to slowly fall out, as if your human form was just a child's body to the monster you would become, your adult chompers just the baby teeth of the demon inside you.

Susan still had all her teeth. Emmett was almost sure of that. So, if Emmett could draw her away from the kids long enough for the rage to run its course, he might be able to save her. Nobody knew, and as long as it didn't happen again, nobody would have to. Snapping the Smith & Wesson's cylinder shut, he told himself that even if he died at Susan's hands before the night was over, as long as the girls survived and nobody saw what happened, he could probably take his wife's deadly secret to the grave. What he couldn't know was how strong his self-preservation instinct would turn out to be. He couldn't know that he, like most folk who try as they might to be the heroes raging against the dying of the light, couldn't pull off saving anybody, including himself.

Jennifer watched her father as he climbed out of the old Prius through the hole where the windshield used to be. He gave her one final look of adoration, nodded to her sister as if to say the baby was her responsibility now, and then stepped into the abyss that had swallowed their lives.

When Jen turned her attention away from her father trudging through the snow and back to her sister, Bobby-Leigh's eyes were open. The little girl stared at her, wide-eyed and breathing hard but not crying. How long had the baby been watching? What exactly had she seen?

Jen unfastened the belts of the car seat and pulled Bobby-Leigh into her arms. Trying to telepathically send her the message to keep quiet, Jennifer huddled with her baby sister in the corner of the front passenger seat's foot well and watched as the turn signal's yellow light lit the snow and then was beaten back by the darkness, over and over again. Its heartbeat rhythm was oddly calming. Hypnotic. Soothing.

Click. Flash.

Click. Flash.

Click. Flash.

Click. . . Bam!

Jennifer and the baby both jumped out of their skin at the sound of the gunshot.

Bam! Bam! More shots, then nothing.

Bobby-Leigh's stoicism finally cracked, and she started to cry quietly as the echo of the shots faded and the ringing in their ears was replaced by the click of the turn signal again.

Click.

Click.

Click.

"Daddy? Mom?" Jennifer called out, but got nothing back in response.

"Da-De!" Bobby-Leigh screamed, only to get the same.

Outside the car, maybe fifteen yards deeper into the woods, Emmett stood shaking from the cold, from the shock, from the truth, with the smoking handgun held out in front of him like a talisman. He squinted and peered into the dark, his ears even more open than his eyes, watching, listening, waiting for. . . for anything.

Click. Flash. Nothing.

Click. Flash. Wind and snow.

His teeth started to chatter as the cold dug into his bones.

Fuck. Had he hit her? Had she already worn herself out? Was it over?

"Honey?" he called out. His voice was immediately taken away and silenced by the wind. Nothing. *Just the clicking of the goddamn blinker.* He wasn't sure if he should go out into the snow and look for his wife, or head back to the car and gather up his children and make a run for the road. Time seemed to be stretching out in front of him, behind him, above him, below—

Jen's sudden hysterical screams knocked the sense back into him. He turned back from the abyss and toward the car just in time to see the red-haired demon who'd once been his wife grab the door frame and roll the just over three-thousand-pound hybrid back onto its wheels like it was a big toy. Then, even faster than it was strong, the berserker moved in to rip her children apart.

Emmett raised the gun and fired. His bullet landed square in the demon's back. The shot distracted it from the girls but left it seemingly unhurt. The berserker turned and leaped into the air. It hit the ground charging. This was his chance. Emmett took it and ran, drawing the monster away.

Back inside the car, Jennifer and Bobby-Leigh curled up against the floorboards and waited for what felt like could only be a painful, inevitable death. But death didn't come.

"It's going to be okay. It's going to be okay. It's going to be okay," the older sister chanted in whispers, not believing a word of what she was saying but hoping that Bobby-Leigh would. They waited. Death didn't come for them. Jennifer finally stopped chanting and listened.

Click.

Click.

The only sound was the turn signal. Slowly, she poked her head up as Bobby-Leigh watched, wide-eyed but calm. Jennifer surveyed the snowy darkness. Trying to capture the images lit by the flashing blinker in her brain, as if they were fireflies on a cool summer's night, instead of potential harbingers of death. But she didn't see anything or anybody. Just the wind and the stupid turn signal's light.

Wait! Was there something just at the edge of the light's reach? Out there in the shadows and swirling snow?

She pressed her face against the driver's side window, which was the only glass in the car not shattered at this point, and tried to make out what was happening, when all of a sudden—

Hoooonk! *Honk*! *Hooooooooonk*!

The sound of the car horn exploded into the night. It caught Jen so off guard that for a long second, she couldn't wrap her head around the idea that it was the horn of their Prius piercing the night. But when that second was up, she whipped around to see Bobby-Leigh in the driver's seat, both hands on the horn, about to really press the thing down and wake up the angels who were supposed to be protecting little girls and their sisters at night, but who had clearly fallen asleep on the job. Jen, who thought she knew better than to believe in angels or Santa Claus or peaceful resolutions to conflicts with bullies, grabbed her sister's hands off the horn and opened her mouth to read the little girl the riot act when—

Smash!

Emmett, the left side of his face hanging off like a half-sliced piece of cheese, landed in a heap on the hood of the hybrid. Bobby-Leigh began to scream as Emmett turned his gruesome visage for what he was pretty sure would be his last look at the two miracles he'd sired.

Survive, he thought as loud as he could, while from the abyss Susan the berserker charged toward them all. Flinching, Jen shuffled back until her head hit the dangling dome light in the middle of the car and knocked it the rest of the way loose.

The light went out. Just the blinkers remained to cut the dark.

Click.

The demon was coming hard and fast, rocketing herself through the snow like a plow, propelled as much by her arms and hands as by her legs. In the strobe-like flashing of the turn signal, what Emmett and his girls saw was more like a series of horrible still photographs than a continuous movement.

Click. Flash. Closer.

Click. Flash. Closer.

Click. Flash—

The berserker grabbed Emmett and yanked him off the hood. He told himself he was ready for the sacrifice he was about to make. He told himself he would gladly lay down his life to save his family. He thought of himself as a hero, and this was what a hero would do. Redemption at last in death—it tasted as sweet as fresh honey in his mind.

But just as the monster that was once Susan was about to tear him apart, Emmett felt the weight of the gun in his hand. He watched himself raise it up and then empty it into the monster's face as it opened its mouth to tear out his jugular with its teeth. He couldn't believe he was delivering death at the last second, instead of receiving it like he'd planned.

What have I done?

What have I done?

What have I done?

The question throbbed out of him with each beat of his heart.

What have I done?

He expected to hear himself answer with something along the lines that he'd only done what he had to do to protect his girls. But the rationalizations didn't come, because in his heart Emmett was sure they weren't true.

The body of the creature thrashed and twitched and jerked as it bled out and died. But what Emmett saw—through the spasms of muscles twitching and jerking as the demon controlling them slipped forever away—was just his wife, her warm blood mixing with his in the snow. It was like the monster had never been there. And as he lay there next to the body of the woman who had been his beautiful wife, the mother of his children, whom he'd not been strong enough to die for, it was impossible for him not to feel like he'd just murdered Susan in cold blood.

What have I done?

You fucking murdered your wife, you son of a bitch!

He stood shakily up and looked at the gaping hole where her face should have been. Her beautiful red hair drenched in even redder blood. He looked at his daughters watching from the relative shelter of the beat-up old car. Their eyes were so wide and wet and full of questions and fear, they seemed like they might pop right out their beautiful, innocent heads. Little Jennifer's face was so twisted by her effort not to cry, to be strong, to not add to the misery of her little sister, that Emmett found himself crying for her.

For them.

For himself.

How the fuck was he supposed to explain any of this to them?

But it turned out he wouldn't have to answer any of his daughters' questions for a long time, because the police had now arrived—finally—and they had questions of their own that would need to be answered first.

* * *

Jennifer and Bobby-Leigh's father was sentenced by a jury of his peers to twelve years for second-degree murder. The judge wasn't happy about it, but he'd be dead soon so in the grand scheme of things, his thoughts on whether or not justice had been done in his court were pretty worthless. The only person in the court that day whose opinion about the proceedings really mattered was Emmett himself, and he had stopped giving a shit the day he'd decided to send the girls away to his brother's place in Fairfield, Iowa.

As he stood and listened to his sentence read aloud, he knew on some intellectual level that he was getting screwed. The jury could have decided that the murder of his wife was a justifiable homicide and just let him go. In most of the cases that made it to court in those days where a berserker had been killed, the mere fact that the victim had HGF in their blood tended to adjudicate the crime as self-defense. It was a get-out-of-jail-free card. But Emmett hadn't played it. Even in the ever-increasing number of instances where folks had clearly planned the murder ahead of time, where they had executed the suspected berserker at a time when they were not in any way going berserk and nobody was in any danger at all, even then, juries almost always came back with not-guilty verdicts.

All he would have needed to say was that he'd been afraid for his life and the lives of his daughters, and he could have gone free. But he'd said nothing. It just didn't matter anymore. So even though Emmett's actions were by all accounts justified, the jury was guided to focus on the facts that he'd been drunk, that he'd insisted on driving, that he'd been the one who crashed the car and set the whole thing off.

By the time the prosecution was done, those twelve men and women sitting in the jury box didn't much appreciate the circumstances that triggered Susan into berserking out, and they held it against him. But they seemed to know on some level that they had been in the wrong with their verdict, so they tried to make it up to him during sentencing. Second-degree murder usually carries a thirty- to forty-year sentence, but to appease the judge, who was notably flabbergasted by the decision (and their consciences), the jury granted Emmet a reprieve due to extenuating circumstances, and he was only sent away for twelve.

He watched the gavel bang down.

His lawyer was saying something about how they would appeal and that he'd be able to put this behind him soon. But Emmett wasn't really listening. He wasn't going to appeal. His mind was stuck in a horrible memory loop: Susan's face obliterated by the gun in his hand over and over and over again. He had no interest in an appeal.

When the paperwork came back with the guilty verdict on it and was put in front of him, he signed it without a second thought. He had been drunk. He had killed the mother of his children. Sure, technically it was self-defense, but as far as he was concerned the court still got the basic facts right—like that he had put a hole through the face of his wife in front of his children—and those were what really mattered. Everything else was just window dressing.

He knew he should call his brother Allen and let the girls know the verdict had come in. He knew he should let them know that he wasn't coming home anytime soon, so they should just drink the Kool-Aid and join the Transcendental Meditation "movement" like his brother had.

But he didn't call.

Emmett felt like just about anybody on the planet would be better at raising his daughters than him after what he'd done, and so he just signed where they asked him and boarded the bus to prison. He simply couldn't bear to see the unbridled hatred in his Jen's eyes or hear it in her voice again. When Allen had brought them to say good-bye before the trial had gotten underway, his already-broken heart had been crushed to dust.

"*You have to tell, Daddy. You have to!*" He could still hear how Jen had screamed at him as Allen stood and watched awkwardly, helplessly, in the tiny interrogation room the cops had let them use for the occasion. "*Please! Let me do it! I'll tell them. I saw it, Daddy. I'll tell them all what happened and you won't be in trouble anymore.*"

She had been there. That much was true. She had seen everything. Bobby-Leigh had too. But they didn't need to relive it all for the jury. They didn't need to have their experiences questioned in a cross-examination. At the very least he could still protect them from that. At the very least he could give them a fighting chance at moving on. But more importantly, Emmett didn't want to be saved; the steel barb of the hook he was on tasted good. It tasted like justice. So, as his older daughter screamed curses at him, he had just shaken his head slowly. No. He would never allow his lawyer to put either of his girls on the stand. Nor would he ever testify on his own behalf.

He was done.

"Go ahead and teach 'em that meditation shit," he'd said to his brother as the man left with his daughters. "If you think it will help them cope with all this. I'm sorry I always gave you such a hard time about it."

It was the last thing he would ever say to him, and though Emmett didn't care about it right then, he'd end up being thankful that his last words to his brother had been relatively kind ones.

By the time Emmett cared about anything again, the final collapse of human civilization would be underway. In the meantime, the grand finale of the apocalypse would drag on for years and years until eventually folks *did* stop going to work, paying taxes, buying HoloLenses, and caring about *Star Wars*. But by then it was too late. The power grids had already started to fail. The water would be shutting off. The gas pumps would soon stop working. All the things that used to make life as we knew it before possible would eventually just stop.

Folks would quickly start hoarding water, weapons, and fuel. They would form gangs and militia. They would rape women and children. They would burn cities to the ground. They would kill their bosses, lovers, and friends and murder their representatives in government.

Eventually folks from one branch of the military or another would get their hands on nukes and take out New York, Boston, Chicago, Denver, Houston, Las Vegas, Los Angeles, San Francisco, and of course Washington, DC, not to mention London, Geneva, Tel Aviv, Paris, Munich, Beijing, Tokyo, Calgary, Perth, and Sydney outside the US. There may have been more nukes set off in other places, but communication would break down once the bombs started popping off, and those would be all that made it into the historical records before folks stopped bothering to keep them anymore.

At some point in the chaos the God-fearing folk would start referring to berserkers as demons. And why not? It was the apocalypse after all. Demonic possession was an explanation that fit just as much as any of the other idiot theories out there. Besides, all the really cool apocalypses had demons at the center of them. Folks would have been disappointed if the language hadn't taken on a more fire-and-brimstone undertone.

Not that any of this mattered to Emmett as he sat in his cell and replayed the murder of his wife in his head. In fact, the only thing that happened for years after the verdict came in that would have mattered to the man was when the girls' yogi uncle was killed over a case of Diet Coke and three Twinkies.

He'd have wanted to know about that.

Likewise, he'd have been relieved to learn that the girls found shelter with a man named Brennachecke, one of his brother's friends, who led a small band of scavengers who had remained in that nutball town of Fairfield after the lights went out for good. He might have even been proud of how the apocalypse ended up looking pretty good on Jennifer as she blossomed into a dead ringer of her mother—a fiery redheaded mess of hard muscles, soft curves, and emerald eyes. He'd have even probably been understanding of the fact that his older daughter to this day simultaneously hated him for taking away her mother and resented him even more for just rolling over without an appeal and sending her and her sister away.

Bobby-Leigh, on the other hand, hadn't really been old enough to understand what had happened in the car that night, or in the courtroom later. She felt only love for her father; in fact, she used to cry most nights because she missed him so much. Emmett would have probably wanted to know that as well, though it would have taken another chunk out of his heart.

Had he known about it, he'd probably have forgiven Jen for insisting that he was dead by now and that even if he wasn't yet, she hoped he would be soon. Just as he'd probably have been crushed to discover that Bobby-Leigh would always have a secret longing for a reunion with her father in spite of her sister's declaration of war on his memory—though he probably would have been dismayed to know that, just like she did with all the secrets the sisters would accumulate while he was in prison and time marched on, she would almost always keep that wish to herself.

By the time he would see them again, he'd want to hear about every experience his girls had had: good, bad, or otherwise. But that would have to wait until the father and his daughters once again shared the same space in time. For the majority of the years Emmett was locked away, he just didn't have the emotional resources left to allow any of that shit to matter to him. Not until he stumbled onto the truth about what—or, more importantly, who—had created berserkers. Once he knew that, gears clicked and his stalled motivation rumbled back to life. Suddenly, something not only mattered. It consumed him.

Not the thought of his daughters, but a chance at revenge.

Part One

Love Hurts

Life's unfairness is not irrevocable;
we can help balance the scales for others,
if not always for ourselves.

- Hubert H. Humphrey

The darkness drops again but now I know
That twenty centuries of stony sleep
Were vexed to nightmare by a rocking cradle,
And what rough beast, its hour come round at last,
Slouches towards Bethlehem to be born?

- William Butler Yeats, "The Second Coming"

Find what you love and let it kill you . . .
For all things will kill you, both slowly and fastly,
but it's much better to be killed by a lover.

- Charles Bukowski (or maybe Kinky Friedman)

Chapter One

The Sisters in the Heartland

JENNIFER GRIPPED the edge of the crappy night-stand for support. The single candle on it flickered, sending shadows dancing across the room as the old wood creaked in response to her rutting. Her red hair hung down over her face in sweaty tangles. Her cheek was pressed down hard against the dirty bare mattress. The boy inside her thrusted jerkily from behind. Teenage sex in post-apocalyptic America was just like teenage sex before the world ended, except that nowadays, kids fucked without regard for their parents' morality, fear of disease, or social stigma.

Jennifer groaned. Mostly in pleasure, which was as good as she'd come to expect from Jimmy Brennachecke. Every once in a while he'd managed to shift his hips, arch his back, or lean—she wasn't sure exactly how it happened—in a way that placed him in the exact right spot and her body would light up in ecstasy. But so far today he'd missed the mark entirely and now his thrusts were getting faster and more erratic, which meant he was getting close, so if he was going to send her over the moon, time was running out.

She shoved her weight back into him and moved her hand from the nightstand to the headboard. And there, suddenly and out of nowhere, he hit it. Jennifer's back arched involuntarily as pleasure consumed her. A howl exploded from her, as if her orgasm was an animal that had just been trapped.

"Fuuuuuuck!" she breathed, seeing stars and starting to shake from the intensity.

Jimmy, who like Jennifer had come of age after the power had gone out for good, was a lean piece of meat. A nice enough kid, sweet, but too inexperienced with women to know when he was doing it right, and when he was just doing it. Hearing the f-word come out of her like that sprouted an ear-to-ear grin across his face. Embarrassed and turned on even more at the same time, Jimmy just prayed his father hadn't heard them, hadn't heard her. Nobody would care about the sex, but his dad was a real stickler for language and hated the f-word like it stung him when he heard it.

Thump.

The sound of someone, or something, bumping into furniture cleared his head of concerns over his girlfriend's language. The room was dark except for the splash of light from the candle. Jimmy couldn't remember what was in the space beside what he could see, which was the bed and the nightstand. He thought there was a chair, or maybe it was a sofa. A coffee table? The Landmark Inn had at one point been restored into a chic small-town boutique hotel, but that was before the lack of power drove most of the people of Fairfield, Iowa, away in search of electric outlets that still worked.

They should have cleared the room before they had started making out. *Oh, man.* They were so stupid! Why hadn't they cleared the freaking room?

He turned his head over his shoulder and tried to make out details in the flickering shadows. It was a pretty standard hotel room, or at least it had been back when the hotel was still operating—not that Jimmy had ever stayed there back then. He could see a dresser, a desk, a love seat, a window covered by dark blackout curtains. The love seat had to have been what had moved, but he didn't see anybody in there with them. Maybe it hadn't been the sound of something moving after all. The place was old and falling apart, maybe it was—

"Hey, where are you?" Jen asked.

Jimmy shook off the feeling of being watched and smiled at her.

"I'm here."

She smiled at him lovingly. Encouragingly.

You hit my special spot, for fuck's sake, don't lose focus now!

He slowly began to move inside her again. Jen moaned to encourage him as the stars began to explode once more. But Jimmy's intuitive muscle was stronger than he gave it credit for. The two barely teenagers were not alone.

In the flickering candlelight a pair of eyes appeared above the back of the love seat and watched hungrily. Staying in the shadows as if it was one itself, the thing watching them slipped around the room toward the bed. For a second the candlelight caught the stealthy form and revealed its human shape against the wall, but neither Jennifer nor Jimmy caught it, sex being the powerful diversion that it is.

Jimmy suddenly groaned involuntarily as his orgasm, short and sputtering, squeezed out of him and into her. It had come out of nowhere and caught him by surprise. He'd always pulled out of her to come before that instant, just to be safe (and because he kind of liked to see it coming out of him), so now he wasn't sure what to do. He wasn't entirely sure if she knew what had just happened. Maybe she just didn't care that he'd ejaculated inside her. He thought she had to have felt it, so he guessed it was okay. Spent, but not really satisfied, he collapsed onto her, his mind going back to the feeling that they were not alone. He tried to be completely still so he could listen, but Jen pushed her hips back, keeping him inside her and knocking them over from doggy-style to a spooning position on their sides. Then she started rocking her hips, keeping him stimulated inside her so that his barely existent refractory period wouldn't kill his boner. Sure enough, less than a minute later, his body flipped the switch back to the on position, and he started to match her movements, ready for round two.

The eyes observing them had positioned themselves just out of the light's reach. They watched as Jimmy reached back and grabbed the nightstand for support, knocking the candle precariously around as he did and sending flickering shadows everywhere. They watched as Jimmy turned his head suddenly, his neck hairs tingling, trying to catch whatever was giving him the feeling he was being watched. But by the time he was actually looking in the right direction, they'd moved under the bed. As the springs creaked and rocked rhythmically, Jimmy was left only with the view that they were alone.

The young lovers jackhammered away at each other, headboard banging, Jimmy's ironclad grip on the nightstand knocking the candle closer and closer to the edge with each thrust.

Back in the troughs of pre-orgasm starbursts, Jen's leg flipped over the end of the bed and hung there, like a piece of fruit on a low-hanging branch of a tree. The owner of the eyes could have reached out and grabbed her if it wanted to, but for the moment it only continued to observe. Jen's toes curled and flexed, her orgasm so close she could taste it hot and oily in her mouth. Still the eyes just watched and waited. But if the watcher was waiting for a better opportunity to grab the young woman, it waited too long. Jen's leg flipped back up onto the bed and into relative safety as Jimmy continued to thrust and knock the candle on the nightstand closer and closer to the edge.

The silent observer slipped out from under the bed and watched as Jen maneuvered on top and grabbed the headboard with both hands, rocking Jimmy's world as he felt himself no longer moving in and out as much as moving forward and back inside her. Then, moments before he was about to come for a second time, it watched the candle fall from the nightstand and its light snuff out upon contact with the floor.

The darkness was instantaneous, thick and suffocating.

The sex stopped immediately.

Both Jen and Jimmy were frozen by a terror only a child of the apocalypse can feel for the dark. They tried to listen in the pitch, but only heard their own breathing. Jen dismounted. The sound of the bed groaning under her movement was impossibly loud to her ears. She and Jimmy waited, ears open, eyes bulging. As if communicating telepathically, they both held their breath at the same time. The silence bloomed as thick as the dark, suffocatingly so, until all of a sudden, it was broken.

Click, click click-clicky click.

A scampering sound on the hardwood. They were not alone. The sound was claws. Neither of them had heard claws on hardwood before, at least not that they could remember, but they still knew it instantly.

In the black, the sounds of movement on the bed erupted and were joined by frantic fumbling and the distinct sound of a lighter.

Phhhhhft. Nothing.

Phhhft. Phhhft. No spark. No light. Nothing.

"It's okay. We're just . . ." Jimmy started, but without light it didn't matter what he said and he knew it.

Phhhhft. Phhhhft. Phhhft. Spark.

Phhhhft-phhhhft. Spark.

Light!

Jen expected to see a berserker-demon or something worse looming over them, but she didn't. In fact, as she scanned the room, she saw nothing out of place. Just Jimmy doing the same thing, with the same results. The room was empty. Or at least appeared to be. The *clicky-click* must have been in their heads.

Jimmy snatched the candle from the floor and relit the wick, adding its flame to the light being produced by his father's Special Forces Zippo, effectively doubling it. Still, they seemed to be alone.

"You must've knocked it over," Jimmy said.

"I must've knocked it over? Fuck you, dude."

They both laughed. It was a desperate, forced, almost manic giggle, like some kind of verbal talisman against the raw nerves and sense of impending doom that had crawled inside their hearts and laid its toxic eggs.

"You got to watch your mouth, babe."

"Seriously? You're taking up that crusade now too?"

"No," Jimmy insisted. "I just . . . I want my dad to like you. More."

"You like me enough. And he's not here . . . so *fucking* relax."

Somehow the teasing, lighthearted way she said it did make him relax. *What's Dad's freaking problem anyway?* he thought to himself, turned on by his rebellion of having sex with a girl who so wantonly swore and cursed, while at the core of his heart he was unable to shake the distaste for profanity he'd been instilled with from birth. Then again, Jimmy was a healthy teenage boy; a suggestively shaped rock could have turned him on. He never stood a chance against the beautiful redheaded potty mouth.

Wishing he hadn't said anything, Jimmy reached his hand over the edge of the bed to where a half-empty bottle of booze and an unopened box of condoms lay in wait. His hand found the condoms first and he pulled them up with a grin.

"A little late for that, dude," Jen said with a wink. Then, seeing the much more mundane fear in his eyes, she added, "I'm about to get my period. You're fine."

It didn't even occur to Jimmy to question if that really meant she couldn't get pregnant. Nor did it occur to him to wonder, with her mom dead and her dad left for dead in some prison two thousand miles away, where she'd learned the birds and bees from. Those kinds of questions didn't matter much to adults anymore, much less horny teenagers.

He reached back down for the booze, knowing the bottle was there, but not its location specifically enough to just grab it. His hand searched blindly. Had he known what was under the bed, lying in wait, inches from his probing fingers . . . Had he known that even the most docile of animals could get you killed in this post-apocalyptic nightmare he was growing up in . . . Had he known that his life was about to end, he might not have been as thirsty. But he didn't know. So when his hand finally found the bottle and he pulled it up, he didn't thank his lucky stars or shed tears of relief at the gift he'd been given of a few more moments of naked stupidity with the girl he loved. He just took a sip, grimaced at the taste, and ogled Jen's naked body.

"Where were we?" he asked suggestively.

"I'm done."

"Oh, come on."

"Seriously. My heart is racing. I'm, like, freaked out, dude."

Jimmy rolled his eyes. "With all the crap that we've seen, babe, you're telling me you're afraid of the dark?"

"Ah, it's exactly because of all the crap we've seen that I'm afraid of the dark, you fucking prick."

Jimmy slid off the bed.

"Where are you going?" Jen asked.

"Relax, I'm just draining the weasel," he said as he walked into the darkness, toward the toilet that was in a little alcove near the door to the room.

Pffffft.

This time the Zippo ignited on the first try. Jimmy saw that he was in the closet space that separated the main room from the bathroom. He saw the box of emergency candles they'd left next to the sink. He saw that Jen had flushed the toilet after she peed (something she always did before sex, but not something he'd ever asked her about) and now there was no water in the bowl. But what he did not see was the little girl who was standing in the back of the closet, watching him.

She was eleven, maybe twelve years old, with unnaturally black hair, the bangs of which almost completely covered her eyes. She wore a dirty bone-white lace petticoat under a Lolita-gothic jumper-skirt, elegantly embellished with ruffles and bustles. Her slim-fitting tailored white blouse had embellishments on the cuffs and neckline. The opaque white stockings that ran up her legs to just over her knees were held in place with frilly garters. She wore black Mary Janes on her feet, and she held a hand ax tightly in her hands like she was some kind of crazed anime lumberjack a blow away from yelling *Timber!* The expression on her painted red lips as she stared up at him, with her black shadowed eyes hidden behind her bangs, suggested she was not happy. But since he didn't see her, Jimmy never got the chance to wonder why.

His attempt to light one of the candles in the bathroom instead extinguished the flame of the lighter and plunged him into darkness again. *Crap,* he thought as the hairs on the back of his neck suddenly stood straight up. Doom pressed in on him as he felt sure the stupid Zippo wouldn't light again, but it ignited without a problem. A half second later the candle was lit as well. But even in the light, the sense of impending doom remained. He turned his head and looked over his shoulder, this time directly into the closet. But the little girl with the ax was gone.

Seeing that he was alone, but not feeling like he was, he shrugged off his heebie-jeebies enough to loosen his bladder. As he listened to the sound of his piss hitting the porcelain change to the sound of it hitting liquid as he filled the bowl up, he fought the urge to look over his shoulder again. A second later, he lost that fight.

Clicky-clack.

He choked the stream of urine off so he could listen. But there was only silence. He couldn't even hear Jen making any noise, which didn't do anything to ease his anxiety. He thought about calling out to her, but he didn't want to look stupid, especially after the dumb thing he'd said about her watching her mouth, so he placated himself to just slowly turning and looking over his shoulder.

Nobody was there.

Of course he felt like he wasn't alone, he told himself, Jen was, like, twenty-five feet away. But somewhere in his heart he knew that she wasn't the presence he was sensing. He unleashed his urine again, but didn't turn back to aim and heard his piss hit the tile floor. *Crap.* He twisted back to the toilet and guided his stream to the place it belonged.

Creak.

The floorboards groaned and this time he was positive he'd actually heard it. His head twisted back around like it was spring-loaded as he prepared himself to look his would-be killer straight in the eyes—but he was alone in the bathroom. The closet hallway was empty. *What's freaking wrong with me?* he wondered, shaking his head.

"Dang, babe, you've got me spooked now," he called out as he let the rest of his urine loose.

On the bed around the corner, Jen smiled at him, then she too heard the sound of claws on the hardwood, or at least she thought she did. Slowly and nervously she turned her head toward the far side of the bed, but nothing was there. She listened hard for a second, but all she heard was Jimmy peeing.

I need a fucking drink, she thought and flopped onto her stomach, poked her head over the edge of the bed to where the bottle of booze was, and reached for it.

Movement in the darkness of the far corner under the bed caught her attention. Her hand froze, fingertips just touching the glass of the bottle. Did she really see something back there or was it just—

Suddenly a huge opossum darted out of the blackness, its sharp, pointy rodent teeth bared to the gums as it lunged at her from under the bed, hissing like a rabid cat.

Jen screamed and launched herself back onto the relative safety of the bed. Jimmy rushed to her, his flaccid penis flopping about, dripping pee everywhere. The opossum, hissing and snapping its teeth at them, scampered into the middle of the room with absolutely no intention of playing dead.

Jimmy reached the bed and pulled the naked, shaking Jennifer into his arms. The adrenaline pumping through his veins triggered his autonomic threat assessment system and allowed him to immediately recognize that the giant rodent, while extremely pissed off, was not really particularly dangerous.

"It's okay, babe." He laughed in relief. "It's just a possum. It's okay." He turned to Jen and pulled her face to his. Her pupils were as big as nickels. "It's okay."

But even as he was saying the words, part of him knew it wasn't true. Part of him knew he wouldn't live another minute. His brain twisted, trying to unknot the certainty of his doom with the situation as he saw it, but he couldn't figure out where death was hiding.

Unseen from the shadows in the far corner of the room, the little girl with the ax stepped out and rushed toward them.

Swack! The ax sunk into the head of the opossum, almost splitting it in half.

The sound of the blow and the sudden silence that followed it drew Jimmy's attention away from Jen. He saw that the opossum was now inexplicably dead—very dead. Blood gushed from its head like from a burst pipe and pooled on the floor around it. But there was no sign of the opossum's killer. Jimmy's brain just gave up trying to understand what was happening, which was probably for the best, because in another thirty seconds Jimmy was going to be as dead as the opossum was. But it wasn't an ax that would do him in. It was the naked girl in his arms.

Jennifer felt it coming while Jimmy was locked with her eye to eye, but she couldn't get the words out of her throat. The warning to run. Her mouth opened, but her vocal cords had seized shut. It might have been part of the change that was about to take her over, but she didn't think so. She thought it was despair that had silenced her. Grief. The certainty that Jimmy was already dead but just didn't know it yet, that no warning could save him, that she was going to be the one to kill him. She felt her lip quiver as sobs tried to get out of mouth ahead of the words, but those wouldn't make it out her either. By the time sound exited her throat, Jennifer was gone and what escaped her was not a warning, not a sob, but a snarl.

Violent convulsions racked her naked body as the veins under her pale, almost translucent, skin bulged up with rushing HGF-filled blood, which was not so much being pumped as blasted through her body with each beat of her heart. She felt like she was burning from the inside out, but the feeling vanished with the rest of her so fast the pain barely even registered. Her muscles engorged with the loaded blood, giving her strength and speed no human being could match. The transformation was impossibly fast. So fast that she was already attacking him before Jimmy could do anything beyond simply flinch reflexively.

His face twisted into a bloody mask, half terror and half realization, as Jennifer grabbed his head with one hand and her nails sank into his skin like knives. She tossed him like a rag doll across the room and commenced with blindly tearing the room to shreds before he'd even made contact with the wall.

Smash!

Jimmy's body crumpled against the wall and dropped like an anchor to the ground. It was a hard blow, but not the deathblow that was coming. He still had the longest ten seconds of his life to get through before he would be granted that grace. Painfully he raised his bleeding face from the dusty floor, and for the first time he saw the little girl with the ax, hiding under the bed. He knew her, but the blow to his head had knocked his memory all out of whack. He wouldn't have been able to tell you his own name, much less hers. But he did know she was Jennifer's sister.

Bobby-Leigh looked at Jimmy from under the bed and hoped he was smart enough to survive this. She liked him enough, but more importantly, she knew Jen would be a disaster if she ended up killing him, because her older sister was in love with the dude. Jen had never been in love before (or if she had, she'd never said it) so if she killed him, well, that would just suck for her on all kinds of levels. Unfortunately, Bobby-Leigh knew Jimmy well enough to know that *smart* would never be an adjective folks would use to describe him.

Though dead *will probably be one soon,* she thought.

Hoping he'd just follow her lead and keep his head down and play dead, like that stupid-ass opossum should have, she raised a finger to her lips and shushed him. The berserker-demon that had possessed her sister for the moment was crushing and smashing and grinding her way through the furniture in the room. She smashed her fists into the walls and ripped and trashed the wires, pipes, and whatever else caught her attention.

"Don't move a muscle. Don't make a—" she tried to whisper to him, but, just like she'd thought, he was not one of the smart ones.

"Dad!" Jimmy screamed at the top of his lungs over and over again as he tried to get to his feet. The berserker immediately stopped demolishing the wall and turned her attention on her boyfriend, whose time was finally up.

Bobby-Leigh watched as her sister tore the naked boy to pieces. "Fuck," the little girl said quietly to herself. "Jimmy, you goddamn idiot."

The berserker tossed the bed, exposing Bobby-Leigh, but the little girl didn't move and, sure enough, instead of grabbing her next, the monster was drawn by the sound of the bed she'd just tossed smashing through the closet wall and into the door. The little girl waited until the creature's back was to her and then scurried into a corner to wait the destruction out, painfully aware that the doorway out of the room was now blocked. But that was okay, because the demon's rage was already starting to dissipate. Jen was wearing herself out. Her final act of violence was throwing the nightstand through the windows and flooding the room with dusty rays of the morning light.

The berserker collapsed.

In the calm that came directly after the *thud* of her sister's fall to the debris-covered floor, Bobby-Leigh heard voices and banging from the hallway.

"Jimmy!" a male voice cried.

Brennachecke senior, most likely, Bobby-Leigh thought.

"Jen! Jimmy!"

"The door's blocked," somebody with him yelled, Ace or maybe Roger.

"I don't give a rat's uncle if it's blocked or not! Get us inside. Now."

That was definitely Brennachecke, Bobby-Leigh thought, as she counted out the mental stopwatch running in her brain.

"One one-thousand. Two one-thousand. Three one-thousand."

She surveyed the devastation in the room as she counted. *Come on,* she thought. *Think! They're going to be inside this room any minute. What are you going to do? What are you going to say? What can you say?*

"Four one-thousand. Five one-thousand."

Jen had collapsed behind a pile of rubble. Only her still-veiny bare foot was visible to her sister. *Come on,* Bobby-Leigh thought, continuing to count. Outside, the "rescuers" had managed to get the door cracked and were hard at work assessing the wreckage barricading it. Bobby-Leigh ignored them.

Whack! Bam! Whack!

The rescuers had found a fire ax. Or somebody had just had one; these were the days when folks did carry those things around—it was like the iPhone of the apocalypse. Wood splintered. They were making progress, which meant Bobby-Leigh was running out of time to get her and her sister out of this.

"Twelve one-thousand. Thirteen one-thousand. Fourteen one-thousand. Fifteen . . ." Bobby-Leigh stopped. "Fuck it," she said to the empty room as she got to her feet. Her eyes involuntarily went to the bloody pile that was Jimmy's shredded body. No part of her wanted to look, but she found herself looking just the same. A huge sigh escaped her throat.

What number am I on? she thought as she slowly approached the monster her sister was trapped inside.

"Nineteen one-thousand? Twenty one-thousand. Twenty-one one-thousand."

At thirty-one one-thousand, Bobby-Leigh was standing over the hulking demon, trying to decide what to do. A dark part of her thought it might be for the best if she just killed her sister right there where she lay. But she didn't think she could do that, even if it would have been a mercy killing if ever there was one. After all, her sister was going to be all kinds of fucked up over what she'd just done, just like Bobby-Leigh thought her dad must have been after he'd murdered their mom. But the twelve-year-old didn't want to be alone. In fact, she'd rather be dead.

Bobby-Leigh nudged the demon's arm with her foot. Nothing.

Come the fuck on, Jennifer! the little girl thought and kicked the monster lying on the ground in front of her as hard as she could.

But still nothing happened.

She'd lost count in her head. She knew from experience that it took at least a minute before an unconscious berserker was safe to approach. She would have needed both hands to count the number of people she'd personally seen torn apart because they'd thought that one was dead, or that the episode had ended, and been wrong.

CRASH!

The doorway would be breached any minute. Bobby-Leigh knelt down by her sister's head. She didn't have any more time.

Phlack!

She slapped her sister as hard as she could across the face.

Nothing.

Maybe she's died somehow. Maybe she's just berserked out too many times to survive. That does happen to folks, Bobby-Leigh thought. *Fuck.*

She lowered her head, put her ear inches away from her sister's mouth, and listened for breath. For a long moment, the little girl couldn't tell if her sister was breathing or not. All she could hear was her own breath and the idiots outside the door breaking in. But it didn't end up mattering.

Jennifer's berserker eyes opened suddenly, and Bobby-Leigh found herself in a staring contest with death incarnate. Jen didn't move. But Bobby-Leigh did. She leaped to her feet and raised the ax over her head, but held fast.

Waiting.

Watching.

Wondering.

A shudder passed through Jen's naked body. As her eyes blinked erratically, Jennifer's pupils constricted to pinpoints and her overloaded body started to seize. A second later the seizure was over and Jen just lay there, eyes open and unblinking, her body frozen and rigid on the floor.

Bobby-Leigh waited. Knowing all too well that it wasn't over yet. Then Jennifer took a huge gasping breath and sat straight up. A human breath. Bobby-Leigh wouldn't have been able to tell you the difference between the inhalation of a human and a berserker, but she knew it when she saw it.

"Thank you. Thank you. Thank you," Bobby-Leigh told the room.

She set the ax down and wiped a strand of bloody hair from Jennifer's face. Suddenly Jennifer convulsed again, hacking and coughing. Bobby-Leigh instinctively rocketed back from her like she was dodging a striking rattlesnake, and raised the ax high to strike back if she needed to. But Jennifer was done for now. Gagging, she spit up several teeth into her hand. Both girls stared at them.

"Are those mine?" Jennifer asked weakly, knowing the answer, but not wanting to.

Bobby-Leigh lowered her ax and looked across the room to Jimmy's crushed skull. None of his teeth appeared to be missing. She answered her sister's question with a nod and looked away as Jen connected the dots in her head.

Like all berserkers, Jennifer had no memory of what she'd done while possessed. But this wasn't her first rodeo ride with the devil inside her, so, as she took in the destruction and chaos around her, including the body of the boy she loved, whom she had obviously and violently dismembered and crushed like an empty soda can, she wasn't surprised by what she saw, just sad.

And hungry. Painfully, nauseatingly hungry.

It was quite possible for a person to die of starvation in the middle of berserking out. The physical demands on the body burned so many calories so fast that most of the time it was physical exhaustion that knocked the monsters out at the end of their episodes. Jen would need to consume thousands of calories in the next hour or so, or she'd likely go into a coma.

They didn't have time for a coma.

As tears dripped out of the naked girl's eyes and she choked her sadness down like it was something to eat, her lizard brain, not to be confused with the berserker one, started spinning and flipping switches. Survival mode was activated.

What was the situation?

She was naked. Jimmy was dead. Bobby-Leigh was not. People were outside. They were trying to get inside. Jimmy's dad was one of the people. Jimmy was dead. The folks outside would realize that either she or her sister was a berserker. No, they would realize that she was the berserker. She was the one covered in blood, so it was going to be pretty obvious Bobby-Leigh hadn't done this to the room, or to Jimmy.

Brennachecke was a reasonable man. He was more than aware that berserkers had no control over what they did when they lost it. But Jimmy wasn't just some kid who'd come in off the street. He was the man's youngest son. And even if he hadn't been, Brennachecke was like a fucking accountant when it came to shit like this. Debiting one son from column A would require crediting column B with Jen's life. It was just math. It wasn't personal. The equation simply had to balance.

Bobby-Leigh dropped a pile of clothes at Jen's feet. She was saying something, but Jen wasn't listening. She was too hungry to focus. Without thinking, the blood-covered teenager pulled on her dead boyfriend's shirt and then her panties from the pile of clothing. Only her lizard brain was currently operational. And it was panicking. They were going to kill her, and then they'd kill Bobby-Leigh, because what the fuck else would they do with her? That was how it worked these days. There was no talking about shit, no trying to come to terms and understand each other. You just committed murder and moved the fuck on.

The threat assessment came in loud and clear: they were fucked.

"Jen, we gotta go," Bobby-Leigh was saying.

But there was nowhere to go. The door suddenly broke open. The busted bed that had been pinning it shut still barred entry into the room, but that was more of a nuisance at this point and wouldn't hold anybody back for long. Through the opening in the broken door the girls could make out Brennachecke, fire ax in hand, and a small, faceless crowd behind him standing in the decrepit hotel hallway.

Brennachecke had been a staff sergeant in the Marines and was a veteran of several of the retaliatory "wars" against the Al Qaeda and ISIS terror networks in the Afghanistan mountains and other hot spots in the Middle East. This was of course back when there was a United States and an Afghanistan, and radical Islamic extremists felt like the worst enemy Americans would ever face. He had been a good soldier then and was a good man now. Not that any of that mattered anymore. Good men did bad things. Evil men did good things. Post-apocalypse, right and wrong were about as arbitrary as which Twinkie you ate first when you were lucky enough to find a pack of them somewhere.

"Jimmy? Jen?!" he called out, squinting against the light flooding in from the broken windows. Bobby-Leigh and Jen didn't answer him. They didn't have to.

A single look at the half-naked girl covered in blood, her strange little sister, and the crushed skull of his youngest son was all it took for the brain in his clean-shaven head to accurately assess what had happened.

Brennachecke blinked once—that was all the time he needed to know what the right thing was to do. He felt no guilt or shame or pity about it.

"Eric," he called over his shoulder.

Reluctantly both Jen and Bobby-Leigh met the eyes of the man who had taken them in. The man who had promised them protection against the horrors of the world, fed them, taught them, and had never asked for anything in exchange for that protection. They both expected his eyes to now stare back at them cold as ice, but they weren't cold at all—just disappointed and sad. They continued to watch as Eric Brennachecke, the spitting image of his father, shaved head and all, pushed his way forward and stepped into the shattered doorway with a homemade flamethrower strapped to his back. Then they stopped watching, turned, and ran for the light streaming in through the broken windows behind them. The elder Brennachecke son (now the only Brennachecke son) opened the valve on his weapon and unleashed a long jet of flame.

The fire launched out across the room like a creature escaping from hell. It billowed and gobbled up the oxygen as it grew and stretched and pulsed—a hot, fanged serpent of flame, consumed by a hunger for destruction as much as berserkers were consumed by rage.

The long snake of burning gas snapped at the girls' heels as they leaped blindly for one of the shattered windows and burst through it into the morning air. The curtains exploded into flames around them as they seemed to hang for a split second two stories above the ground. But the fire would only singe the girls—it was the fall that was going to be dangerous.

Time sped back up, gravity kicked in, and down they dropped.

The hotel room overlooked one of the narrow little alleyways off Fairfield's main square. Below the window was a green plastic-lidded dumpster that was still half-full of garbage from years ago. The last vestige of humanity, throwing out the trash, had apparently lasted longer in Fairfield than the last vestige of civilization, picking the trash up. This turned out to be a lucky break for the girls. They smashed through the plastic lid of the dumpster into a much softer mess of dusty long-lost refuse, and ended up relatively unhurt aside from the superficial, though stinging, cuts from the glass. The landing wasn't the part of the fall that was the problem, though.

Adrenaline exploded into Jennifer's system. It exploded into Bobby-Leigh's as well, but the little girl didn't have a history of turning into a monster because of it, so she wasn't the issue. Shaking off the fall as fast as she could, the little sister grabbed the bigger one and locked eyes with her. Jennifer's pupils dilated to the size of nickels.

Fuck, the little girl thought. Berserking out again so soon without eating might actually kill her sister right here and now. But if it didn't, then being trapped with her in such a confined space was definitely going to end up getting Bobby-Leigh herself killed.

"Breathe. Breathe. In. Out. Close your eyes. Just listen to my voice. You're safe. We're safe. Find your mantra, Jen," Bobby-Leigh whispered as calmly as she could manage to her sister.

Bang! Pachink!

A gunshot bounced off the side of the dumpster.

Fucking hell! Bobby-Leigh thought as she looked up at the burning hole above them where the window used to be and saw Brennachecke standing in the billowing flames, pistol outstretched, recalibrating his aim. She closed her eyes, expecting to die, but the man was forced back inside before he could get the shot off. The fire was spreading fast. Bobby-Leigh heard wood inside the building pop and opened her eyes in time to see a puff of ash and flame explode out the hole. She hoped that was the end of Brennachecke. Not that she didn't understand why he was trying to kill them, or that she even disliked him for it; she just needed to focus and the motherfucking gunshots were extremely distracting.

In her arms, Jen twitched. Her big sister was obviously doing all she could to fight the change, but it seemed unlikely she would be winning the battle.

No, goddamn it! the little girl screamed in her own head while she slipped behind her sister, wrapped her in her arms, and held a karambit blade—a small curved knife that resembled the claw of a bear and which she had seemingly pulled out of thin air—to the bigger girl's throat.

The convulsions started.

"We're okay," she soothed. "Jen. We are okay. Find your mantra. It's so easy. Effortless. Remember? Just like breathing. Just like a heartbeat."

When she spoke her voice was calm, in stark contrast to the rest of her, and full of authority she didn't actually feel. She sounded like one of the Transcendental Meditation dudes her uncle used to have over for dinner, not like a little girl in a dumpster holding a knife against her sister's jugular.

Then, by the grace of a god neither girl really believed in (or simply due to the fact that Jen just didn't have the fuel in her to berserk out again), Jennifer's body calmed. Her pupils contracted back to normal. She blinked. Blood ran from yet another superficial wound, this one caused by the razor-sharp blade her sister was holding against her throat, but that was the extent of the damage inflicted.

Almost.

Jen spit blood into her hand, then reached up and probed inside her mouth for a second and pulled out another tooth. She looked at it without emotion, then touched the knife against her throat, signaling to Bobby-Leigh that she could lower her blade.

Clink.

Jen flicked the tooth against the side of the dumpster.

"Are you kidding me?" she whispered to her sister, as if the little girl was somehow responsible for all this, and tried very hard not to cry.

"We gotta find Dad," Bobby-Leigh said, putting the smaller knife away and grabbing her ax from the rubble.

"Fuck that shit, dude. I have to eat." The words came out stronger than she thought they would, so she added, "Besides, there's no way he's still alive anyway," as if that made anything better.

She was sure he was dead. Pretty sure, that was. The only way he'd have been able to survive would have been if he'd broken out of jail. Or if somebody had let him out, which she supposed might have happened.

Well so what if he is alive somewhere? she thought to herself as she climbed shakily out of the trash. He was dead to her.

"They're going to come after us, Jen. We've got nobody now. If you don't want to try to find Dad, then what do you think we should do?"

"I don't know! I'm fucking naked, standing here in an alley, Bobby-Leigh! I, I just killed my . . . Jesus, fucking Mary and Joseph, I just killed— I've got blood all over me. I'm fucking starving. What the hell do you want from me? I do *not* have a plan!"

Jen expected Bobby-Leigh to burst into tears, but she should have known better. Bobby-Leigh hadn't cried since she'd survived being snatched at a Walmart, and that was years ago. Besides, a little screaming from her big sister was pretty insignificant when it came to the long list of things that were actually worth shedding tears over these days. So Bobby-Leigh's eyes just stared back at her, like their father's used to when Jen would throw a temper tantrum. Back before he'd started really drinking. Back when mom had still been alive. Back when everything that went wrong hadn't ended up being her fault, and when her fucking sister didn't dress like she'd just stepped out of some Japanese anime program. Her little sister was as immune to her ranting as her father used to be before everything Jen loved decided to start dying on her.

But somebody needed to cry over this shit, so if Bobby-Leigh wasn't going to do it, she would. Jen sobbed quietly while Bobby-Leigh watched indifferently and waited, until she heard men shouting in the distance.

"They're coming," she said quietly.

"I have to eat," Jen said, but didn't move.

Her heart going out to her teary-eyed big sister, Bobby-Leigh firmly took Jen's hand and dragged her away. They slipped unseen around the corner and across the street to the bookshop café their murdered uncle used to love, now long out of business. A place that was once called Revelations.

Chapter Two
The Last Guard in Maine State Prison

AS MUCH AS JENNIFER wanted him to be—or at least thought she wanted him to be—Emmett Kessler was not dead. Nor had he been freed or been able to escape. He was right where they'd left him: 1,700 miles away in Maine State Prison.

If there had ever been a bad time to be sent to prison, the end of the world was certainly it. Had Emmett been a little more thoughtful in the middle of his guilt and grief, he may very well have reconsidered his refusal to appeal. The moral high ground of punishing yourself for not saving your wife's life and instead blowing her face off—even if it was in self-defense—crumbled a little bit when the guards stopped showing up for work and you got left there to rot.

The logic behind Jennifer's thinking Emmett should be dead was sound. He should have been and in fact would have been if it had not been for one man, a fifty-two-year-old veteran corrections officer by the name of Captain Bill P. Waters.

Captain Waters had worked Maine State ever since it was moved from Thomaston to Warren. For decades he'd tried to just "do his eight and hit the gate" like everybody told him to, but the man was cursed with a conscience.

Even before folks figured out the world was ending and started abandoning their short-sighted, self-centered, consumerist ways for equally short-sighted and self-centered survivalist ones, the prison was a place where psychopaths and sadists walked on both sides of the bars. But Captain Waters steadfastly refused to partake in beating the inmates or falsifying reports. He even asked the prison staff that he shared his shifts with to refrain from being verbally abusive. Sure, the worst offending COs just got their shifts changed and went on doing what they did. Sure, most of the cats he worked with thought he was just going easy on the black inmates because he was black himself. Sure, he spent most hours on the job waiting for the assistant warden to come up with a justification to fire him. And sure, he drank himself stupid most nights after work to keep himself from breaking down in tears of frustration and humiliation. But in spite of all that, he woke up every day, ironed his uniform, polished his shoes, showered, brushed his teeth, and arrived fifteen minutes earlier for his shift than he needed to.

Captain Waters believed in rehabilitation, and, despite the systematic failure of his superiors and colleagues to stop the rampant abuse of the clientele, he'd worn his uniform with pride. Besides, the uniform was ninety percent of the job; looking the part was how he earned the respect that kept him alive among rapists, thieves, and murderers. He was a stern, honorable man who stuck by the rule book more religiously than the pope stuck by the Bible. He was a man who did what he could when he could as long as it didn't end up risking his job, and in the US criminal corrections system that was doing a lot. For that, cats called him "Black Jesus" behind his back.

The apocalypse slowly eroded normal life for everybody. Prison was no exception. Eventually, the whole facility was on twenty-four-hour lockdown seven days a week, mostly because the COs one by one stopped showing up for work, until there was only a handful of staff left to manage the 950 inmates, give or take. Then the paychecks stopped coming and the supply deliveries stopped coming, and that handful quickly dwindled down to one.

Black Jesus could have just released all the men and walked away. Actually, he could have just walked away and left all those cats there to die. That was pretty much what everybody had told him to do, and what they had all done themselves. Even the inmates couldn't understand why he was hanging around, enforcing rules that clearly didn't mean shit anymore. But he did. He single-handedly kept the prison functioning, or at least kept the inmates alive, for ninety-three days.

Then riots started and black and white turned gray and red. Amid the smoke and chaos, Black Jesus kept the doors locked tight and let the fury and flames burn themselves out, as if the prison itself were a berserker. Hundreds and hundreds died at the hands of their cellmates. Hundreds more from the fires themselves. Captain Waters had done what he could to mitigate the carnage, but short of releasing everybody, there was simply not much one man could do once the ball got rolling. By the end of the hundredth day, only seventy-seven inmates were still alive.

Black Jesus had slowly and methodically cleared C Block of the dead and burned them in the staff parking lot. Then he had one by one moved the survivors in. It had taken almost a week to do—the man just wasn't as young as he used to be.

* * *

As Captain Waters had walked Emmett in shackles from the death stench of B Block to the relative cleanliness of C Block, Emmett had been pretty sure the man had lost his marbles. But he'd been wrong. Mostly.

"Captain Waters, sir. Why don't you just let us go? There's no way you're going to be able to keep us here, alive anyway."

"Did I ask for your opinion, inmate?"

"No, sir."

Black Jesus had stopped and given Emmett a strange look.

"I don't have the authority to let inmates out, Kessler. I know that may seem ridiculous to you, all things considered. But it is not ridiculous to me. You will do your time. Everybody here will. And then you'll be released."

"Do you even know how much time I have left?"

"Five hundred and ninety-six days."

Emmett had sighed and then muttered, "Great. So, basically, we're all going to starve to death."

"Not if I can help it. Now shut up and walk."

Black Jesus had decided to put Emmett in a cell with a twenty-eight-year-old berserker who was once named Wiley DuPont, but was now known almost exclusively as "Beast." When they'd arrived at the cell door, the monstrously muscled giant of what used to be a man had looked at Emmett with its simple, confused eyes. This was what became of folks once they'd berserked out too many times. The rage would sleep unless provoked, but whatever had once been DuPont—his personality, his loves and hates, his soul—those were lost inside the hulking muscles of Beast. Emmett had always pitied the poor thing. Whoever DuPont had been, he'd surely had more going on inside his head than he did now. Beast currently had the mental capacity of a toddler. He couldn't read. He couldn't write. He couldn't focus on anything for more than a few minutes. He also didn't seem to be bothered by it much. In fact, he might have been the happier of the two of them, Emmett had thought that day—but that didn't mean that he wanted to share a cell with the poor bastard.

"Can't you put the berserkers together?" Emmett had said as he'd met the hard eyes of Black Jesus.

The rationale, to say nothing of the procedure, for transferring the inmates was a complicated one. Captain Waters had thought long and hard about the best way to maintain order, considering he was the only one left to maintain it. The prison was not designed to be run by a single person; in fact, for safety reasons it was designed specifically *not* to be. And it was also not designed to be run without power for a prolonged period of time. Finding fuel for the generators was already taking a big part of Waters's day. He also needed time to find and stockpile food for when the kitchen storages eventually ran out. The riot had improved the food situation significantly, but he had cats who had life sentences to serve. No amount of rationing was going to make what they had last long enough. Things were pretty fucked. Frankly, he didn't really know how he'd managed to keep the place going as long as he had already. Still, he had no intention of walking away or releasing anybody early.

Of the seventy-seven convicts left, he had twenty-two berserkers and twenty-five basically nonviolent offenders that he more or less trusted not to kill him as soon as an opportunity presented itself, which left him with thirty clients potentially plotting to kill him and escape at any given second. The worst of those he'd put in the isolation cells, but he had decided to bunk the rest with a berserker cellmate in an attempt to keep everybody manageable. Captain Waters had hoped that the fear of provoking a berserker into raging out, which undoubtedly would lead to the non-berserker's death, might keep a lid on things. But he didn't tell Emmett any of that when the man questioned the new sleeping arrangements.

"Arms out, convict" was all he'd answered with. Then he'd cuffed Emmett to the bars and asked DuPont to come forward.

Berserker management was something the correctional system had had to figure out fast, because you can't send monsters to prison unless you have a method of controlling them, or at least subduing them. To that effect, all the COs in Maine State Prison had carried military-designed PharmaJet needleless injectors loaded with a mix of propofol and ketamine. Berserkers could usually survive a large number of doses in rapid succession without OD'ing on the stuff, but multiple doses didn't actually speed up the effect, which was to knock the monster out and make him forget the rage. However, the thirty or so seconds it took for the drugs to get to the brain and do their work was a long time to have a raging berserker in front of you. So, to mitigate abuse, the PharmaJets held only a single dose.

Back before everything fell apart and society stopped even bothering to send berserkers through the system, each berserker inmate had been assigned a "trainer" who, in addition to the standard-issue handheld injector, carried an eight-foot-long version of the device. The PharmaJet didn't hurt, so there wasn't any danger in administering it to a berserker if you could catch him before an episode started, as long as he was not caught by surprise.

"I'm going to give you your medicine, DuPont," Black Jesus had told the looming but docile creature. DuPont had known the drill, and less than a minute later the Beast was out cold and Emmett had been shoved inside with him.

"It's this or isolation, Kessler," Captain Waters had told Emmett. "Be grateful you'll at least have somebody to talk to."

The old black man had looked wearily at him, expecting Emmett to shoot his mouth off, but the cat just smiled at him sadly. Then, just as Waters had turned to go, Emmett called out to him.

"Captain, you may very well be the last righteous man on Earth, you know that? I can't say I agree with what you're doing or understand why the hell you're doing it, but there's a part of me that's glad—no, honored—that you are."

Captain Waters knew better than to trust anything that came out of an inmate's mouth, but he'd smiled just the same.

"All that time in the library. You ever read the Bible, Kessler?"

"No, sir. Though, considering the times, maybe I ought to have picked one up."

"'And the Lord replied, "Should I find fifty righteous men in the world, then I shall spare all on their account." And Abraham said, "suppose only ten can be found." And the Lord answered "for the sake of ten, I will not destroy the world."' Genesis 18 something or another."

"Looks like we came up a little short in the end on that one. About nine short, by my count."

"It does feel that way sometimes, inmate," Captain Waters had said over his shoulder as he walked back toward B Block to get the last of his wards moved in.

* * *

That first night, Emmett tried to sleep in the bunk above his new cellmate, but the monster's garbage disposal–like snores made it impossible. Exhausted and bored, his mind browsed through memories like a bored old drunk in a bookstore killing time before happy hour.

He rubbed his bloodshot eyes and attempted to squint and blink the weariness out of them. *Folks are addicted to the illusion of understanding things,* he thought, or remembered thinking at some point. His memory had been slowly handing the baton to his dreams, jumbling up the past with the present. *We track our steps. Measure our sleep. Count our calories. We have data for everything. Yet folks don't know shit about how anything actually works.* He could feel the rant building in his mind, but then suddenly sleep grabbed his pillow and smothered him into unconsciousness.

In his dreams that night, he was back in the prison library, researching obsessively. Folks all had their way of passing the time while they were incarcerated. It was as important as food when it came to surviving in prison. Plotting to kill, rape, or smuggle in contraband were the most popular pastimes, followed by finding religion and getting an education. Trying to figure out how not to get raped or shanked took up a lot of the time in the beginning, but folks either learned that quickly, or they didn't and one or the other happened to them. Until the library was shut down, Emmett had clocked most of his days exploring and developing his theory of where berserkers came from.

Had Emmett been incarcerated half a decade earlier, the depth of his investigation would have been impossible. When the United Nations all the way back in 2011 declared that Internet access was a fundamental part of the human right to free expression and opinion, they were not concerned with the civil rights of prisoners in the United States, but that decision planted a seed—a seed that was then watered by Time Warner, Facebook, Google, and other powerful lobbying interests, until the thorny concept of neutrality had grown into such a convoluted root system that it spurred a lawsuit against the California Department of Corrections over the email-only access to the Internet the US Department of Justice instituted when it enacted the Trust Fund Limited Inmate Computer System (TRULINCS). The case worked its way up to the Supreme Court, and in a five-to-four split decision the US joined a number of European nations in allowing limited Internet access to inmates for educational and legal defensive purposes, which was all Emmett needed.

On the surface there was nothing about his explanation that made any more sense than anybody else's rationalizations—except that Emmett happened to be right and the fact that he was made his theory stick in the craw like the melody of a children's song after a day at summer camp. Not that it mattered; being right would only bring him trouble, never the peace or closure he'd hoped to find at the end of its fickle rainbow. He was not a scientist, so most of the hows and whys were way over his head, but the way he saw it, after World War II mankind ended up in this kind of bizarre evolutionary period. The number of reproductively viable men in the world had been cut down so drastically and so fast that there was a blip of sorts in the human genome. Had nothing else changed and had folks just gone back to having babies again, the blip would have been just that, a blip. But things did change—a lot of things.

Science got a little out of control during the twentieth century. Food processing, genetically modified organisms, baby formula, electromagnetic radiation, drugs (both recreational and medical), pollution, and a thousand other "advances" in technology came year after year. When folks figured out that cigarettes caused cancer, and then, in rapid succession, horrifyingly discovered that just about everything else in the modern world did too, fear of "the big C" took over the world and things calmed down a little. But cancer was such a slow-acting death sentence, it never really scared anybody enough to really change their behavior, much less correct the collision course they—we—had set for the apocalypse. Only when folks were pretty much used to the cancer did they start to realize it was just the tip of the iceberg. And no warning labels or education could save us from hitting it.

The end really began with the world's refusal to accept the fertility issues that came with the toxicity of what was now the twenty-first century. Of course, a causal relationship between any one thing and infertility could almost never be convincingly established, but the fact was, for generations our collective biology had tried to respond to the world we were creating, and natural evolutionary adaptation just couldn't keep up. And so humanity found itself in a unique position in the history of life on our planet: pockets of human genetic polymorphic sympatric speciation erupted around the world and went unnoticed by the scientific community.

Emmett didn't understand as much of the science as he wished he did. But he had finally gotten his head around what polymorphic sympatric speciation was and why it was manifesting as fertility issues. Polymorphism in genetics, at its very core, was the existence of different versions—or morphs—of a species within the species as a whole. The most common and obvious example of this is the separation of humans into male and female versions. The existence of blood types is another example. At some point, polymorphism had split the human species into a new set of subgroups: those with the berserker gene and those without it.

Polymorphism happens all the time and wouldn't have been a problem, at least not an end-of-the-world problem, except that sympatric speciation, which is when a new species evolves within the population of one that already exists, was forced on the human population when those with the berserker gene and those without turned to science to overcome their hidden genetic incompatibility.

It seemed so obvious once Emmett had gotten his head around it: The two different morphs of the human species that made up the baby boomer generation would have had difficulty producing kids—just like how Rh negative blood in a mother with an Rh positive blood-typed fetus can make birth problematic—but the berserker gene morph made things a thousand times worse, because if that baby did manage to survive, the child would technically no longer be human. And yet, it'd still be genetically close enough that with a little scientific encouragement this new non-human could still produce offspring with a regular human—though with a few quite literally monstrous side effects.

He'd tried to get further into the biology to understand more about how this all worked but always ended up grinding his teeth and wanting to bash his face into the cement walls. But he didn't have to understand it all. He got the point: an increasingly toxic world had forced humans to rapidly genetically adapt until we became a hybridized species population.

Of course, people totally oblivious to the genetic failsafe that had been activated inside their DNA still wanted to have babies. Frustrated parents-to-be, of which not only Emmett and Susan had to be counted among but also Susan's parents as well, collectively said *Fuck you* to their biology and turned to science to fix it. Never mind that nobody really understood what the *it* was that they were trying to fix. Never mind that when you say *Fuck you* to her, Nature—who is not nearly as impartial as she's thought to be—almost always says *Fuck me? No. Fuck you, motherfucker. Fuck you!* and then fucks with you right back a thousand times worse. (Just ask the idiots who introduced rabbits to Australia.) Even now, humanity, or what was left of it, still hasn't grasped that concept yet. Maybe folks never will.

Back in the seventies, Susan's mother had tried for years to get pregnant, and just as she was about to give up, a Dr. Weiss had come along and *cured* her by taking her eggs out of her body and manually introducing them to Susan's father's sperm. Nobody asked about or cared about what nature was trying to safeguard folks against by keeping them from reproducing. Nature had been the enemy and Dr. Weiss the conquering hero. Susan had been born healthy, beautiful, and perfect in all the ways that could be measured at the time. So when Susan and Emmett had trouble conceiving themselves, Grandma had introduced them to the man who had made miracles happen for her, and Dr. Weiss had done his magic again. A year later, after a couple of failures that Dr. Weiss had used to tweak his work, Jennifer was born, just as healthy, beautiful, and perfect as her mother.

The first inkling of the idea had crept into his subconscious the night Emmett had killed his wife. Back in the bar, when life still seemed like it had somewhere to go. Back when Emmett had just seen Julie Barnes on the news. She'd been a fellow patient of Dr. Weiss. And if Emmett remembered correctly, Julie's mother had been a patient of his as well—just like Susan and her mother. The news report had been about how Julie had berserked out and killed her family—just like Susan would less than an hour later, the only difference being that Emmett would murder his wife before she could rip their girls apart, and apparently Brad, or whatever Julie's husband's name had been, hadn't found the opportunity to do that himself.

It had felt like a pattern, and Emmett's theory had started forming in the dark corners of his brain as soon as it landed in his subconscious. Trying to pass the time those first couple of years of his sentence (the time he should have spent filing an appeal), Emmett had started looking into just how many of Dr. Weiss's other patients had berserked out. It had seemed like a stupid line of inquiry at the time—the activity of a guilty mind desperate to find somebody else he could hold accountable for what happened. He'd known it was stupid. Everybody had told him it was stupid. But the more he dug, the less stupid it had become, at least to him. In no time, he'd found himself falling down the research rabbit hole.

The memory–dream jukebox in Emmett's head then suddenly flipped to the only significant interaction he'd ever had with Wiley DuPont, no doubt triggered by the monster's snoring. The day Beast had almost killed him.

* * *

Emmett had been sitting at the computer.

A couple of notepads had been open next to him, filled with his tiny, precise scrawl. In one was a list of all the patients of Dr. Weiss he'd been able to find over the man's considerably long career as a fertility specialist in the United Kingdom, South America, and then the United States. Almost all the names had a check mark next to them, indicating that either that woman's child or somebody related to her had been documented as having a berserker episode.

In the other pad were the notes he'd taken as he attempted to understand the science. He'd chewed absent-mindedly on his pen as he glanced over his scribbles, trying to put it all together. His eyes focused on the name *Dr. Julius Weiss* written at the top of the page, and then shifted to the crux of his theory, spelled out in all capital letters in the middle:

DIFFICULTY IN CONCEPTION = NEW HUMAN SPECIATION?

Emmett tapped on a link in the browser of the computer and his screen filled with an abstract from one of Dr. Weiss's papers. This wasn't the first of Dr. Weiss's research he'd tried to read, nor would it be the last, but it had been the most important to his theory. Not because it explained anything in a way Emmett could understand, but because this was the paper that had given Emmett a reason to carry on. A reason to live. This was the paper that had convinced the grieving father who had turned his back on his own children that there was somebody else he could hold accountable.

The paper was titled "Declining Fertility in the Modern Age Due to Increased Genetic Incompatibilities in Women Born after 1942." And as he'd read through the detailed summary, one thought had rattled around his head like a loose screw: *You knew, you fucking son of a bitch.*

"In this day and age there is no good reason why a woman at your level of health should not be able to have a baby," he'd recalled Dr. Weiss's words to them at some point. His almost nonexistent German accent twisted into a grotesque and clichéd caricature of Hitler's in Emmett's memory.

While caught up in his daydreams, the eight-foot brick house of a berserker that was Beast had bumped into him, snapping Emmett out of his angry, mocking sarcasm. Beast had looked at him like the main attraction in some kind of monster zoo would look at a schoolboy on the other side of the glass.

"I bumped you," Beast had said slowly, his words coming out garbled and gummy from his lack of teeth.

"It's okay, Wiley."

There were about three dozen full-on berserkers that Emmett knew about in the prison at that time, and they were all legends. Like some sick and twisted version of high school popularity, all the inmates knew their names and at least some of their stories. They'd all entered the system before chain reactions had started to become such a common complication that it became impractical to incarcerate every poor son of a bitch whose switch got flipped. But Emmett had never bothered to keep up with developments on shit like that when he was on the outside, and once inside, he'd never wondered why no new berserkers ever arrived on the block. Those were the kinds of observations a caring person might make, and in those days Emmett still didn't give a flying fuck about anything outside of the theory he was developing and the vengeance it promised him.

Still, Emmett had known, if only by osmosis, that Wiley was a Bostonian who had berserked out for the first time (as far as the official record went) at a nightclub on Tremont Street called the Royale. No chain reactions had been triggered. He'd been a small (or at least normal-sized) man then, but had still managed to kill thirty-one people and had been responsible for the injuries of at least a hundred more. Emmett had also heard through the prison walls that when Wiley's incarceration began he wasn't anywhere close to the size of the colossus he was now. Apparently it had only taken three months in prison for the poor bastard to have been provoked into berserking out so many times that the radical physical changes in his physique occurred. Prison had taken the man and, in less time than it took Time Warner to cancel your cable for nonpayment, turned him inside out, so that the monster that once hid inside him was now all that was left. Convicts had made him into what he was as sport. It blew Emmett's mind that somehow COs like Black Jesus genuinely believed that rehabilitation was still possible for assholes who would do something like that for fun.

Emmett had glanced over to where Black Jesus was monitoring them with disapproving eyes. Murderers, thieves, even rapists he agreed could probably be rehabilitated, given enough time and the right system. But folks who demonstrated cruelty like that? Emmett would have preferred those dickheads shot.

"I bumped you?" Beast repeated, as if suddenly unsure whether or not he actually had.

Emmett smiled up at him and had been about to say something when a big book hit Beast squarely in the head.

Fuck.

Emmett jumped to his feet and stepped protectively in front of Wiley as three Aryan Nation types, all not much more than kids, approached them slowly with books they had no intention of reading in their hands. Emmett recognized the leader by the death's head swastika on his neck and thought his name was Borman or something.

"You dropped your book," Emmett said to him, as Wiley bent down to pick up the volume that had been thrown at him and handed it back to Borman with what he obviously thought was a helpful smile, but which had mostly been just terrifying because of how his HGF-flooded system had built up his jaw muscles and caused his teeth to fall out.

"Oopsie-poopsie, dropped your booksie. Oopsie-daisy-doodle-o," Beast sang like a child.

The Aryans laughed, then the asshole on Borman's left had drawn his arm back and launched a new book in their direction. Again Beast was hit in the face. Confused, he bent to pick it up, still seemingly oblivious to the fact he'd been attacked.

"Oopsie-poopsie, dropped the booksie, need a hooksie, daisy-doodle-o," he'd sang like an old man with dementia.

The CO trainer that was supposed to be monitoring Beast was now chatting with a female officer a couple of rows away, and both had missed the whole thing. The only other CO in sight was Black Jesus, but the do-gooder had been too busy disapproving of the fraternizing between the other two coworkers to notice the misbehavior of the inmates right in front of him. Emmett knew they'd all be there to put Beast down in a heartbeat if these assholes were to succeed in triggering the poor guy into having an episode. But by the time it was taken care of, somebody would surely be hurt, or dead, and that somebody would probably be him. Plus, this shit was just cruel and pissed him off.

"Do you really have to do this bait-the-berserker shit in the library, folks?"

"You the fuckin' librarian now, Kessler?" The dickhead on Borman's right had asked, his thick Boston accent turning "now" to *nah* and "Kessler" to *Kesslah*.

"This is the only computer that still works," he answered, trying to find a balance between pleading and commanding in his tone.

Black Jesus had finally realized trouble was brewing and had pulled himself away from the affair his colleagues had been trying to have.

"Borman, I know you and your friends can't read, so put the book down before we have a problem here."

The Aryan threesome had moved as if to comply, but then Borman himself suddenly lunged forward and smacked Beast hard across the face with the book in his hand. Beast's face contorted. His pupils dilated. Then with a fury and quickness his previously slow, shy demeanor would have made seem impossible, he had exploded in an all too familiar violent rage.

In Emmett's memory of the incident, time had slowed down.

"Fuck," both he and the CO trainer assigned to Beast said at the same time, the word elongated and its pitch lowered by the time shift. Emmett then watched in excruciating detail as the CO trainer lunged with his pole-like PharmaJet weapon and dosed the berserker in the shoulder. Beast didn't even notice the injection going in, his focus had been so sharp on getting a hold on Borman.

Time jumped back into gear and in the next blink of Emmett's dreaming eye, Beast had swung the Nazi up into the ceiling and jerked him back down like a towel being snapped in a boys' locker room. Then the monster had turned and charged at the next closest person, which of course had been Emmett.

He'd tried to leap out of the way behind the desk with the computer, but his merely mortal speed had just not been enough to escape being swatted down by one of Beast's huge, overly muscular hands.

Emmett went crashing to the floor, his head hitting the ground hard, his mind shifting to an old memory like a 45 skipping to a new song.

* * *

"What do we do?!" Susan screamed at him.

It was over a decade earlier, in the old farmhouse on the High Road in Cornish, Maine, and everything was going wrong. Emmett, a cell phone to his ear, had been on the phone with Dr. Weiss trying to figure out exactly that. The doctor had asked if Susan was bleeding, which she was.

"But there's not . . . I mean there's . . . there is some blood, but not a lot," he said as he watched his wife groaning and twisting next to the toilet with one hand on the sink and the other on the lid. She wore a man's undershirt (Emmett's), and the reddest blood Emmett had ever seen was trickling down her leg in a long thin line.

"We're losing it . . ." Susan said between breaths. Defeated. Exhausted.

"Not necessarily. Some folks get cramps. You've spotted before—" Emmett started to say, but a huge racking half sob, half sigh came out of Susan's mouth, cutting him off, as she'd dropped heavily to the floor.

"Can we see him tomorrow?" she breathed.

"Can we see you tomorrow?" he asked Dr. Weiss on the other end of the line. And of course they were able to, first thing. "Nine?" Emmett had asked.

Susan nodded. Then, suddenly, she flung the toilet seat up and vomited into it.

"Morning sickness. That's a good sign," Emmett said, trying to comfort her.

Susan breathed heavily and just looked at him. She wanted to believe him. Dr. Weiss, still on the other end of the line, remained silent.

"I feel better . . ." Susan said. She slowly stood, leaving a bloody mess on the tile beneath her.

Emmett was listening to Dr. Weiss's reply and relaying the message to his wife. "Dr. Weiss says it could still be okay, he—"

But then something had caught Emmett's eye in the blood on the floor. In his heart he knew what it was, though he couldn't understand it. As his vision tunneled, he'd put the phone on the counter and reached for it.

"Is that . . . the baby?" Susan asked in horror, as her husband delicately scooped up a chunk of jelly-like human tissue from the floor.

It was.

Emmett turned to the sink and caught his eyes in his reflection. On the other side of the bathroom mirror he could see the prison library, and Beast flinging a computer monitor through the glass separating his dreams, shattering it to pieces. His home in Cornish vanished down the abyss of his mind once again—at least for now.

* * *

His notebooks lay open on the old carpeted floor next to him, their ripped pages strewn about like leaves hit by the first winds of winter. Emerging from one nightmare right back into the other, he scampered to gather them. Beast had been subdued by the dose his trainer had hit

him with in the shoulder, and Black Jesus was now busy
pulling the female CO, as well as a couple additional
officers who'd shown up for the fun, off the unconscious
Beast, as they continued to stab him with their PharmaJets.

The angry *hiss* of the heavy-duty tranquilizers being
injected into Beast over and over again—even after he
had been clearly put down—was testament to how little
Black Jesus had actually been able to stop the abuse he
witnessed on a daily basis.

With Beast subdued and his precious notes now
gathered up, Emmett took a second and surveyed the
damage. It looked like a bomb had gone off in the library.
Borman and one of his Hitler-wannabe provokers had
looked pretty dead. Emmett surmised that prison Nazis
tend not to be a particularly emotionally bonded group,
because the one who remained alive and whole looked,
at best, merely disappointed by the demise of his captain
and presumptive friend.

Emmett wanted to punch the guy in the face,
but he didn't. Instead he said, lamely, "I needed that
computer, you fucking asshole."

"Why, Kessler? Nobody's gettin' outta here. Ain't you
watchin' the news? Staff's just gonna stop showin' up soon
'nuf. We all gonna *rot*. Whatever ya stupid project is, it
ain't gonna do ya no fuckin' good."

Emmett turned and looked at the officers standing
around Beast, like big-game hunters still high from
their kill. Sure, he'd seen what was happening at other
prisons on the news just like the Nazi had, but those
had felt like isolated incidents. Of course, the future
would ride in on such isolated incidents—he could
still remember when berserkers had been considered
just isolated incidents—but the idea that the prison

would shut down and they would just be left there to die seemed too outrageous at the time to be creditable.

Emmett had missed the fact that over six hundred inmates had been left in filthy chest-high water for four days at the Parish Prison Compound in New Orleans after the staff fled for safety during Hurricane Katrina. And he'd missed the controversy over the fact that Riker's Island in New York, which held more than twelve thousand prisoners, some of whom were just awaiting trial and had not even been convicted of a crime yet, didn't have an evacuation plan in place in the event of an emergency.

Had Emmett been aware of the long history of correctional institutions' abandoning inmates to their deaths during natural disasters, he might have reconsidered his stance on what was creditable and what was bullshit. He might even have changed his mind and filed for a last-minute appeal, if it wasn't already too late. (It was.) But he wasn't aware.

He was going to find out the hard way soon enough.

"Don't eyeball me, convict. Pick Mr. DuPont up with your friend there and get him back to the pod," Black Jesus told him.

"You provoke him again and I'll shoot both of you stupid pieces of shit in the head," the female CO added, pulling her service weapon and pointing it at Emmett. Black Jesus seemed visibly dismayed by her threat, but his insistence that such language and posturing was unnecessary had been met only with ridicule.

"I didn't—" Emmett had started to say.

"Don't talk back to the lady, inmate," the woman's would-be co-adulterer shot back at him before he could finish, not about to miss an opportunity to get himself into her good graces—and by extension, into her pants as well. From the way her smile beamed back at him, Emmett had been pretty sure it had worked.

Not that it mattered.

The CO trainer, whose name Emmett's dream-state mind now couldn't recall, must have not liked the smirk on Emmett's face, because he'd smacked him in the head with a vicious swing of his now empty eight-foot PharmaJet pole.

The blow transcended the dream, and knocked Emmett awake with a start and a cry.

* * *

Captain Waters was exhausted. His clientele were now all accounted for in their new living arrangements. All safe. All healthy. And he was confident he could keep them that way.

He had decided to move into C Block himself. The small town of Warren, Maine, was still probably safe enough to scavenge in, but the chaos of the cities had been spreading. Every second exposed would be another chance for some asshole to show up and try to take what he had. Black Jesus had no interest in looking for trouble, or in making it easier for trouble to find him.

It was now a few months since the nukes had gone off, and everything had gone to hell in a handbasket faster than he'd have thought possible—a fact he had no intention of telling any of his clients. He figured the prison was probably the safest place to be at the moment. It seemed secure and defendable. He had an industrial pantry still half-full of food, and, now that only C Block was using power, enough diesel to keep the emergency generator going for weeks, so long as he rationed the electricity like he had been rationing food.

Although he was acutely aware that the obligation to perform his duty as a corrections officer was pretty much only in his head now that the world had ended, and that he was probably crazy not to just walk away like all those other cats, he'd never felt better about anything he'd done in his life than he had about his commitment to seeing that his men finished their sentences.

Besides, he thought, he probably stood a better chance of surviving by just continuing to carry out his duties here in the prison than his colleagues did out there in the shit.

But of course, he was wrong.

Chapter Three
The Pedophiles at Walmart

BOBBY-LEIGH AND JENNIFER fled up Iowa Highway 1 toward their dead uncle's farm, figuring it was empty and would provide them a safe place to regroup. The idea that the land and farm and all the promise it held no longer belonged to them hadn't so much as crossed their minds.

While possession had been nine-tenths of the law back when the rule of law still had some sway over folks, now, that nine-tenths belonged not to possession, or deeds, or proof of purchase, or anything else to do with owning something. Now it came down to just firepower. Possession, paperwork, and legalese were things of the past, as was the girls' time on the farm. Even if they'd stayed there, they wouldn't have had a means to keep it; the fact that their uncle Allen had built the house from the ground up, cultivated the land, and owned a piece of paper in a safety deposit box somewhere in town that said it was still his meant nothing.

They'd been sheltered, first by their uncle and then by Brennachecke's group, for so long that they'd missed a fundamental shift in the landscape of what used to be called society—a landscape that was now made up of whatever was left over after folks lost what remained of their collective humanity.

The yogi and the old soldier had been like fathers to the girls, and in this new world of horrors, the men had done what all fathers of little girls have done since the beginning of all this: they kept them from knowing the full extent of the depravity that was sweeping across land and sea as much as they possibly could. Traveling rape camps and small bands of cannibals were the least of the plagues to be avoided—and the least of the things both men had kept the existence of as secret as they could.

The girls just didn't need to know how bad the world had gotten. They didn't need to constantly live in fear of their fellow man. It was enough that anybody you saw—stranger, friend, enemy, lover, sister—any of them could be a berserker and be triggered into a deadly violent rage so powerful it would obliterate any connection you had and get you killed just for being nearby.

So when the rumors and whisperings of something being out there that even berserkers were afraid of started floating in on the breeze, they'd kept the girls in the dark, for their own good. Or at least that's what both men had told themselves at the time.

Unfortunately those sentiments were just sexism in disguise. Ignorance was not bliss. Ignorance was dangerous. Thanks to the girl's uncle and Brennachecke, they were now out in the wild completely ignorant and utterly unprepared for what they were about to face. All because their benefactors had failed to warn them about blood pirates.

A transfusion gone wrong—or right, depending on how you looked at it—had revealed the secret not long after the nukes had shut civilization down like cops showing up at a high school party. Who was giving blood to whom, why and where, had been lost to the wind, but word of mouth about the effects of injecting berserker blood into a non-berserker's bloodstream traveled far and wide, and fast.

The metamorphosis from human to berserker was still not very well understood. *HGF* was really just a generic term for something in the blood that made people radically stronger and faster. The truth was that nobody understood why or how this worked. Not that it mattered, because nobody really cared about the whys and hows of much of anything anymore. Maybe folks never really had. They had data. They had results. During an apocalypse, that was more than most folk felt they could hope for.

It wasn't even clear that it was the HGF in the berserker blood that basically turned it into a PCP-laced drink from the Fountain of Youth when swapped out for human blood in a normal person. And there was no satisfactory scientific explanation for how it restored and rejuvenated regular human flesh like a touch from God, and sent normal brains on a rocket ride up into the higher realms of perception. (At least, that's how folks described it—not that there were any rockets being launched anymore to compare the experience to.) Yet a pint of O-negative berserker blood was worth more than just killing for. (Just about anything was worth that—a Twinkie, a shower, two AA batteries; things that were worth killing for were a dime a dozen.) For men and women who bought, sold, or swapped it, O-negative berserker blood was worth cutting your own leg off for—maybe even your arm too—especially if the blood had been taken during an episode, which for some reason made the effects even stronger.

The men and women (though mostly men) who hunted berserkers for their blood tended to be the worst of what was left of us. Blood pirates generally didn't bother testing blood for HGF. That took too much time and required at least a little knowledge of hematology—plus it was a lot less fun. Instead, what most of the pirate outfits did was capture potential stock and torture them. Any berserkers in the mix would inevitably berserk out and would then be separated to be bled, and anybody who didn't turn out to be a berserker got to provide some entertainment. Either way the pirates won. The whole operation was savage, dangerous, and bloody.

Obviously it would have been easier to hunt only the berserkers who had changed physically enough to be visually identified—and those poor bastards did certainly get hunted. But for the evil motherfuckers who were drawn to this particular trade, the satisfaction of torturing, raping, and slaughtering their own kind as part of their search was more than enough compensation for the dangers inherent in pursuing less obvious targets to harvest blood.

Jennifer and Bobby-Leigh didn't know any of this as they headed up 2nd Street, under the railroad bridge and past the old all-natural and organic foods grocery once called Everybody's, whose shelves had long since been looted. They had no idea where Brennachecke's group was, but both girls knew they were still out there looking for them. Folks had time for things like hunting down women and children these days. In fact, most days, life during the apocalypse was pretty boring for scavenger groups like Brenna-checke's. The world wasn't so far gone yet. Food, gas, ammo: these could still be found without too much effort—maybe not in stores like Everybody's so much anymore, but certainly in the stockpiles left inside folks' homes. Scavenging was the most popular of activities. But there were also groups out there that were farming. There was trade. But mostly there was violence. Groups of marauders roamed like packs of rabid dogs from town to town. Farmers protected their crops with automatic weapons and booby traps. Scavengers stayed on the move.

Farmer.

Scavenger.

Marauder.

Dead.

Those were the options. All folks were one or another. There was no gray area. No in between. No exceptions. At least that's how it had felt to Jen and Bobby-Leigh's uncle, Allen Grant Kessler, who had he lived would have been forty-two, a decade younger than Emmett.

He had been a farmer of organic, sustainably produced, and overpriced non-GMO crops before the power permanently failed in town. He'd then moved with the girls off his own land to join forces with some of his better-armed neighbors once nukes got set off and the locals' remaining hope ran dry.

But lawlessness swept across the county like a storm, and "better-armed" had turned out to really just mean you were more likely to get noticed. Realizing this, Allen gave up farming altogether and moved on with the girls, though it didn't save him in the end. On his first official scavenge he'd been murdered trying to protect a pack of Twinkies and a single can of Diet Coke he'd found and intended to surprise Jen with for her birthday. With nowhere else to go, the girls found themselves passed unceremoniously into Brennachecke's care.

Meanwhile, in a stand so short it hardly counted, the farming collective they'd joined was burned to the ground and its people scattered or killed. Even though the girls had not witnessed the latter event with their own eyes, they'd certainly heard all about it. A small town is still a small town, even after the end of the world has driven most of the people elsewhere. News traveled and secrets were hard to keep.

Allen's old farm was still standing. The problem was that it was almost ten miles outside of town. Jennifer had found enough food in a back pantry of Revelations to sustain her, but she was still basically naked. Even though it was summer, an odd cold front had moved in overnight and now lingered suspiciously, sucking away at the usual heat this time of year and making it feel like winter.

Jen was shivering uncontrollably by the time they came up on the apartment dorms of the Maharishi University of Management, off 4th Street, where the girls took their chance to get out of the open and find Jen some clothes and maybe some more food. Across from them, on the north side of the campus, the golden men's meditation dome still stood relatively untouched. Although, without the thousand or so residents and student practitioners who once worked, studied, and participated in the Transcendental Meditation movement centered around the campus, the huge structure, as well as the women's dome behind it, was now just an empty shell.

Allen had been a part of the TM movement for most of his life. The girls' uncle had done his teacher training with Maharishi himself in Mallorca, Spain, in his twenties. Then he'd gone on to Fairfield when the movement bought the old Parsons College campus and started the Maharishi University of Management. To say TM was a huge part of his life would be an understatement. So when his brother had sent Jen and Bobby-Leigh to him, he'd have introduced the girls to the daily practice even if Emmett hadn't given him permission to. Both of the Kessler girls had taken to it like ducks to water.

Unfortunately, when it came to the battle between enlightenment and the chaos of the apocalypse, the movement just didn't have the numbers to hold off the end of the world eternally, though they certainly did try. The fact that the two golden domes still stood was probably a testament to the effectiveness of what the yogis called the *Maharishi Effect*—the measurable positive effect on society of the collective human consciousness raised by a large number of meditators all practicing together in the same place and at the same time. Then again, the world in the end had still fallen apart, and within the TM community in Fairfield there seemed to be just as many berserkers as anywhere else. (Jen was a testament to that fact.) Skeptics would say that this was just further proof that TM was nothing more than a cult and basically full of shit. But to such critics, Allen and most of the TM community in Fairfield and all over the rest of the world would have responded that it was perhaps exactly because of the TM movement's efforts that the civilized world lasted as long as it did. But the debate didn't matter now. In fact, it hadn't really mattered then.

Jennifer, for her part, had been able to use her meditation practice as part of a tool set to keep the monster inside her contained. Thanks to her uncle's teachings, as long as she could see the threat coming, she could for the most part keep from berserking out. It hadn't saved Jimmy, obviously, but it had saved others, most importantly her sister.

Seeing the domes still standing lightened both girls' hearts for a couple beats. It wasn't much, but this had been a really suck-ass day thus far, so any reprieve was welcome. Bobby-Leigh smashed a window and climbed inside the ugly yellow-brick dorm building. Jennifer quickly followed, trying not to cut her bare feet on the glass.

They were obviously not the first ones to ransack the building. Doors had been knocked down, random stuff was strung about, and they probably could have found a window that was already broken if they'd bothered to look, but it didn't matter—a little extra broken glass was not going to make their presence there stand out. Luckily they were looking mostly for something Jen could wear, and clothing was not a very popular item to scavenge for, so the previous looting most likely wasn't going to be a problem. They went a little deeper into the building just for cover, and then entered an apartment.

A significant portion of the students at the Maharishi University of Management came from overseas, mostly China and India. The apartment the girls had ended up in apparently belonged to a Chinese woman, because there were a huge number of burned CDs with Chinese writing scribbled on them in black permanent marker, as well as an old Sony Walkman CD player and earbuds, lying on a bed that was covered with a pink comforter and topped by lots of pillows. Men just didn't do pillows like that, not in the US, not in China, not before the world ended and certainly not after, so they knew the apartment once belonged to a woman. By the time the world ended, CDs were a completely outdated technology in even the smallest villages in China, so whoever had once lived there was kind of a freak. Being in the room of another outcast, Bobby-Leigh instantly felt an intense sense of kinship with the CD-listening Chinese girl. She felt safe there. It was totally irrational—maybe even dangerously so—and she knew it, but that didn't stop her enjoying the sensation while it lasted.

Bobby-Leigh looked through the CDs, not completely sure they were what she thought they were, as Jen looked through the closet and the clothes already conveniently dumped on the floor for something to wear. The Chinese woman had been more or less Jen's size, so prospects were looking good that there would be something here she could wear.

"These are music CDs, right?" Bobby-Leigh said.

"Probably. Why?"

"I don't know. There's so many of them."

"Yeah? So?"

Bobby-Leigh looked up at her sister, stung by Jen's dismissive response and hoping she'd seize the chance to apologize. But she didn't.

"They're CDs, kid. Not mysteries of the universe."

"You don't have to be mean."

"I'm not being mean. I'm just saying, dude."

"Have you ever even listened to a CD?" Bobby-Leigh asked, her tone now edged.

Jen opened her mouth to answer. *Of course I haven't fucking listened to a CD before, they hadn't been sold in the US since before I was born, for shit's sake,* or something equally snarky formulating in her brain, but she started crying instead of saying anything.

Bobby-Leigh sighed heavily and cursed Jimmy silently to herself. Of course she hadn't listened to CDs before. But Jimmy had. Bobby-Leigh had even listened to her and Jimmy talk about them before. Jimmy had been a tech nerd and was obsessed with how inefficient old technology like CDs—or even worse, *tapes*—had been. It was one of his favorite rants, for Christ's sake. *Why did I say that? Stupid. Stupid. Stupid.*

For as long as they'd been together, every time Jen and Jimmy found something media related, they disappeared into a corner together to try to consume it. Jimmy would joke about how even though old tech had been ridiculously complicated to use, it had been built to last. With the power out and the Internet off, media that was not stored locally was just gone, and Jimmy loved to point that fact out as they watched whatever it was, be it an iPad with a movie on it and enough charge to get through it or a book from the Harry Potter series. The two lovebirds never excluded Bobby-Leigh, though she often excluded herself just to get away from their lovey-dovey crap.

Jesus, why couldn't that stupid boy have just laid low like she told him to? Brennachecke would have probably still exiled them from the group because living with a berserker was generally considered to be a death wish, but he wouldn't be after their blood. He wouldn't be trying to kill them. And Jen wouldn't be a basket case.

"I'm not a basket case," Jen said, wiping her eyes.

"I didn't say you were."

"You were thinking it pretty loud."

Folks often think the five stages of grief occur linearly, but they don't. Jen wasn't progressing one by one through denial, anger, bargaining, depression, and then finally finding peace in acceptance. She was bouncing around between them like a pinball in some demented arcade in hell. At the moment, anger was smacking her around the machine—anger directed at Bobby-Leigh, who'd just sat there and watched as Jen ripped Jimmy apart. The little girl had lived through Jen berserking out more than once.

She obviously knew how to do it. Jimmy wasn't an idiot; she could have shown him what to do to survive. His death was really on Bobby-Leigh's hands, Jen told herself. She couldn't help what she was, but if her little sister hadn't been such a selfish bitch . . .

Jen felt the emotional roller coaster bank suddenly in her heart. The pinball shot away from anger and landed on acceptance for a second. Bobby-Leigh was a lot of things, but selfish was definitely not one of them. Jen knew it. She knew it wasn't her sister's fault, or her own fault in a premeditated, first-degree-murder kind of way. It wasn't anybody's fault. Not even that stupid possum's.

For the first time in years, Jen found herself wishing she could talk to her dad. She suddenly felt the capacity to forgive him for what happened to their mother bubbling up inside her heart. Just a hint of it. Not that she ever would ever actually absolve him for it.

Actually, she found herself thinking, *ultimately Jimmy's death was Dad's fault.* And away the pinball spun, through denial, toward anger.

"Did you find something that fits?"

She had. A pair of jeans, some tennis shoes, and a coat, all of which fit well enough to get them where they were going. Jen looked at her sister as she finished getting dressed. Uncle Allen's death had triggered a shift inside Bobby-Leigh, and then what had happened later at Walmart had locked those changes in. And the changes were deeper than the goth makeup and dyed black hair. She just wasn't a little girl anymore. She didn't laugh. She didn't play. She didn't crush on boys (or at least Jen didn't think she would—it'd been a while since they'd seen a kid her age).

Jen knew that she was just as responsible as the murderers that killed Uncle Allen for her little sister's fucked-up state of mind. It had been her stupid idea to tag along with Cooperman, Ace, and JP when they went out to the superstore in the first place. It was all her fault, but she didn't know what to do about it.

"Want to see if we can find a doll or something?" Jen asked as they looked through the rest of the left-behinds for anything worth appropriating.

"Seriously?"

"A book? Maybe she has the next *Twilight* one?"

"You're the one who likes those, not me. Besides, everything here is in Chinese. If you wanted a book you should have grabbed one at Revelations."

"I don't want a book. I thought you might want one, or something to play with. You know, because you're a fucking little kid and all."

"I'd have grabbed a book there if I'd wanted one."

"Okay, okay. Doesn't have to be a book."

"When's the last time you saw me play with toys, Jen?"

"Doesn't have to be a toy either, shit. I just . . . I don't know."

"You just what?"

I just want you to be happy for like ten seconds, Jen thought, but then she suddenly realized Bobby-Leigh was actually happy most of the time. It wasn't an innocent or childlike happiness, to be sure, but her little sister certainly wasn't miserable. It was Jen herself who wanted to find something to distract herself from the pain. She was just projecting.

"Look, we've got a whole building's worth of apartments to find shit in. Maybe you'll find something you'll want to hang on to. That's all I'm saying. We should spend the night here anyway. Give Brennachecke a chance to lose our scent."

The two continued to rummage in silence for a minute or so, until Bobby-Leigh broke it. "How long do you think he'll chase us?"

Jen thought about Jimmy's father. She remembered his eyes as he took in what she'd done to his son less than a day ago, and realized that he'd given her the same look he always had. The man's eyes had never been angry when he got upset with her, which was often. They just got sad and maybe a little disappointed. She'd expected to finally see anger in them when they'd locked on her and Bobby-Leigh standing over Jimmy's body back in the hotel room. If ever there was a time for the man to be angry with her, surely that was it. But he hadn't looked at her any differently than when he asked her to lay off the swearing.

She wondered what that meant. Maybe he'd always hated her with all his heart? Yet somehow she didn't think that was true. In fact, while she was positive he would kill her now, and probably Bobby-Leigh too, if he found them, she knew from experience that their murders would not be motivated by hatred, or even love. Brennachecke would kill them out of obligation. *The equation has to balance,* the man had told them whenever the time came that he had to spill blood in the name of protecting, or avenging, his people. Except that Bobby-Leigh complicated the shit out of the math in this particular equation. Her involvement turned what would have been simple first-grade eye-for-an-eye arithmetic into some kind of bizarre human calculus even Einstein would have struggled with.

"He'll track us until he can't find a trail to follow anymore. Then he'll start trying to pick up the trail again by going to any and every place we might go."

"So we're not going to be able to stay at the farm when we get there?"

"No. Not for long anyway."

"That sucks."

"Super sucks. Especially if the batteries are still working."

Bobby-Leigh was rummaging through a dresser drawer as they talked. She smiled, Jen saw it and couldn't help but smile herself. It was such a rare thing for her little sister to do.

"Speaking of batteries," Bobby-Leigh said, and pulled out a huge bulk box of Energizer AAs, which had been passed over by the looters before them.

"See if those are the right size for the CD player."

They were.

The Chinese girl's CD collection was quickly spread out between them like a picnic. Neither girl had ever heard a single song in it, including the ones they could see were in English, but that only made it better. They spent the rest of the day listening, sitting on the bed together, and sharing the earbuds between them. Jen had the left side and Bobby-Leigh had the right.

It was a meaningless moment in the grand scheme of things, but the best times in life are not always the ones that tip the scale one way or the other. Sometimes folks' best memories are what they are exactly *because* they don't matter. But even in the midst of making a good memory, Jen found herself recalling a bad one. One that *had* tipped the scales forever in one direction. One that *had* mattered. One that she often found herself returning to.

Her thoughts were drawn back to that day at the Walmart.

* * *

"Oh, fuck you, potato! Fuck you and the horse you rode in on!" Jen looked at the thin trickle of blood oozing out her finger. "Fuck you up the asshole twice!"

Jimmy watched her, hypnotized by her language as much as by her looks. The new girl had said the f-word three times in less than ten seconds. And she didn't even seem to care that she was swearing. He found himself blushing for her. Blushing and looking guiltily around the room to see if his father was close enough to hear the language she was using. He didn't want to look, but he couldn't help himself. It was ingrained in his survival instinct at this point.

"Ah, you might want to watch your language just a little bit—"

"Your dad doesn't fucking scare me."

"He should."

"Yeah, well . . . he doesn't, dude."

The division of labor in Brennachecke's group was skill based. Those with real firearm experience and those who knew the area like the back of their hands did the scouting.

Those who were technologically and mechanically inclined did the scavenging. Those who were young enough to warrant shielding from the horrors out there—namely Jimmy, Jennifer, and Bobby-Leigh—did the cooking.

On this particular day, a week or so after Uncle Allen had been murdered, Brennachecke had traded fertilizer to a small farming group to the south for potatoes. They ate a lot of potatoes. The girls felt like pretty much all they'd done since Uncle Allen had spent his dying breath telling them how Brennachecke would take care of them, was cut potatoes, boil potatoes, mash potatoes, and eat potatoes. They complained about it, like all kids do about chores, but didn't mind nearly as much as they acted like they did. Bobby-Leigh felt safe in the kitchens, and Jen had quite a love–hate obsession going with Jimmy. Brennachecke, still cautious around the new arrivals, often positioned himself in the doorway just out of sight, cringing at Jen's language, but enjoying seeing his son crush on a girl who was age appropriate.

"Cooperman said he might take us on the next trip to Walmart," Jimmy said.

"Really?" Bobby-Leigh asked. Ever since Uncle Allen had been killed she'd basically stopped talking, so Jennifer jumped at the opportunity to bring her sister back out from the shell she'd hidden in.

"Yeah! He told me about that. I don't know if you're old enough to come, though." She smiled, hoping to get a rise out of her sister. Bobby-Leigh looked crushed and lowered her head. Inside her heart, Jen screamed, *Fuck! Come on, Bobby-Leigh!*

"What do you think, dude?" she asked Jimmy. Jen was desperate enough to reach out for an assist from the boy she'd been working hard at hating since she arrived.

Her reasons for hating him had been lost to the wind days ago, but the hormone-stoked emotions lingered like smoke after a fire. And if there was smoke, her brain told her, there must be a reason he rubbed her the wrong way. So her brain invented new, petty things to be upset about.

"How old are you, Bob?" Jimmy, who had no idea why Jen was always so quick tempered with him, said with a smile, just grateful for the opportunity to be having a civil conversation.

Bobby-Leigh sighed, defeated. "I'm just nine."

"You know, I went to Walmart when I was nine."

"You did?"

"Yeah. And I wasn't nearly as mature as you are."

"You weren't?"

"Nope."

Jen had disliked Jimmy almost from the second she'd met him. It had been one simple exchange that had set her off. If she could have remembered it, she'd have laughed at how stupid it had been for her to be so upset by it. She'd just burned her hand on a pot of boiling water and, exaggerating the pain a little bit for effect, dumped a bottle of nearly frozen ice water over the wound. It wasn't a bad burn and the ice water had done the trick just fine, but Jimmy had had the nerve to suggest that she should have used warm water instead of cold. He'd cited some fucking Swedish study nobody had ever heard of as his source.

Warm water. Yeah, right. Seriously, what the fuck is wrong with this dude? she'd thought. It was a pretty smug-ass thing to say after she'd already treated the burn with *cold* water. *I mean, what the fuck am I supposed to do with his little nugget of knowledge from fucking Sweden? I already treated the fucking burn!*

The only reason she'd been able to see for him to have volunteered information like that after the fact was to make her feel stupid, which was a pretty asshole thing to do when you're just meeting somebody. And all of that was beside the main point that *everybody* knows you treat mild burns with cold fucking water, except apparently the stupid Swedes. She'd been so pissed that she'd unleashed a whole hellfire of expletives at him at the time, but since then, her hormones, the lack of any other suitable potential boyfriends, and a little bit of honest attraction had muddled the whole thing up until she couldn't place the source of her hatred for the boy anymore, yet clung on to it for dear life just the same.

Jimmy was a genuinely kind-hearted boy and had never intended to hurt her feelings. Not that it mattered, since her wrath had not stopped him from crushing on her in the slightest. In fact, her vulgarity had had the opposite effect on his young heart.

Brennachecke knew his son had the same beautiful heart his mother did. He'd found it frustratingly useless in the daily routine. But at that moment, while hiding in the doorway, he realized it was that seemingly infinite capacity for empathy that had made him fall so hard for the boy's mother in the first place. Watching from the shadows, he decided to let Cooperman off the hook for promising the boy something the man had no authorization to give. In fact, he decided to suggest that Cooperman take the kids out himself. Walmart was basically empty at this point. The risk was pretty low. He could send Ace and JP with them just to be safe.

"Tell you what, dude," Jen said. "I'll talk to Cooperman."

"You will?"

"Fuck yes, sister."

"Okay."

"Yeah?"

Bobby-Leigh nodded and smiled. This was before the goth makeup and dyed black hair. Before the little girl had started carrying an ax like it was a security blanket. This was back when Bobby-Leigh was still a virgin to killing men. She had looked fragile and innocent back then. They would soon all learn that she was anything but that. However, for now there were potatoes and a momentum of communication with her sister that Jennifer wasn't about to let go of.

Jen saw a light in the little girl's eyes for the first time since they'd watched it blink out of their uncle's. She racked her brain for something else to say, anything that would keep it going, but nothing came to her for a long time. Finally, looking at the stupid spud in her hand, she remembered a piece of trivia that might work.

"Did you know that potatoes were the first vegetable grown in space?"

"Why would you want to grow potatoes in space?"

"This was back when dudes did shit like that."

"Why?"

"I don't know, dude."

"Probably for the same reason the farmers are growing them now," Jimmy chimed in. "You see, Bob, my dad says potatoes are kind of like this superfood. Easy to grow. Lots of calories, lots of vitamins."

"Don't call her that."

"What?" Jimmy said, confused by the quick turn toward anger the conversation had taken.

"Don't call her Bob."

"It's okay, Jen."

"No, it's not," Jen told her sister. "That's not your name. We've been here for almost two weeks. The dude should know your name."

"I didn't mean anything. I just— Bobby-Leigh, Bob . . . it just seemed like—"

"It seemed like what?"

"Nothing. Forget I said anything."

"Bob is short for Robert," Jen said.

"So is Bobby," Jimmy said. "See where I was—"

"Her name is Bobby-Leigh, dude. That's what it says on her birth certificate. It's not fucking Robert."

"Yeah, okay. I was thinking more like Roberta-Lee. Like maybe she was named after Robert E. Lee, the Confederate general or something like that."

"We're from fucking Maine, dude. What kind of fucked-up New England parents would name their daughter after the general of the separatist states?"

"I don't know. Lee was a brilliant commander. West Point even has a barracks named after him. In fact, he didn't even really support the breaking up of the Union, he just happened to be born in Virginia so he—"

"Look, whatever, dude. Her name's Bobby-Leigh. I don't need a fucking history lesson. I just need you to get her fucking name right."

Brennachecke, who was still eavesdropping, smiled in the shadows. *The lady doth protest too much.* She obviously liked him and just didn't see it yet. Why were women like that? Always making things so much more complicated than they needed to be. And what was with this girl's mouth? He was going to have to pull her aside and talk to her, again.

"So if we got to go to space, we'd still have to eat potatoes?" Bobby-Leigh asked, desperate to change the conversation back to something more civil.

"Fuck. Probably," Jen said, still tweaking with adrenaline. Not the kind that could set the berserker inside her loose, but the other kind. The kind that made her feel warm between her legs in a way she'd never felt before, and a little sick to her stomach.

Jimmy looked at her, pleading with his eyes for her to cut the swearing out and give him a break. He'd just been trying to help her, for the love of Christ, why was she tearing him a new one?

The message was received loud and clear, but she tried to ignore it. When she smiled at him, she told herself it was to cover her own thoughts. What the fuck was he doing anyway? She'd never asked him for his help. She didn't need his stupid-ass assistance. Her sister was her problem. She'd fix it. By. Her. Self.

Jimmy blushed, and somehow that defused the hormone bomb Jen's body was driving her crazy with. Or maybe she'd just run out of steam. It didn't really matter.

"I wouldn't mind. At least we'd be in space," Bobby-Leigh said, still trying to break the tension.

"True that, dude." Jen smiled. "Fucking space, can you imagine what life would be like? All weightless and shit. Just fucking floating around, like some asshole without a care in the world—because the motherfucking world would like fucking be, literally, beneath you, dude."

"Jennifer!" Brennachecke yelled from the doorway, no longer able to turn a deaf ear to the language spilling like toxic waste from the girl's mouth.

"I warned you," Jimmy whispered, to which Jen just rolled her eyes.

"What?" she said, feigning cluelessness as to why the old army dude was so mad.

"Do you know what separates humanity from animals?"

"Uh, there's like some many things, dude."

"No, Jen, there really isn't. There is just one thing. Language."

"Okay," Jen said. She'd heard Jimmy go on and on about how much his father hated cursing, but he'd never explained why. She was genuinely curious because, all things considered, it seemed so fucking stupid to get upset over.

"Do you know why you like to curse so much?"

"I wouldn't say I like it. It just comes out that way."

"No, it doesn't. You like it. It makes you feel good to talk that way," Brennachecke explained. "Swearing triggers a chemical response in the brains of people who say those kinds of words. And it triggers a similar response in the people who hear them. Language like that connects straight into our fight-or-flight response. It momentarily numbs our pain and triggers adrenaline."

"That sounds like a good thing."

"Wrong. It's not a good thing," Brennachecke said. "Language like that pushes us into a more instinctive, animalistic headspace. It literally makes you, and those listening to you, less human."

"Whatever, dude," Jen said, incredulously.

"There is a real lack of humanity out there these days, in case you hadn't noticed. Every f-bomb you drop, it makes it worse. See, our language is one of the clearest reflections of who we are. And you're not an animal, Jennifer. You're not one of those beasts masquerading as a person. You're not a sadistic killer, like the ones who murdered your uncle. You're one of us. You're part of the legacy of greatness that put a man on the moon. That wiped out smallpox and polio. That brought any number of species back from the brink of extinction. That worked tirelessly to right the wrongs, inequalities, and destruction around the world." He looked at her and could tell that he wasn't getting through. "That went to space and grew potatoes."

Jen looked at him. *But I do have a monster inside me,* she thought. Not that she'd ever tell him that, but it was just as true as it was a secret. If she'd known he'd find that out the hard way and that Jimmy would be killed by it, she may have changed her mind about all the secrecy. But the only part of the future she could see in that moment was that there would undoubtedly be more potatoes to peel tomorrow.

Brennachecke looked back at her.

Jen guessed she could try to curtail her bad language around the old man as best she could. Just because she respected him and was grateful for his shelter and protection, even if by his own argument there was a reason she spoke the way she did—which was the message she took away from his little speech.

She looked down. The weight of her secret was heavy in her heart.

"Language is our connection to who we are. It hurts me to hear you defecate all over that every time you open your mouth."

"So . . . am I going to be punished?" Jen wasn't sure she wanted to know the answer to that. Particularly if the answer was yes.

"No," Brennachecke said heavily. Why did he even bother? Maybe he *should* punish her. But he didn't have the slightest idea of what an effective disciplinary action would be for a teenager in the middle of an apocalypse. A little soap in the mouth seemed idiotic, and cutting her tongue out was not something a civilized man worthy of the human legacy he'd just told her about would do. Everything he came up with fell either on the side of the idiotic or the downright uncivilized. Frustrated, he rubbed his face and just stared the little potty mouth down.

"I'll try to do better," she told him. "I really will."

Brennachecke smiled sadly at her and touched her cheek. His sigh of frustrated disappointment let her know that he wasn't really expecting her to be able to change anything. She didn't know what she was supposed to have said to his little rant, but clearly she'd missed the mark, which really sucked because she had tried to be as respectful as she could. And she'd meant what she'd said too. She really would try to do better, at least around him. She was just too young to understand the difference between not getting caught doing something and not doing it at all in the first place. But she wanted the old soldier's approval—there was something about Brennachecke that just brought that out in folks.

Jennifer didn't really understand what integrity was. Sure, she knew the dictionary definition and could use the word in a sentence well enough. But the depth of character required to consistently act with integrity? The best of folks out there failed daily at that in the best of times. She craved Brennachecke's approval because the man didn't give it out lightly. You had to earn it.

Integrity.

Righteousness.

Honor.

Folks had to have it to get it reflected back, and Brennachecke did exactly that. He was a big mirror of uprightness that Jen simply couldn't see herself reflected back in. It threatened to break her heart, but she didn't let on.

"That goes for you too, Bobby-Leigh," The old man said to the little girl, trying to make a joke. The little girl hadn't said so much as twenty words to him since they'd taken her and her sister in, and not a single one of them had been a curse word, so he'd hoped she would find it funny, maybe even finally really talk to him. But she didn't get the joke. She just nodded solemnly.

* * *

Walmart was on the east side of Fairfield. It was one of the first places to be looted in town when the plundering began, just after the National Guard Armory on Stone Avenue, neither of which any longer had any of the obviously useful items like guns, munitions, camping gear, batteries, blankets, and nonperishable food, to say nothing of the drugs in Walmart's pharmacy, but the superstore was hardly empty. It was ninety-four thousand square feet of building. Even after years of steady and rampant looting, you still could always find *something* at Walmart. Sam Walton would be proud.

Cooperman, Ace, and JP escorted the kids across the empty parking lot toward the looming building. Cooperman was in his sixties, a former wood craftsman, a cabinetmaker of sorts. He was extremely good with his hands and was now the group's doctor, self-taught. Ace was in his late twenties and nobody knew or cared what he used to do for a living. It was his hunting and fishing skills that folks identified him with now. He, along with Dan Patterson, was one of the few hunters of the group. While Ace couldn't shoot a bow and arrow or hit a target like Dan, he could track and find fish and game better than just about anybody left alive in the country.

As for JP, the balding man in his forties had been a cook at one of the local joints, but nobody knew that. He was one of the small minority in Brennachecke's group that practiced TM; like the girls' uncle had been, he was a trained Transcendental Meditation teacher, but he'd come to Fairfield after Marharishi's death in 2008. Though Jen and Bobby-Leigh were both meditators themselves, the girls didn't like JP much because that was all he ever talked about, and the culty, new-agey, overly positive language he used drove both of them nuts and cheapened their own experience of the practice.

As they crossed the pavement, Bobby-Leigh was actually smiling. The sun was out. Ace had said he was pretty sure that nobody else—friend, foe, or otherwise—was around. It seemed like the kind of day where nothing could go wrong. The kind of day where everybody comes home alive and in one piece. The kind of day that could almost make you believe things would eventually get better. That civilization was not lost. It was the kind of day where Jennifer didn't feel compelled to drop f-bombs into every sentence that came out of her mouth—a good day that quickly gets forgotten. At least, that's how it had seemed as the six of them slipped in through the shattered glass doors in the front of the store. But by the time they would make it back outside to the parking lot, it wouldn't seem that way anymore. It was going to become the kind of day none of them would be able to forget, no matter how badly they wanted to.

Walmart, in an effort to be more energy efficient, had skylights throughout the retail space of the store, so even without power, the inside of the building was not dark. This was the only reason Brennachecke had allowed the kids to go on this little field trip. If the store had been dark, he'd never have let them go. Bad things happened in dark places. Unfortunately, bad things also happened in places lit by skylights.

They stayed together as they looked around. The place was a mess, but that only made it more fun for the kids. The bulk of what was still left in the store was clothing, so that's where they went first. But they quickly discovered that while there were a lot of clothes left, there were good reasons nobody had taken them. Still, they managed to find a frilly jumper-skirt and a pair of Mary Janes that fit Bobby-Leigh. Not that she'd ever wear them, or so she thought.

They had better luck in the toy section, where Jimmy found a whole stack of board games. Most folks would have been surprised to learn the importance of board games during an apocalypse, but when you can't escape into virtual reality, play video games, watch YouTube, or use your smartphone, there is suddenly a remarkably large quantity of time in the day that needs to be filled. So much so that JP, Cooperman, and Ace were almost as excited as Jimmy by the find.

"Man, I never even thought to look for these!" Ace told Jimmy as they all looked at a deluxe edition of Clue.

"You know, they made that one into a movie in the eighties," JP said. "No meditators involved, but . . ."

"But what?" Cooperman said, irritated by how JP always brought the conversation back to TM, and not for the first time.

"Nothing. There's just a lot of actors and directors and producers who meditate, but none of them worked on Clue, to the best of my knowledge."

"Who cares?"

"That's the tone that hurts my feelings, Cooperman."

"Is the game any fun?" Jen asked.

"Honestly, I don't remember."

Bobby-Leigh watched the conversation until she saw that there was a whole aisle of dolls, completely untouched, just a few yards away. Ace and JP spotted a Scrabble and snatched it up, as Bobby-Leigh slipped slowly down the aisle toward the dolls.

"I would totally kick all of your asses at that one, dude," Jen declared.

"Oh, really?"

"You know you can't use swear words, right?" Ace said.

"Yes, you can," Cooperman said.

"No, you can't. You can only use words that are in the dictionary," JP said.

"You don't think the word *fuck* is in the dictionary?" Ace said.

"Mmm, pretty sure it's not."

"Mmm, pretty sure it is."

"Dudes, there's probably a fucking dictionary here. We can just find out."

"I will bet you a million dollars that *fuck* is in the dictionary," Ace said.

"What would I do with a million dollars, Ace?" JP asked snarkily.

"You could shove it up your stupid fucking ass," Ace replied.

"That's the tone that hurts my feelings."

"You sound as bad as her, Ace. Better not make it a habit," Cooperman said, pointing at Jen, making her smile. "Look, I'll go find a dictionary and we can settle this once and for all."

Cooperman marched off toward the books.

"You shouldn't go alone, man," Ace called after him, but the old man just waved him off. The place seemed deserted, so Ace let it go. Besides, the man knew what he was doing. This wasn't his first trip to Walmart. Just as Cooperman turned the corner out of sight, Jen realized Bobby-Leigh was no longer with them.

"Where's my sister?" she asked, and then shouted out Bobby-Leigh's name before anybody could respond to her. Silence was all that answered, until it was broken by screams.

* * *

There were so many dolls to choose from, Bobby-Leigh was completely overwhelmed, and yet the hairs on the back of her neck were tingling. She could hear Jen and the guys talking, so she knew she was okay, but she didn't feel that way. Maybe it was all the dolls looking at her with their plastic and painted eyes that were creeping her out. Maybe it was the lingering rotten, musky smell that had started to assault the back of her nose as she strayed farther and farther from the group. She looked around to make sure nobody was sneaking up on her, but the doll aisle was empty. She relaxed, or at least told herself that she should.

It's just the bigness of the store that's spooking me, she thought. The smell had to just be the remains of an animal of some kind, probably killed a long time ago. Ace would have known if somebody or something else was here with them. He'd have said something. Besides, she could hear him swearing at JP now, so obviously he wasn't too concerned.

Still, she had a nagging feeling that she was being stalked, but then she saw a doll named Carla and forgot all about everything else. It took Bobby-Leigh about thirty seconds to get the doll out of the box. Its eyes blinked. Its strawberry-blonde hair was so soft. She pulled out another doll named Molly and immediately facilitated a conversation between the two human-shaped pieces of plastic. When the man's hand closed over her mouth and the arm yanked her up against his chest and held her so tightly against him that she couldn't breathe, much less move, much less call out for help, she was taken completely by surprise.

Her assailant's hot breath washed over her neck as he carried her soundlessly away from the voices of her sister and the guys. It was rancid and wet. Bobby-Leigh tried to cry out, but his grip on her was too tight for her to draw breath. Against the back of her thigh she could feel his erection as she bounced against him while he ran. Though she'd never seen a penis, flaccid, hard, or otherwise, she knew what was poking her in the leg, and she knew what it meant.

Another man holding a candle opened a door and smiled at her in the wash of the flicking light, like he'd just won the apocalypse lottery. She could feel his breath too as they passed him and it was just as bad as that of the one who held her. Hot. Wet. Rancid.

Another door. Then another. Until they were somewhere in the back of the store where there were no more skylights, just the darkness beyond the reach of the single candle that was lighting the way.

A final door opened and Bobby-Leigh was tossed like a bag of trash into a room that was probably a manager's office back before the shit hit the fan. All the furniture seemed to have been moved out. The carpet was wet and it stank, but she could smell the thick body odor and rotten breath of the two men above the musty mold below her easily. Desperately trying to get her bearings and calm herself down, Bobby-Leigh rolled as she hit the ground and came up sitting on her knees.

The man who had snatched her pulled out a nasty-looking hunting knife. The other man held up a hand ax menacingly. They seemed confident that the display would ensure that Bobby-Leigh would do what they wanted her to. They were both sickly thin. Their mouths and arms were covered with sores. Their hair was flat and greasy. The ax man was in slightly better shape, but both obviously had caught something, and it was something bad. The candlelight glinted off the blade in each man's hand. She'd never get past them to the door, and that was the only way out of the room, so Bobby-Leigh waited for them to come to her, just like her uncle had taught her to.

The man who had grabbed her dropped his pants and pulled out his erection. The flesh of his manhood, covered with the same sores that were on his face and arms, was her first real look at a penis, and she didn't like it one bit. It looked like a terribly malformed finger to her, not just because this one in particular was so diseased, but because of the way it just pointed up there like that from the ugly tangle of hair between the man's legs. She couldn't imagine a woman wanting a baby bad enough to put one of those things inside her. Penises seemed like horrible wastes of flesh that didn't belong on a body at all—like some kind of elongated growth or a weirdly shaped wart. Boys were truly disgusting creatures. She didn't know the name of the venereal disease that had produced the sores, but she knew enough to know what the men wanted from her, and that if they got it, they'd make her just as sick as they were.

Uncle Allen had told Bobby-Leigh this day would come, and he'd done what he could to teach her and Jennifer how to fight and get away when it did. "Girls, I don't want to scare you," he'd said completely out of the blue one day, not long after the nukes started popping off. "But I do want you to be prepared. One of these days, a man, or a group of men, is going to try to force you to have sex with him."

The bearded surrogate father had been dressed in a red Hawaiian shirt that completely contradicted the gravity of the lesson he wanted to teach, a fact he had seemed aware of when he looked at Bobby-Leigh and asked, "Do you understand what I'm talking about?"

"Rape," Jen had said.

"Exactly. He'll try to put his penis in your vagina, or your mouth, or somewhere else, or he'll try to put something else in you, his fingers, his tongue, the details don't matter. He'll probably try to hurt you as well. Sex is what I'm talking about here, girls. But not normal sex. Rape is different. It's about power as much as it is about getting off for these guys. So it'll be very scary. And you'll be tempted to just close your eyes and not fight back, to just pretend like it's not happening. You may even be tempted to think it's somehow happening because of something you did, or that you deserve it for some reason."

Bobby-Leigh had started to cry at that point, but Uncle Allen had not stopped, nor did he pull any punches. As far as he had been concerned, this was a perfectly appropriate time to cry.

"But you listen to me now. I'm serious. I need you to really hear this: No matter what happened to get you in that situation, it will not have been your fault. You are *not* to blame that it's happening."

"What if—"

"No. Listen to me. If it happens to you it will *never* be your fault. Never. If it happens, it's because the man, or men, are bad. Evil. That is it. No exceptions. No matter what you did or didn't do. No matter what you said or didn't say. No matter what you wore or didn't wear. You get to decide what happens to your bodies, girls. Period. Full stop. Okay? Nobody else has the right to make you do something, or to make you *feel* like you have to do something sexually with them, or with anybody else. Ever. Ever, ever, ever.

"But they'll try. Maybe not anytime soon, but eventually, a man is going to try. And when it happens, no matter how scared you are, you have to fight. You can't just close your eyes and pretend like it's not happening, or like it's okay for some reason. You have to fight. Because if you don't fight, a part of you, a very important part of you, is going to break, and I don't know if, in the future, broken parts like that will be able to be fixed. And I can't have that. I can't live with that."

"We'll fight," Jen said.

Bobby-Leigh nodded, but didn't look like she'd put much fight up if it came to it. *But what eight-year-old does look like they'd be ready to take on the pedophiles and rapists of the world?* Allen had thought, still not believing his birds-and-bees talk had come to this. When his father had had the talk with him, it had been centered around making the girl happy before you make yourself happy, treating women like people, not objects, always wearing a condom and not getting anybody pregnant before you were married. But times had changed. None of that mattered anymore. The talk was now entirely focused on how to kill, or at least incapacitate, your inevitable rapist before you got violated. Good times. But he had known that Emmett would want his girls to be able to take care of themselves in this world, and of course he had been right—though Emmett would never find out about it.

"I'm going to give you both a special knife," he had said next, taking out two small, lightweight, and extremely sharp curved karambit blades, each with a rugged rubber hilt and a finger hole at the bottom to prevent slippage and aid in welding the tiny weapon.

"This knife was inspired by a bear claw. It's very effective for women when it comes to self-defense," he told them. "And that's what it's for. Nothing else. Do you guys understand? You are not to use this for anything else. Nobody should even know you have it, because you are never going to take it out, unless it's to use it as I'm going to show you. Maybe if you're lucky you won't ever have to take it out, have to use it at all. But these are not the kind of days to count on being lucky. You are to have this knife with you at all times. Do you understand me? At all times."

Emmett's younger brother stared the girls down until they both looked away.

"You hold it upside down. Your index finger goes through the hole in the bottom here. Held like this, the most effective way to use it is with a punch then slash kind of movement. Like this." He showed the girls how and then made them do it themselves.

"Good. See how the blade will cut both as it goes up as well as while it comes down? And how hard it is to see in your hand. You can use all that to your advantage, okay?"

He showed a little more and corrected them as they practiced themselves for a few minutes, before he continued. "There are four major arteries that you need to know about. One of these will almost always be accessible in the kind of situation we are talking about, and if you can cut one, the man attacking you will be dead in less than a minute. Now, you'll be tempted to whip this out and try to use it to scare the man into leaving you alone. But never do that. Because, what did I just tell you?"

"Never take it out unless we are going to use it," Bobby-Leigh said.

"But aren't we using it to scare the dude?" Jen asked.

"No. Look, as far as you are concerned, this knife only has one use, okay? Slicing arteries. So you don't take it out until you are sure you can use it like I am about to show you."

"Why?"

"Because you'll need the element of surprise, girls. And you never know who is watching. Most girls get raped by people they know. Did you know that? I don't know if that is still true anymore, but you're not going to take any chances. This knife is a secret weapon, *secret* being the key word. So no showing it off, no using it for other things, and if the moment comes that you think you are going to have to use it, no matter how scared you get, you wait for the opening you need."

"What if we never get an opening?"

"Then you haven't waited long enough. One will always come. And until it does, you fight them with whatever else you can find. You use your hands and feet and teeth if it comes to that. But you *do not* take this blade out until you know you can sever a vein. Promise me."

"Okay," Jen said.

"I promise," Bobby-Leigh said. She had stopped crying, which made Allen smile. There was a seed of toughness inside her, and he could see it just starting to sprout. He wished Emmett could see it. The girls were going to be okay. His brother could stop blaming himself for destroying their fragile young minds when whatever happened with Susan had happened.

Allen had thought then, just before he'd started to teach the girls about blood flow and the anatomy of the circulatory system, that maybe it was time to head east to see his brother, even if he'd expressly forbidden him from doing so. The world in which Emmett had sent the girls off to live with him was gone now. Surely agreements made in that world held less sway in this new one.

But Allen hadn't gotten the chance to take the girls east in the end.

Bobby-Leigh now looked at the disease-ravaged pedophiles in the candlelight and hoped her uncle had been right about everything he'd shown them. Weeks and weeks of practice and training had left her confident in her abilities to defend herself. But this was the first time she'd ever had to use the deadly art she'd been taught, and she was at least as nervous as she was scared. In her right hand she stealthily palmed the secret blade, like Allen had shown her, while with her left she punched the man who had grabbed her, the man with his cock out, as hard as she could in his hairy ball sack. She hated the feeling of his warm erection as it brushed across her hand, but she loved the sound of her tiny fist *smacking* into his flesh and the shock on his face that a little girl like her was so hell-bent on fighting back.

"Hold her!" the man with his dick out croaked to his partner as he dropped to one knee in pain. Before he could stand back up, the quick little bitch hit him again, this time in the neck.

Fucking motherfuck! The young ones were supposed to be easy, what the fuck is wrong with this stupid little cunt? he thought, completely unaware for a solid second or two that Bobby-Leigh had just slit his carotid artery.

The man's partner, however, saw the blood spraying out his cohort's neck into the darkness, and, totally confused as to how the girl had managed to cause so much damage so fast, just let his instincts take over. His ax swung down as the first snatcher finally realized his blood was shooting all over the room and he was going to die. Spraying blood extinguished the light and his screams filled the darkness.

* * *

"Bobby-Leigh!" Jen screamed as she searched franticly down the near-empty sporting goods aisle, with Jimmy, JP, Ace, and Cooperman hot on her heels, their guns drawn, trying to cover her. The screaming had stopped before they'd been able to determine where exactly it was coming from, and now they were just haphazardly going through the store. It hadn't sounded like the screams of a little girl, but a person's screams—real screams—never sounded like folks thought they would. Grown men sounded like little girls. Little girls sounded like grown men. Bobby-Leigh was gone. Somebody was screaming. Jen found it hard to wrap her head around the possibility that it wasn't her sister's cries they'd heard.

"Maybe we should split up?" one of the guys behind her said. She was working so hard to keep herself under control that she couldn't tell who it had been, but she thought it must have been JP, because he was the only one stupid enough to suggest something like that. Cooperman must have agreed with her.

"Not unless you want us all to die," the old man said.

"This is a big store, Cooperman."

"Exactly."

Jen turned down the next aisle and froze.

"This way!" she said.

Bloody footprints were all over the floor. They were fresh, small. They had to be Bobby-Leigh's. She followed them to the back of the store, to a door that said "AUTHO-RIZED PERSONNEL ONLY." When she finally made out a complete footprint, she realized she'd misread the tracks.

Fuck! She should have let Ace lead, he was the fucking tracker! What the hell was she doing?

Fuck! Fuck! Fuck!

This was the way Bobby-Leigh had come from, not the way she was going. But that was probably a good thing, Jen realized. She remembered Uncle Allen's lessons on how to defend themselves with the karambit knives he'd given them. A knife she herself had strapped to her back at that very moment and had spent every day since her uncle had been murdered dreading having to use. She'd never asked Bobby-Leigh if she was carrying hers, but of course she would be. Bobby-Leigh had taken those lessons to heart. Uncle Allen had scared the shit out of her, but she'd listened, through tears at times but never without her complete attention. Jennifer suddenly wished she'd listened better herself, because whatever had just happened, her little sister had fought back and was now alive because of it.

Probably.

Maybe.

Unless it was Bobby-Leigh's own blood that she was tracking all over the store.

The pride she'd felt a second ago flickered like a florescent light bulb that needed to be changed. Her mind jigged and jogged through scenarios of what could have happened. She let the images come, but didn't hold on to them. As long as they flowed through her and then out, she'd be fine. If she grabbed one and let her mind nurture it and grow it to an obsession, she'd lose it. She'd berserk out. She still had hope now. So she let that hope calm her mind and let the rest of her thoughts and emotions just run though her like water in a river.

Her sudden turn as she reversed directions caused her to collide with Ace, who had been right on her heels, trying to tell her she was probably going the wrong way the whole time. The collision knocked the sawed-off shotgun he carried out of his hands and onto the floor.

"We're going the wrong way," she said.

"That's what I was trying to tell you."

Jimmy tried to give her a reassuring smile as she

passed him, retracing her steps. But she ignored it. Maybe he wasn't such an asshole, she thought. But until they found her sister, she didn't give a shit about whether she'd misjudged him or not. No matter how good looking he was or that her heart tingled a little bit when her eyes met his.

But even though she didn't smile back at him, their eyes locked, and in that connection what had been nothing but a mixed bag of teenage hormones suddenly became something else. Seven minutes before they found Bobby-Leigh, Jennifer and Jimmy fell in love, though it would still take a long time for them to realize it, and even longer to actually accept it.

They finally came upon the little girl in the hair-care aisle and froze, the way someone would if they'd spotted Bigfoot in the woods. The little girl's clothes were soaked with blood. Her hair was matted to her face. She had a cart with her and in it were the jumper-skirts they'd seen earlier, as well as several pairs of Mary Janes, a couple of pairs of knee-high stockings, and some makeup. The two spiked black dog collars were the only particularly odd items in the pile of goods. It would have been a cute scene, if not for the blood and the ax she was holding so tightly in her hands that her knuckles were white. Bobby-Leigh turned and looked at them. She didn't say anything. She didn't move. She didn't smile. She didn't cry. It was hard to tell if she even really saw them or not.

"Bobby-Leigh?" Jen asked, not sure what she should say or how she should proceed. She could tell the little girl had been traumatized, but she didn't look physically hurt. In fact, it looked like the blood she was covered in all belonged to somebody else. Her clothing wasn't ripped or cut, just very bloody. Bobby-Leigh looked at her for another couple of seconds, but it felt like she was looking through her, or past her, or . . . Jen didn't know exactly how to interpret that look. It was cold. That was all she could nail down in her mind.

Cooperman knew it, though. It was the look folks got after they'd killed somebody, justified or not. It was the look that comes only after a person has realized that there really is no such thing as sanctity of life. That killing is just another thing a person can do, like eating a cupcake. It was hard to see that look in such a little girl, but he preferred it overwhelmingly to the look girls usually had after somebody snatched them, the one that came after a girl had been violated for the first time. That one meant she'd internalized the violence of the rape to the point that she'd never see herself as anything more than the human-shaped piece of meat she'd been treated like. Bobby-Leigh had fought back—and somehow won—and while, yes, the little girl would never be the same again, she was still whole. Unbroken. The old man wanted to cry in relief, rush to her and pull her into his arms, but he didn't. He knew better. Instead, he nodded to Jen to approach her sister and with a look told the rest of the men to keep back.

Bobby-Leigh watched all this without any response of any kind. Jen took a step toward her, desperately trying to think of the right thing to say but coming up with nothing as her sister went back to what she'd been doing when they found her: looking at hair dye.

"You find anything good?" Jen asked softly, immediately wishing she'd said just about any of the other things she'd thought about saying before she decided to say that. Bobby-Leigh ignored her. Jen didn't know what to say next, so she just approached slowly and silently.

"Thinking about a color change, dude?" the big sister asked the little one.

"I want black. But they don't have black."

Jen looked at the boxes of hair dye. There were at least seven different kinds of black, so she didn't know what the fuck Bobby-Leigh was talking about.

"What about this?" she asked, showing her sister a box of Revlon that said "Soft Black."

"I don't want soft. I want black."

Jen pulled down the box next to it.

"Blue black?"

"No. Black."

"Okay. Well, I'm sure they have one that is just black," Jen said, totally confused about what was going on in her little sister's head, and terrified of finding the answer at the same time.

"This one just says 'Black,'" Jen said, pulling down a box of Clairol and handing it to her sister.

Watching them from the edge of the aisle, Jimmy turned to Ace and asked what he thought they were doing. Ace told him he had no idea. Cooperman told them both to shut up.

"That looks good. Thanks," Bobby-Leigh said, putting the box in her cart.

"I see you got a couple new outfits there, dude."

Bobby-Leigh looked at her sister with a look Jen couldn't read.

"Well, I can't really wear what I'm currently wearing out of here, can I?"

"Dude, I wasn't trying to give you a hard time or anything. I think this stuff is nice." Jen didn't think the stuff was nice at all. It was creepy, like some kind of doll outfit. And what was up with the makeup? And the dog collars? She wanted to ask what had happened, but she didn't. Maybe because she knew that the answer, whatever it was, was going to scare the crap out of her and change the way she looked at her little sister forever. Maybe because it just seemed like such an out of place question in the moment. Maybe because she thought there was a chance that Bobby-Leigh would break if she talked about it.

"The dressing rooms are going to be dark," she said.

"No, they won't, the tops are open," Bobby-Leigh countered.

"Really?"

"Yes."

"Um, yeah. Okay. Let's get you some new shit, dude. Let me just tell the guys what the plan is."

Jen walked over to the guys and tried to communicate with her eyes that Bobby-Leigh was okay, but not okay. Maybe *really* not okay. Jimmy touched her hand and she didn't pull away, at least not immediately.

"She wants to change her clothes."

"Okay. That seems pretty reasonable."

"Do you think anybody else is here?" Jimmy asked nobody in particular.

"No. But that doesn't mean that there isn't. Obviously, we weren't alone before when we thought we were," Cooperman said and shot Ace a look making it clear that he held the young man personally responsible for dropping the ball on this one.

"Don't let us out of your sight. But maybe, you know . . ." the implied instructions to follow at a distance were directed at all of them, but it was only Ace who answered.

"We got it."

"Thanks."

Jen went back to her sister, who without a word headed off toward the dressing rooms. The guys followed but kept their distance. Jen checked back over her shoulder several times, wishing one of them could somehow signal to her what she should say or do, but even if they could have sent some kind of message, they didn't know how to deal with what had happened to Bobby-Leigh any better than she did.

At the dressing room, Jen moved as if she was going to enter the little room with her sister, but Bobby-Leigh stopped her. The little girl had been right. The rooms were all open at the top and the skylights actually did light them just fine.

"I'm okay," Bobby-Leigh said.

"I know, dude. I just . . ."

"I'm really okay," she said, and Jen felt tears welling up in her eyes and a sob climbing slowly up her throat.

"I'm not," Jen said. "Can I just come with you, dude? Please. I'm afraid to . . ." She didn't know what the end of that sentence was. *Afraid to let you out of my sight again,* she guessed, or maybe it was *Afraid to not be there when you need me again.*

But Bobby-Leigh didn't care what the rest of the sentence was. At the moment she didn't really care about anything except being somebody else as quickly as possible, and if that meant her sister had to watch her metamorphosis, well that was just fine with her.

"Whatever."

When the girls exited the dressing room, Bobby-Leigh was decked out in her first attempt at the Lolita-goth look she'd carry through her coming teenage years and then some, except for the dyed black hair, which Jen would do her best to fix that night when they got back to camp, though they'd never be able to get all of her original red out.

The risqué clothing and dark makeup made the folks back at camp uncomfortable—well, that and the ax that never left the little girl's side from that point on. But the only part of the whole thing that bothered Jen were the two dog collars her little sister insisted on wearing around her neck from that point forward.

Bobby-Leigh never volunteered what had gone down in the back of that superstore. She never offered any explanation for any of the elements of her outfit, and, in spite of her fear and curiosity, Jen never asked. In fact, she made sure nobody else ever tried to talk about any of it with her little sister either. Jennifer Kessler had firsthand experience in keeping demons locked away, and respected the practice.

* * *

Night had come. The girls took a break from listening to the Chinese greatest hits to meditate, then they set off to find something to eat, which took them several hours of going through six different apartments, and even then all they ended up with was a bunch of candy bars hidden away in some chick's closet—the secret stash of a hidden eating disorder, no doubt. They were stale, but still sweet. It was enough to keep them going. In fact, it was kind of a treat after the potatoes Brennachecke's group ate on a daily basis.

"I lost my knife with Jimmy," Jen said as they ate and flipped through a photo album of their absentee Chinese host, trying to guess who was who in the pictures.

"What knife?"

"*The* knife," Jen said.

Bobby-Leigh smiled and pulled the karambit blade she'd held against Jen's throat in the trashcan earlier out from somewhere in her dress.

"You mean this knife?" she said.

"Lucky. You still have yours."

"I know," Bobby-Leigh said, then laughed. "But this one isn't mine. This one is yours. I grabbed it before you even berserked out. Uncle Allen would be pissed if I let you lose it."

"You're a rock star, dude."

"Yeah, I *am* pretty cool."

"You know what I like most about you is your modesty, though," Jen teased.

"I know, right? I am amazingly modest."

Both girls smiled. For the thousandth time, Jen almost asked her sister about what had happened at Walmart, but didn't. Instead, she turned back to the CD collection and the photo book and tried not to think about Jimmy, or her father, or Uncle Allen, or Brennachecke.

Before they'd had a chance to realize how exhausted they actually were, the girls had fallen into an uneasy sleep. The sounds of muffled Chinese hip-hop spilled from the earbuds by their side as they drifted away, making for some extremely strange dreams.

The next thing they knew it was dawn.

Chapter Four

The Blood Pirates in Vedic City

BRENNACHECKE STOOD in the bookstore café once called Revelations waiting to have one himself. It'd been pretty easy for Ace to track the two this far because Jen was bleeding. But they'd tended to their wounds with book pages and now the trail was harder for Ace to follow. Brennachecke's intuition told him they'd go to their uncle Allen's farm. If not right away, eventually. It was the only place left for them.

Brennachecke had actually learned TM himself just as the shit hit the fan. His wife had been on him to do it, and twenty minutes twice a day was a small price to pay if it made her feel more connected to him and got her to shut up about how great it was. Meditating had made her happy, and knowing he was doing it too had made her even happier. But she was dead now. And he didn't meditate anymore. It wasn't that he'd disliked it. He just always seemed to have something more pressing to do. Still, the TM community in Fairfield was a close-knit one. Brennachecke hadn't exactly been friends with the girls' uncle, but he'd known him. More importantly, he knew where the man's farm was. Brennachecke also knew that a particularly large band of blood pirates had set themselves up in a TM community known as Vedic City on the outskirts of town and that they were actively hunting along Highway 1.

All the nonviolent groups that were active in eastern Iowa knew better than to travel on, or too close to, the interstate highway. It was the equivalent of a suggestively dressed drunk young woman walking alone through New York City's Central Park late at night—back before the park was burned to the ground by a nuclear blast, along with the rest of Manhattan. Sure, maybe you'd get through it okay, but if you did you'd be one of the lucky ones. And the number of folks left who got by counting on being one of the lucky ones was thinning quickly. Luck, it would seem, was suffering from a catastrophic drought.

Folks had been using Highway 1 to move around for a few years now and word had traveled. News of the safer route to and from Cedar Rapids had then found its way into the more violent communities, and they'd descended upon Fairfield to harvest the misery as best they could.

The blood pirates, being the worst of the worst, had arrived shortly thereafter and soon were the only nearby marauders to Fairfield's north. Brennachecke would have traded them for a thousand of the earlier hostile groups if he could. But they were here to stay. Vedic City had been upgraded over the years, and now the western parts of the community were nearly completely off the grid. It was sustainable. It was defendable. In times like these, it felt like a paradise—as long as you were one of the pirates. Folks who ended up there as "guests" were a little more likely to find themselves envying the damned in hell.

Brennachecke fully intended to kill Jennifer Kessler, but he had no intention of being cruel about it. If he could get them before they got beyond the MUM campus, things would be pretty easy. But if they made it up Highway 1 and ended up in Vedic City, or Blood City as it'd been rechristened, then the plan got all muddy. His people, all fourteen of them, would follow him down any road he led them. But getting too close to the blood pirate stronghold put everybody at incredible risk. Even if it hadn't posed such a threat, the futility of saving Jennifer from being tortured, raped, and mutilated while they milked her of her monster blood, only to put a bullet in the back of her head, was painfully apparent. And yet, if they couldn't find them that was exactly what he intended to do.

"Eric," he called out and the boy appeared by his side instantly. "After dark, you're going to go up B Street, past the burned-out Eco Village where Sweetwater used to be, get on Mahogany Avenue, and head up to the farm that's just past 110th Street. That's Allen Kessler's old place. That'll be where Jennifer and her sister are heading. You wait for them."

"By myself?"

"No. You're going to take everybody. You're in charge. If the girls show up, just watch. Don't let them know you're there. Don't do anything to them. Just wait for me. If the farm's been destroyed, you still wait for me before you do anything. Understand?"

"What if they come and then leave? You still want me to wait?"

"I'll only be a day or two at most behind you."

"But what if that's all the time they stay?"

Brennachecke smiled. Eric had a good head on his shoulders. Always had. Never got emotional. Never got wrapped up in relationships. Never failed to do right by his father. Eric would be able to lead the group just fine if something happened to him. Jimmy on the other hand, well, Brennachecke wasn't surprised at all that Jimmy had been taken first. He'd always been his mother's boy.

"Track them, but send runners back in relays until I get there," Brennachecke said, and almost added, *Unless it takes me more than a week to show up, then put a bullet in Jen's head and move out toward Cedar Rapids like we've been planning, because I'm not coming. I'm dead.* But he didn't say it. He didn't say it because he didn't have to. Eric knew better than to stay in one place for too long. Brennachecke told himself that they'd all be safer on this mission than on the suicide one he was going on to enter Blood City and attempt to negotiate for the girls. But *safer* was not by any means safe.

The old soldier called the rest of his people over and explained the plan, reminding them to stay off the road and use the dead cornfields for cover. Daniel Patterson, a thirty-seven-year-old real estate salesman in his former life, insisted on coming with Brennachecke to infiltrate Blood City.

"We're not going there to stir up trouble, Dan."

"I understand."

Brennachecke believed him, but he also knew that after the blood pirates had taken Vedic City, Dan's fiancée disappeared. It was a logical assumption that she'd ended up there. However, if she'd been snatched it wasn't logical to think she'd still be alive. Daniel obviously saw a chance for revenge.

"I'm serious, Dan. If you come with me and do something that puts what I need to do at risk . . ." He didn't finish the sentence.

"I understand the mission, sir," Dan said.

Brennachecke thought it over. If he ordered Dan to head to the farm with Eric, he knew the man would do as he was told. At the same time, he was about to walk into hell, and a little backup might be what allowed him to walk back out again.

"Okay, fine," he said. "We'll head out at dusk. Let's get ready."

Brennachecke sat down as his group began what at this point was a familiar routine of moving camp and setting up in a new building. His mind drifted to Jimmy. To Jen. To Jimmy and Jen together. His head dropped to his hands as grief consumed his heart like an infestation of maggots. But no tears dripped from his eyes. His mouth didn't tremble. He held his pain tight in his chest and let himself feel its weight, but he showed no sign of it on the outside.

His youngest son was dead. He'd failed as a father, just like he'd failed as a husband to protect the boy's mother. But the worst part of it all was that he'd loved watching his boy fall in love with the pretty potty-mouthed girl. And Bobby-Leigh, though weird as hell ever since the incident at Walmart, was the toughest little girl he'd ever seen, and smart as a whip. He'd been excited to watch her become the powerful matriarch of the group one day. He knew that Jennifer hadn't intended to murder his boy. If it was in him to forgive, she might even have been allowed a second chance. Unfortunately, the old soldier's heart was broken long ago, and while he had compassion and even empathy for the possessed girl, it was duty that moved the blood through his body now.

He called Dan over and the two men set about making a plan. Dan was an amazing bow hunter. With a compound bow he could kill a deer easily at a hundred yards, and he'd taken game down from as far away as 240 yards. The problem was that a bow does not make for a particularly well concealed weapon. The pirates were not going to allow them to walk into Vedic City and address the Man-in-Charge with Dan armed like that. But at the same time, a bow—especially at distances like Dan was capable of—could take out an enemy pretty much completely undetected. It was a lot like having a sniper rifle, only there was no sound of a gunshot. No muzzle flash, no smoke. In the right position, Dan could pick off folks until he ran out of arrows and probably never have his location pinned down. That was the only advantage Brennachecke was going to have, aside from what he intended to offer in exchange for the girls.

* * *

At dusk, the air was extremely cold for a July evening in Iowa. Brennachecke's group could see their breath as they said good-bye to Dan and the old soldier. Eric watched his father and the real estate salesman head out to infiltrate Vedic City. Dan was loaded down with a bow and arrows, and Eric's father was apparently armed with only his service pistol—a well-worn M9—and a hunting knife.

Eric's eyes burned as he watched them disappear into the shadows. He would never openly question his father, but this whole business was fucking bullshit, he thought, purposely thinking words his father would not approve of. As if somehow that little act of rebellion, even if it was only in his own head and heart, mattered when he was just going to do as he was told anyway.

Getting killed trying to save the girl who killed his brother, just so he could kill her himself—what the fuck was that?

Whenever they'd lost people over the years his father had always avenged the death if it had gone down in a way that was anything less than fair and square. In fact, Brennachecke's reputation for responding with an-eye-for-an-eye justice was a huge part of what kept the group safe from the lesser marauders who remained in the area. His father's vengeance was surgically dealt and only fell on the head of the one responsible. There was never malice behind it, just an obligation to balance the scales.

When Dan's fiancée went missing, the poor man had wanted to go on a killing spree, but Eric's father had held him back. Suspicions were not enough. Yes, it had probably been the blood pirates to the north who had taken her, but they had no proof. Nobody had seen it. The woman had just vanished in the night without a trace. They'd spent months reaching out to the hundreds of groups in eastern Iowa, trying to find out what had happened to her, but never came across a lead. There was nothing pointing to the blood pirates as the perpetrators of her disappearance and presumptive murder. But the idea that it couldn't have been anyone else was a hard one to shake.

Of course, there was also the possibility she'd left of her own accord and simply didn't want to be found, though nobody ever openly admitted to it.

Eric knew that Dan was frustrated. He sympathized, but Eric also knew his father was right to hold the man back. He knew this because he knew something about Dan's fiancée that nobody else did: The woman had been a sexual deviant. A predator, almost. And Eric knew this firsthand. He was embarrassed by what he'd done with her, even more ashamed of it because she was another man's woman, but what kept him from telling his father about it was that he'd enjoyed it. Worse yet, he missed it. Fear of judgment kept his mouth shut as the searching began, but he suspected the whole time that she had left in the middle of the night because she was simply unsatisfied by what both Dan and Eric had been able to offer her.

Regardless, Dan was surely going to get a chance to kill some blood pirates now. It would not end up being justice, but since the man would never know the truth, Eric figured Dan would probably get some pretty intense satisfaction out it. What that meant for his dad was not something Eric was prepared to deal with yet.

The group traveled light. No vehicles. No animals. Society and civilization had fallen like Humpty Dumpty and broken into a million pieces, but the world was hardly a wasteland. God had just stomped on the anthill that used to be humanity, and all the angry little motherfuckers who survived were spilling out everywhere without any sense of purpose, community, or civility—biting and climbing and crawling and killing and running and hiding, until order could be restored.

Eric wore his homemade flamethrower rig on his back as he guided the dozen men and women his father had promised to protect away from the town square and up

B Street. The little ignition flame of the rig on his back was the only light they had to follow except for the stars and moon that occasionally peered down on them from between the clouds.

Ace and Cooperman walked with him. JP held the rear, mostly because Eric couldn't stand the man's constant babble about TM. The nine people between them ran the gambit of what pre-apocalypse life had been; the group had construction workers, a bank teller, a librarian, and a bartender, that Eric knew of, plus a bunch who never talked about their past lives. But there were no children. Bobby-Leigh had been the only child among them. Children didn't fare so well in the world after the power turned off and the nukes exploded. Folks with means couldn't protect themselves. Children without means didn't stand a chance.

"I get that Brennachecke feels like he has to put Jen down, but . . ." Ace began, and then couldn't finish. The question of what would become of Bobby-Leigh weighed heavily on all of them.

"Maybe she didn't know she was a berserker," Cooperman said.

"She knew," Eric said. The men spoke in hushed voices, trying not to disturb the cover of darkness.

"You don't know that," Cooperman said.

"It doesn't really matter, does it?" asked Eric.

"Of course it matters," Cooperman replied. "It's not like she murdered your brother in cold blood, Eric. Your father's vengeance has always been just, you know? I just don't see the justice in this."

"If it hadn't been your brother, I—"

"My father is a lot of things, Ace," Eric cut him off, starting to get angry. "But he is not a man who acts on emotion. If Jen had killed any of you instead of his own flesh and blood, he'd be doing the same thing he's doing now. You know that."

"Do I?"

"You don't have to stay with us if you don't like what's happening," Eric said coldly, effectively ending the discussion. In his heart, Eric agreed with Ace, but the young man had locked his heart away the same night Dan's fiancée had vanished into the night.

They walked on in silence for a few miles until they came to the dirt road between the dead cornfields, just past what was left of the Sweetwater Bunkhouse property and Eco Village—a reminder of why it was better to keep moving.

There were lots of these off-the-grid farms all over the US. Or at least there used to be. The folks who lived on them quickly found themselves with targets on their backs, and as the properties changed from one bloody hand to the next, their old inhabitants would do their best to rip them apart, either in an attempt to keep the technology even though they were losing the location, or just out of spite, so nobody else would be able to enjoy the benefits of having electricity. It was the latter that had ultimately resulted in the destruction of Eco Village.

Fucking assholes, Eric thought, as they slowly and cautiously moved into the thick dead corn. Again the language in his head was an expression of his frustration and anger at his father. He'd never use those words out loud. Just like he'd never tell Ace that executing Jen didn't feel like justice to him either. Just like he'd never tell Dan about being fucked by his wife-to-be.

"Bobby-Leigh is still one of us, as far as I'm concerned," Eric said softly to the corn.

"Amen to that, brother," said Ace.

"If your father kills the girl's sister, do you really think she's going—"

"No, of course not. But that choice is on her."

"But it's not like you're just asking her to pick a glass of wine to go with dinner," said Ace. "What options does she really have? I mean, do you seriously think she could watch your dad execute her only living family left and then forget it ever happened and just pop back into the kitchen and start peeling potatoes?"

"She's not going to do that," Cooperman chimed in.

"She'll defend Jen to the death. You know that," Ace said.

"Probably," Eric agreed.

"Look, man, I feel like I need to be explicitly clear here. I am not okay with hurting that little girl, no matter what your dad says," Ace said. "If that means I need to leave, then I don't know what to tell you, Eric. I guess that means I'm gone."

Cooperman didn't say anything, but Eric could tell he was in agreement with Ace and just didn't want to say it out loud.

"Me too, brother," a voice from the back said. Eric knew that voice belonged to Roger Halburn, a thirty-odd-year-old former bartender at the Arbor Bar and one of the original group his father had pulled together in the months that followed Fairfield losing power for good. Roger had followed his father through thick and thin up to this point. His dissent was a dangerous tipping point, and Eric knew it. Mutiny was as dangerous on land as it was on the high seas—not that these folks would attempt to violently remove his father from power. They'd just leave in the night, like Dan's fiancée most likely had. Brennachecke's group would be weakened by the losses, but what was worse, if the deserters couldn't find another group to join, they'd be picked off like tin cans at shooting practice. This was a lose-lose situation in the making, and the making was happening fast.

Eric really wished his dad was here. Nobody would be questioning anything if he was. Deep down in the pit of his gut, Eric was not completely confident his father would make it out of Vedic City and back to them. He took a deep breath and felt the weight of the world pressing down on his shoulders.

"Nobody is suggesting we hurt Bobby-Leigh, guys."

"No, but—" Ace began, but Eric cut him off.

"Listen. I don't have orders to execute Jen. You all know my dad isn't going let anybody pull that trigger except him. Whatever happens, it's not going to happen until he meets back up with us. But no matter what, Bobby-Leigh isn't going to be punished for something her sister did. I won't have it any more than any of you will." The words came out louder than they should have, then without thinking he added, "In fact, if it were up to me, I wouldn't be punishing Jen at all."

As soon as it came out of Eric's mouth he knew he'd messed up. It was bad enough when other people broke ranks with his father by questioning his command decisions, but it was pure treason for any disagreement to come from his mouth. He should say something to negate it, he thought. Something like *But it's not up to me, my father's in charge and this decision is his to make as a commander and a father.* Yet he didn't say that, or anything else. The words just hung there in the oddly cold night air, waiting for him to fix this situation. But he didn't want to fix it. This wasn't like any of the other times the group had participated in eye-for-an-eye justice. Jen was one of them. Eric liked her. In fact, if his brother hadn't been so obsessed with her, he might have even pursued her himself in a year or two, when the age difference had grown a little less creepy.

His words hung in the air unanswered until they were lifted away by the cold air, into the night. *At least I shut everybody up,* he thought as he moved forward through the corn. It wasn't much of a consolation, all things considered, but deep down he was starting to not care anymore. They weren't soldiers in the army after all. They were just a bunch of people trying to stay alive. Military hierarchies of command didn't even really make sense under the circumstances.

He took a deep breath and for the first time realized just how much he resented his father for leaving them to pursue the Kessler girls. It obviously wasn't the first time Eric had been angry with the man, but he suddenly was hit with a strong feeling that it might be the last, and his resentment evaporated instantly.

* * *

Vedic City had—ironically considering its current occupants—originally been built to facilitate world peace and had boasted a population of over a thousand people before everything fell apart. It was home to a resort-style golf course. It had a town center, a capital, and several hotels. It was more than just a community. Technically, it was almost its own country. It even had its own currency, not that anybody actually used it. It hadn't been designed to be off the grid originally, but as the second and third generations of the TM movement returned to Fairfield from all over the country to raise their own kids, it had slowly become more and more green. Most importantly, it was next to the tiny municipal airport—and it was the airport that was going to be the key to Brennachecke's negotiation with the vile dregs of humanity who had taken over the place.

The airport was in remarkably good shape, all things considered. When things had started to go bad, the folks who'd known how to fly and had the means to do so had flown away toward Canada, where there were fewer guns and more wilderness to hide in. Then there were those who didn't have the means to fly north and who were stupid enough to try to put avgas into their cars and trucks. Some of those idiots had ransacked the place for fuel in the months of panic after the power failures and the nukes, but those folks were low in numbers and the airport fuel tanks were not empty.

Being stupid didn't equate to living a very long life these days. Without power, the gas pumps didn't work and that was enough to send a lot of folks off to find alternative sources for fuel. Of course the pumps could be hacked with a car battery, or if that was too technical, the gas could simply be siphoned from the underground tanks with a hose. But not everybody was that resourceful. Unfortunately for those who did try to use avgas in their cars, the relatively high lead content and chemical additives used to make the fuel safe for planes at higher altitudes slowly destroyed their ground vehicles' engines. The morons tended to inevitably get stranded in the kinds of places death found them quickly.

Smarter folk knew there were better places to find the things they needed than a municipal airport. In fact, there were still planes in hangars just waiting to be used. Brennachecke had seen them with his own eyes and knew how to fly most of them. Since nobody had seen a plane in the sky for years, he assumed the blood pirates did not.

It was deep into the heart of the night by the time Brennachecke crossed over Jasmine Street and the Vedic City line. He was alone. Dan was perched with his bow high and away, watching with field glasses, out of danger and for the next few hours out of range. The whole plan was risky as hell, but this was the most dangerous part of it.

Brennachecke stealthily moved down Village Center Drive, angling to cut through the thin green strip of trees between the houses and the Ayurvedic hotel and spa once called the Raj, which he'd heard through the wind was now the blood pirates' command center. This approach allowed him to come at the building from the side instead of straight up the driveway, but it was debatable if a less direct approach would make anything easier.

Blood City was asleep for the most part—the drunken shouting of a pirate resident somewhere sight unseen notwithstanding. There were no security patrols that Brennachecke could see, which meant the pirates either had grown complacent with the size of their numbers or were just plain stupid. Either way it was a good sign. The voices in the wind put their numbers at over a thousand, but like most rumors that seemed to be an exaggeration, unless there were full-on barracks somewhere Brennachecke hadn't seen yet. With only a couple of exceptions, the homes he was passing now as he approached the green belt around the Raj were obviously empty. He wondered if Vedic City had solar batteries or not. And if they did, just how prevalent they were. Tesla's Powerwall batteries had dropped to a price point that residential installs had almost started to make economic sense. But then the world had ended, and Brennachecke didn't have any idea how many homes had power storage beyond a few kilowatts for emergencies. These homes did not appear to have any power, but speculating as to why was just a waste of time.

As he got closer to the Raj, however, it was clear that unlike the homes he'd just passed, the spa hotel did have power. In fact, it glowed softly with light as if the intentions behind its Sthapatya design had finally found fulfillment in the darkness of the world it now existed in. But as he looked closer, he quickly saw that the opposite was true—the structure had been tragically misappropriated by forces significantly darker than the night around it, and the light radiating out from within now only shone forth in irony. Dozens of bodies, naked and all female, had been strapped to the pillars at the hotel's entrance with barbed wire. At first Brennachecke thought they were corpses, but they weren't. The women lived, their flesh a bloody and rotting mess. He wasn't sure if they were strung up as a punishment or as warning. Probably both. His instinct was to put them out of their misery, but he didn't dare—at least not until he knew what had become of Jennifer and her sister. The women for the most part were stoic in their agony, or at least they were until one recognized that Brennachecke was not one of the pirate residents of the city.

"Please," she whispered. "Help me."

The woman was missing most of her left foot, and gangrene had clearly set in. Her entire left leg was rotting, and the stink of sepsis was nauseating. She was dead, but just hadn't stopped breathing yet. Brennachecke looked around to make sure nobody was watching except for the other women lashed to the pillars, and then pulled out his long hunting knife from the sheath on his arm. The woman nodded and smiled. Tears of relief poured out of her eyes and down her bloody cheeks.

The knife cut through the space between her ribs and pierced her heart almost effortlessly.

"Please," the other women called out to him.

"Please."

The commander in Brennachecke knew very well that putting an end to the suffering here would complicate his mission. He hesitated to euthanize them.

"Please."

They begged in rolling waves of pleading that washed over him and threatened to erode the resolve on which he stood. Threatened to pull him under, fill his lungs with sorrow, and make him drown. Then one started to scream and things got complicated in a hurry. Brennachecke realized what they were. They were a test and an alarm built into one. And he had failed.

The two men who came out of the Raj carried AR-15s— arguably one of the best assault rifles in the United States, which was a country that had more guns than people even before the apocalypse. Brennachecke smiled at them and held up his hands. *Here we go,* he thought, as the nerves that come from years of being on the front lines of one war after another clicked coldly into place.

"Morning, gentlemen," he said as the two pirates looked him over, both having a hard time believing the balls on the guy, but also perfectly willing to put him down without a word. Brennachecke wanted them to speak before he said anything more, but before either of them did, the taller of the two noticed that one of the strung-up ladies had been prematurely killed.

Complications upon complications. And it was all because of women he had only been trying to help. Why couldn't he just stay out of things? Brennachecke was not the least bit bothered by the sexism in his own thoughts.

He wasn't going to have the luxury of waiting for them to speak. He could see it in their eyes, even before the tall one started raising his weapon. The mental calculations flashed by in a heartbeat; there was only one way left to go, and he didn't waste any time wondering if this was going to escalate things beyond the realm of a possible positive outcome or not.

It would be what it would be.

As the men with the AR-15s started to come up, Brennachecke stepped forward and pushed the barrel of one of the assault rifles into the chest of a tall pirate so fast the man didn't even know it had happened. In fact, it wasn't until Brennachecke's leg launched out behind the guy and swept his own out from under him, sending him down to the ground backside first and leaving his gun in the hands of the old solider, that he even realized he'd been attacked.

A boot to the head cut that realization short.

Brennachecke didn't pause long enough to even take a breath before continuing the attack. The other, shorter, pirate was not any faster and found himself without his weapon and with the stranger's hunting knife against his throat before his friend on the ground had even started to bleed.

"Kneel," Brennachecke said. The short pirate complied without a word. Never taking the blade away from the man's neck, the old soldier checked the pulse of the pirate on the ground and stripped his gun away from him.

"He'll live," he informed the short one.

"Maybe. But you're fucking not gonna," the pirate hissed.

Brennachecke smiled and nicked the man's neck, not enough to sever an artery, but enough to make him feel it. "There's no need for that kind of language. I have an offer for your boss. You can take me to him, or you can die. Choice is yours."

The little pirate didn't say anything, which didn't surprise Brennachecke in the least. The man was obviously trying to calculate his chances, but without the years of practice and training Brennachecke had, the man's doubts were getting the best of him. Brennachecke had seen it in a number of soldiers over the years on his tours of duty. *The pirate wouldn't have lasted long on a real battlefield,* he thought. He knew that was probably going to be true of most of the men he was about to be facing off against. In fact, he was counting on it.

"Take me to your leader," Brennachecke commanded after another second or two of waiting for the man to decide what he wanted to do.

The short pirate finally moved. In his head, Brennachecke breathed a sigh of relief. He needed to be in front of the Man-in-Charge before the tall one woke up, or he'd end up having to kill one, if not both, of them. Murdering folks only made things harder. This was already complicated enough.

With the two AR-15s slung over his shoulder, his knife digging into the soft tissue of his hostage's neck, and ice water in his veins, Brennachecke walked into the light spilling out of the lobby of the Raj.

"Kill me," the women strung up on the pillars behind him cried.

"Kill me, please!"

"It hurts so bad. Please! I can't take it anymore!"

"Curse you, you fucking cruel son of a bitch."

One of the women managed to spit up a bloody chunk of something at him, but it didn't make it very far from her mouth and just ended up dangling off her swollen and bruised lips, more a testament to how much she wanted to die than to how angry she was at the man for not fulfilling her wish.

Brennachecke ignored it all. He didn't look back even once at the women screaming for death behind him. But they certainly looked at him, and their continued curses would prove to be remarkably prophetic.

* * *

Eric looked through the brown long-dead stalks of corn at the Sthapatya Veda house that legally belonged to Jen and Bobby-Leigh's uncle. He could see his breath in the cold night air and was shivering, but thoughts about how odd the weather was for a July night in eastern Iowa had been pushed out of his brain for the moment. He was preoccupied with the sliver of light he could see coming from the windows of the house and what that meant. Jen and Bobby-Leigh were already there. Or if not them, somebody else was, which would be worse.

The cold, even if he wasn't wasting time wondering about the weirdness of it, did actually matter (or at least it would soon). It meant they couldn't just wait outside indefinitely like his dad had ordered them to do.

They'd all dressed for a cool summer night—light jackets over short sleeves—not expecting the temperature to continue to drop like it had. It wouldn't be long before hypothermia became a real issue.

"What are we doing?" Ace asked.

"Waiting," Eric said flippantly.

"For?"

"I don't know."

"Well, it's cold as fuck out here, man."

"The house is not empty," Eric said.

"Jen and Bobby-Leigh wouldn't leave a candle going like that," Roger said.

"I was thinking the same thing."

"So what are we doing?" Ace said again.

"I'll go and see if I can get a head count," a woman's voice said. The voice belonged to Maddie Love—or "Mad Love" as most of them called her—a fifty-nine-year-old former librarian who was probably the smartest woman Eric had ever met.

Folks had always underestimated women, and the end of the world hadn't changed that fact. Mad Love would not appear to be a threat to anybody. If she were spotted doing her reconnaissance, she'd probably be able to stall until Eric and the rest of them could get to her. It was a good idea, but before Eric had a chance to agree to it, the door opened and an occupant of the house came out.

"Eric Brennachecke!" the voice of the dark figure on the porch shouted. It was a voice Eric had never heard before, and he would have remembered it if he had. The distinctive accent (was it African?) of the woman on the porch was as strange in eastern Iowa—even in the once eclectic little town of Fairfield—as the cold front they were experiencing in July.

"How do you know me?" he shouted, stepping out into the open but signaling to the rest of his group to wait in the shelter of the corn.

The Sthapatya Veda architecture endorsed by Maharishi and popular in the TM movement had a number of features not particularly common to farmhouses in Iowa: geometrically proportional rooms, east-facing entrances, and a *brahmasthan* space at the structural center of the building among them. But the feature that suddenly caught Eric's attention in this moment was the little steeple on the top of the house, called the *kalash*. On this home in particular the kalash was atop a tiny glass-windowed belfry-like structure, which at the time Allen Kessler had built it had been designed to light the brahmasthan inside with shafts of sunlight during the day, but now apparently served as a crow's nest for a sniper with a laser-guided targeting system. Eric saw the tiny red eye of the beam blinking at him from the darkness above and looked down at his chest to find the telltale red dot of light painting him as its target. The dot then disappeared, but Eric knew that the gun was still tracking him. Modern laser-targeting no longer required a continuous beam to follow home; these days snipers just used the red beams to mark the desired impact point for the bullet. After that the trajectory guidance circuitry of the gun would take over and a miss was just about impossible regardless of what the victim did.

"I need your people to come out of the corn," the African voice said. "So long as your intentions are peaceful, nobody needs to get hurt."

Eric didn't know if his intentions were peaceful or not. The house was supposed to be empty, or if occupied, it should have been with the Kessler sisters, not this foreign lady with her snipers and all-seeing eyes. From the doorway two more blinking red eyes of laser target painters popped on, and two more dots appeared on his chest and then vanished.

Jesus, he thought, *who are these people? Military?*

He didn't think so. Those guys were usually only interested in occupying cities, where the resources were plentiful, not tiny towns in Iowa. Or so he'd been told. Brennachecke's group hadn't crossed paths with a military faction even once in the entire time they'd been together. They'd heard stories about them, of course—horrible stories, second only in depravity to the ones folks told about blood pirates—but they'd had no firsthand experience. If this woman and her group were military, he reasoned that they must have been deserters. That would explain the apparent firepower and tech. Eric liked the potential poetic irony of coming across a group of real deserters while members of his own group were threatening to leave him, but his intuition told him this woman was not a soldier, at least not in any formal sense.

"We come in peace!" Eric shouted. "But my people are not coming out into the open until we know who you are!"

There was a long pause before the African voice responded. From the distance he was to the house, Eric couldn't make out any words from the discussion she was having with her people, but he knew what they were talking about it—or at least he thought he did.

"Where is your father?" the lady finally asked.

The question had so much wrapped up in it that Eric almost just didn't answer it. As his mind raced to quickly unpack its significance, he found that he had no idea what the right answer was because her question begged a bigger, broader, more pressing question of his own: *How did she know his father was not with them?* And that question quickly spawned an avalanche of additional ones: *Did she know who* was *with them? Did she know all their names? Did she know what they were packing? Did she know about*—The questions rolled down his mind until they threatened to cover everything else.

Maybe she can somehow see through the dark and the corn, he thought, but even if she had some kind of night-vision tech working for her, that didn't seem like it would give her the intelligence she was obviously in command of. And if it wasn't technology that was giving her the information, then what was? Was she a witch? A psychic? Satan's sister? Eric didn't know, so he did the only smart thing a man could under the circumstances. He told the truth.

"He's trying to find the Kessler girls in Vedic City."

"What the fuck are you doing?" Ace hissed from the corn behind him.

Eric wished he knew, but since he didn't have any answers, he just ignored him. Two spotlight beams suddenly shot out of the open doorway, blinding him. He squinted into the light, trying to shield as much of it away with his hand as he could. There was movement on the porch. Somebody—the woman, he guessed—was approaching him. He heard Ace pulling the hammers back on his shotgun, ready to fire.

"Stand down, Ace," he whispered. But the man wouldn't, Eric knew that as well as he knew they were in way over their heads here. "Our side does not shoot first," he said, loud enough for his whole group to hear, but hopefully still quiet enough to not share the order with the lady and her people marching toward them from the house.

"Your father took James and Daniel with him to Vedic City?" the woman asked when she got to Eric, her people still shining their spotlights in his eyes so that he couldn't make her out.

"Jimmy is dead," Eric said, relieved that the woman didn't know everything after all. Then suddenly his adrenaline surged again when he realized that, while she may not have known that Jimmy was dead, she did still know that both he and Dan were not with them, and that normally they would be. *Who the—*

The lights lowered, suddenly breaking his train of thought and allowing him to see again. There were three people standing in front of him, a woman and two men, but it took him a second to register that the woman was actually a woman. Her body and face were obviously female, attractively so, but her hair was cut so short, his own shaved head had almost as much hair as hers did. Had she been white, Eric probably wouldn't have done the double take. But she was black. And not TV-appropriate Tyra Banks and Kerry Washington black either; this woman was dark-skinned African black. The kind of black that the predominately white mainstream-media gatekeepers could barely tolerate in men and almost never allowed significant screen time for in women.

This was the first black person Eric had talked to, or even seen up close in person, in years. Even before the apocalypse began, Iowa's black population was just barely over one percent. Eric wasn't so much racist as he was naive and sheltered, but nonetheless, he stumbled back, nearly falling to the ground, when he saw her. This was a reaction the woman must have had before, because she just smiled a sad, knowing smile and sighed loudly before she spoke again.

"My name is Anoona," she said. "The Kessler women are welcome here if your father gets them out of that cesspool, as are the rest of you, but understand this in no uncertain terms: this farm belongs to us now. If you can't agree to that, then you'd best be on your way."

Eric just stared at the black woman, trying to make sense of what was happening and coming up short. Anoona and the two armed men with her patiently waited for him to respond.

"How do you know me and my father?"

"I need you to acknowledge what I just told you and agree to it before I can answer any of your questions, Eric."

"Okay, yeah, just give me a second here. How did you know that Jimmy wasn't with us? How did you know that my people are in the corn? Who are you?"

"Eric, like I said, I am happy to answer your questions. All of them. But I need you to acknowledge your understanding that this farm is ours. Right now, before we do anything else. Because I am well aware that it *used* to be Allen Kessler's. I'm going to need you to convince me that you understand and agree to our ownership rights here, so that if your father shows up with Kessler's nieces we can have a reasonable expectation that nobody in your group—those young ladies included—is going to attempt to challenge our position here. Of course, that is not to say that your group is not welcome to join us. We have the capacity to take you in either short term or permanently, whatever you'd like. Just as long as you understand that this place is ours."

Eric agreed.

* * *

Standing in what was once the library of the Raj, Brennachecke decide once and for all that he hated women. Sure, some might be okay. Some might even be freaking great. But it wasn't enough to make up for how miserable they collectively had made his life.

The short pirate had taken him to see the Man-in-Charge just like he'd asked, but the man wasn't at all what he'd expected. The square-faced, beady-eyed leader was a plump, redheaded man sporting a comb-over even Donald Trump would have called him out on. He looked too soft and slow to be running things, and yet here he was. But the real surprise was that the man was not alone.

Dan's fiancée was with him.

And as far as he could tell she was not a prisoner. No, not a prisoner at all; she was sitting pretty just like a modern-day Lady Macbeth. As he silently took in the scene, it seemed to Brennachecke that she might even be the one running the show, with her soft whispers into the eager ears of power. After all, she was the one who spoke first, not the supposed MIC.

"Sergeant Brennachecke," Dan's fiancée said.

"Beverly. You look good, considering most of us thought you were dead."

The woman laughed without any humor, but her eyes sparkled. Both Beverly and the MIC were hooked up to blood bags, getting transfusions of berserker blood. Some kind of nurse was attending them, but the man's mouth had been sewn shut and he wore a collar that looked like it probably had an explosive charge in it of some kind, so he guessed the man was not there willingly—though if that was true, the attendant didn't let on. Brennachecke was actually a little surprised at the clinical nature of the whole thing. He'd expected something much more gritty, dirty, more horror-show like, but to an untrained eye this would have looked almost civilized. It almost didn't even feel out place here in the Raj, where back in the day all kinds of Aryuvedic treatments had been offered. It was like they'd just added berserker blood transfusions to the list of standard spa services.

Brennachecke thought protecting the health spa aesthetic must have been Beverly's influence. He had always been aware of the probability that Dan's fiancée had run off rather than been snatched. The fact that they'd never found so much as a trace of her pointed in that direction. When folks were taken against their will, there was almost always some evidence left behind. Signs of a struggle. Blood. Witnesses. Rumors. Something. Beverly had just vanished into thin air.

"Mmm, so . . ." she said. "How's Dan?"

"Probably better off thinking you're dead."

The woman laughed again, it was still humorless, but now held a seductive undertone. "For sure," she said. "You know, for years and years I wondered if he'd ever figure out who he was really with. What kind of woman he'd been about to marry. But then you know what? One day I just woke up and didn't give a fuck anymore. I mean, seriously, how do you stand being around him? The man is such a bore."

"Oh, I like the man, Beverly."

"Really? Okay, well, how about this, then? And tell me honestly too because your opinion really does matter to me here: What did you think of my sirens out the front?"

She knew Brennachecke would know she was referring to the dying women strung up around the pillars at the entrance to the Raj, but the man didn't give her the satisfaction of letting her know it. Apparently he didn't want to engage in a debate as to what was appropriate and what wasn't during an apocalypse.

Oh well, fuck him. She knew her brilliance and wit even if he wouldn't acknowledge it. *I mean, come on!* she thought. *I am using naked dying women to lure good men to their deaths just like in an old Greek myth, for the love of God. It's fucking brilliant.* Inside her head, she growled. If Brennachecke didn't start being more fun real fast or at least have something worthwhile to offer, the asshole would have to die in the arena. And then after that maybe she'd send a squad out to kill Dan too just for the hell of it.

"What the fuck do you fucking want, Brennachecke?"

"I'm trying to find the Kessler girls."

"And you think I'd tell you if they were here?" She laughed.

Brennachecke didn't bother to answer. He just waited. Dawn was breaking outside. In an hour it would be morning, and if the girls were not here yet, they surely would be by the end of the day. His gut told him his little hostage was not going to be much of a deterrent if push came to shove, so he was going to have to manage to keep Beverly from escalating this, which he could see she clearly wanted to do.

What was it with women?

It was a task he wasn't exactly confident he was up to. Beverly had been hard to read even before she'd slipped quietly into the night, cast off her sheep's clothing, and been reborn as the rabid wolf sitting before him now.

Dealing with somebody strung out on any kind of drug made things more difficult, but there is still a logic and a thought process at work in an addict's mind. If a man could tap into it, negotiation was still possible.

As he waited for her to react to his silence, he reviewed every encounter he'd had with the woman while she was with Dan and part of his group. There had to be a moment that would in hindsight give him clues to her true nature, but he couldn't bring any up out of the dark. She'd been quiet, reserved, never overtly cruel, but not particularly kind either. He now realized that she'd been basically just like Gacy, Dohmner, and the other psychopaths out there, or at least how they were typically described by neighbors in interviews after their carnage had been revealed.

Suddenly Beverly laughed and whispered something into the Man-in-Charge's ear, then disconnected her IV line from her blood bag. As the nurse hurried over to put it away, the Man-in-Charge smiled, cruelty dripping from his lips.

"Answer her," he said in a breathy, gravelly voice.

Brennachecke sighed and pressed his knife into the little pirate's throat, just enough to make the small man squeal. He didn't want to be having this conversation and hoped the trickle of blood now oozing around the blade would drive that point home and get them to take his request seriously.

"I think they headed this way from town, up Highway 1," he said, biting his words like they hurt his mouth.

"Oh, do you? Well, I'll make sure we keep an eye out. We can always use new toys around here. Thanks for the heads up."

Beverly slid off her seat next to the Man-in-Charge and walked up to her one-time friend and his hostage. She was wearing an expensive-looking long cashmere robe. It had been folded over her body while she'd been sitting, but apparently it did not have a tie, because it opened up as she moved off the couch, unabashedly exposing her naked body underneath to everybody in the room. She may have been hard to read, but Brennachecke was pretty sure by how she walked toward him that the woman enjoyed the men's reactions to seeing her naked flesh. This was a show. Sex was power too. Especially when it came to bad men.

When she got to him, she slowly reached out and touched his hostage's lips, and then ran her finger up the line of blood dripping down his neck and tasted it. Brennachecke eyed her, not sure what she was doing but not about to let whatever it was get to him.

Suddenly, she thrust her hands forward and pushed the blade of the hunting knife deep into the throat of his hostage. The knife severed the small pirate's jugular vein and let loose an enormous spray of blood all over Beverly, who closed her eyes, tilted her head back, and seemed to take sexual pleasure from the sensation of its warmth splashing against her naked skin.

Brennachecke was caught off guard. He'd thought he was prepared for anything, but he hadn't been prepared for that and certainly was not ready for what happened next.

Beverly's hands rubbed the blood over her naked breasts and down her flat stomach to her porn-star trimmed privates, where she rubbed at her clitoris, gently bringing herself to climax in a matter of seconds. Brennachecke's hostage died before her berserker-blood-fueled, human-blood-soaked orgasm had finished shuddering its way through her body.

The Man-in-Charge, grinning ear to ear, politely waited for her to return to the real world from the ecstasy overload she was experiencing, so she wouldn't miss his men taking Brennachecke out, or the satisfaction he knew she'd get from watching the bloody smears being laid into the carpet as they dragged away the bodies.

The world switched into slow motion for the old soldier. His mind flashed through what he'd just witnessed, grabbing on to details he wished he could let go of forever.

Blood. Splashing across Beverly's face.

Her hands. Rubbing furiously between her legs.

Her breasts. Undulating as her body shook.

AR-15s. Pointing at him. About to fire.

"Wait!" he said.

The Man-in-Charge held up his hand slightly, and the pirates in turn held their fire.

"There are still planes and fuel at the old airport next door. I can teach your men, or just you if you prefer, to fly them," Brennachecke blurted out, hating the way his voice sounded in his own ears, almost as much as he now hated women in general.

* * *

The morning was still crisp but finally starting to warm up enough to dispel the visible vapors of Dan's breath. Last night had been cold and uncomfortable. He hadn't expected Brennachecke to return anytime soon (or maybe at all), so he'd tried to get some sleep before the sun came up. Curled up in the small departures and arrivals building with no heat and only his thoughts, however, he'd found rest elusive. Instead he spent the night fighting a constant tug-of-war in his mind between his urge to flee (if only to find a place he could actually get warm) and his urge to rush into Vedic City and get Brennachecke out before it was too late, because the likelihood of the old man coming out of this mission in one piece felt lower and lower with each breath he watched come out of his mouth. But he'd managed to stay put, just like Brennachecke had told him to.

Now, basking in a shaft of sunlight pouring in through the one remaining pane of glass in the wall of windows facing the runway, he soaked in the warmth on his face and hands and wondered if this bizarre cold in the middle of July was just a fluke event or the new normal.

He remembered reading something (or maybe watching it) about global warming and climate change and how it didn't always mean things would get hotter. He couldn't remember the details—something about the directions of the ocean currents reversing when the amount of freshwater displaced the amount of salt water, which was happening because all the polar ice caps were melting and falling into the ocean. Or maybe it had something to do with the greenhouse gases in the atmosphere. He'd seen that movie Al Gore had made while folks were still trying to deny the facts, the one with the stupid title, which he couldn't for the life of him remember at the moment. All that had stuck with him was the idea that global warming was making the weather more and more extreme and might somehow cause an ice age. The hows and whys may have been over his head, but he sure as hell could say one thing: it was colder than a witch's tit in a snowstorm last night, and it was the middle of July.

He pulled a Tupperware container out of his pack and opened it. Boiled potatoes. Breakfast of champions. He popped one in his mouth, packed the rest away, and stood up, trying to stretch the stiffness out of his body. He climbed up a ladder and through the access hatch in the ceiling, then scrambled onto the roof of the building. He could see the edges of Vedic City poking up behind the trees to the west. The place was still asleep, most likely, but he put the field glasses to his eyes to check it out just the same. He could see only a few homes and not the Raj from his vantage point, but the structures didn't interest him much anyway. He cared only about the roads, and there was no traffic on them yet.

He turned and looked out across the runway to Highway 1 in the distance where there too all was quiet. He looked to the hangar Brennachecke had chosen. They'd opened the doors and rolled a Cessna 172 out last night before they'd split up. Dan didn't know much about planes, but Brennachecke obviously knew what he was doing with the thing. Dan wondered why the old man hadn't taken advantage of having aircraft at his disposal, but then he realized that it was probably for the same reason the group hadn't settled down on one of the farms. Nomadic scavenging was just safer. If crops and electricity put a target on your back, Dan could only imagine the unwanted attention a plane would bring. He wondered if Brennachecke had that in the back of his mind when he planned this little invasion of his. Was he trying to bring down the blood pirates by making them draw more attention to themselves? That seemed too convoluted to be the actual plan. Besides, they were there to get Jen Kessler and her creepy little sister. Brennachecke had expressly said so. *But as an added little bonus?* he thought. *Hell yes.*

Though Brennachecke didn't actually seem to be doing much crusading against the squatters in Vedic City, Dan thought. And for that matter, the pirates had left them pretty much alone too. Not that his group had sought out conflicts with them—at least not until now. After Beverly had been snatched, Brennachecke had actually refused to inquire if anybody in Vedic City knew anything without some kind of evidence pointing in that direction. Dan had been pissed off for weeks about that, but once the old soldier made his mind up about something, God himself couldn't change it.

Dan looked at his watch. It was almost nine. Not that it meant anything anymore, but he found it comforting to keep track of the time. He popped another potato into his mouth and grabbed his bow, arrows, and field glass from the floor. It took him a second, but he eventually found a nice spot in the sun to wait for something to happen.

He didn't have to wait long. Old routines and schedules still haunted the lives of most folk. The collective consciousness of America still had 9:00 a.m. ingrained into it as the time when work was supposed to start. It still had noon ingrained as the time to eat lunch. It still had 11:00 p.m. ingrained as the time by which folks should be in bed. It was the circadian rhythm of a society that no longer existed, one that had no real purpose anymore—except maybe for the folks who farmed—but it survived nonetheless. Even for depraved and psychotic folks like blood pirates, the daily routine was remarkably ordinary. By 10:00 a.m. Vedic City had gone to work.

Dan watched a small convoy of vehicles drive out of the town and head toward him. He smiled, ready. But the convoy didn't turn into the airport; instead it kept going out to Highway 1. He put the field glasses up to his eyes and watched as the four cars and two vans set up to intercept folks who didn't know better than to take alternative routes. Folks like the Kessler girls. Dan shifted his observation toward the MUM campus just on a whim. He was too far away to make out anything. Even the glint of the golden domes in the distance was beyond the range of his vision. But he found himself suddenly convinced that Jennifer and Bobby-Leigh were not captives or victims of blood pirates just yet. He didn't know where this intuitive hit was coming from, but it was strong.

Had they jumped the gun? Had Brennachecke gone into the beehive and shaken things up before the honey had even been made?

If the girls were not in Vedic City, Dan wasn't sure how the plan would play out. He supposed that Brennachecke could still make his offer. He'd probably have to just to get out of there alive. But then what? It seemed unlikely that the pirates would be inclined to do much for them once they'd gotten their flight training.

Suddenly, Dan realized he didn't even know how long it took to teach somebody how to fly. He assumed it was like driving. The mechanical part was easy enough to learn quickly. Right foot on the gas, left on the brake and working the clutch. Clutch in while you shifted. Clutch out when you accelerated. But what really mattered was experience. You had to learn to feel for how long it takes to stop at different speeds. You had to learn to feel the clutch engaging and disengaging and how that worked with shifting and applying the gas. You had to learn to feel how fast you could take a corner without losing control. How much of that coaching did the old soldier intend to do?

He should have asked more questions. All Dan knew was that Brennachecke was confident he could get the pirates to take him to the airfield, and from there it was up to Dan to make a hole to escape through if it became necessary. They'd never talked about how long it would take. Dan had just assumed it was something that could be done in a day.

He looked out toward the meditation domes again and saw a disaster in the making. Two lone figures, one significantly smaller than the other, were just visible on Highway 1 through his field glasses. Jen and Bobby-Leigh. Of course, he couldn't be sure, at least not in any kind of scientifically accurate sense of the word, but he'd bet the house (if he had one to bet) on it if he could. It had to be them.

They were still a couple of miles away from the blood pirate's ambush point, but they were definitely going to be walking right into it.

Maybe Brennachecke had gone out with the road crew. Maybe when he'd asked for the girls and been told that they weren't there, he'd managed to convince them to let him—

He couldn't even finish the thought it was so ridiculous. Whatever plan they had was fucked. End of story.

But he was wrong. It wasn't the end of the story at all. This was just the midpoint of the first book in the chronicles of a very long apocalypse.

Part Two

Blood Pressure

Give man a fire and he's warm for a day, but set fire to him and he's warm for the rest of his life.

> - Terry Pratchett, Jingo

Those who have hunted armed men long enough and liked it, never really care for anything else thereafter.

> - Ernest Hemingway, "On the Blue Water"

The blood of the covenant is thicker than the water of the womb.

> - Source unknown

This is the way the world ends
Not with a bang, but a whimper.

> - T.S. Elliot, "The Hallow Men"

Chapter Five
The Beast in the Wild

EMMETT WAS REALLY not a bad man. He was really not a bad father. Really not a bad husband. A bad brother. Friend. Prisoner. He just wasn't particularly very good at being any one of these either, which was about as kind as folks could be when it came to referencing a guy who'd gotten drunk and driven his whole family off the road and then proceeded to shoot his wife to death in the snow.

That said, the man did have one thing going for him. He could talk. Not in a car salesman kind of way, or a therapist kind of way, or a politician kind of way. It wasn't something folks would be able to put their finger on, or would even notice for the most part. He talked to folks the way hot-bodied cheerleaders talked to rough and rowdy football fans. Emmett (once he'd quit drinking) opened folks up and stoked their inner fires in a way not very many people left on the planet could. Black Jesus had found that conversations with him would stir the pot of whatever stew was cooking inside his brain. It wasn't in what he said or how he said it. Emmett's gift was in what he didn't say. How he heard what folks meant, instead of just listening to the words that exited their lips while waiting for his turn to talk.

Black Jesus was committed to doing his duty by all the convicts in his care, regardless of what he thought about them or the circumstances that had put them behind bars. But over the last few days, he'd started to actually like Emmett. Not enough to release him early or anything like that, but enough to come up with reasons to pass by his cell and have conversations.

Unfortunately, today's conversation was not one of the good ones. Emmett's obsession with his wife's fertility doctor had reared its ugly head again, and now Black Jesus was having a hard time finding an opening through which to walk off without being rude—which was utterly ridiculous and he knew it. There were no rules of etiquette when it came to COs talking with inmates. Inmates talking to COs, on the other hand, was an entirely different matter. In that case the COs might as well be gods and the inmates ants.

And yet, this particular god didn't want to hurt the ant's feelings if he could help it. Kessler's obsession made Black Jesus uncomfortable. It was obviously unhealthy and didn't serve him. And it would certainly wind up getting the man in trouble if he couldn't reconcile with it before he was released. But, if he were truly honest with himself, Black Jesus simply didn't see how listening to another rant on Kessler's theory of the apocalypse would help the cat move on.

That said, the inmate's notion of why the world had fallen apart was much more interesting than the general bullshit everybody else had to say about it. So even though he didn't want to stay there and listen to him go through it yet again, part of him kind of did. It was crazy, sure. All the theories out there were. But once you started down the rabbit hole with him it was hard to tear yourself away from the logic of it all. Unfortunately, it was that very logic which was biting Emmett Kessler in the ass, and Black Jesus didn't know if he could keep from trying to explain that to him again.

"If your doctor man was inclined to partake in blood swapping, he could be in pretty choice shape still, even at—what would it be? Almost a hundred years old?"

"Oh, I'm sure he's doing that. He probably was the one who invented the fucking shit," Emmett said.

Black Jesus had been extremely troubled the first time he'd run into blood pirates and witnessed the brutality of their harvesting. Emmett had been the one he'd confided in. That conversation had been one of the good ones. Maybe even the best one. By the time it was over, he'd come to terms with how he felt about what he'd seen and felt like a better man because of it. He wished this conversation would take a turn in that direction, but he supposed Emmett needed to be heard as much as anything else. Though what he really needed to do was *listen*, even if just to himself, the CO thought, as the man's words continued to gush out of his mouth. Emmett was picking and choosing the dots he was connecting, and you just couldn't do that. Not if you really believed what you were saying.

"I still don't think you can hold one man responsible for all of this, though," Black Jesus couldn't help himself from chiming in.

"Did I tell you he worked with Josef Mengele in Brazil in the fifties? Mengele's a fucking Nazi war criminal. Just because the world's gone to shit, that doesn't mean nobody can be held responsible anymore."

"Look who you're talking to, inmate. And how could you possibly know that anyway?"

Emmett smiled.

"Internet. Found an old photo of them together on a site documenting Nazi war crimes. Josef Mengele was a monster, man. He did thousands of human experiments on Jews in concentration camps. But, you know what? My guy, Weiss? Weiss is actually worse. It's one thing to experiment on folks, but at least the results of Mengele's work didn't fuck up the human genome and get passed on for generations and generations to new victims he never even met. Weiss took innocent, unsuspecting families and turned their *children* into monsters."

Black Jesus sighed and shook his head. He was surprised a Nazi-related site, even one just documenting war crimes, hadn't been flagged and scrubbed by the Department of Justice filters, but just a little—it's not like this was the first time he'd ever heard of an inmate getting access to questionable content after the DOJ switched over to managed access from the near-absolute ban.

"That's not exactly the conclusion I'd draw from what you've told me." He wondered why the man couldn't just let it go, and then, not for the first time, why he himself couldn't let go of his not letting go. Why did he care so much about what Emmett thought? Why did he keep engaging? Why didn't he just walk away like he wanted to?

"Well, then I must have not told you enough, Captain. Because I learned a lot in the years I've been researching this and let me assure you: Weiss is one evil Nazi prick."

"Kessler," Black Jesus began, but considering the cat had steadfastly refused to see the point he was trying to make (again), he decided to attempt a straight-up honest approach, but hoped to soften him up by using the convict's first name.

"Emmett. I understand you're angry at the man, but you came to him. You paid a lot of money and went through a lot of effort to be able to have the two children you have. So even if you're right about everything, how is Weiss any more responsible for the world than you are yourself? You were the one so desperate for a child of your own that you refused to accept the biological facts of your infertility. Couples like you and Susan were the ones who sought out, paid for, and ensured the evolutionary process was going to be corrupted by technology. You and Susan, her mother and father, the hundreds of thousands of other couples over the years who refused to accept that they could not have children—at the end of the day, it was you cats who created and raised the monsters that laid waste to the world. Quite literally, brother."

This honest approach did seem to keep Emmett from getting angry with the captain over what he was saying, but he was past the point of being able to be influenced by such talk—straight up, sideways, or otherwise.

"Now you're just being an asshole."

"No, brother," Black Jesus said. "I'm just speaking truth. If you kill that cat when your sentence is up, then by your own logic, don't you have to kill yourself too? You really think Weiss knew any more than you did? That somehow he was aware you fools were maligning the whole human race's evolution? I never met the dude, but I'm sure this wasn't the future he wanted any more than you did. Nobody in his right mind, or even not in his right mind, would have wanted this. So if you're really some kind of victim here for having been forced to kill your wife, then isn't he just as much a victim for having inadvertently, accidently, *unintentionally* made her a berserker?"

"First of all, *he* is not a victim. Not in any way, shape, or form. And just to be clear, sir, I am not a victim because I put down my wife. I am a victim because when Susan and I, and everybody else who was part of this, when we were dying of thirst in the desert for a child of our own, Weiss poisoned the fucking water in the well and then told all of us we could drink it. I mean, for fuck's sake, Captain, somebody has to hold the man accountable," Emmett said, then added, "I would have thought you'd understand, you holding me accountable in here and all."

"Apples and oranges, convict," Black Jesus said, finally able to pull himself away from the conversation. He'd tried to be softer this time, but he'd still probably been harsher than he should have if he really wanted to get through to the fool. The inmate was clearly dealing with a huge amount of guilt over what he'd done to his wife. He was just trying to help the man. But he could have been gentler. Should have been gentler.

This is probably why they weren't supposed to talk to the inmates in the first place, he thought, a split second before—

KA-boom!

The explosion shook the building to the very foundation and caught them all completely by surprise. There was a long ear-ringing second of stunned silence throughout B Block, and then the screaming started.

Instantly Waters regretted pairing berserker inmates with the regular convicts. What had been a precaution to keep those he couldn't trust in line quickly turned into a bloodbath when the block was breached and started filling with smoke. Before Black Jesus could see any of the men attacking the prison from the outside, he had twenty convicts beaten to death by their berserker cellmates, their horrible screams for help rattling almost as loud as the sounds of their bodies being smashed, ripped, and thrown, until one by one they were cut short.

Those deaths are on me, he thought as he raced to his makeshift armory, past the carnage and rattling cells being destroyed by the out-of-control raging demons inside.

The air was colder outside than in. The warm air pushed the smoke out of the hole made by the explosion and cleared the visibility inside enough for him to just barely make things out. Finally, he got his first look at the men breaking *into* his prison. They seemed to be in uniforms of some kind.

Army? he wondered. *Probably not, up here in Maine. Private security was more like it. Rent-a-Cops turned rogue militia.*

Captain Waters saw five men advancing in a standard cover formation through the haze, past the burning Ford cargo van they must have use as an IED for their breach. Slowly the fire inside the building overtook the physics of the vacuum drawing the smoke outside, and the fumes started to lazily shift direction. He smelled ammonium, which meant it was a homemade bomb, most likely.

Definitely not military, he thought. The Rent-a-Cops had automatic shotguns, not machine guns, and, well, the military didn't really do shotguns.

They still knew what they were doing enough to be dangerous, for sure. But if they didn't have access to the resources of professional soldiers, maybe he had a chance, even though he'd been caught with his metaphoric pants down. Waters's brain was working quickly.

Assessing. The smoke was more dangerous than the cats with guns.

Strategizing. Escaping the smoke was going to require getting past the cats with guns.

Implementing. He needed to deputize some cats of his own and give *them* guns.

He grabbed the milk crate with the gear and weapons he'd set aside for his potential deputies. Deputizing the inmates he felt he could trust was his catchall disaster plan in a nutshell, but there were only four of them in total. Now in the moment, he was suddenly far from convinced this plan was actually a good one. Trusting an inmate not to kill you while he's locked up is one thing, but letting him out, putting a gun in his hand, and asking him to assist you in defending the prison you and he both knew you were just going to lock him back up in when all was over was asking a lot, to say the least. Yet that was exactly what he was about to do. Black Jesus believed that men would rise to higher expectations if they were given a chance. Maybe not all men, but his chosen four would. Emmett might even rise to the occasion as well, but Waters wasn't confident enough of that assessment to make him his fifth man. With four deputies and a little (or perhaps a lot of) luck, he'd be able to evacuate the prison and still retain control of it—or so he hoped.

The milk crate had seven Glock 9mm handguns, stacks of pre-loaded ammo clips, five gas masks, and ten tear gas grenades. The box was heavy. But heavier still were the ever-growing doubts that clouded his vision worse than the smoke now thickening all around him. Pushing the bad thoughts aside as best he could, he headed for the cells of his most trustworthy clients. With each step he tried to convince himself he was prepared (at least on paper) for this exact situation. He'd put his "trusted" men in the cells closest to his so he could arm them quickly if he needed to. But as he unlocked the doors and passed out the weapons and gear, he couldn't help but chide himself for being a fucking idiot and not factoring in the berserkers' response to the breach.

Goddamn it! He should have known better. Kessler had known.

The man was right when he suggested all the berserkers be housed together. All those convicts are dead because I just—

Before he could finish the thought a sound drew his attention.

Crash! Clack-Crash! Clack!

Three of the berserker cell doors broke open in rapid succession and the monsters came scurrying like rabid bulls toward the smoky light of day that spilled in through the hole in the wall on the north end of the block.

"Fuck," Black Jesus breathed. *The explosion must have knocked the doors loose.*

Suddenly he was extremely thankful he hadn't listened to Emmett after all. If all the berserkers had been housed together, he'd probably have more than two dozen monsters smashing everything in their path. And *everything* would have surely included him.

He slipped down behind a wall, motioning for his trusted, now-armed deputies to do the same. This new realization didn't do anything to lessen his responsibility for the deaths of his wards or his guilt about it; that was still on him.

They waited, trying to be as unnoticeable as they could as they watched the three escaped berserkers move toward the intruding assault team, smashing everything in their path as they crashed forward in a tidal wave of rage. Captain Waters and his band of merry little deputized convicts went unnoticed, but when the Rent-a-Cops with shotguns opened fire without realizing what they were up against, the trio of berserkers certainly noticed them. It only took a few seconds for the squad of assailants Waters had identified to be torn to pieces. Black Jesus wondered if the Rent-a-Cops had even known that there were berserkers incarcerated here. It certainly didn't seem like it.

The fire continued to billow and thicken the inside of the large cellblock with its smoky, deadly poison. Black Jesus slipped his gas mask on and motioned for the others to do the same. He'd intended to use the masks in combination with the tear gas he had, but at this point, popping the tear gas would be a waste. Nobody could breathe with all the smoke as it was. Visibility was shit and getting shittier. His whole plan, which had seemed so foolproof on paper, felt like it was falling apart as he pivoted it from a defense plan to an evacuation plan. He estimated they now had only a few minutes left before his entire clientele still behind bars died from asphyxiation. He was already responsible for the deaths of at least twenty of the inmates, plus the berserkers he could hear now being cut down outside. He wasn't about to be responsible for losing the rest of them.

Gunfire and screams echoed through the smoke. He heard men on radios and the sound of trucks. The Rent-a-Cop militia was apparently a sizable force.

This is not going to end well, he thought. *Not a chance.*

He turned to the squad of men he'd decided he could trust and handed one of them the keys to the cells. He didn't know who he'd given them to—everybody looked the same wearing gas masks in the haze—but it didn't matter, he told himself.

"Unlock as many of the doors as you can," he said to the man now holding the keys, but the man just stood there staring at him. "Fuck," Black Jesus said, snatching the keys back. "Really?"

The convict raised the gun and pointed it at the CO, the man who had had enough faith in human nature to have put the gun in his hand in the first place—faith that, Black Jesus realized now, was an absolute fucking terrible mistake. Humanity was dead.

"Really?" Waters said again, still dumbstruck by his disappointment in them. *If I get killed by an inmate I put a gun in the hand of,* he thought to himself, *I'll fucking kill myself.*

But the inmate didn't kill him. He just slipped quietly away. The other "trusted" deputies followed the first's lead without missing a beat. *So much for my ability to judge character,* Waters thought, not sure if he was happy to still be alive or not.

Time was ticking. He could decide if he was happy to be alive or not later.

He ran the opposite way his deputies (now traitors) had gone, toward the occupied solitary cells on the far end of the block, where he'd placed the worst of his human offenders. One by one he opened the concrete and steel cells.

"Listen to me carefully, convict," he told them each in turn. "You're not being released. But this block has been compromised and I cannot keep you safe here. There are armed men coming in from the north side. Avoid them as best you can, but get outside before the smoke gets you. I expect you to meet me in the east yard in one hour. I'll find you if you don't."

Each convict nodded, not really listening to a word the CO was saying. As soon as the old guard stepped aside, they each made a run for it. Black Jesus didn't expect to see anybody on the east lawn in an hour, but he still felt obligated to say it. Whether or not he'd hunt anybody down later was not something he was prepared to decide one way or the other at the moment.

Letting the berserkers out was a whole different ball game. No speeches. No appeals to civil obligations. Just unlocking the cells and letting the raging creatures figure out on their own that the door was open, all while trying to be invisible. That was until he got to Emmett's cell.

Wiley was no longer berserk. The cell was trashed, so obviously he had been, but now the big creature was lying in the middle of the floor, snoring. At first Waters didn't see Emmett at all, but then he spotted him hiding under the iron bed frame, which was half-ripped from its bolts in the wall. It only took a couple seconds to get the door open and Emmett out.

Bam! Bam-bam-bam!

The two men looked at each other for longer than they had time for as more gunshots echoed around them, followed by unintelligible shouts.

Screaming.

A second explosion.

Emmett was coughing fiercely in the smoke, but managed to wheeze out the words that would change his relationship with Captain Waters forever.

"We. Can't leave. Wiley," the convict said. Waters had not intended to leave him. In fact, he was actually just about to tell Emmett the exact same thing. *Thank God I'm not trying to survive on my ability to judge character,* he thought and grinned ironically, because that was exactly what he was trying to do at that moment.

"Help me get him up," the CO said, the tone of his voice changed with newfound respect.

They pulled the big creature up and half carried, half dragged him toward the only exit they had, the hole made from the breach. If Wiley woke and berserked out on them, they'd both be dead before either one could crack corn, so on the list of stupid things that Waters had done today, this would have to be right up there at the top. But it was the *right* thing to do, and for the first time since everybody had stopped showing up for work and he'd had to run things himself, he was not alone in his conviction of what was right and what was wrong. Black Jesus had been so alone for so long without even realizing it that he was shocked to feel his throat closing and actually had to fight back tears.

"Wait," he told Emmett as they were about to pass the cell the CO had turned into his own housing. Waters slipped out from under Wiley and grabbed two more gas masks, a machine gun, two large backpacks and all the PharmaJet doses he had. After quickly injecting Wiley (just to be safe), he squeezed a gas mask onto Beast's face, then handed the other one to Emmett, plus a backpack, though he did not give the man a gun. He'd already made that mistake today and he wasn't about to make it again. Emmett didn't miss a beat. He donned the mask and the pack, then slipped back under Beast. Waters nodded and the men continued toward the exit, unlocking the remaining cells as they went.

For most folk under the circumstances there wouldn't have been time for speeches and orders to meet in the east yard in an hour, but Captain Waters was not like most folk. Every convict under his care was explicitly told they were not being released from their debt to society and that they were required to rendezvous with him once it was safe. Emmett could have made things difficult. But the convict just held the bulk of Wiley's weight on his shoulders and smiled encouragingly as the captain went about doing the closest thing to right he could under the circumstances. Waters wished his deputies had been half as honorable as Emmett had turned out to be. Not for the first time, he wondered what the fuck he was doing.

* * *

The Rent-a-Cop army had been a solid fifty or so men strong fifteen minutes ago. But they'd obviously been totally unprepared for the number of raging-out berserkers Black Jesus had locked up in the block. By the time the old CO and Emmett made it outside with Wiley, there was no one left to shoot at them. There were also no convicts standing around waiting to be locked up again. No surprise there. Outside, there were just dead bodies, blood, viscera, abandoned vehicles, and small fires to greet them as they lowered Wiley's still-unconscious body down to the pavement.

Emmett counted fourteen berserker corpses, which meant a bunch of them had actually escaped. *Good for them!* he thought. The purely human convicts didn't fair quite as well, but he was still pretty sure a lot of them had survived and escaped too. *All in all, Black Jesus's plan to see out the sentences of each and every one of us has to be over,* Emmett thought as he took it all in. But then he saw Waters take a logbook out of his pack and start going over the bodies, making notes.

"What ya doing, CO?" he asked.

"Roll call."

"Seriously?"

Black Jesus didn't have to answer. As far as Emmett knew, the man was always serious, so he didn't know why he'd even bothered asking. He sighed heavily and walked over to an inmate body and flipped it over.

"John Connelly," he said. Black Jesus made a note of it.

It wasn't like Emmett had anything pressing to do. His only agenda was to find and kill the monster maker, Dr. Weiss, which could wait a day or two (or two hundred). The world he'd left behind when he'd gone into prison was obviously gone. The idea of making his way to Texas to fulfill his mission alone was frankly terrifying, especially since he didn't really know how the world worked anymore. Black Jesus was a good man. Emmett could trust him. He could trust Wiley too, he supposed. But the old captain was a much better conversation partner. Regardless, if his CO wanted to inventory the losses, Emmett might as well help. The hard conversation about what was going to happen now was inevitable, but this would postpone it some. Maybe give him enough time to come up with an argument for murdering Dr. Weiss the old black man would actually accept.

He moved some debris off an inmate with his face too shot up to identify. He checked the serial stitched on his prison uniform.

"54-69-8-90."

"William Martinez," the Captain said after a short pause and made a note of it in his logbook. Emmett looked at him with an impressed smile and chuckled to himself. The man had apparently memorized all their convict serial numbers. *Why the fuck?* he thought, but it didn't matter why. Not really. All that mattered was that Emmett was really starting to like the guy and was dreading more and more the talk they were about to have. A talk he needed to be prepared for.

Next to one of the dead Rent-a-Cops, a combat shotgun was lying on the ground. Emmett knelt down and checked the dead man's pockets. He found a handful of extra shells, which he slipped into his socks one by one as discreetly as he could as he went about the business of identifying the formerly incarcerated dead.

When they were done with the inventory, Emmett circled back to the shotgun, knelt, and checked the circular clip. It was loaded. Apparently the poor bastard had gotten only a single shot off before one of Black Jesus's deputies put a bullet into his chest. He carefully watched the CO finish up making his notations in the logbook. Of course, Emmett had no way of knowing anything about Captain Waters's trusted convicts turning out to be not trustworthy at all—at least not yet. But if he had, it wouldn't have changed anything. By the time the captain looked up, Emmett was already on his feet looking as innocent as a choirboy at his first Communion.

"Fifty-nine accounted for," the CO said, "including Mr. DuPont and yourself."

Emmett slipped his foot under the shotgun as he nodded. "What's the thinking here?" he asked.

"We wait to see if any of the inmates circle back here like I—"

"Captain, that isn't going to happen, those folks are gone."

"Probably, but I'd have expected you to be gone about now as well, and yet here you are still. You never know who is going to surprise you. You just never know."

"Yeah, about that . . ." Emmett started to say, but then didn't know where to go with it. What exactly did he want here? He didn't really want to face the future alone. Wiley would probably come with him, but Beast wasn't exactly the best company. He wished there was a way this could end in which he and Black Jesus rode off into the sunset together as friends. But everything he knew about the man told him that was extremely unlikely. So what the hell did he want to have happen?

"We need to talk" was what Emmett finally said as he kicked the shotgun up to his hands. He didn't point it at Black Jesus. He hoped he wouldn't have to. Somewhere in the back of his mind he still hoped they'd end the discussion they were about to have as friends.

Captain Waters looked at the shotgun in Emmett's hand and shook his head. He deserved whatever was about to come. After all, he'd broken the cardinal rule of inmate management so many times today, it was inevitable that he'd eventually pay the ultimate price for it. He'd started to trust Emmett. How many corrections officers were in the ground because they'd done the same? Hundreds? *Probably more*, he thought. Without a word, the last of Maine's prison correction officers unsnapped his holster. But he didn't raise his gun at Emmett—maybe because Emmett hadn't raised his at him. Maybe because, just like Emmett, he too hoped that somehow this exchange could end with friendship instead of dead bodies. Maybe because he was just so goddamn tired after keeping this place functional for weeks on end, only to have it all blow up in his face, that lifting his arm was just too much. Maybe it was the fact that he couldn't escape the utter ridiculousness of killing a convict for escaping, considering the current state of things. Maybe on some deep, dark level he actually wanted Emmett to shoot him. He didn't know. He didn't care. As long as the shotgun was not being pointed at him, he planned to keep his own weapon aimed toward the ground.

"I'm disappointed in you, convict," Black Jesus finally said.

"I get that, but . . ." Emmett started to say, but again found himself unable to decide how to proceed. Black Jesus waited silently with irritatingly calm patience, just staring him down. Inside the prison something exploded, as the fire found footing and began to devour the structure from the inside out. "The prison is gone, Captain. Hell, the whole world as we knew it is gone. Any debt I owed to society has to be gone too, man, because society itself is fucking gone. You get me?"

Their eyes locked. Black Jesus didn't say anything for what felt like a long, long time. But it was Emmett's turn to wait a response out, so he stood there in silence as the seconds turned to minutes, until at last the CO relented and spoke.

"Convict, I'm going to need you to put that gun down. I hear that you want to talk things over, and I'm willing to entertain a discussion of some sort considering the state of things at the moment, but I can't do it with you holding that shotgun."

"Can't do it, man. Me having this gun is the only way this talk stays between equals."

Black Jesus didn't respond, but he didn't turn away or shoot him either, so Emmett continued. "I like you a lot, Captain. I admire your commitment to your duty as a corrections officer. I admire the fact that you didn't just let all of us die. I was willing to go along with your plan to carry out our sentences as long as there was a reasonable expectation that you could uphold your side of that deal. Keep us fed and healthy. Safe. That's the unspoken contract between prisoners and guards, you know? The inmates give up their freedom in an effort to atone for their sins, and the guards ensure that they survive the ordeal. Good guards, like you, try to safeguard the inmates' dignity and humanity in the process, while the bad ones try to strip us convicts of everything that separates us from the animals. But regardless, there is a social contract in place that governs our relationship here. Can we at least agree on that?"

Black Jesus did actually agree with that, but he'd been very clear that he was not going to talk with Kessler as long as he was holding the shotgun, so he kept his mouth shut.

"That contract is invalidated the second you can't uphold your part of it, man. Look around you. The

fucking prison is burning to the ground. Half the convicts are dead and the other half have escaped. Food.
Water. Protection. Even if it's just Wiley and me left, do
you really think you're going to be able to provide that
with us locked in some cage somewhere? And if you do,
where is that cage? You did your duty, man. You did it
longer and with more integrity than anybody else working here. You didn't just leave us locked up to rot, like
your colleagues did. You didn't just let us all suffocate to
death when the shit hit the fan either.

"Do you know that we all call you Black Jesus
behind your back? Wanna know why? Because you're
just like the messiah, man. You could be counted on
to do the right thing. I don't know if you know how
fucking rare that is in prison. Some of the guards
here were worse than the prisoners, man. But not
you. Not Black Jesus.

"So if you can convince me that you can still uphold
your side of the social contract between us, as prisoner
and guard, I will fucking put this gun down and serve
out my sentence as you direct me to. I'll do it, because
my wife's blood is on my hands and whether I am behind
bars or in the wild, my heart will ache the same. My guilt.
My shame. My debt. These stay with me, man. They're
the real bars. They're the real prison.

"On some fucked-up level it's actually easier to live
with what I've done with you overseeing my sentence.
At least with you it will end, and I know the date that
will happen. Without that, then there's nobody left to
tell me it's okay to move on, you know what I'm saying?

"So, fuck me, Black Jesus, I will serve my sentence
out with you if you can honestly carry it out with the
same integrity and dignity you've had up to this point.

But if you can't, then we need to have a different kind of conversation, you know? Because I like you, man. And in this new fucking world we're in, it just seems—at least to me—that having a friend with you on your journey is probably a fucking good idea."

"Put the shotgun down."

Black Jesus wasn't going to have a conversation until the gun was no longer in Emmett's hands. Nothing Emmett said, no matter how much Waters agreed or disagreed with it, was going to change that fact. But the old corrections officer did want to talk. Even if all this was just an act to get him to lower his guard, Emmett did really seem to understand him and to appreciate what he was trying to do. Or had been trying to do—God knows what he was going to do now.

He couldn't imagine a world where letting a prisoner go free when he didn't absolutely have to was the right choice, and yet, what was the alternative here? He could kill Emmett and Wiley, he guessed, but that didn't seem like a particularly righteous move. Killing a prisoner in the middle of an escape attempt may technically be a justifiable discharge of an officer's service weapon, but it felt like murder under these circumstances. That was unless Emmett gave him no choice, which was a possibility so long as he was holding that goddamn shotgun.

"Kessler. Please don't give me a reason to put you down, brother," he said.

"Seriously? You would shoot me in cold blood?"

"Putting you down in self-defense during an escape attempt is hardly in cold blood, inmate."

"I'm not going to hurt you, Captain."

"Then put your weapon down."

"As soon as we come to terms on what this new relationship of ours is, I'm not going to need a weapon anymore. So I'll put it down then."

"The only reason for you to have a weapon in your hands is that you intend to do me harm."

"Look, dude, that is not my intention here, I promise. I just want to have a conversation."

"Then put the gun down."

"Goddamn it, man! I am not going to put the gun down. Just fucking shoot me if you have to, but I am not—"

BAM!

Black Jesus moved fast, like a gunslinger. His aim was nowhere near Emmett when he pulled the trigger. But that was intentional; he did not want to shoot the man, just shut him up and motivate him to comply.

"Fuck! Okay. I'll put it down," Emmett said and tossed the combat shotgun to the ground.

Bluff. Called.

"Now we can talk about things," Black Jesus said.

"My fucking ears are ringing."

Black Jesus looked at him and waited for a second for their ears to recover.

"The question is, can I continue to function as a corrections officer without the resources of the prison? The answer is, I can't."

"This is why I needed to have the fucking shotgun, man!"

"Emmett, I honestly don't know what the right move is here. I can't just let you and DuPont walk away, but I'm also not willing to use lethal force to keep you from doing so. That said, if you don't walk away, I don't know how to uphold my end of the social contract between prisoner and CO you talked about, which, for the record, I do believe in, very much. I am not going to shoot you in the back if you want to leave."

Emmett couldn't tell if that meant Black Jesus was letting him go or not. He doubted the captain would ever do something like that. So where did that leave them? He could walk away, but Black Jesus wanted to be sure he felt as guilty as possible about it if he did?

"What I want, man, is to go to Texas and find Dr. Weiss so I can hold him accountable for what he's done and then find my girls and try to put my life back together."

Black Jesus sighed and bit back the frustrated and near-hysterical laughter that was building up in his chest. *This has to be one of the most ridiculous tête-à-têtes two cats have ever had.* And yet he kept talking. "I can't let you just hurt somebody, Kessler. No matter how we end this conversation. I can't let you go if I know you're going to murder somebody. I might not shoot you in the back, but I will stop you if I believe you have criminal intent."

Emmett took a look around at the dead bodies everywhere and in less than a second, thought of a hundred sassy, sarcastic things to respond with, but he didn't say any of them. Black Jesus was just trying to do the right thing. Emmett knew it. Hell, he even respected it. The man didn't need to have his balls broken over the ridiculousness of the situation. He needed a way out of it, and the longer Emmett played antagonist and didn't help him find one, the more likely this was going to end badly.

Wiley stirred, drawing both men's attention. The drugs were wearing off. This needed to get wrapped up fast before Beast woke up, or things were going to get a whole lot more complicated (and violent). Looking at a lone pair of handcuffs lying in a puddle of blood next to one of the Rent-a-Cops, Emmett suddenly had a solution.

"Come with me to Austin," he said. "You can make sure I don't hurt anybody when I get there—or along the way, for that matter. And, if you'll agree to allow me to at least confront that bastard Weiss, I'll stay in your custody, so to speak, for the remainder of my sentence. And I'll help you with Wiley, so that he doesn't give you any trouble."

Black Jesus didn't think allowing Kessler to go to Texas was a good idea at all, but if he was going to compromise something, that seemed like a small concession in light of everything else. The man had proven himself to be honorable when it counted. Sure, it could just be an act, but he didn't have an idea he liked better. And this was infinitely better than putting him and DuPont down.

"You've got five hundred and eighty-four days remaining, Kessler. DuPont has a life sentence. When I release you from custody at the end of your stretch, you'll have to give me your word that you'll stay on with me as a deputy until I can come up with a way to facilitate DuPont's sentence. You'd be working with me as a free man at that point, of course, so I wouldn't force you to stay for long, but . . ." Black Jesus sighed and wondered if he would think back to this moment and realize he had been making a deal with the devil as much as he was making one with Kessler. He hoped not, but only time would tell. "If you can promise me that you'll do that, then I guess we have an understanding."

"As long as we can spend that time going to Austin and then finding my girls, I am fine with that."

"Okay, then. Don't ever call me Black Jesus again."

"Never to your face, boss," Emmett said with a smile and headed over to where DuPont was waking up.

Beast was very frightened when he saw the carnage around him and completely discombobulated by the fact that they were outside in the wild, as he kept calling it. The repeated pumping through his bloodstream of the hypersteroid-like super-cocktail of hormones, endorphins, and whatnot—otherwise known as HGF—had caused brain damage well beyond what Emmett and Captain Waters were aware of. But as Black Jesus and Emmett talked him through what had happened and what was going to happen next, Emmett realized the full-grown man's mind was still in there somewhere. *Maybe there's a connection between the berserkers and the rampant rise in autism spectrum diagnoses over the last few decades,* he thought. *Maybe not.* Regardless, the poor bastard was terrified in a way Emmett had only witnessed once before, when his own father's rapid descent into dementia stripped away his familiarity with the people he had nurtured and loved his entire life. It was like he knew he should understand what was happening but just couldn't, which was what had made it so hard to watch.

"I do that?" Wiley said for the fifteenth time as he noticed once again all the dead around him, like he'd just opened his eyes.

"No, man," Emmett said. The whole conversation was going to repeat again. Fucking hell, he thought they'd gotten through to him this last time. They should have cleaned up the area before he came to, but who knew the once-human creature was going to freak out like this?

"I in the wild?" he asked Black Jesus.

"No, inmate," the Captain said softly. "I'm here. I'm your CO. We're just going to be outside of the facilities for a while. Think of it as extended rec time, yeah?"

"I in the wild . . ." the huge creature said and suddenly started to sob, mumbling, "Oopsie-daisy-doodle-o, I kill 'em, deadie-day-oh," through his tears.

"Wiley," Emmett said, touching the monster's shoulder. "Captain Waters is going to take us on a trip. He isn't going to let you, or me, hurt anybody. That's his job, buddy. So as long as he's with us, you'll always know that you're not hurting anybody."

Black Jesus and Emmett shared a look.

"You're a good man, Wiley. You just got caught up in some unfortunate circumstances, you know? But I promise you, the captain here, he's going to make sure you don't do anything you need to feel bad about, okay? And you know what? I'm going to help him, alright?"

The same speech he'd said before, just different words. Emmett suddenly flashed back to a discussion he'd had with Jennifer before his world had been turned upside down. Back when she was three, or maybe four. Back when Susan was still alive. Before he'd really started drinking. Before he'd shot his wife in the face, failed to file an appeal, and survived being in prison when the end of the world kicked into full swing.

Jen had just pulled the leg of their little pug—Emmett couldn't remember the dog's name at the moment—but his daughter had yanked so hard that the dog's shoulder had been dislocated. Now, she'd had no intention of hurting the little animal, she had just wanted to play, and when the dog suddenly starting yelping and frantically limping around her, trying to get away, his little girl had burst into tears and screamed for hours, utterly distraught over the realization that she'd hurt this creature she loved so much.

That same innocence was hiding behind the eyes of Beast, and just like it would have been ridiculous for Emmett and Susan to have punished their daughter for hurting the dog—Bobo, that was what she'd named it, Emmett suddenly remembered—it seemed equally ridiculous to ever punish Wiley for any of the deaths he'd caused. But at the same time, he supposed he wouldn't want the ticking time bomb that was entangled in the psyche of all berserkers to go off again in public. If the government hadn't collapsed and society hadn't cannibalized itself, he wondered if they'd have eventually figured this out and created a separate facility for berserkers, one that wasn't a prison, per se, but that still separated them from the general population.

"Berserkers don't belong in prison . . ." Emmett muttered to himself as he wiped the big creature's tears. "They should have a special place for them."

"Like a camp somewhere?" Black Jesus asked.

"Yeah."

"Like a camp where you could concentrate them all in one place."

Emmett looked at Black Jesus, suddenly realizing what the man was saying. "That's not . . . I don't mean a fucking concentration camp, boss."

"Yeah, that's probably exactly what the Nazis said when they first started rounding up Jews."

"You're a fucking asshole, Captain." A day ago, Emmett would have been nervous about the consequences of calling Black Jesus an asshole to his face, but the etiquette felt like it was looser now. Still, Emmett waited for Waters's reaction. There was a long pause, or at least what felt like a long pause to him. But Captain Waters was acutely aware the circumstances had changed and was okay with a little friendly banter between him and Emmett. In fact, as the seconds ticked by without a response on his end, Waters decided that the decorum from inside the concrete walls that now only housed smoke and flames wouldn't serve them so well out here in the wild. He looked Kessler in the eye, held him there for a second longer, and then finally spoke.

"Says the white male suggesting to an African American that internment camps are a humane solution."

The tension broke. Emmett could have laughed out loud, but he didn't. "Do you really think prison is the right place for these guys?" Emmett asked, breathing a huge sigh of relief inside.

"I don't think it matters anymore. But, you know, they actually did stop sending them to prison. They didn't put them in camps, though. They just put them down."

"Are you shitting me?"

Black Jesus shook his head.

"How'd I miss that?" Emmett asked, but they both knew the answer. "I guess I'm not surprised."

"Suppose we've all kind of been in the wild for a while now."

"I in the wild?" Wiley half asked, half screamed in terror.

Emmett sighed. Black Jesus's shoulders slumped and he covered his face with his hands. Both men knew the conversation with Wiley was going to go another round.

Fuck.

"You're not in the wild, inmate," Black Jesus said.

"No?"

"No, man," Emmett seconded.

"Officer-bossifer doodlie-do?"

"Doodlie-do, my brother."

Beast breathed a huge sigh of relief. Maybe they'd finally gotten through to him after all.

"Captain, do you know if there is any kind of paint anywhere nearby?" Emmett asked. "I need to leave my girls a message if we're going to leave, just in case they come here looking for me."

"Maybe in the maintenance building over there."

Black Jesus nodded to the only building not on fire: a small cinder-block structure with no windows.

"Are the keys . . . ?"

Black Jesus looked at Emmett like he was a crazy person. "Stay with DuPont. I'll see what I can find for you."

"I can go . . ." Emmett began, but then realized that to the captain, handing over the keys to the facilities to an inmate was just not something he was willing to do. He didn't bother reminding the boss man that he'd actually already given Emmett keys when they were opening the cells of the prison on fire. Nor did he mention that since they were leaving anyway, there really wasn't much value in locked doors and keys at all anymore. He knew it was just one of those reflexive habitual rules the man had internalized over the years, not really a reflection on how much the man trusted Emmett—not that Black Jesus would ever admit trusting him. Or that Emmett actually deserved that kind of trust.

Apples and oranges, inmate. Emmett impersonated Waters in his head and smiled. The truth was, he was happy to stay with Wiley while the man looked for him. It would allow him to put a little insurance policy in place while the captain's back was turned. Emmett didn't have a formalized plan yet, but he knew that once they got to Austin he was going to do more than just confront Dr. Weiss. He was going to kill the bastard. The truth in his heart weighed on him a little. Not the intended murder—that he'd been comfortable with for years—but the fact that he'd lied right to Black Jesus's face. Just because his eventual betrayal once they got to Austin was premeditated, strategic, and inevitable didn't mean Emmett got to feel good about it.

Ninety minutes later they were climbing into one of the Rent-a-Cops' armored vans and pulling out of the double rows of barbed-wire fencing that surrounded the still-burning remains of Maine State Prison. As they headed out into the wild, toward Texas, Emmett was in the driver's seat, Black Jesus was beside him, and Wiley was in the back with as much food, gas, and ammo as they could carry.

On the rock sign next to the first checkpoint folks saw when they entered the facility from the street, right in front of the main entrance gate to the still-smoking concrete prison block they used to call home, and over the now meaningless words "Maine State Prison," was the message, crudely drawn in neon-blue paint:

JENNIFER AND BOBBY-LEIGH

HI GIRLS! I AM ALIVE AND GOING
TO YOUR UNCLE'S FARM IN FAIRFIELD
I HOPE TO MEET YOU THERE

LOVE, DAD

Chapter Six
The Man in the Pilot's Seat

THE GIRLS BEGAN THE DAY with their twenty-minute morning meditation just like they'd been taught to. Technically, Bobby-Leigh hadn't been supposed to learn the sitting version of TM until she was ten, but Allen Kessler had taught it to her early, almost as if he had known he'd not be around to do it when she was of the proper age.

Up to this point in Jennifer and Bobby-Leigh's lives, the girls had more or less gotten by just on doing what they were told, going where they were told, and thinking what they were told (for the most part). Emmett had sent them off to Iowa to live with their uncle Allen. Uncle Allen in turn had told them (with his dying breath) to find Brennachecke's group. And until two days ago, Brennachecke had managed their lives from morning to night—except for the moments where Jen was fucking his son and swearing like a sailor. But now they were on their own. As they prepared to head out up Highway 1 toward Allen's place, the magnitude of that change was slowly starting to sink in.

Little decisions like what to eat for breakfast were suddenly complicated. No longer was it a choice of potatoes or cornmeal like it had been with Brennachecke. It wasn't even a choice anymore. They didn't have any potatoes, nor did they have any cornmeal. All they had was what was left of the small pile of junk food they'd found stashed in a shoebox in some closeted overeater's crap. The girls loved the sweet goodies, but cookies, candies, and snack cakes just made them want to eat more cookies, candies, and snack cakes. So they'd ended up eating the entire stash before they had finished packing up for the long walk ahead of them. Had they had more experience being on their own, they'd probably have taken an extra hour and scavenged up at least enough food for the day. Had they had more experience, they might have decided on an alternate route to their uncle Allen's place—one that was less exposed and offered more cover, for example. Had they had more experience, they probably would have left the CD player and the Chinese CDs behind. Had they had more experience, Jen certainly would have tried to camouflage the fact that she was an extremely attractive teenage girl.

None of these things would have made a difference, of course—except maybe taking that alternate route—because what was waiting for them on Highway 1 didn't give a shit if they were hungry, or how they were dressed, or what kind of music they were listening to as they walked. And while the standard blood pirate torture protocol tended to have a sexual bent when it came to pushing folks into berserking out, being ugly (or trying to fake that you were) wasn't going to ameliorate the nature or severity of the violence. The only thing that would matter if they discovered Jennifer Kessler was a berserker was that she would bleed.

"I wish we could have a dog," Bobby-Leigh said as they put the dorms behind them.

Jen looked at her, stung but trying to hide it. There didn't seem to be any malice in her little sister's voice, but Jen still wanted to smack her in the face. Jimmy was enough to feel bad about at the moment, thank you very much. She didn't need fucking Bobo added on top like a goddamn cherry on her self-loathing ice cream sundae.

"I know we can't. But still . . . you know?"

Jen did know. When she looked past her guilt, she missed having a dog too. Unfortunately, she also knew that blindly loyal, misguidedly selfless four-legged companions didn't understand how to lie low when they were faced with a berserker, and didn't fare too well in the encounter.

"We had a dog," she reminded her sister.

"Yeah. But Bobo was fucking stupid. If we could get a smart dog and train it . . ."

"Bobo wasn't stupid," Jen said, suddenly realizing that her sister might not know what had actually happened to Bobo after they'd arrived at Uncle Allen's.

"He picked a fight with you when you were berserking out," Bobby-Leigh said.

Okay, Jen thought. *I guess you do know what happened to the damn dog.* She didn't know why, but it really bothered her that Bobby-Leigh thought the dog was stupid. That somehow it was the dog's fault for getting killed, not Jen's fault for tearing it to bloody pieces.

"That doesn't make him stupid," she said.

"Really?"

"Ah, I love the smell of an emo twelve-year-old's sarcasm in the morning," Jen said, badly impersonating a young Robert Duvall.

"What?"

Instantly the joy of being witty was crushed, as she was hit in the chest by the truth that Jimmy was not around anymore to appreciate her clever old-school movie references. He was not around, because just like Bobo the fucking pug, he'd been too stupid to take cover when she berserked out.

"Nothing. You're right. Bobo was fucking stupid. Just like Jimmy. They're all fucking fuckhead motherfucking idiots."

"I didn't mean it like that."

"Doesn't matter."

"Uh . . . I think it might matter a little bit," Bobby-Leigh said.

"Robert Duvall said he liked the smell of napalm in the morning."

"Who is Robert Duvall?"

"A dead actor."

"I am so confused right now."

"In the movie *Apocalypse Now.* He said— It's a famous line from the movie."

"Oh, is that the one with the zombies that—"

"No."

"Aliens from—"

"No."

"Is it the one where that virus—"

"No, it's the one— Never mind. Forget I said anything."

The girls walked for a while in silence up Highway 1. Just as they were passing the Fairfield city limit sign at the edge of the MUM campus, Bobby-Leigh couldn't help herself and blurted out, "It was one of Jimmy's favorites, then?"

"Yeah."

"I'm sorry, Jen."

"Why? I'm the one that fucking killed him."

"That's not your . . ." But Bobby-Leigh knew it didn't matter what she said, so she went back to the topic of conversation she'd started before. "I read this book about a dog named Chance—or Chase, or Choice, or something—and that dog was so smart he knew like over three thousand words. I bet you could train a dog that smart to do the right thing when you berserked out."

"I'm not going to berserk out anymore, Bobby-Leigh."

Bobby-Leigh knew her sister couldn't promise something like that, no matter how much she wanted to. But the wishful-thinking center of her brain reasoned that if she really didn't think she'd ever do it again, then maybe, *maybe*, they could get a dog after all. Jen turned and looked at her, reading her mind.

"That doesn't mean we're going to get a dog."

Bobby-Leigh sighed.

"We need to find Dad," the little girl said out of nowhere.

"Why?"

"I miss him."

"You hardly even knew him."

"I still miss him."

Jen was about to say something cruel to nip this conversation topic in the bud, but before she could, she was distracted by a glint of the sun in the distance and the sound of a convoy of cars coming toward them.

Cars were luxury items now, at least ones that worked. The networked, self-driving electric vehicle revolution had saved tens of thousands of lives and reduced air pollution all over the US before everything fell apart. These new vehicles had slowly replaced gas-powered ones, until more than half the cars and trucks on the road were both self-driving and electric powered. Companies like Uber then turned the whole auto industry on its head by combining their on-demand car service with the self-driving vehicles. It became so convenient, at least in the cities, to just push a button and have your autopiloted Uber show up at your doorstep two minutes later that city folk quickly stopped buying cars of their own altogether. A whole generation of kids grew up without knowing how to drive, much less wanting to own a car.

But then the power grids had failed. For a while the solar-fed charging stations carried some of the weight, but overuse and lack of maintenance eventually killed most of those too. There were still plenty of gas stations, and most of them still had gas, but the electronics of the pumps didn't work without power, so even if you had a car that you could drive, you still had to know how to hack the circuitry of the gas pump to make it go. So when Jen saw a half dozen vehicles racing straight for them, she quickly pulled her sister to a stop as alarm bells went off in her head.

But it was too late.

From the strip of woods on either side of the highway, men exploded from the brush like jackals flushing game and rushed toward them. The men didn't yell. They didn't call out to one another. They just sprinted toward them silently, coldly, rehearsed, like they'd done it a thousand times before. The steel cable net that exploded from some kind of custom-fitted gun took the girls completely by surprise as it tangled them up. They still hadn't recovered seconds later, when the men started dragging the girls toward the vehicles now in front of them.

Jen closed her eyes, brought her mantra to the forefront of her mind, and focused on it. Her breathing steadied. She felt the blood pumping through her with each beat of her heart. The cycle of thoughts rolling up and her mantra taking her back down washed through her like waves rolling through the deep ocean, far away from land. For the moment she was still in control of the berserker within.

Tangled in the net as they were, Bobby-Leigh wouldn't last five seconds if she lost it.

Mantra.

Bobby-Leigh had to be doing the same math in her head.

Mantra.

She could feel Bobby-Leigh moving around frantically, no doubt trying to get to her ax, but she knew the little girl's ax had been ripped out of her hands by the thick wire net.

Mantra.

It was tangled up and completely out of reach. Bobby-Leigh was not going to be able to sacrifice her older sister to save herself like Jen had made her promise she would hundreds of times each day in the weeks after the pug Bobo lost his life at her hands.

Mantra.

She wouldn't let something like that happen again to anyone. Not this time.

Mantra.

Not ever again. Jimmy would be the last. Her mantra came and went effortlessly.

"Breathe," she heard her sister whispering. "It will be okay. Just close your eyes and step away."

When Bobby-Leigh saw her sister's eyes open again, she knew that Jen was not just meditating anymore. In addition to her TM practice, Allen Kessler had trained Jen to mentally detach herself from her body and mind—to quite literally step outside of herself and become a simple observer, as if she were watching a movie of her life instead of being an actively emotional, feeling participant in it. It was for times exactly like this. After Bobo had died, and he'd witnessed Jen's big deadly secret for himself, Allen had spent a lot of time with her. Bobby-Leigh remembered very clearly that at the time, she'd been extremely jealous of all the extra attention her big sister was getting, but now that it might just save her life, she was only grateful. For now, it was working, but the worst was yet to come and she knew it.

More men jumped out of the vehicles. For a few more seconds everything continued to happen in eerie silence. Through the tangled wire, Bobby-Leigh managed to slip the earbuds into her sister's ears, attempting to dull her sense of the real world with Chinese pop music. The pirates formed a ring around the girls in the net. Several carried eight-foot-long razor-tipped pikes. They approached, grinning. It was a look Bobby-Leigh knew, and it made her shudder. She'd not seen anybody look at her in that way since Walmart, and in the superstore there had only been two of them. Now there were two dozen at least.

Her hands slipped to where the karambit blade was hidden. She didn't draw the weapon yet—it was too soon for that—but she was relieved that even while tangled in the metal mesh she could still get to it. She'd be ready when the time did come.

Bobby-Leigh met the cruel eyes of one of the men with the long spear-like weapons and took a deep breath, but before the fun could set off, everybody's attention was drawn to the sky as a small plane flew by overhead and started circling. The small motor roared over the excited hooting and hollering that burst out of their capturers, breaking the deadly cold silence and precision they'd operated with up to that point.

* * *

Brennachecke had never actually seen how Beverly's blood pirate army took their victims down on Highway 1, and while it wasn't exactly irony (except maybe to Alanis Morissette) that the first time he would witness it, their prey would turn out to be people he knew—one of whom he himself intended to kill—it was something. *Fate? Poetic justice? Fortune?* He didn't know what the right word was. He didn't really care either. Had he been a different man, he'd have just settled on *fucked up* as his descriptor of choice, but he wasn't ever going to sway into language like that. Besides, the bigger question, and the only one that he did care about, was how he was going to manage the situation now.

The cards were on the table. The players were all in. One by one the cards would turn. No more bluffing. The strongest hand would take it all. Everybody else would be dead.

It had been decades since Brennachecke had played a high-stakes game of Texas Hold'em, but still, that was where his mind immediately went. As long as Beverly was back at the Raj, and the MIC was with him in the air, and nobody on the ground did anything stupid, he still might get what he wanted without a fight. But even as the thought came to him, he knew how unlikely that was. The MIC had pulled a full house on the river, and his king-high straight wasn't worth the price of admission anymore.

But that wasn't actually the truth, he realized. Finding the girls like this was just a reshuffling of the cards. They were now back to the game he'd thought they were going to be playing from the beginning. Still, as he circled the plane around for another pass and tried to hold on to the sense of hope he'd had when he and Dan had set off for the airport a day ago, he felt his confidence flicker. Maybe he should smash the plane into the heart of the abduction scene they were witnessing from the air and just kill everybody and be done with it. But as tempting as it was in that moment, that was not actually something the old soldier had it in him to do.

"Those the two little twats you looking for," the MIC yelled into the radio headset. It wasn't a question, but it wasn't a statement either.

"Yes" was all Brennachecke responded with. *Twat* was a particularly ugly word to his ears. It left his self-righteousness ringing and moved the needle in the smash-the-plane-into-the-ground direction (if only in Brennachecke's head).

Flying a plane was exponentially easier once it was in the air and before you tried to put it back on the ground, so that had been where the old soldier had decided to begin his small-plane aviation *crash* course with the blood pirates' Man-in-Charge.

They'd been airborne for almost an hour and a half already. The MIC was picking things up quickly, though how much the man retained of the instructions for emergency procedures Brennachecke had rattled off throughout their time in the air, he couldn't begin to guess at. Not that he really cared. This was going to be a quick and dirty kind of deal. It was all he had time for. Now that the girls were in the pirates' clutches, even this speedy version of flight training might take too long.

He had intended to show the MIC how to take off, keep the plane in the air in good weather and without any mechanical issues, and put the plane back on the ground using a stabilized approach and without killing himself. He'd get him to the point where he could do it on his own once, maybe twice, walk him through how to maintain the aircraft, and then get the heck out of there before his luck ran out. He'd intended to just mention that things were much harder in the wind and verbally walk him through how to adjust his landing, manage the flare, and execute the rollout to deal with it, but that was back when he was just trying to get out of Vedic City alive. Now that the girls were actually in the picture, he'd need to revert back to the original plan, which meant actually teaching the man how to land.

"Our deal only stands if they remain unharmed," he said to the MIC over the headset. "If your men down there hurt them, or if I find out they've been mistreated back in Vedic City, I'll make sure neither you nor any of your people ever get off the ground."

"Oh, you will, now? Well, that's unfortunate, since I can't exactly stop anything from happening from up here," the MIC mockingly shouted through his headset, knowing how empty Brennachecke's threat really was;

the old man was going to teach him how to fly one way or another. If these little bitches made it easier to get it done, then so be it, but regardless of what happened to them, the MIC would see to it that his little army took to the sky.

Brennachecke could see everybody on the ground below looking up at him, momentarily distracted by the shiny plane in the sky. But they were not going to stay distracted by the plane for long and the MIC was right—if Brennachecke wanted the man to control his men, he needed to get him on the ground so he could give the order. Brennachecke circled around the cheering and shouting blood pirates as close as he could without crashing, making sure they could see that the MIC was with him. More than just with him, the Man-in-Charge was actually in the pilot's seat. Brennachecke hoped it would look like their leader was already an ace in the sky and not just sitting there in the seat observing the trick moves the actual pilot, he himself, was now making. He circled wide one more time, calculated his approach, and prepared to put the plane on the ground as close to the action as he could without getting tangled up in the power lines over the road. If he'd been able to only show the MIC the stabilized approach method of landing, he was confident the man would never have known that it could be done any other way. But that was no longer a viable option.

"There are three stages to landing a plane," Brennachecke said as he set his airspeed and stabilized his pitch and roll with tiny adjustments to the throttle, ailerons, elevator, and rudder. "Landing starts with an approach. Key factor here is airspeed. Try to always fly into the wind if there is any. You try to land with the wind hitting you from the side and the odds of maintaining a good approach without a lot of experience are pretty bad. And that means you'll probably bend some metal and die. As we do this, remember that the headwind changes your ground speed. We're going seventy knots here, and we've got a ten-knot headwind, so our ground speed is sixty knots.

"See how I'm smoothly leveling off using elevator control and reducing my power toward idle? This is called the *flare*. I'm attempting to fly as close as possible above the road as I can without actually touching it while my airspeed drops to a stall. Your airspeed is crucial here, but notice how I'm not actually looking at the indicator during the flare. That's because at this point you've got to be watching what's happening around you. Keep the plane just a couple of inches above the ground until you run out of lift."

As if on command, the plane's wheels softly touched the pavement of the highway. The MIC laughed like a little boy. To the old soldier, it was obvious that the man was genuinely impressed by Brennachecke's skill as a pilot and happy to be learning how to fly himself (and most likely relieved to have returned to ground safely as well). He hoped that those feelings would keep this exchange going smoothly to the end, but as the plane rolled down the highway, he knew better than to depend on it.

"Just because your tires touched the ground, that doesn't mean you've landed yet. You've still got to do the final part. We call this the rollout. You let your guard down here and you'll still crash. Your flight controls are less effective on the ground, and that makes maintaining control throughout the rollout harder than you think it will be. You're going to need to increase the upwind aileron deflection here. Your instincts will tell you to reduce it, but I promise you, neutralizing your flight controls on touchdown is a surefire way to bend some metal."

As the plane finished its rollout, Brennachecke added, "If your airspeed is too high in the flare and you think you don't have enough runway, pull back up, circle around, and try again. You start pushing forward on the yoke, or releasing the back pressure, in an attempt to force the plane onto the ground before running out of runway and you're going to get a nosewheel-first touchdown that'll bounce you and jump from wheelbarrowing into severe porpoising in less time than it takes your heart to beat. You'll lose directional control, collapse your nosegear, and smear your plane across the runway. You never force it. Just take her back up and try again. Got it?"

"Aye, Captain!" the MIC shouted through the headset, sounding for the first time like the pirate he actually was, as the plane finally came to a stop.

* * *

If they hadn't been so distracted by the plane, the blood pirates would have been readying themselves for what they called the *bloodeo*. Because the effects of berserker blood were so much more potent if the blood was drawn in the middle of a breakout, and because there was no way to know when berserkers were going to reveal themselves, blood pirates had to be prepared to harvest the sweet red monster nectar at any time during their capture process. To that end, IV lines would be attached to the heads of their pikes and run to storage banks. This tubing would carry the berserker blood from the host to bags that were kept in temperature-controlled coolers. The pikers, as they liked to be called, would then stand by while the other members of the ambush crew pulled the long cable out of the back of one of the fortified vans and clipped it to the rings at each corner of the steel net that held their captives. But none of this happened, because Jen never berserked out, and the plane rolled right up to them, thoroughly sidetracking the entire capture protocol.

Bobby-Leigh coldly watched the blood pirates react to the plane, trying to decide if she was better off staying and risking her sister berserking out, or looking for an opportunity to strike and run away. It was a question of chaos or control. She didn't know what she was dealing with. They were significantly outnumbered and outgunned. With those kinds of unknowns the argument for control was pretty weak. If she waited to act, she might not get a chance to act at all.

Never in her life did she think she'd wish she was back in that stinking dark room in Walmart facing those two diseased pedophiles, but she'd much rather be there than where she was now. At least in Walmart she'd known what to do. Uncle Allen's training had been perfectly tailored for that situation. But this current situation had not been in the don't-get-raped handbook at all. *What the fuck are these assholes doing with those weird-ass spears?* she thought. *And where the hell did they get a goddamn airplane?* Control seemed like a joke. But embracing chaos was suicide.

Lost in the turmoil of her thoughts, Bobby-Leigh hadn't noticed that Brennachecke was in the plane at all. She didn't see him step out with the fat, redheaded stranger. She didn't hear the Mr. Bad Comb-Over tell his men, who would not stop cheering, to shut up and stand down. It wasn't until she heard her old surrogate father's voice that her mind was able to wrench away from the paralyzing indecision that was consuming her.

"I don't suppose you'd just let me take them now?" Brennachecke said.

To Bobby-Leigh, his words were like a hard slap in the face, followed by a bucket of ice water over her head. The blood drained from her face as all the questions in her head fell away and were replaced by just one: *How is Brennachecke here?*

The voice of the man who wanted to kill her cut savagely through Jen's meditation, through her out-of-body exercise and into the cushion of Chinese hip-hop. Her eyes focused and cleared in an instant. She popped the earbuds out so she could hear clearly, all the while doing what she could to control her breathing, her heart rate, and the amount of adrenaline pumping through her veins. She didn't bother trying to make sense of things. Doing so would require too much of her attention. It was taking all she had to keep the berserker inside her from erupting out. She took a deep breath, once again went inside her head, and took a step back outside of her own body so she could watch everything as if it was happening to somebody else.

For all the time she'd been working on perfecting her uncle's practice of detachment, this was the first real test of its worth. The incident with Jimmy had simply gone down too fast for her to try it. *So far, so good,* she thought vaguely, as she watched herself smile at her would-be murderer through the metal webbing.

I could shoot her in the head right here and now, Brennachecke thought, as he looked at the knowing smile
slowly spreading across Jennifer's lips. Taking a gun from
one of the idiots standing around would be easy enough,
but the aftermath was hard to predict. Everybody was
amped up. Trigger-happy. He could right the scales of
justice for his son's life easy enough, but he'd end up in
a vicious little firefight as soon as it was done, for sure.
He knew he'd be able to shoot his way out, but Bobby-
Leigh almost assuredly wouldn't make it out with him. He
wouldn't have time to free her and still have a reasonable
chance of surviving the escape. And if he left her, even
if she survived the crossfire of the gunfight, which was
unlikely, the pirates would take her. Leaving a little girl
to be raped and mutilated—especially a little girl who
had been like a daughter to him only a couple of days
ago—didn't exactly right the cosmic scales.

"What would you do if I just stomped their little cunt
brains out right here in front of you?" the MIC asked
him casually with a goading smile.

Brennachecke didn't answer, but he didn't have to.
The MIC didn't expect him to. The cruel Man-in-Charge
just wanted a chance to watch Brennachecke. Study him.
Get a look into his machinery.

"Maybe we just fuck 'em to death right here, eh?
Maybe we see how many dicks the little cunt can swallow
until she chokes to death? Maybe we shove your cock
in there too, huh? Bet you'd like that, wouldn't you?
Bet that's why you want them so bad, ain't it? They run
away from your little surprise fuck party?"

One look at Brennachecke made it clear that he was
not in the least sexually interested in the girls, which only
seemed to make the MIC happier.

"No? Well . . ." He took a moment to find the words that would cut through the man's stoic facade the most effectively. "Then maybe we chop your dick off first and you can just watch the little one choke on it while you bleed out."

The man was just trying to get a reaction. Brennachecke knew it. As long as the MIC wanted to fly, he was confident the man would keep his side of the trade healthy enough to make the deal worth his time. But enough was enough.

"Maybe if you don't watch your mouth, we'll all just die right here and now," Brennachecke said, turning to stare down the MIC with his cold blue eyes, drilling in the very real possibility that if the man didn't heed his warning, he'd find a way to make it happen.

The MIC laughed at him.

"You want to learn to fly or not?"

Still laughing, the MIC looked at his abduction squad and rolled his eyes mockingly, effectively showing that he was still the authority here. His men laughed the way subordinates do when their bosses make a joke, even if the joke isn't funny. "These two little bitches are going to let us fly, boys. Like fucking angels. Blood angels, motherfuckers. You like the sound of that, don't you? Yeah, you do! Take 'em back, put 'em somewhere safe until you hear from me, yeah? And 'cause Daddy Daedalus here is a fucking party-pooper, you keep your hands off 'em or you'll answer to me, you fucking degenerates. He wants them whole and unsoiled."

Brennachecke didn't point out that suggesting he was Icarus's father didn't bode well for the MIC's ultimate success as a pilot, but he *did* wonder who the idiot was trying to impress with his obviously faulty knowledge of

Greek mythology. Then he remembered Beverly's reference to her sirens out in front of the Raj and smiled in spite of himself. When a man continues to behave in a way that he thinks might impress a woman he's sexually interested in, even when she is not there to witness the behavior, then it's pretty safe to say the woman has the power in the relationship. If he had had any doubt before about whether or not Beverly was really in charge of the whole show, it was gone now. Though he'd never used the term himself, Brennachecke knew that the MIC was as pussy whipped as a rich but ugly freshman at senior prom. He also knew that Beverly didn't care one way or another if the Vedic City pirates learned to fly or not, and that might end up being a problem.

The abduction crew quickly clipped the cables extending from the van to the net and flipped the switch on the power winch inside. Before either of the girls or Brennachecke could respond, the cables whipped taut and yanked Jen and Bobby-Leigh across the pavement and into the van. Once the net and everything in it was hauled up and the van doors had swung shut, the old soldier and the Man-in-Charge turned and silently walked back to the plane. The abduction squad loaded up and returned up Highway 1 to Vedic City.

"I'm going to need to see with my own eyes that they are okay when we get back."

"Yeah, sure. Whatever," the MIC said. "Walk me through taking off again."

Brennachecke sighed deeply. This was his bargain. He'd set the terms. He'd done the math. He'd thought it through backwards and forwards. And yet, if Beverly was the one who really had the power here, he'd done this all wrong. Suddenly, he couldn't shake the feeling that things were inevitably slipping slowly toward the edge of a great abyss, and at the bottom of that deep, dark hole there would be no justice to be had, for the only thing waiting for him would be the fury of hell.

* * *

Dan had watched unseen at the airport while Brenna-checke and the MIC went over the plane. His bow had been ready, but the old sergeant hadn't needed it. The small posse of men the MIC had brought with him had all been too excited about the possibility of flight to adequately examine the area. He could have probably stood straight up on the roof and waved at them and still have gone unnoticed, but of course he didn't do that.

He had hidden. He had waited. Brennachecke knew he was there, and occasionally they'd shared a secret glance or two in which Dan assumed the man was telling him all was going according to plan. But then when he'd watched the plane land on the highway a couple of hours later, he'd suddenly not been so sure.

Why the hell would Brennachecke land on Highway 1?

But he had known the answer even before the question had completely formed in his mind. The one question that he couldn't fathom the answer to, however, was how this affected their plan.

He'd watched the abduction crew return to Vedic City and then had just waited until the plane returned, circled several times, and landed with a couple of hard bounces on the runway half an hour later. By the time Brennachecke stepped out of the cockpit, Dan was almost shaking with adrenaline. He desperately wanted to know what the fuck was going on, but there was no way for him to ask. All he could do was watch and be ready for anything.

When folks want something to happen, it is amazing how slowly time seems to progress for them. Dan saw Brennachecke and the MIC exit the plane and talk to the excitedly waiting men. He watched as they went over the post-flight maintenance. He watched as they went over how to refuel. He watched as the MIC whipped his dick out and took a steaming piss all over the runway. He watched and waited desperately for Brennachecke to look up at him or give him a signal of some kind. But it didn't happen.

Brennachecke took out a small pad of paper and wrote some things down on it, then showed it to the MIC and his men, all of whom nodded. He wrote something else, but seemed to not like the way he'd written it and crumpled up the piece of paper. Then, as Dan watched, he suddenly looked directly up at him as he tossed the ball of paper to the ground and started again. It was all Dan could do to keep himself from jumping up and running down to snatch up the supposedly discarded trash in front of everybody. But he had to wait. For almost another hour he toiled in mental agony as Brennachecke reviewed flight procedures with the MIC and his men.

As they talked, the wind, which had been nothing more than a cold whisper on his exposed skin for most of the day, started to kick up a notch. He watched as it drove the wadded ball of paper slowly down the runway and toward the rows and rows of dead abandoned corn. He knew he should be monitoring Brennachecke with the hostiles, but he couldn't focus on anything but the message he knew was scribbled on that piece of paper. If Brennachecke had signaled him before he left with the MIC and his men back to Vedic City, Dan missed it; he was too obsessed with the note that had now been blown into the thick of the corn. But the old man was still alive when he left, and Dan had overheard plans for an early start tomorrow, so he didn't really care.

Once they were gone and he was alone again, he scurried off into the corn and grabbed the note. Anger flashed through him as he read it, though he couldn't for the life of him understand why. He was expecting more, he supposed. But that was stupid. The man had only had a second to write it. So the fact that it just told him to get food and stay warm shouldn't have really come as a surprise. He just felt so in the dark that it was hard not to take the minimalist instructions personally. Nothing could stop him from resenting the fact that there was so obviously something of significance going on and that he didn't know what that *something* was.

The plan hadn't changed. That was the gist of the message. But the feeling that Brennachecke had new information and that, even though he'd found a way to securely communicate, he was still withholding that information from Dan spun irrationally around in his head.

What are you hiding, Brennachecke? he wondered over and over. *And why?*

Fuck this, Dan suddenly decided. He'd do some reconnaissance tonight and get his own answers

Chapter Seven

The African in the Corn Belt

THE KESSLER FARM was gone. Sure, the buildings were still there, as was the land, but the artesian organic core wrapped up in the nice Maharishi-approved Vedic shell that had made it what it was had been replaced the way a surgeon might pop a pig heart into a little boy to keep him alive if better alternatives didn't present themselves (and these days, better alternatives never presented themselves). The pig heart the farm got transplanted with was strong, and once in, it beat and beat and beat away, transforming the place into a freak of nature that could survive. So while everybody, including the small clan that had taken it over, still referred to it as "the Kessler farm," it certainly no longer warranted that particular namesake.

Neither Anoona nor any of her people were practitioners of Transcendental Meditation or part of the TM movement. None of them were even from Fairfield. They had found Kessler's farm on the Internet—or what remained of it in the chaos after things started shutting down—and had sought it out as a sanctuary against the rising uncertainty in Grinnell, where the group had all attended the university.

"Who are you guys?" Eric asked, his mouth agape as he took in an overwhelming amount of technology he'd not seen since he was a child, and some he'd never seen before at all. His people had been led into the house by Anoona and her two guardsmen, Rodney and Hamm, but everybody was too shocked by what they saw once inside to make it much further than the foyer. Every one of Brennachecke's people was wondering the exact same thing as Eric, but none of them could find the words.

"Seriously, who are you guys?" Eric repeated, but this time his question wasn't directed at them as much as it was to himself. Anoona's crew appeared to consist of only seven people. There was Anoona, Rodney, and Hamm. Then inside there was the fattest man Eric had ever seen—who he would later find out was ironically called "Tiny" by everybody. There was a little girl, who was maybe twelve years old and obviously Anoona's daughter—or at least Eric thought it was obvious, since she was the only other black person in the crew. As they all slowly filed into the house, a young lesbian couple named Sarah and Rachel came out of the kitchen to greet them and to round out the number to seven. Though Eric had never seen lesbians before, it wasn't the people that were blowing his mind at the moment; he didn't even register that the two women were rather intimately holding hands and wrapped in each other's arms as they joined them. His brain was too busy trying to process what he was actually looking at in the space all around them.

The living room had been converted into a state-of-the-art command center, where Tiny—overflowing out of his chair—was running what looked like several computer systems at once. There were twelve huge monitors mounted on the wall, and at Tiny's fingertips there were two complete keyboards and a variety of versatile touchscreen controls. Tiny himself wore a pair of augmented-reality glasses and haptic gloves, but Eric didn't recognize either of those things for what they were yet.

One of the monitors was divided into sixteen video grids, and it was those that had caught his eye almost immediately. Each one was a live video feed of some kind. He saw the dead cornfield they'd walked through. He saw Highway 1. He saw several angles of the exterior of the Kessler farm and its buildings.

His gaze jumped from feed to feed until he suddenly saw something so beyond his experience of the world that his whole face twisted up in a knot of confusion. He was looking at a video feed from what looked like some kind of warehouse filled with racks and racks of something green and plantlike. Surrounding the racks, buzzing around like giant insects, were four tethered robotic drones. All of this was under rows and rows of what looked like oddly colored florescent lights. The racks were automated to rotate whatever the plants were, tray by tray, into the light. Hoses fed misting sprinklers below the trays, feeding the plants—he thought they had to be plants—water and nutrients. It was an automated factory farm of some kind, he supposed, but it was so far from anything he'd known existed that he couldn't be sure.

His eyes moved to the next video feed over. He saw what looked like another warehouse, only this one was full of chickens—shelves of them. In fact, the shelves looked just like the ones holding the plants in the other feed, just without the water hoses. More of the automated tethered drones tended the flock.

In the remaining video feeds he saw empty rooms in the house, and then in the last frame of the grid he saw himself and all his people staring dumbstruck at it all. There was a little square graphic around each of their faces with their names and other key information next to it. One of the screens had a detailed 3D-rendered map of Fairfield and the surrounding Jefferson County. There seemed to be some cross-referencing between the information generated next to the squares around their heads and the map, but exactly what information was being passed was impossible to tell. Anoona's crew was being captured by the video system as well, but instead of squares, her people's faces were surrounded by circles.

Anoona followed Eric's gaze and smiled.

"Facial rec. We've got most of the people in the area in our system."

"I don't . . ." Eric began, but then just closed his mouth and shook his head.

"Where are the cameras?" Ace asked.

"Exteriors are JIYs handing off at twenty-minute intervals in algorithmic sweeps," Tiny said. "Interiors are mounted." He pointed up and Eric and Ace saw a black lens mounted high in the corner of the room. The camera was so small, if Tiny hadn't pointed it out to them they'd probably never have noticed it.

"Jesus, man, how do you have the power to do all this?"

Tiny laughed good-naturedly. "We've got almost fifty megawatt hours incoming, if the weather's friendly."

It was Hamm that spoke next, saying, "Kessler had a bunch of solar panels already. And we brought a bunch more with us. Since we got here, we've also been scavenging from local sources like Eco Village and MUM. We're up to over three hundred cells at this point."

No sooner had Hamm spoken than Tiny touched something and Eric suddenly saw them for himself on one of the monitors. Where Allen had once sown his organic heirloom seeds now stood panel after panel of solar cells. The Kessler farm had quite literally been converted to a solar farm.

"But the real kicker is the shit ton of storage we got in the basement," Rachel added with a smile.

"Yeah, we managed to appropriate a shipment of Tesla Powerpacks on our way here," her girlfriend, Sarah, explained with a distinct note of pride in her voice, but Eric, Ace, and the rest of the new arrivals had no idea what she was talking about.

It was all too much. They may as well have all been cavemen visiting the space station. Eric, for his part, had still been a child when Fairfield had gone dark for good. The only electrical power he'd experienced in a long time was produced by a Honda gas generator, the use of which his father had rationed so severely that it was almost as if they hadn't had it at all. His head was spinning and he was sure he wasn't the only one with his mind blown.

Who are these people? he thought to himself, and then his wonder shifted to more important questions: Why had they revealed themselves? And what did they want with him and the rest of his people?

They didn't seem to mean them any harm, but these were not times when such instincts could be given the benefit of the doubt. *No,* he thought coldly. These were the times when anything that seemed too good to be true, as a rule was exactly that: too good to be true. There was undoubtedly a catch here. He didn't know what it was yet, but he was sure it was coming. He just hoped that when it did finally jump out from the shadows at them, they would all live to tell about it.

Anoona smiled at him and chuckled. Her teeth were blindingly white against the darkness of her skin. She was beautiful, he realized suddenly, as the novelty of her blackness wore off a little. He found himself blushing in embarrassment for no reason he could understand. His throat felt tight. His lungs didn't seem to be able to get enough air into them to keep the oxygen flowing sufficiently to his brain. He felt his skin prickling.

"It's a lot to take in, I imagine," she said.

Eric was so distracted by the tech, by how black she was, and by how strikingly beautiful he found her, that he had a hard time hearing her words through the naive, if not slightly racist, fog that was enveloping his brain. He couldn't respond, so he just nodded. Nobody else said anything either, so he guessed he wasn't alone in his stupor.

"There's a bunch of couches downstairs. Why don't you all head down and make yourselves comfortable. Sarah makes some pretty solid hooch. Hamm and I will bring down a bottle and some glasses and we'll try to answer whatever questions you guys have."

* * *

There were indeed a number of couches downstairs, seven of them to be exact, all arranged in a big circle that took up most of the space of the main lower-level room. It was enough sitting room for the twelve of Eric's group as well as Anoona and Hamm to be comfortable. Anoona's little girl had come down with her mom and now sat on her lap.

Nobody spoke.

Nobody drank the hooch that Hamm had brought down and passed around.

It was an awkward moment that stretched and stretched, until at last Roger put his glass to his lips and tasted the alcohol. Ace reached out to stop him, but it was too late.

"We're not trying to poison you," Hamm said with a sympathetic smile.

Ace blushed, but didn't say anything in response. His eyes were glued to Roger to see if in fact Hamm was telling the truth or not. Roger, for his part, just rolled his eyes at Ace and smiled as the liquid spirit passed his lips and pleasantly burned its way down his throat, warming his belly.

"Wow," he said. "That is some silky-smooth oaky goodness right there." Roger looked at Ace and smiled as if to demonstrate beyond any doubt that he was not poisoned, but the smile just wasn't enough.

Sarah, who had been watching the awkwardness from the stairway (in easy reach of her AR-15 assault rifle that was waiting just out of sight in case things took an unfortunate and unnecessary turn toward violence), revealed herself and spoke up.

"Yeah, Anoona just calls it hooch to break my balls. You've all got full-on, properly distilled and aged straight bourbon in your glasses there."

She was obviously proud of her work. Somehow that obvious pride calmed Ace's nerves and fears about poison enough for him to try it himself. Unprepared for the burn, he coughed as the spirit went down his throat.

"Nice," he managed to croak. Everybody laughed and, magically, just like that the tension broke. Eric tried it, then Maddie Love, the librarian.

"It's my granddaddy's recipe," Sarah continued as everybody else finally tipped their glasses and had a taste. "Just cracked the first barrel a month ago."

"So," Anoona said. "Where shall we start?"

"Who are you guys?" Eric asked for what felt like the thousandth time.

"The six of us all met at Grinnell in an Agricultural Technology class. Rodney had just finished an internship at FarmedHere, and Rachel and Sarah were on their way to work at SpaceX when they graduated. Tiny, the big guy running the computers, was just interested in the subject, I guess. I was here studying abroad from Zimbabwe and Hamm, was . . ." She paused and smiled a private smile. "He was just the guy I was seeing at the time.

"But as the shit hit the fan and it became more and more clear that the world was about to make a sharp left turn into an even deeper pile of shit, we decided we'd preemptively make a doomsday plan. The rolling blackouts had started already at that point, so we knew we couldn't count on the grid or the traditional infrastructure for power or water. Also, the level of violence was quickly getting out of hand, and I'm not just talking about the berserkers. The cops—even in the little town of Grinnell—had started to not show up for work. People knew they could get away with things, but they were also scared, which is never a good combination. The government hadn't declared martial law yet, but we knew it was coming and as small as Grinnell is, we still knew it would eventually get out of control, especially if the power one day didn't come back on, which of course is exactly what happened. When it did, just like here in Fairfield, most of the people who left did so to find someplace where the lights were still on. But not us.

"We had been researching where the best spot to wait out the shit might be when we found the website for the Kessler farm. Turns out Fairfield and Jefferson County have a surprisingly high amount of solar adoption for such a small rural community. And so, while everybody else fled to the cities hoping to find power grids that still worked, we appropriated the gear we needed and headed here in two big old semitrucks.

"By then, of course, the Internet was for all intents and purposes down, but Tiny built us a local network here and he has been steadily increasing the connectivity as best he can. We've been able to monitor—though just to a limited amount—what's left of the net in Cedar Rapids and a few other places. But as you can guess, security is always a concern, so we're just doing it passively for now. We've taken a census of Fairfield and most of Jefferson County, which you saw earlier up on the monitors. Nobody here in the area has anything close to what we do as far as tech and power goes—at least as far as we know. If they do, they're even better at hiding it than we are, which is a scary thought, but we're pretty confident our position here is a uniquely strong one.

"Hamm is a mad scientist of a mechanical engineer and built the drones you saw tending to the crops and chickens. He was also the one who modified the JIYs for Tiny to keep watch over us."

It was a lot of information, but it didn't really satisfy Eric's curiosity. He realized suddenly that nothing Anoona said probably would.

"So . . . you're from Zimbabwe?" he said, as if that was the most important piece of information in the history she'd just recounted. Anoona smiled at him and nodded.

"JIY?" Cooperman asked.

"It's a drone," Hamm said. "Nobody knows what the hell it stands for. Something in Chinese, I think."

"What's SpaceX?" Ace asked. He expected Hamm or Anoona to answer, but it was Mad Love who chimed in.

"Before he was killed, there was a man named Elon Musk who was this outrageous Tony Stark–like industrialist. He started Paypal, which you've probably never heard of, Solar City, and the Tesla car company—do you know Tesla?"

Ace nodded, but Eric didn't.

"Doesn't matter, the point is he had all these companies working on making mankind's existence more sustainable, and one of those businesses of his was this private space flight company which was on this mission to colonize Mars, and that was SpaceX."

"Mars, like the planet?" Eric asked.

"Exactly."

"You think things suck down here, just think about the twenty-odd astronauts who got stranded on Mars when the lights went out," Sarah said.

"I'm sure they're all dead by now, so maybe they're actually the lucky ones," Matt Knowles said.

Matt was not somebody Eric knew very much about, even though he'd been with his father's group for years. He was in his early forties, or at least that was how old he looked to Eric, and he was a quiet man who preferred to read books (the physical paper kind) over talking with others.

"Well, aren't you just a dark motherfucker," Sarah said from her perch on the stairs, then added with a wink, "Just my kind of man."

"Mom said that you didn't like men," Anoona's daughter said out of the blue.

"Exactly, sweetheart," Sarah chimed back without missing a beat.

"But if you don't like men, then how can this guy be your kind of man?"

"She's just making a joke, honey," Hamm said.

Anoona's daughter sighed loudly and looked around the room to see if anybody else was as confused by this exchange as she was.

"But . . . why is that funny?" she said a little too loudly, obviously frustrated.

"Hush now," Anoona told her daughter. "I promise I'll explain it to you later. Right now we're trying to catch up our guests."

"So do you know what causes the berserkers, then?" JP asked.

"Well, there are two camps on that," Hamm said. "Those with a religious predilection tend to gravitate toward explanations that involve some kind of demonic possession. Those with a more rational, scientific background tend to like the idea of a viral infection of some kind.

"What the truth is at this point is anybody's guess. Most of us here never have been the kind of people to put much stock in the Bible, or religion in general, so we tend to lean more toward the virus side of the debate. But from what we've read and heard, the odds that it is actually a virus are pretty slim. There's no berserker antibodies being made. No immune response to it. It's a mystery on a scientific level. We don't even know what it is about berserker blood that makes it do the amazing things that it does. If you pull the HGF out and give it to somebody straight, it seems to just get absorbed by the body without any of the magic. Maybe it'll give the person a little bit of a steroid-like bump, but nothing like what happens if you give them the blood as is. So we can definitely confirm for you that there is something unique and powerful in berserker blood, but I'm sure you already know that. At this point there is frankly just as much evidence for the demonic possession argument as ours."

"That's not true," Anoona chimed in.

"Isn't it, though?"

"There *is* some science in what we know about berserkers. It's not all mysterious huffelpuff."

Hamm smiled awkwardly at Eric and the rest of them. He hadn't intended to start a debate and now just wanted to shut it down, but he never knew what was going to stick in Anoona's pudding. She was ridiculously smart and seemed to take it personally when somebody said something that was less than accurate, but then at the same time she was often mortified by what she called Hamm's "lack of tact." He'd never been successful at just placating her with unearned indulgences. Most days this feistiness was something he loved about her, but sometimes it was annoying as hell. This was one of the annoying times. He didn't like looking stupid and being corrected like that when he was just being dismissive to be funny. Why did she not get that?

He tried to clarify his earlier statement. "The fact is, they've never been able to predict who is likely to go berserk—at least not in any kind of scientifically accurate way. You can test for HGF in the blood, but with the number of normal people using berserker blood like a drug, you are going to get *a lot* of false positives."

He looked to Anoona for permission to continue, assuming this statement was accurate enough for her. She nodded. It was.

"The bottom line is that even though there's hundreds of groups out there claiming to know who the berserkers are and who they aren't, no real evidence so far has shown up to support any of the claims. Mostly there's just a bunch of rhetoric being used to isolate and murder the people who the guys in power don't like for one reason or another."

"Well, that's disappointing," Cooperman said.

"Yeah. Sorry."

"Are any of you berserkers?" Ace asked.

"Not that we know of," Anoona said. "How about you and yours?"

"Well, it turns out Jennifer Kessler is, or was . . ." Eric said. "She had a, um, episode and, um, killed my brother a couple of days ago."

"So that's why your dad is—"

"Yep," Eric said, cutting her off.

Anoona took the hint and dropped it. Brennachecke's reputation for an-eye-for-an-eye justice had reached her and her people even though they'd been doing their best to stay invisible.

Hamm changed the subject by asking if anybody in Eric's group knew anything about the nukes. They'd heard rumors, of course, but never anything concrete. Hamm took a deep breath and then filled them in.

"We don't know what the story was outside of the US, but New York was the first place hit here in the States. The berserker incidents had long been out of hand. The nukes came after months and months of people being too afraid to leave their homes to do things like go to work, or to do just about anything in public, frankly. The economy was crumbling all over. Officially the US was under martial law by that point, but it didn't matter because it seemed like everybody had a gun and was shooting first and asking questions later. The maintenance of the infrastructure that had been supporting modern life more or less eventually got so neglected that it just fell apart. Power grids, water treatment, communication satellites, law enforcement, public health—it all just crumbled.

"The military forces in a couple of the large cities, the ones who were enforcing martial law in the name of the government, stopped taking orders from the politicians in Washington. Then, in DC, a popular general by the name of Walter Thomas, who might have even been retired at the time, simply declared himself the leader of the United States and marched on Congress with like twenty thousand troops and just killed anybody that stood in his way. The president was in New York at the time of the coup, so General Thomas launched a nuclear strike on the Big Apple to take him out.

"Then all hell broke loose. The collective armed forces of the United States fractured into a bunch of dictator-led groups, all of whom claimed to represent the *true* United States government, and, following that bastard Thomas's lead, started throwing nukes at each other. We know for sure Chicago was hit and we're pretty sure Los Angeles was too. But by then real information was pretty hard to come by and what you could get your hands on couldn't be verified anyway, so exactly what the state of the union is at the moment is anybody's guess."

"Jesus Christ," Ace said.

"Oh yeah. And then somebody discovered the whole berserker blood thing, and blood pirates started popping up everywhere. And that's pretty much where we're at now," Anoona said.

"What do you guys know about the berserker blood thing?" Mad Love asked quietly. "I know about Dr. McCay's experiments in the fifties and the resurgence of his research a few decades ago at Stanford—or maybe it was Harvard—where they showed that giving old mice blood transfusions from young mice had these incredible rejuvenation effects. I've always thought there must be a connection between that and the effects berserker blood has on non-berserkers?"

"I'm sure you're right," Hamm said. "But I'm afraid none of us here can really tell you much more about how it works. Nobody here has tried—what do they call it? *Blood swapping?* Well, at least as far as I know."

Eric's eyes met Anoona's and he finally asked the question that had been bothering him since they'd started talking. "Why did you take us in? What do you want from us?"

"Nothing," Anoona said.

"Well, that's not exactly true," Hamm said.

Here it comes, Eric thought and braced himself.

"We have the capacity to support up to maybe forty adults here at the moment. As I'm sure you've noticed, the weather is changing. Tiny has talked with some guys in Cedar Rapids who think we're about to have a very long period of extreme cold. Not another ice age or anything, but they think it's going to get pretty bad and stay that way. I mean, just look outside right now. It's snowing and it's July.

"We need more people to keep up with the maintenance and defense of this place, especially if the weather cuts into the yields of the solar fields and we get to the point we can't support the work drones anymore.

"We're actually planning on quietly recruiting some key people we've been tracking for a while. A couple of doctors, a vet, and a bunch of farmers and mercenaries. There is also a mechanic who has a little group of pretty skilled tinkerers holed up in a camp behind the old car wash by Walmart."

"Fesler's people," Cooperman confirmed. "Yeah, we've done business with them. They're solid."

"Exactly."

"So you were already going to recruit us to join you guys for this long winter you think is coming, when we just showed up on your doorstep?" Eric asked more than just a little incredulously.

"Um, well, to be honest, Eric," Anoona said, "your father's group was not really on our list. No offense."

Funny thing about people saying "no offense," Eric thought. *It almost always comes after they've said something that could only be taken as one.*

"Why not?" Ace asked.

"Well, we made our list with particular skill sets in mind. Doctors, people skilled with engines."

"We've got skills," JP said. "Does anybody in your group practice TM, Transcendental Meditation?"

"Oh for the love of God," Eric groaned. "Shut up, JP! Now is not the time."

"No. No, it's okay. I get it," Hamm said. "And to answer your question, no, JP, none of our group practices TM at the moment. But we *are* aware of it and its connection to the community here, or at least to the community that used to be here. However, the priority for us is survival at this point, not enlightenment."

"You'd be better served reevaluating that one," JP muttered under his breath, but everybody heard him.

"So we're not on your list, but you still wanted us to come in," Eric said.

"Not exactly," Anoona said, dodging the question.

"Just tell them!" Sarah shouted from the stairwell.

"Your relationship with Beverly is a pretty serious risk factor for us and what we've got going here. Until you showed up and gave us no really acceptable alternative, we had no intention of bringing any of you in," Hamm said.

Eric felt the blood drain from his face in embarrassment. How did Anoona and her people know that he and Beverly had slept together? Jesus, was there anywhere in Fairfield safe from their spying camera drones? He felt like he had to respond. Had to deny. Had to explain. Had to—

"Way to soften the blow there, jackass," Sarah said, but Eric was too overwhelmed to hear her, or to see Anoona throw up her hands with an awkward shrug that sent the message that, though she was frustrated by Hamm's lack of tact and wished he'd said it better, everything he said was the truth.

"I don't understand," Eric blurted out before he could finish getting his panicked thoughts in order.

"Well, it just comes down to the fact that, frankly, nobody in our group at the moment is much of a cold-blooded killer. I mean, maybe in self-defense, but preemptively? That's not who we want to be," Hamm said.

"Oh my God! What the fuck is wrong with you?" Sarah said, her hand now on the AR-15, ready to yank it up and open fire on the newcomers if they went for their weapons—which if anybody ever listened to her they would have left upstairs.

Eric was still too totally stuck on the idea that Anoona knew he'd slept with Beverly that he missed the meaning behind what Hamm had just said.

"Lucky us?" Ace said in an attempt to break the tension and counting his blessings that Anoona's group had opened their doors to them instead of cutting them down where they stood.

"Beverly's gone, probably dead, so what relationship are you guys talking about?" Matt Knowles asked while he too counted his blessings to still be alive.

Eric opened his mouth to say something, anything to keep the truth of his betrayal locked away in the darkness, but Anoona got her words out before him.

"Is that really what you all think?"

Silence filled the room as her words sank in. It was Ace who finally broke it. "She's not dead?" he asked.

"No, she's definitely not. Nor is she gone. Do you guys really not know that she's the *Blood Queen* of the pirates that took over the west side of Vedic City?"

Eric's world, which was still spinning out of control at the thought Anoona knew he'd slept with Beverly, suddenly stood perfectly still. Everything he thought he knew about who his father was and what he was doing was suddenly launched into space at 1,038 mph, which was still not fast enough for him to avoid being swallowed up by the oceans of doubt that kept moving all round him, even after the ground under his feet halted to a stop.

Did his father know that Beverly was a blood pirate? Is that why he would never let Dan go looking for her? Is that why he thought he could get Jennifer and Bobby-Leigh back? *No! There's no way he knew!* he thought. His father just didn't do dishonesty. He didn't lie about things. Even when it would make life easier not to, he spoke the truth.

Anoona watched Eric intently, reading him like a book as he struggled with the information bomb that had just blown his world up. From their reactions, it was now obvious to her that Eric and the rest of his people had not known what happened to Beverly after she'd left them. But—

"Surely your dad at least knew? I mean, isn't that why he's there now, negotiating for the Kessler girls' release? How else would he expect to be able to just walk in there and talk to them? Why else would he have taken the woman's fiancé with him?"

Eric wished to God he had answers for her, but he didn't. His hand covered his mouth as he looked around the room at his people. *At least they don't know about me and Beverly after all,* he thought, as he shakily poured himself a glass of Sarah's bourbon and choked it down, hating himself for his thoughts.

* * *

Almost a day had passed since they'd been welcomed into the new operations at the old Kessler farm instead of being murdered in the cornfield at the property line. He didn't know what would happen if they tried to leave (yes, he did), but that was fine because he was pretty sure his father was dead somewhere in Vedic City (no, he wasn't), and if that was true, then there was nowhere better to go anyway.

Anoona's daughter sat silently with him. They were on the back deck watching the striking contrast between the warm sun setting to the west and the massive storm clouds moving in from the east like a column of advancing troops armed with cold and flurries of snow. Sitting in two of the four big blue rocking chairs outside, the son of one man and the daughter of another watched the vapor of their breath drift out into the world.

Eric was thinking about how much colder it was now than the night before, and the night before had been cold. Ridiculously cold, considering it was freaking July. He was trying to ignore the much darker, hurtful thoughts that lurked just under the surface of his consciousness.

Wrapped in coats and blankets but still not exactly comfortable, he wondered what had compelled Anoona's daughter to join him after she'd brought him the blanket. Surely the little girl had better things to do than mope in the cold with him. And yet, he was grateful for her awkwardly silent company. Behind them, inside the warmth of the house, his people and Anoona's had already merged into one, it seemed, which was for the best, all things considered.

"What's your name, kid?" Eric asked just to break the peace and quiet that was starting to drive him crazy, because at the moment he didn't feel peaceful or quiet. The little girl didn't answer him for a long time. He'd almost gotten lost in his own thoughts again when she finally spoke. Instead of answering him, she asked her own question.

"Do you miss your daddy?"

"Yeah, kid. I do."

She nodded as if his answer confirmed something she'd suspected all along, and then was quiet again for a long time. Eric hoped that she wasn't going to ask him if he missed his brother next. He didn't think he'd be able to answer that one without losing it, and he desperately didn't want to lose it in front of these folks. Though, what difference would it make if he did? He couldn't have said.

"My name is Marinda," she said. "But everybody just calls me Mari."

"Eric," Eric said and held out his hand.

"I know that, silly," she said, but shook his hand just the same.

"I used to know another little girl like you," Eric said. "Well, not like you, but your age."

"Yeah, I know. Bobby-Leigh."

"Of course you do," Eric said, still confounded by the reach of Anoona's people's technology and surveillance. Behind them, the door opened, but Eric didn't hear anybody come out.

"Your dad's alive. So are the Kessler girls, at least for now, though it seems your dad actually beat the ladies to Vedic City," Tiny said from behind him. Eric looked up at him, wondering how such a big guy could move so quietly, but grateful for the information just the same—though he was so emotionally drained from the last twenty-four hours that his face hardly showed it.

"Just thought you'd wanna know," Tiny said with a twinge of disappointment in his voice. He'd at least thought the man would ask how he knew what he knew.

Tiny was very good at what he did, but that didn't mean he didn't still crave affirmation. The fact was that Tiny's self-esteem was almost entirely dependent on the approval of others—approval he hardly ever seemed to get, it felt like. He found himself trying to remember if there were any Little Debbie snacks (Star Crunches, preferably) left in his secret stash, but he didn't think so. He'd already pilfered the various cases of snacks Sarah and Rachel had brought in years ago to the point that he dared not take anything else, lest somebody notice that he was hoarding food. *Anoona and Hamm wouldn't really care,* he thought. It's not like they'd try to punish him, or banish him, or anything like that. He was irreplaceable and he knew it. It was just the potential disapproval he'd have to face if they found out . . . They'd want to sit down and talk about it, and he just couldn't take that kind of humiliation. But—

"We got a couple cases of Little Debbies in the pantry if—"

"Tiny!" Marinda said, cutting him off with a tone that wonderfully imitated adult disappointment. "Remember that Mom said sugar turns you into a snapping turtle? Remember?"

Eric smiled in spite of his private dark thoughts.

Tiny said, "You ever hear the expression 'Feed the pain,' Mari? It's what *Americans* do. And, it's not for me, okay? Our boy Eric here looks like he needs some cheering up, and—"

"I heard Mom and Hamm joking about feeding the candida. Is that the same thing?"

Tiny snorted and rubbed his forehead.

"Look, little girl, everybody knows sweets are comforting when you're sad. Do you want him to be sad?"

"No."

"It's okay, I'm fine," Eric started to say, but Tiny cut him off to continue his argument with the 03-old.

"His brother just died like two days ago. We have snack cakes. What's the problem?"

She looked up at him disapprovingly. Tiny stared her down right back. *What kind of kid is against eating snack cakes?*

"Tiny, if you eat a Little Debbie, I'm going have to tell Mom."

"Or," Tiny said with a huge smile, "you could just have one too."

"No," the little girl said, hopping to her feet and heading inside. "I don't think that'd be right."

Tiny made an exaggerated *whatever* gesture with his arms that shook his whole body. In his mind, he was already forming the various responses he could give if Anoona, or Hamm, or anybody gave him shit about offering one of their new friends a little piece of individually wrapped sugary goodness. *Fucking food Nazis.*

Eric didn't even know what a Little Debbie was, but the insight into the power dynamics of the group was fascinating. Anoona's crew seemed like a big, though slightly dysfunctional, family. He supposed he and his group were lucky to have been adopted by them, especially considering the alternative, but the sloppiness of the hierarchy and chain of command just made him miss his father more. If his father said you couldn't have a snack cake, then you didn't eat a snack cake. But at the same time, Brennachecke would never have bothered to dictate what you should or should not eat, except maybe indirectly through the fact that he set the priorities for scavenging and snack cakes would have never made it onto the get list. Maybe there was more merit to the whole military chain of command, iron fist of authority thing than he'd thought.

"Seriously, though, we do have snack cakes if you're interested," Tiny said once Mari was out of earshot.

"Are they that good?"

"Oh my goodness, man. Have you never had anything by Little Debbie?"

"I don't think so."

Tiny clamped him on the shoulder with one of his fat-fingered hands and squeezed. The big man's conspiratorial grin was infectious already, but it was the way he nodded his head, somehow both saddened by Eric's lack of experience with the power of high-fructose corn syrup–infused sweets and ecstatic at the possibility of sharing something he desired so much with somebody who may just appreciate it as much as he did, that made Eric actually laugh.

"Eric, my new friend, I'm about to show you what civilization actually tasted like before . . ." He paused, looking for just the right word.

"The flavor apocalypse?" Eric suggested.

"Oh, I like you, buddy." Tiny squealed like an excited schoolboy. "I fucking like you, man!"

Chapter Eight

The Blood Queen in the Cashmere Robe

BOBBY-LEIGH LOOKED at her sister and smiled with a sad but overwhelming sense of pride. Jennifer had not berserked out (yet). Things were steadily snowballing from worst to whatever was worse than worst, but her sister was still in control. Sure, she was now huddled in the corner of the cage, still caught up in the now loose netting that had been used to drag them into the van for transport to Vedic City. Sure, she was mumbling what Bobby-Leigh assumed was her TM mantra like a crazy person. Sure, her eyes were squeezed shut, as if she believed that what she couldn't see couldn't hurt her—something both of them knew was absolutely not true. Sure, she was sweating even though it was cold enough to be snowing outside. But none of that mattered; she was still in control and that was amazing. More than amazing, it was a testament to how much Jennifer loved her sister, because if she did lose it while tangled in the cable net inside this home-made reinforced and barred metal crate, Bobby-Leigh was sure to die.

When they arrived in Vedic City and the van's rear doors opened, the sisters found themselves in a small field looking out at a large pond. The Raj was directly behind them, though they couldn't see it yet. One of the pirates smiled hungrily at Jen as he waited for the big forklift, its poorly maintained gasoline engine roaring and smoking, to pull the cage from the van and drop it onto the grass. The two pirates who'd driven in with them started to pull the metal net off the girls right through the bars and repacked it in the van with the efficiency and well-practiced skill of men who'd done it enough times to leave most of the task to muscle memory.

"There's no way you're going to get to," one of the netting pirates, a man with a long beard and black hair, said, continuing a conversation they'd obviously started earlier as they worked.

"Oh, there's a way," the beardless one replied.

"How?"

"Maybe I'll just ask."

"You'll just ask?"

"Yeah, why not?

"You don't think they've already got their own plan for who gets to and who doesn't?"

"Maybe they do. Maybe they don't."

"Maybe you're an idiot."

"Are you saying you don't want to do it?"

"Of course I want to do it. But that doesn't mean I'm going to *get* to do it."

"We've been here for three years. If anybody is going to get to do it, it should be the people who've been here the longest."

"Maybe it should be, but it never works that way."

"I know! That's why I'm going to ask."

"Mmm, I think there's a reason they're not asking for volunteers."

"Like what?"

"I don't know. Maybe there's some kind of physical requirement or something."

"To fly? I don't think so, except maybe eyesight or weight, which wouldn't matter for me."

"What, you've got some kind of perfect vision?"

"Yeah."

"Really?"

"Yeah, man. I got 20/20 in both eyes."

"How do you know?"

"I got tested in school, man."

"What if it's changed since then?" the long-bearded pirate said, slamming the rear doors of the van and moving to get into the driver's seat.

"It hasn't."

"How do you know?"

"I just do," Beardless said as he jumped into the passenger seat and closed the door, ending their conversation, or at least the girls' ability to overhear it. When the van sped off, only the forklift driver and the pirate lecherously staring at Jen were left.

The girls now had a much better view of where they were. Theirs was not the only cage out there on the grass. There were rows and rows of them. Some were stacked two high. Some were broken open and dragged haphazardly out of the ordered lines and off to a pile on the side. Some were empty. But some of them were occupied with folks snatched off Highway 1 just like them.

Maybe I'll have a chance if I just curl up in the corner and play dead, Bobby-Leigh thought. If it came to it this was exactly what she planned on doing, but a chance was just that: one chance in maybe a hundred. Maybe a thousand. She didn't like those odds very much, but the only other alternative she really had would be to murder her sister with the karambit before she berserked out.

Jen had made Bobby-Leigh promise to do just that if a situation like this ever came up, and to the little girl's credit she'd almost done it less than seventy-two hours ago in the dumpster, after Jennifer had thrashed the boy she loved to death. But in that dumpster, Bobby-Leigh now realized, she'd learned something very important about herself: she simply didn't have what it took to slit her own sister's throat to save herself. She'd had the chance to open her sister's jugular and had hesitated. If Jen had berserked out then, Bobby-Leigh would have missed her opportunity to put her down and save herself. But the fact was that Jen hadn't berserked out. So if Bobby-Leigh *had* drawn her blade across her sister's throat, ending her life, she'd have killed her for nothing.

So if things did escalate, her only real option was going to be to play dead, and then most likely become dead for real, which just sucked. What sucked even worse was knowing that she would be leaving the aftermath of her broken promise behind with her body for Jen to deal with. Bobby-Leigh hated that part of the plan significantly more than the part where she more than likely died.

The two men guarding them laughed in the way men who are about to do something evil laugh, drawing Bobby-Leigh out of her deliberations. The little girl watched helplessly as the perverted-looking one leaned into the bars behind Jennifer, suddenly grabbed her breasts, and used them as handholds to pull her back against the bars. Squeezing them roughly, the man then stuck out his big fat tongue and sloppily licked Jen's ear.

"You wanna watch what I'm going to do to your sister?" he hissed.

Jen's eyes flashed open and her pupils suddenly dilated until the pretty green of her eyes was almost completely gone. Her body twitched as she struggled against her instincts and the sweet oblivion of berserker rage that threatened to overwhelm her, the coping and management strategies that had gotten her this far breaking down and falling apart around her head.

This was about the time Bobby-Leigh would need to slip in and position her blade against her sister's throat if she was going to do it. But the little sister didn't move, not only because she didn't have it in her to fulfill her promise, but because she also didn't want to reveal to the motherfuckers threatening to rape them that she had a knife hidden away with her.

But she had to do something.

Bobby-Leigh launched herself at the man assaulting her sister through the bars of their cage, convinced it would be the last thing she would ever do. As her mouth opened and her teeth sank into the meat of his exposed arm, she stole a sideways glance up at Jen's eyes and was amazed to see her pupils had contracted back to normal size. She was regaining control. She didn't know how Jen was doing it, but the results spoke for themselves.

While Bobby-Leigh's teeth were clamped down on her assaulter's flesh with all the strength she had in her, Jen suddenly thrust herself forward and twisted around. The man's grip, loosened by pain, was broken and Jen rocketed free from his lecherous touch, retreating to the center of the cage, out of reach.

Taking her sister's lead, Bobby-Leigh lunged for the middle of the cage too, but she didn't release her jaw's vicelike grip on the man's arm when she moved. The flesh tore with a wet, tacky sound and by the time the would-be rapist had a chance to process what was happening, a seven-inch strip of flesh from his forearm had been ripped off. He fell back onto his ass and just stared at the two girls in barely comprehending horror as he held his bloody limb against his body. It was several seconds before the shock wore off enough for him to even scream.

But scream he did. It was shrill and loud and sad, not that the girls had any pity for the bastard. It also drew a crowd. In what felt like seconds, their cage was surrounded by men laughing and jeering as much at their fallen comrade as they were at the girls huddled together just out of arm's reach on the other side of the bars. Nobody helped the injured man up. Nobody saw to his wound. In this broken society of jackals, there was no place for sympathy, no place for mercy, and certainly no place for weakness.

"You fucking idiot!"

A large red-bearded pirate howled at the wounded pervert as he kicked him brutally over and over again in the legs and back until the suffering man managed to scuttle back and up to his feet. The crowd laughed and jeered at the indignation while they shoved, punched, and pushed the bleeding pirate as he attempted to flee to safety. Once he was gone, however, there was nothing to occupy the evil bastards' attention except for Bobby-Leigh and her sister.

Jen looked at Bobby-Leigh and smiled as if there was not a mad, depraved mob of rapists and murderers surrounding them.

"You're amazing," she said.

Bobby-Leigh didn't know how to respond. It was impossible to focus with all the catcalls and violent threats being hurled at them. She didn't know how Jen was doing it, but she did know that whatever it was she was doing to keep calm in the middle of this was the reason she was not berserking out. *You're the one who's amazing,* she thought, seconds before a man's hand found one of the rings on Bobby-Leigh's dog collar choker and snapped a chain on her.

Is that a fucking leash? was all she had time to think before it was yanked and back she tumbled toward the bars. In the next seconds, the leash got help. First one strong hand grabbed her. Then the one became two, then three, then four, until there were so many hands pawing at her she couldn't isolate them individually anymore. They pinned her hands up against the bars before she could get her secret weapon out. They pinched and squeezed. They poked. Her jumper-skirt was ripping. Fingers were staring to push their way toward places she did not want fingers to go.

Jennifer's eerie, almost creepy calmness no longer seemed so amazing to Bobby-Leigh. Suddenly that calm smile seemed more dangerous to her than if her sister had lost control and berserked out right then and there. As the hands of the men tore at her, intent on violating anything of the little girl's they could get inside of, Jennifer watched from her happy place as if she had no intention of helping. Humiliated and seconds away from being violated right there through the bars, Bobby-Leigh thought she understood the horrible truth behind those brilliant-green eyes—there was simply nothing her sister could do for her at this time. She felt erect penises brush and bump into her now exposed skin from behind. Her panties were ripped away. Bobby-Leigh closed her eyes and screamed.

* * *

It had taken Jennifer a long time to finally find her way to a place of transcendence above the physical brutality she and her sister were up against. She'd stepped outside herself as the cable netting closed around them back out on Highway 1, but it wasn't enough to keep the monster inside her in check for long. She could feel the chemistry of her body shifting and stirring, trying to wake up the blinding rage that would wash out all other experiences for her until it had run its course.

The part of her mind that was still connected to her body was meditating like she had been for years. That was the easy part, the familiar part, the part she knew the limits of. But there was more to what she'd been learning than basic Transcendental Meditation, and this was the first time she'd really had a chance to test the out-of-body self-projection strategies Uncle Allen had suggested she study up on. She'd spent thousands of hours training herself to self-project and could at times certainly achieve something like an out-of-body experience. Unfortunately, every one of those successes had been in a private, calm space. Not under duress. Not tangled in metal cabling. Not en route to Blood City.

The experience was much like manually focusing a camera lens with a very shallow depth of field. Micro-adjustments of less than a single millimeter would throw the whole image out of focus. Shaky hands. Uncontrolled breathing. A pounding heart. Everything joggled the focus ring. As the net snapped tight and pulled them into the van, Jennifer realized that she'd never achieve and maintain the focus she needed for her self-projection to be successful if she continued to try to do it manually. It was just impossible.

What she needed to do was find a way to switch this metaphoric camera into autofocus. But there had been nothing that explained how to do that in the books she'd been studying. Nobody she knew of had ever even described the split-body experience she had going for herself right now. Her guidebooks were all like photography books that walked you through how to use a camera and then explained the elements that made a good picture, but never actually described how you connected those two to produce a good picture yourself. Now she was left wondering if maybe good pictures were just accidents.

Uncle Allen had been the one to suggest she try to learn the whole out-of-body thing, but he'd never been able to do it himself. *Maybe nobody ever actually has,* she thought in her detached mind as the van bounced down the road toward Vedic City. Maybe everything she'd read was just fucking theoretical and she was the first person in the history of the universe to actually do it herself. There were days she thought enlightenment might actually be like that, because for all the descriptions of transcen-dence and bliss the old TM dudes—including her uncle Allen—talked about, for all their lectures on the power in those amazing states of bliss that can be found when the mind travels down to the very source of consciousness, for all the hopping the TM Sidhi-trained meditators did under the name of "yogic flying," that oneness of universal consciousness, as far as she could tell, might just be something that can only be witnessed in glimpses out of the corner of your mind's eye, not actually experienced.

How can you know, ever really know, you are actually fully experiencing something? she wondered. *What does it even mean to be enlightened?* And yet, as the van doors opened and the pirates pulled the netting off them through the bars, she realized that she did know those answers. Recognizing the duality of knowing without knowing for the universal truth that it was suddenly allowed her to take the next step and switch the focus on her out-of-body self-projection from manual to automatic. Ironically, just like the authors of her books, she couldn't have explained how the mechanics and the result were connected either. They just were. You had to experience it to understand it. You had to be doing it to be able to learn it.

So, as she felt the hands of the man on her—the bastard her sister would momentarily be ripping the flesh from with her teeth—as she felt him pulling her against the bars of their cage by her breasts, as she felt the adrenaline explode inside her and push her inner chemistry past the tipping point, as she felt herself falling into the fugue berserker state she'd been so terrified of, she just flipped the switch in her consciousness. It was effortless. Her inability to articulate the hows and whys of it all did not impend her implementation of it in the slightest. Her focus fluttered for a split second and then, with an almost audible snap, sharpened automatically to perfection and stayed that way.

In an instant there was no stress. She was perfectly calm. The adrenaline pump in her brain shut off. The monster inside her rolled over and settled back into its precarious slumber. Effortlessly, she turned and moved out of the weakened grip of her assailant and watched as he fell back. She smiled as her sister spit out the big chunk of his flesh and scrabbled to her arms.

You are amazing, Jen thought, or said. It was hard to tell which in her current state. She watched as the crowd of evil men drew in around them. She watched as the man who had assaulted her was assaulted himself and shamed away into the coming cold dusk of the day. She watched one of the men get a hold of the collar around her sister's neck and snap on a chain. She watched her get dragged against the cage wall, her hands trapped, making it impossible for her to defend herself. She watched as the groping, disgusting hands seemed to give birth to more and more of the same. She watched as Bobby-Leigh's jumper-skirt started to tear. She watched as the little girl's panties were ripped off her body and the evil men's cocks started getting pulled out, stoked into erections, and pressed against Bobby-Leigh's exposed skin. She watched as her sister closed her eyes and screamed.

She looked at the beautiful whiteness of her sister's teeth, and marveled that even in all this violence and filth and evil, her teeth could be so perfect. But even in her nearly transcendent state, she'd reached the point where she couldn't just watch anymore—not when she could act.

Like a switch, she flipped the focus button in her mind and snapped out of it—or back into it, as the case may be. Still in control of her inner demon but no longer floating away and above herself on a cloud of bliss, she pulled her own karambit blade from its hiding spot and started to cut.

* * *

When an erect penis is severed from the body of the man who was once attached to it, the spray of blood is not at all like a fire hose, as folks often think it would be. It is actually more akin to a water balloon exploding. The blood supply is ample, but the pressure, once released, is just not anything like what causes an arterial blood spray. This fact turns the mere seconds it takes to bleed out when folks have their jugulars severed into several minutes when their erect penises are removed. If the man in question kept a level head after the impromptu penectomy and was able to stop the bleeding and put the removed organ on ice, surgeons would most likely be able to reattach the member, just like if it was a finger.

Vedic City did not have any surgeons, but even if the blood pirates had set up the most pristine surgical center possible in post-apocalyptic Iowa and filled it with the most highly decorated staff and the most sophisticated equipment money and violence could procure, not a single one of the bastards trying to rape Bobby-Leigh would have been able to get their cocks put back on. The chaos and confusion, to say nothing of the screaming and yelling, that followed Jennifer's extremely targeted cutting left those motherfuckers' dicks simply lying in the bloody mud to be trampled on by the crowd.

The men who were once attached to those penises didn't fare much better. Falling to the ground in horror, they were also trampled in the bedlam. All three men bled out and died before anybody realized what had actually happened. And even then, not a single pirate in the jeering crowd actually saw Jen's knife. All they saw was the big (hot) sister rush to the little (creepy) one and start to pull her away from the onslaught of rapists groping her from the other side of the bars. Then, as far as any of them could tell, dicks just started exploding and falling off.

The prevailing theory on the cause of the apocalypse among the blood pirates had up to that point been *Who gives a flying fuck?* But the old cultural and religious roots still ran deep even in these ungodly men. Not a man among them would have questioned the theory that berserkers were, in fact, demon possessed, nor for that matter would they have questioned a more scientific explanation. It had not been in their dark natures to wonder about the hows and the whys of things. Up until then, they'd existed only to take and to hurt—so much so that folks might even have said the blood pirates, not the berserkers, were the demonic agents of this particular apocalypse. But when penises seemingly just started to fall off of their own accord, leaving their rapist owners to bleed out screaming, suddenly it seemed there was an answer to the pirates' prevailing *Who gives a fuck* question. Suddenly each and every one of them gave a very big flying fuck, because as it turns out, nothing makes a man start asking questions like lopping off the cock of the man next to him.

As the men realized that several of their own had just lost their fun sticks right as the fuck party was about to get started, and the dots between those losses and their attempted violation of Bobby-Leigh got connected in their brains, a stunned calm swept through the crowd.

Abruptly, no man there any longer dared to take the risk of losing his manhood to what they all suddenly and collectively concluded could only be magic.

"Witches!" one screamed at them, already retreating.

"Witches!" another echoed.

It would take less than an hour for almost every single person in Vedic City to hear a version of the "witch girl" incident, and in turn pass it on with a few new, fantastic embellishments above and beyond what had happened. By the time the story got back to Beverly, the witch girls had gone from victims to perpetrators and the attempted gang rape had become a mass seduction wherein the sisters had lured ten poor, unsuspecting pirates in by stripping themselves naked and performing some kind of ritualized satanic lesbian sex act—a sex act that cast a spell on anybody there, a spell that would make any man's penis that grew erect explode if he watched. From the common threads of the various ridiculous descriptions given of these witch girls, Beverly put together that the story could only be about the Kessler sisters, whom she knew with a good amount of certainly were not witches in any way.

"How many boys lost their dicks?" she asked the two men in front of her for the second time.

"At least ten," one man said.

"I think it was more like fifteen," said the other.

The blood bag she was swapping with was almost empty. The Man-in-Charge was still out learning to fly with Brennachecke. She knew that if the girls were significantly harmed the old solider would refuse to continue the flying lessons the MIC was so excited about. She might get to kill the old man then, or better yet pit him against one of the berserkers in the arena. But then the MIC would be all pouty, and she hated dealing with that shit. Absently she wondered (as she often did when the Man-in-Charge wasn't actually with her) how much longer it would be until she felt secure enough in her authority over the pirate army there to finally take over and just get rid of the fucking waste of good berserker blood.

Certainly not yet, but that day was coming.

She smiled and pulled the IV line out of her arm. When she got up, her bloodstained cashmere robe opened, exposing glimpses of her unnaturally youthful and toned naked body to the two men who had been summoned to explain to her what the fuck all the commotion was over.

"Alright, then, let's go see what these two little fuck-cunts have to say for themselves," she said.

The men hesitated.

"What? Are you morons fucking afraid of them too?" she asked, her tone sharp with ridicule.

Neither man answered, but neither one moved either, which in its own way was answer enough. For all the positive effects berserker blood bestowed upon those who swapped it out with their own, patience was not one of them. Beverly desperately wanted each and every man in her pirate army to unquestionably obey any and all commands she gave. Every little hesitation was an affront to her position and more evidence of the fact she was constantly hoping would change in her favor: the men in Vedic City as a whole were simply not yet willing to follow her. It was just another reminder that even though she had actually ruled Vedic City from behind the scenes for some time now—the MIC really being just her little lapdog at the end of the day—the perception of the men she wanted dominion over was that she was just a blood-hungry whore.

A familiar anger filled her temples, making her head hurt, but she knew what would calm her impatient soul. These two assholes just needed a little demonstration of her authority. *After all,* she thought, *there is only one woman in Vedic City with enough real power to cut off a man's cock and throw it away like the useless thing it is.* And it wasn't the fucking Kessler bitches. It was her, goddamn it.

Her hand reached out and snatched the closest man's hair. With the added strength from just having swapped blood, the small yank she gave was enough to pull the man off balance and drop him to his knees in front of her. She buried both her hands in his thick hair and smiled down at him.

"There is only one woman in this city you ever need to be afraid of," she said and twisted the man's head savagely to the right, snapping his neck. As his body crumpled lifelessly onto the floor, she looked up at the other man, her wicked smile never wavering.

"You do know who that woman is, right?" she asked the man who still lived.

"Yes, ma'am," he said instantly, his fear now secured away in the right place.

"Good. Now take me to those little cunts you morons think have magic powers."

There was no hesitation this time. Beverly was, at least for the moment, satisfied. She was actually excited to see the girls. So what if she couldn't allow herself to hurt them physically? She could still sure as hell wipe the stupid innocence Brennachecke had so endeavored to safeguard in them off their pretty, stupid little faces. Since most of the folks that were snatched from the highway who didn't turn out to have berserker blood flowing through their veins got left to the men as party favors, a reward for following orders, she had very few people to show off to when it came to all the work she'd put into the place. None of her people appreciated the cold precision she'd applied to Vedic City's operations. None of them appreciated the recruitment trials she'd started up. In the few years she'd been secretly running the show, their band of pirates had grown from fewer than a hundred to almost a thousand. And she'd been the one who got the power turned back on. Sure, electricity wasn't in all the buildings yet, but they had lights and hot water in the Raj almost 24/7, which was a significant improvement over the daylight emergency power shit they'd started with. She was the life force behind their current strength. She was the unappreciated proud mama bear of a literal army of degenerate cubs.

Hell, if I hadn't been there, she thought, *the MIC probably would have just fucking killed Brennachecke when he'd showed up asking about the Kessler girls.* So if they did end up getting airborne, she'd get to take credit for making that happen too. In short, she was a little light in the public-affirmation-and-awe department and was looking forward to collecting on some long-overdue bragging rights.

* * *

"Fucking witches!"

The crowd of men around the girls' cage had shifted from lecherous to fearful and angry. Jennifer and Bobby-Leigh hadn't decided yet if that was actually a good thing or not. Nobody was reaching in to molest or violate them, but as the number of men grew, so did the boldness of the mob. Rapists were frankly easier to fight against.

A rock bounced off the bars and landed just inside. This wasn't the first thing that had been thrown at them since Jen had saved her sister from being fucked against her will, but it was the first thing to make it inside the cage. The crowd was a swirling, ever-shifting mass of male bodies. Jen kept expecting to get used to the smell of blood and body odor and shit (both of her now dick-less victims had emptied their bowels as they bled out, and nobody seemed to care enough to remove their bodies, much less clean the mess up). It was impossible to identify who was throwing things at them. And even if they could see who it was, it was not like they were in a position to do much about it.

Despite the impending violence, Jennifer Kessler felt in complete control. Whatever she'd discovered in the out-of-body self-projection she'd experienced while doing her TM practice under duress remained with her still. She could feel the focus ring of the lens inside her mind, and though she was back to manually controlling the field of view, she'd now have her finger on the auto button at all times and she knew she could flip it in a heartbeat if required. It was a powerful feeling after being at the mercy of losing control over what hid beneath for so long. *If Jimmy had only lived another couple days,* she found herself thinking, *he might have never been in danger at all.* It was a thought that weighed heavily on her heart, but those private, self-reflected lamentations would have to wait for quieter, calmer times to be addressed. Things were about to escalate—Jen could feel it in the air, and one look at Bobby-Leigh told her she could feel it too.

"Burn them!" somebody in the mob shouted.

"That's not very original," Bobby-Leigh said under her breath.

She was pissed. The near gang rape wasn't what was bothering her, though—at least not on the level at which she was mentally processing things; Jen cutting those fucks' dicks off and leaving them to bleed out and shit themselves went a long way to even that particular score for her. But her clothes, and the image of herself that went with them, had been her armor against the evil in the world and had taken a long time to put together. Now her whole outfit was all torn to shit. Even her panties were ripped and hanging off her. To make matters worse, they'd taken her ax in the van, so now she was facing down these bastards with her ass literally and figuratively in the wind.

Where am I going to find another outfit? she screamed in her own head. It had taken her almost a year to collect the pieces of this one. *A fucking year!* The gothic-subgenre anime styling she'd managed to pull off with the combination of the knee-high stockings and the vintage lacy jumper-skirt would have made Japan's Harajuku girls proud. But now this witty (and creepy) juxtaposition of Lolita, death, and innocence, which she had cultivated so painstakingly and wrapped up her mental image of herself so completely in, had been literally torn away. She was exposed. Vulnerable. Cold as hell. And she didn't like it one bit.

Bobby-Leigh was pissed, but she was not afraid. Jen seemed to have conquered the beast within her, and for Bobby-Leigh, that monster had been the only thing she was really afraid of. Not because it could kill her, but because whenever it got out, somebody or something Jen loved died—and she was pretty much the only thing her sister had left. Men with their nasty erections and probing fingers bled and died easily enough. Fire could be put out, burns treated, bullet holes sewn shut. Thoughts of pain, even death, didn't make her lose any sleep. Those were just physical changes to the body. But the soul-crushing aftermath of Jen feeling responsible for what the berserker did? Any more of that would completely and irrevocably break her sister's heart, and the fear of that is what kept Bobby-Leigh up at night—especially now that she knew she was too weak to put Jen down like she'd asked her to. As long as the berserker could stay locked away, Bobby-Leigh didn't think she'd ever be afraid again.

Fearlessness begot confidence and confidence begot peace. Peace in turn begot faith. This was not where she and Jen would die; though all evidence pointed to the contrary, she just knew it in her heart. So as a torch appeared in the crowd and was thrust between the bars and the pirate mob screamed for them to burn in hell, she just smiled. Jen shot her a look, eerily calm herself, and whipped her jacket off in a smooth motion. She deftly wrapped it around the torch as it came clumsily at them, smothering the flame.

The crowd roared, but, before they could do anything else, Beverly showed up and put a stop to the craziness. Bobby-Leigh was right; today was not the day they would die. However, in the grand scheme of the universe no promises could be made about tomorrow. Death was coming and the Reaper wasn't nearly as picky as folks tended to think he was.

* * *

A short time after she first bedded the MIC, Beverly had christened herself the Blood Queen, but up to now, at least as far as she knew, nobody had ever actually referred to her that way. Even the MIC refused to call her that, and he was wrapped pretty tightly around her little finger. As she approached the holding cage with the Kessler sisters in it, she marveled to herself how ridiculously superstitious her army of chanting, fear-mongering morons was.

Could this be the opportunity she'd been looking for to establish her Blood Queen title with the men? A little shock and awe in the face of this collective hysteria might just bring the whole thing together.

She stood back quietly and observed.

Too scared of losing their penises to witchcraft, the idiots had settled on cautiously pushing a long torch into the cage in an utterly idiotic attempt to light Jennifer Kessler on fire. If they got their heads out of their asses and actually managed to do something that stood a snowball's chance in hell of actually working, she'd have to step in and pull the little cunt out, but so far that seemed unlikely.

The pretty teen is just as smart as she is fuckable, Beverly thought and smiled as she watched Jen deftly smother the flames of the ridiculous torch with her jacket. Her men, however, were decidedly not as smart. Beverly was no stranger to the fact that fear of the unknown makes folks stupid in ways that can seem unbelievable to more rational minds, but she'd never seen anything like this before. There was a gasp from the mob as the torch failed to light the girl on fire.

"The devil protects his own!" a man screamed.

Beverly mentally made a note of who the shouter was so she could deal with him later—some assholes were just too stupid to be allowed to continue living. She then stepped forward into the crowd and held up her hands.

"Gentlemen!" she shouted in a voice that left no room to doubt who was in charge. "These girls are under my protection. They belong to me. Your *Blood Queen*. Any man here who would dare contaminate their virtue; any man here who would dare mark their flesh, spill their blood, fuck those soft, delicious holes of theirs; any one of you who would so much as take a single hair off one of their young heads will"—she smiled and paused for effect—"will no longer be a man."

The mob was silent.

The sisters were silent.

Beverly had everybody right where she wanted them.

Why does that woman look so familiar? both Jen and Bobby-Leigh wondered as Beverly continued to slowly approach them. Her open robe fluttered in the cold, though her naked skin didn't seem to feel it.

"Beverly?" Jen said breathlessly, utterly shocked.

Beverly smiled in acknowledgment.

"They call me the Blood Queen here," she said and as the pirates gathered around the cage started whispering to one another, her self-bestowed title suddenly became a reality. The satisfaction she felt hearing it murmured by the morons of her pirate army was disappointingly underwhelming. Still, it was a box that had to be checked on the grand list of things she needed to do before she dared publicly assert her leadership and rout the MIC from power.

"Understand the words of your Blood Queen," she said to the mob. "Hear and obey, or I will separate you from your cock, and your life, just as these men here have been." She pointed to the dead men with shit in their pants and their dicks no longer attached. "These two little girls are not witches. They have no special powers. They cannot hurt you."

She turned to the sisters and winked conspiratorially at them, as if she was doing them a favor by making them seem harmless. Though that was hardly the primary purpose of her words or the intention behind claiming their perceived magical powers as her own, she was in fact doing them a favor. Rendering the Kessler girls harmless would save them as much as it would put Beverly in a better position and set the foundation of her title as Blood Queen in the morons' minds. It was a win-win.

"But there *is* one woman here who *can* hurt you," she continued, turning back to the mob. "Is there a man here too stupid to know who that woman is? Well, I'll spell it out for you just the same. I am the one you should fear around here. Me, your *Blood Queen*, and only me. Fail to understand that, boys, and you'll experience a suffering that these poor dead, lecherous fools would only envy. Got it?"

Nobody there doubted a word she said, except for maybe Jennifer and Bobby-Leigh, who didn't so much doubt Beverly's words as much as they just didn't understand what was happening.

"Doubt me at your own peril, gentlemen," Beverly repeated, just to drive the point home one last time. Then she grabbed the pirate closest to her—a scrawny, long-haired man who didn't look like he could grow facial hair—and pulled him to her. Beverly was strong, but it was fear that brought the man to his knees in front of her, fear that made the Blood Queen's loins burn with lust. For the first time, she felt like she might truly have power over these men. She smiled at him as he quaked under her gaze.

"Open it."

The Blood Queen's command was almost immediately obeyed.

The cage door came crashing down. Beverly beckoned to the girls. Jen looked at her sister, for the first time truly seeing the tattered remnants of her clothing and just how close she had been to being raped right in front of her. Tears filled her eyes, but she fought them back. Bobby-Leigh locked eyes with her as she shivered in the cold. The little girl was angry, defiant, and totally confused by what had just happened. Neither girl knew what to expect next. Every ounce of Jen's being told her Beverly could not be trusted, and yet she had put an end to the violence against them and secured their release.

Back in town, before Beverly had disappeared and had been presumed dead, before Bobby-Leigh had drawn blood for the first time in that back room at Walmart, before her beloved Jimmy had been beaten to death by the demon inside her, Jen had not really known the woman who was now calling herself the Blood Queen. In fact, she'd been such an insignificant part of their lives while under Brennachecke's care that Bobby-Leigh still didn't recognize her beyond a nagging feeling that something about her was familiar.

Cautiously the Kessler girls exited their confinement and entered the unknown. As they stepped free of the cage, Beverly stepped between them and put an arm around each and led them away.

"Let's get you cleaned up. And then, oh my God, girls, have I got some amazing things to show you."

"Aren't you cold?" Bobby-Leigh asked under her breath in a tone that implied the real meaning of her words was more like *Go fuck yourself.*

Beverly smiled at the little girl with her jackal smile and thought about how much fun she was going to have bathing in her virgin blood after this little charade of politeness came to an end. Brennachecke was going to die. These two little ungrateful cunts were going to die. The MIC was going to die. The Blood Queen's time was coming.

As they entered the lower-level restaurant of the Raj, the coy flurries of falling snow that had been playing hard to get all day finally stopped their teasing, stripped naked, and took a hit of ecstasy as serious snow began to fall.

Holy shit, Beverly laughed to herself, *it really is going to be Christmas in July.*

* * *

"I'm going to need the knife," Beverly said.

They stood in the double room next to the queen-sized beds. Bobby-Leigh was wearing a Raj-branded white cotton robe over her tattered clothing. It was so long it dragged on the floor and covered her hands, but she was grateful to no longer be so utterly exposed. The Blood Queen, or Beverly, or whoever she was, obviously didn't share Bobby-Leigh's sense of modesty, as she hadn't bothered to shut her robe once since she'd appeared out of nowhere in the nick of time and released them. Bobby-Leigh had never witnessed such a lack of shame around nakedness in her whole life. She wanted to interpret that lack of modesty as liberating, but she couldn't. There was something off about Beverly that she just couldn't shake, something dangerous just behind her eyes and at the corner of her smile. Though she'd been nothing but kind to them thus far, the Blood Queen's refusal to cover her privates just added to that feeling that something was not right with her.

From the emotional telepathy only siblings can understand, she knew that Jen shared her misgivings. She also knew Jen recognized the Blood Queen as somebody they knew, but for the life of her Bobby-Leigh couldn't remember who Beverly had been. She didn't know strategically how to respond to her demand, so she left it in her sister's court while she tried to place this new person, who wasn't actually new, in their lives.

It was just the three of them in the room, but outside in the hall, four of Beverly's more trusted personal guard stood waiting—armed, alert, and ready to kill on command. It felt like they were there to ensure the girls' compliance as much as they were there to safeguard their virtue. But again, Bobby-Leigh wasn't sure where those feelings were coming from.

"What?" Jen asked. She wasn't trying to be impertinent; the request had just caught her so off guard that she genuinely needed to hear it again to process it.

Beverly, though, was already tired of playing nice and couldn't help but take the question as anything but insolent. Still, she smiled and kept her tone in check. The training of all those years of hiding her true nature from the world had served her well. She could play her cards so close to her chest that folks would mistakenly think she wasn't even in the game if she had to.

"The knife, girls. Or are you two really witches after all?"

Jen locked eyes with Beverly, trying desperately to read what was behind them, but aside from the general sense of untrustworthiness she'd always felt toward the woman, she couldn't glean anything more specific. Uncle Allen's admonition to never reveal their little weapons of last resort rang in her ears so loudly it was like he was in the room, telling her in person. It had been repeated so many times that it'd become instinctual to the point she felt physically ill at the thought of handing it over to someone, much less someone she was almost certain was at best not trustworthy and at worst . . . *Fuck me,* she thought, *the possibilities are endless.*

"Why do you need it?"

"You know why."

"I don't."

"We can't have you cutting any more dicks off while you're here."

"As long as everybody keeps 'em in their pants, that won't be an issue."

"It's a security threat, dear."

"Are you kidding me?" Bobby-Leigh burst out. "You've got four dudes with, like, automatic weapons in the hallway, and you're worried about—"

"One little knife?!" Jen finished, cutting her sister off before she could say anything that would reveal there was more than one weapon between the two of them. Bobby-Leigh looked at Jen and immediately got the play her sister was making.

"I know it doesn't seem fair," Beverly soothed. "But I promise, as long as you're under my protection you have nothing to fear. Frankly, girls, there's really no reason for you to have a weapon here at all. I, on the other hand, do have things I have to, *need* to, be afraid of. That's why my boys have the guns. They'll protect you with them too. That's their orders, you can be sure of that.

"But one of those things that I am afraid of is that you'll have some kind of misguided overreaction if you should see something that doesn't agree with you while you're here. And I just can't risk that. Pretty big fires can get started with the tiniest of little sparks. I've seen it. Hell, you girls just saw it for yourselves."

"What kind of things would we see that wouldn't agree with us?" Bobby-Leigh asked, now morbidly, genuinely curious.

"Let's just say there's a number of philosophical differences between how the Man-in-Charge and I run things here, compared to how that goody-goody Brennachecke manages your little group of pack rats."

"We're not part of his group anymore."

"Really?" Beverly said, desperately trying to contain the cutting sneer that wanted to ride out on her words and cut the little bitch down. *Then why is the old bastard risking his life to teach us how to fly just for a chance to get you two bitches back into the fold?*

"We had a falling out," Jen said vaguely.

"It's none of my business," Beverly said. "That knife of yours, however, is. This is only temporary, I'll give it back as soon as I'm convinced you two have a strong enough stomach to handle what we do here."

Beverly smiled her jackal smile.

Jen smiled back.

Bobby-Leigh didn't smile at all.

The silence stretched out and out between the two girls and the woman until it engulfed them. Beverly's smile spread from her lips to the corners of her eyes as genuine satisfaction bloomed inside her. It was so much more of a challenge to manipulate women, especially girls, than it was to manipulate boys and men. She could tell that Jen's instincts were screaming at her not to trust anything Beverly said. She could tell that the young woman was hiding something more than just the knife. There was a real legitimate battle of wits happening here behind their smiles and their words. It was exhilarating. She'd still kill them in the end, of course, but for now she was relishing the change of pace.

With boys and men, sex was almost always, one way or another, an effective weapon. Given enthusiastically, promised but repeatedly withheld, offered to a rival instead, allowed to be taken by force—there was always a way to use sex to influence those who peed standing up. Beverly was a master at it. It was easy. In fact, just having her robe open the way she did was enough to give her an edge in almost every interaction she had here in Vedic City—an edge that no doubt was instrumental in her survival. She knew very well that her numerous lies and acts of duplicity would have been long ago detected had the men around her not been so distracted by the constant brazen full-frontal view of her naked, toned, and seductive body.

But with girls, that all went out the window. Even lesbians didn't respond to seeing somebody they wanted to have sex with naked the way men did. She supposed that was because when women got aroused their blood didn't need to fill up an entire cock, just the button of their clit, and so the extra was left to rush to their brains, which in turn must make them more perceptive.

Fucking lesbians, Beverly thought, as her mind began to wander in the tension of the silence. This difficulty staying focused was happening more and more to her, but like always she blew it off as boredom instead of connecting it to its true cause, which was of course the ever-increasing amount of berserker blood she swapped into her veins. The fact was she was anything but bored. She wanted to just reach out and slap the little bitch and see what would happen, but knowing Jen had somehow managed to cut the dicks off three men without anybody seeing it happen, and then conceal the tool she'd used to do it, kept her in check. The Kessler girls had already proven themselves worthy of a certain amount of guarded respect. Beverly was not one to underestimate folks.

Finally Jen sighed in that unique way only an American teenage girl can and rolled her eyes as she said, "Fine. Give her the knife, Bobby-Leigh."

"Really?"

Jen knew that Bobby-Leigh wasn't actually questioning her but was just playing along with the ruse. She was proud of how quick her sister was. They'd need to be quick, she thought, if whatever was happening in this place might really drive them to resort to their sacred secret weapons—or weapon, as the case may be now. She knew perfectly well that the only way they'd get Bobby-Leigh's knife back was if Beverly was dead. But she could live with that. She'd give her sister hers if she needed to.

"Yeah, give it up."

Bobby-Leigh reached into the folds of the too-large robe she was wearing and from someplace Beverly couldn't fathom the location of, she pulled out the surgically sharp karambit blade and flipped it open. There was a soft *click* as the knife locked into place, ready to be of service. An almost uncontrollable, instinctual urge to launch herself forward and plunge the knife into the woman's jugular suddenly threatened to overtake her, but Bobby-Leigh managed to convert all that distrustful bloodlust into a jackal smile of her own. She handed the weapon over, hilt first.

"Well, now aren't you a little magician," Beverly said, still trying to figure out where the girl had hidden the knife on her person. She took the weapon and admired it for a second. It was perfect in its design. Beverly instantly decided she'd follow the little girl's lead and keep it on her, hidden, as a weapon of last resort. Her promise to return it was forgotten without a second thought.

"We've got hot water and heat. Clean yourselves up. I'll see about finding you some new clothes and have some food sent up. Make yourselves at home in here. Brenna-checke is going to insist on seeing that you're okay once they get back from the airport, which should be any—"

"Brennachecke wants us dead," Bobby-Leigh said, cutting Beverly off. "Or at least he wants my sister dead." Jen smiled and shrugged, revealing nothing beyond the feigned flippant attitude of an ordinary American teen-age girl.

"Interesting," the Blood Queen said and smiled. "Well, fear not, ladies. My protection of you here is against any kind of violence from any man, Brennachecke included. And it is absolute. I'll cut his cock off myself if he tries anything."

Jen and Bobby-Leigh couldn't tell if Beverly was being serious or if the threat to their surrogate father was just hyperbole. Had anybody else said it, it would have been an obvious exaggeration, but with this woman who called herself the Blood Queen it didn't feel like an overstatement.

Jen knew full well that Brennachecke intended to take her life, and yet the idea of this woman hurting him, especially in her and her sister's name, for some reason made her sick to her stomach. The thought of her own karambit blade hidden in its secret spot against her flesh stirred so vividly that she could suddenly feel the knife's pressure against her skin. Unbidden, her mind tossed out a clear picture of herself saving the man who was coming to kill her, by killing the woman who had saved them. The image was a very, very satisfying one, but try though she might, she couldn't make any sense of why.

Chapter Nine
The Cuckold on the Other Side of the Glass

D AN SHIVERED in the darkness as he looked through his faint reflection in the one remaining window of the little airport, out toward the road to Vedic City. He couldn't believe it was snowing outside, really snowing, like *Fire up the damn snowplows and get those roads clear or folks aren't going to be able to get to work in the morning* kind of snowing—not that folks were going to work anymore, or that there was anybody left to drive the plows even if there had still been folks who needed to use the roads.

He also couldn't believe Brennachecke hadn't given him more detailed instructions. *Can the flying lessons even continue in this?* he wondered. When Brennachecke had left with his little band of pirate flight students just a few hours ago, he'd convinced himself that he should go into Vedic City and find out what the hell was going on. But now, with the snow tumbling out of the sky like it was February instead of July, he wasn't so sure.

First of all, he would leave tracks. If the snow continued coming down like it was, that wouldn't really matter; they'd all get covered and nobody would be the wiser. But if it stopped . . . And it had to stop; it was the middle of summer after all, so surely no amount of climate craziness could produce this radical a change from the norm for any kind of extended period of time—or could it? If it stopped, then he'd end up leaving a trail right back here and fuck up the entire plan. Assuming that the plan was still the plan.

And even if the snow didn't stop, and his tracks were covered up, it was maybe twenty degrees outside. God knows what that became when you factored in the windchill. Dan was prepared for a couple of cold July nights—nights in the forties, or even the high thirties. He had a solid jacket and some thick canvas hunting pants, but they were hardly enough to weather a freak blizzard for a significant amount of time. He knew his hands would be too cold to accurately shoot his bow with any kind of speed by the time he got across the cornfield and into Vedic City, never mind by the time he actually found anything out. He had a knife, but using it as a weapon under the circumstances was a bad joke.

What do you call the man who brings a knife to a gunfight?

A dead man. Ha, ha, ha. (Not.)

"Fuck me," he muttered to himself and turned away from the glass, just as unsure about what to do as he'd been an hour ago.

* * *

"It's not impossible, but it's a lot harder," Brennachecke said, looking out the library window of the Raj over the little balcony and at the freak July snowstorm hell-bent on covering the ground with white. "The cold makes your engine harder to manage, at least initially. Stiffens the rest of the plane up. But the ice is the real problem, and the wind, of course."

The Man-in-Charge frowned. This was not what he wanted to hear. The powerful effects of the berserker blood he was swapping out as they talked about the next session of Brennachecke's flight school didn't actually do much to settle his tingling nerves. Flying was exhilarating. The idea of stopping because of a little snow was so ridiculous he wanted to scream and break things.

As gravity pulled the stolen red AB blood down from the IV bag and into his spiked vein, his frown deepened and deepened. He preferred AB to O when it came to swapping. The universal donor essence of type O blood felt cheap to him. It couldn't be as good if anybody could use it. AB, on the other hand, would kill, or least really fuck up, anybody with another blood type. It was special. It made him special. Swapping with AB made him feel so much better than just settling for O. Or at least he thought it did. Both made him stronger. Both healed his wounds. Both filled him with confidence. And he was feeling strong and healthy and confident. But AB made him less frustrated. Calmer. More in control. Or at least he thought it did.

He looked again at the bag hanging next to him and at the big handwritten letters on it, confirming for the third time that this was AB and not O. Maybe it wasn't any better after all. He just didn't know anymore. The MIC was not the kind of man that typically wondered these kinds of things, and so the very fact that he had these questions only made it all worse. He wordlessly motioned to the attendant who was doing the blood work to set him up with another bag. The man set to work on it immediately without needing any further clarification, but the MIC needed more than just a new bag of blood, so he grabbed him and dragged him over to his side and whispered something in his ear.

Brennachecke turned and looked at the MIC just as the private instructions were ending. He felt the hairs on the back of his neck prick up. "I can still go over procedures and we can work in the plane on the ground, inside a hangar or something, but there's just no way I safely put you in the air until this stops."

The MIC nodded, but said nothing.

The man seemed distracted, and Brennachecke didn't know if that was something that would end up being in his favor or not. What he did know was that he needed to check in on the Kessler sisters. Since they'd landed, Brennachecke had not seen any indication the MIC had made it clear to anybody other than the men who had actually picked the girls up that they were to be left alone. *Would the message have been reliably passed on?* he wondered. *Not likely.* He had no gun and no knife anymore. In the plane he had had leverage. He could easily enough just crash the thing and kill everybody; none of the pirates, the MIC included, knew enough yet to stop him from doing it. But they were not in the plane anymore, and Dan was back at the airport being snowed in more and more with each minute that passed.

Brennachecke was at the mercy of the deal they'd made. Deals made with less than honorable men even in the best of times tended to be trouble—and these were anything but the best of times. He felt sick to his stomach at the thought of what could be happening to Jennifer and her sister right now under his very nose. He still intended on putting a bullet in Jen's head at some point soon, but he didn't want her to suffer before he did it—or after, for that matter.

"I need to see those girls."

"You need to figure out how to keep our little fight school up and running in the weather," the MIC said as the attendant slipped out of the room.

"I told you what I can do down here," the old soldier said. "I'm sure the snow won't last and we'll be back in the air in no time. It's July after all."

"Then I'm sure it will be no time until you see your precious little cunts."

"My concern is that they'll be . . . damaged when I see them."

"Then you better figure out a way for us to fly tomorrow, old man."

Brennachecke sighed. This was the third time he'd gone through this conversation with the MIC, and the stubborn man simply would not give. He looked out the window again at the snow tumbling down from the sky and then at the four guards with AR-15s in the room with them. He didn't even know where the girls were being held.

"Please."

The MIC smiled sadistically. The two men's eyes locked. Neither one liked what they saw down there in the wells of the other's soul.

* * *

"Screw it," Dan said. "Screw it, screw it. Screw. It."

He opened the door and marched out into the snow, hoping to God that he was not making the biggest mistake of his life, but also not really caring anymore if he was. This plan of Brennachecke's had been risky to begin with, and that was before the snow started falling. Maybe the pirates would think his tracks were a deer's. Surely they were not that stupid, but maybe Dan would get lucky. He was due for some luck. *Long overdue, actually,* he thought. Of course, that wasn't how luck worked, so far as such a thing existed, and Dan knew it. As far as he understood it, luck was just a selective viewing of random chance happenings. Folks just didn't recognize the randomness over the emotional power of the "lucky" event.

"Success and failure are in the hands of God, my love, not your own." The words were his mother's. They suddenly came to him unbidden and without any love behind them.

"Yeah, that's why you're dead and I'm not," he muttered in response to himself, feeling colder on the inside because of it. *God didn't fucking save you in the end,* he thought as the emotional shreds of his mother's passing stirred up around him like leaves in a whirlwind.

"Yes, my love. He did. He took me just as he took all the faithful of His children to live forever by His side in heaven. It's you and the other sinners He left behind to fend for yourselves in hell."

"Shut up, Mom."

It didn't matter anyway. Lucky or not. Good idea or bad one. Blessed by the Lord or cursed. Dan needed some answers, and he was going to get them. The snow was accumulating fast. Each time Dan looked back as he made his way through the cornfield that separated the airport from Vedic City, there was a little less of a trail for somebody to follow. He smiled in the cold.

* * *

Beverly was already on her way there when the stitched-mouthed attendant found her and passed on the message, which he'd written on a page in a small notebook as he looked for her, that the MIC wanted to see her in the library. She came in and closed the door behind her, smiling as she watched Brennachecke and the MIC staring each other down. For a moment, she just enjoyed having secrets. Then she went to her lover's side.

This had been one of the best days she'd had in years. Strides forward had been made in the preparations for her coup. The Kessler girls had proven themselves to be powerful and intelligent and she was excited to have beaten them into giving up the knife, and even more excited about the idea of bathing in their blood. Then again, she considered now, if she did decide to let them live, the idea of twisting and molding their young and naive little minds into her own sinister tools for maintaining power was pretty exciting too. Her dreams felt so close. But then, as if the MIC could tell his demise was imminent and knew he needed to remind her who was in control, the rug was suddenly yanked out from under Beverly's feet.

"Suck it," the MIC said to her as he continued to stare Brennachecke down.

"The Kessler girls are—" Beverly began proudly, not hearing what the man had said, or even registering the fact that he'd spoken in the first place.

"Suck it," he repeated and pulled his penis from his pants, his eyes never leaving Brennachecke's.

Beverly looked at Brennachecke, who did not break the invisible beam connecting the two men by returning her look. She smiled her jackal smile. This time it was coy and seductive, as if to say the performance she was about to give was really for his benefit and not for the man whose penis she was about to take into her mouth. Then she placed herself between the legs of the Man-in-Charge and did what he had asked, while inside and in absolute secret she burned in both humiliation and anger. The MIC grabbed her roughly by the hair and forced himself deeper and deeper down her throat until tears filled and then dripped out of her eyes. She fought for breath, but did so elegantly, never once betraying the appearance that this was exactly what she wanted to be doing.

Brennachecke didn't flinch. He didn't break eye contact. He knew that somehow this juvenile, sadistic staring contest would determine if he saw the Kessler girls before he finished teaching the MIC and his pirates how to fly. Beverly was just being used as a ploy to break his attention.

Beverly, for her part, even while the MIC brutalized her mouth, understood what was happening too. This wasn't about her. It wasn't about sex either. Brennachecke needed to be broken and the MIC was demonstrating how powerful he was. Even as she felt his hot, slippery ejaculate wash down her throat and was tossed aside like a penny fuck whore, Beverly didn't take it personally. She'd play the part, for now. Then one day soon, she'd use the karambit claw knife the Kessler girls had been so reluctant to give up to split the man from asshole to throat.

One day, she thought. *Soon.*

She smiled up at her abusive partner and seductively wiped her lips. As she sat on her chair, her robe open, fully exposed, she cocked her head and shot Brennachecke a look that said she'd take him that way too if he wanted. His reaction almost made the humiliation worth it for her. Almost.

The MIC had broken eye contact when he'd blown his load, but somehow because of the way he'd done it he hadn't exactly lost the battle of wills, nor had Brennachecke exactly won. He watched as Beverly turned to the MIC and whispered in his ear like she hadn't just been sexually assaulted by him. He laughed. She whispered some more and then she laughed herself.

"So, no flying until this fucking crazy storm passes, huh?" Beverly said to Brennachecke, absently playing with herself.

"No, not after just a single day behind the stick," he said, wishing the woman would cover herself up and stop trying to titillate him. "Flying in weather like this takes a seriously advanced skill set."

"Mmm," she said. "And as long as the girls stay untouched, then you'll teach that skill set to our people here, yes?"

"Of course, eventually, but you've got to start at the beginning. And that is still where we are here. Now look, I've made good on my end of our deal. I know you took the Kessler girls in today, we saw it happen. So I think it's time I got to confirm that they're okay."

"Oh, they're okay. Confirmed."

"I need to see them with my own eyes."

"Why? Don't you trust me?"

"Not at all."

Beverly laughed. Brennachecke and his stupid honesty was actually rather refreshing after the constant mind games she'd been playing here.

"Tell me something, Brennachecke. What do you intend to do with little Bobby-Leigh after you murder her sister? Are you going to kill her too?"

Brennachecke was too stunned by the question to answer it, which was just fine because Beverly didn't really care what the answer was anyway. She'd just wanted to see his reaction. She smiled, until movement outside the window on the little balcony caught her eye and she turned toward it. The smile on her face widened into a goblin-like grin as she suddenly recognized who was outside watching them in the snow.

"Dan! Oh, Brennachecke, you brought friends! Why didn't you tell us!"

Brennachecke turned his head toward the balcony to see what Beverly was talking about, but the cold steel of his well-seasoned soldier's instincts already knew exactly what he would see. In the instant he saw Dan through the glass, those same soldier's instincts also knew exactly what was going to happen next. There would be no more flight school for the pirates. There would be no more staring the MIC down. No more sexual exhibitions by Beverly. Not that any of these things were really great losses. The really great losses would be coming soon enough, though.

This plan of his had been moving sideways since he'd arrived, so he guessed part of his mind had already been mentally preparing for a disaster. There was not so much as an inkling of surprise in his heart when Dan kicked in the French doors.

With a flurry of cold and snow, the man who once used to be in love with Beverly entered the room, drew an arrow from his quiver, and nocked it. He didn't say a word as he drew the string back and let the arrow loose in a smooth, almost beautiful movement. Brennachecke didn't know how he knew who Dan would be aiming at with that first shot, but he did. Still, even though he could see it coming, the old soldier was only fast enough to avoid being killed instantly. He wasn't fast enough to avoid being hit.

The arrow landed with an audible thud just below his shoulder and ran through his body and nearly six inches out the other side before coming to a vibrating stop in his chest. This was the first time Brennachecke had ever been shot with an arrow and it hurt a lot more than he thought it would. But even as the pain exploded through his chest and shoulder, he could tell that the piercing tip of the bolt had missed anything immediately vital. In his experience, immediately mortal wounds were not quiet or sneaky about their natures, though somewhere in the back of his mind he did note that there was an awful lot of blood oozing around the arrow shaft.

Regardless of how serious of a wound it was, he had to keep moving. He closed his eyes and mentally shut off the pain and threw up blinders to the blood. Odds were that everybody in the room would be dead in the next five minutes, and if he was going to buck those probabilities, he needed to get his hands on a gun, and fast.

* * *

Dan trudged through the thick snow like an insect. He was unaware of being pulled forward by forces he couldn't really understand. Unaware that he was moving steadily toward his own death. Unaware that the loss of his life would seem both completely unnecessary and inconsequential to all the folks who witnessed it. Unaware that his consciousness was the equivalent of a single cell in the follicle of a single strand of arm hair on the pilot of the B-29 that dropped the first atom bomb. Unaware that he was insignificant in all the ways that mattered, and yet remained an integral part of the complex clockwork of chaos that maintained the very fabric of the whole of existence.

He wasn't alone in his ignorance. Humanity was never designed to comprehend even the smallest pieces of the big picture. How can a single cell in a person's body understand its role or its importance in the actions that person's body will take years from now? We are all just cells in the great body of the universe. Our purposes are locked into the way we carry out the daily functions of what we are designed to do. Do you think a liver cell understands the significance of what it does day in and day out in terms of protecting the organism as a whole? It most certainly does not. It just wants to keep up with the liver cell next to it. Man is no different, not that folks will ever stop trying to make sense of things. That is the curse that balances the power of our intellect.

Dan was no exception to this human need to make sense of things. His mind was its own cold storm of thoughts. He told himself he just needed to know what Brennachecke wanted him to do now that it was fucking snowing in the middle of July. He told himself that he just needed to know for himself if the Kessler girls were actually here or not. Maybe he could just break them out and they could all just go home. *Sure, that wasn't the plan,* he thought. But the plan didn't make any sense to him anymore.

He got all the way to the front of the Raj without seeing another soul, or so he thought. Beverly's sirens—the naked, disfigured, and left-for-dead women secured to the front pillars—had been at last put out of their misery by the cold. The snow had covered them enough to disguise their true natures from a distance. Dan didn't recognize them for what they were as he stood in the parking lot flanked by the rows of trees on either side of the long driveway. The limbs of the trees were breaking under the pressure of the heavy wet snow on their thickly leaved branches. Dan felt oddly sympathetic toward them. As he looked up at the Raj washed in the soft yellow glow of the lights in the windows, he wondered if maybe he was breaking under the pressure too. But even if he was, he didn't care anymore. He was cold and wet and the only thing that would warm him up would be knowing what the hell he should be doing. When he was finally close enough to see that the snow-covered pillars at the entrance to the Raj had dead bodies wrapped around them, it still took him a second to understand what he was seeing.

"Jesus!" he squealed as he fell back down the steps in horror, immediately looking around to see if his outburst had drawn any attention. The Raj was buttoned up tight against the snow and the cold. He was safe from discovery. Standing up again, he looked at the lit windows and weighed his options for gaining entry.

It was surprising, even to Dan himself, how quickly he settled on climbing the frozen limbs of the sirens to get to the balcony on the second floor. But it seemed like the best course of action because the only two real alternatives were going in through the front door or going around and finding a service entrance out back, both of which would not allow him to observe much before he inevitably ran into a pirate of some sort or another, who would surely end up sounding the alarm. He wanted information, not a body count. Or so he thought, as he climbed up the ladders of frozen dead human flesh. He quietly pulled himself over the balcony and peeked into the window, not suspecting for a moment that everything was about to change.

He saw Brennachecke standing closest to the balcony doors. The man seemed to be in an intense staring contest with one of the men who had been learning to fly, a man who was now swapping blood and getting blown by some woman. Quite obviously this was the Man-in-Charge. There were about a half dozen bored men with guns in the room as well. Dan supposed they were bodyguards of some kind. The doors to the library were closed. He didn't have the slightest idea what kind of sicko shit was going down in there, but he figured Brennachecke was explaining why they couldn't continue their little pilot school and that it was not going over too well. Why the Man-in-Charge needed to be blown while he received the information was beyond him. Blood pirates were crazy. That was the only explanation he could come up with. And it didn't matter; it's not like he cared who had the man's johnson in her mouth. Brennachecke obviously didn't care either, which was perfect because if the old soldier would just look over he'd be able to signal him without anybody else being the wiser.

He watched the Man-in-Charge blow his load in the lady's mouth, then felt his blood drain as the woman stood up and smiled like she'd just been given a diamond ring for her birthday, daintily wiped her mouth, and turned around to flirt with Brennachecke.

Beverly?

It wasn't a question. He had no doubt that he was looking at his lost wife-to-be flaunting her naked body at a man he'd trusted his life with.

Beverly.

Alive.

Sucking the cock of some other man.

He felt something stir inside him.

Something wild.

Something dangerous.

She wasn't a prisoner. She wasn't being raped. She wasn't missing. The thoughts were like daggers in his heart and they kept coming faster and faster. She'd left him. She'd left him to be a fucking blood pirate. *No, to* fuck *a blood pirate. King of the blood pirates, apparently.*

The cage door inside his mind that had been holding that dangerous, wild something back was suddenly flung open. *And Brennachecke's known the whole goddamn time.* Somehow in Dan's mind that betrayal was even worse than anything Beverly had done. He'd almost expected this of her, he told himself, even though it wasn't at all true. But Brennachecke? The man was his friend.

Had been his friend, he corrected himself, literally frothing at the mouth, seething with anger now. *That's why he never wanted to come here looking for her. He knew we'd find her here. He knew I would go fucking nuts and start some shit. So instead of helping his friend deal with the truth, he took the easy way out and just lied to my face.*

For almost a year!

The man had lied to him for 345 days. Right to his face. Over and over again. The whole time saying that doing the right thing, even when it was the hard thing, was what made man worthy of his fellow man.

Dan sucked in a hissing breath of freezing, damp air and felt the coldness spread inside him. It seeped from his lungs into his blood and then rocketed into his brain. But the cold did not bring calm for the cuckolded man. He would not be calm again until death finally put him out of his anguish.

Fucking hypocrite!

Dan was breathing so heavy at this point, his breath had started to fog the glass of the French doors. *Brennachecke,* he thought. *You're going to fucking die.*

Beverly suddenly looked over at him and laughed.

Laughed!

That was it. Dan was done. Though only human blood flowed in his veins and he had no demonic monster hiding inside him, ready to knock him out and destroy everything in sight, he went as berserk as his human body and mind would allow. He kicked in the French doors, drawing an arrow from his quiver as he did so, and allowed himself to be consumed by a new mission objective.

Everybody in that room was going to die.

But Brennachecke was going to die first.

* * *

"She could have at least found me something black," Bobby-Leigh muttered loud enough to make her sister smile and open her eyes. They'd finished their twenty-minute meditation a few minutes ago and were now in the resting state, slowly coming out of it.

"Your choker goes good with the pastels, dude."

"You know that's not true."

Jen laughed. Of course it wasn't true. Why her sister couldn't part with the dog collars after all the trouble they'd caused her was not something she'd ever understand. Why had she worn them religiously since that day at Walmart? What could they possible represent for her? These were all things she knew she'd never talk to Bobby-Leigh about. Things she would never understand. She almost suggested taking them off, but knew better. Besides, she actually didn't look that bad. Bobby-Leigh was just like her sister; she looked good in just about anything, spiked dog collar chokers and pastel yoga shirt and pants included (well, almost). But looking good and feeling good about how you look are two very different things.

"You're like a ray of sunshine on a dark and stormy morning."

"Fuck that."

Jen laughed again. Bobby-Leigh didn't want to smile, but she couldn't help it. Her sister's laugh was infectious. It took her a few seconds to get her familiar scowl back in place. With the exception of the raven-black dye job that still held fast among the streaks of her stubborn natural red hair and the ever-present spiked dog collar chokers, the little girl's entire identity had been washed away in the hot water of the shower, which, for as good as it felt after everything they'd been though, was not much of a consolation to her.

Who the fuck is this girl looking back at me? she thought as she eyed her reflection in the bathroom mirror from her position seated on one of the beds.

The yoga pants, rolled up at the hems because they were too big, and the organic cotton long-sleeved yoga shirt burned her pride like holy water. *Jesus Christ.* She couldn't imagine a more inappropriate outfit. Her painstakingly cultivated Lolita-goth stylings were just not something folks who stayed at Ayurveda health spas like the Raj wore. And even though she knew the priority had been to just get her naked body covered again, she still felt ridiculous and vulnerable.

I'd almost rather just be naked, she thought, but that wasn't true.

"I wish I at least had my makeup. I mean, shitballs, there has to be makeup here somewhere, right? She could have at least brought me some lipstick and eyeliner."

"Beverly doesn't even wear clothes anymore, you think she's thinking about makeup? She doesn't give two shits about that stuff, dude. We're lucky to have anything more than those stupid robes to put on."

"Whatever, you look good in anything and never cared about clothes anyway."

Jennifer was wearing almost the exact same outfit as her sister, except for the collars around her neck. The torn, soiled, and dirty clothing they'd arrived in was in a pile in the corner of the room.

Bobby-Leigh was right, of course. Jen didn't care at all about how the clothes looked on her. All she cared about was that she was able to find a place to secretly strap the remaining karambit blade to her body and that the shirt and pants were loose enough to not restrict her movement. *It's probably healthy for Bobby-Leigh to take a break from the emo goth thing for a day or two anyway,* she thought to herself. *Nobody's identity should be that wrapped up in what they wear.*

"Do we have a plan for when Brennachecke comes?" Bobby-Leigh asked, already knowing the answer was no.

Before her big sister could confirm it, though, the sound of automatic weapons being fired came blasting through the hallway of the Raj. Immediately, both Jennifer and Bobby-Leigh knew exactly what to do. They didn't need to talk about it. They didn't need to prepare for it. Although neither of them had ever heard a gunfight before, to say nothing of one with automatic weapons, they had no misconceptions about what the sounds were or what they meant: It was time to go. Time to take advantage of the confusion and get the fuck out of Dodge before they had to deal with Brennachecke, or something worse.

"Shoes," Jen said.

Bobby-Leigh was already moving off the bed toward the pile of dirty laundry before her sister had even opened her mouth. She tossed Jen's bloodstained sneakers out of the pile to her sister and slipped on her own Mary Janes, hating how the filthy shoes clashed with her new ensemble almost as much as how it clashed with the dog collars, or more accurately how her new ensemble clashed with the dog collars her filthy (but perfect) shoes. As they huddled at the door, Bobby-Leigh suddenly ran back and grabbed their robes as well. They'd need all the layers they could get for the weather outside.

Somebody screamed. A man, but not Brennachecke. Both girls knew he was not the kind of man who screamed. Jen wondered whether their surrogate father was even in the building. Maybe they'd manage to slip away without ever seeing him again. But somehow she knew in her heart that was not how this was going to play out.

Bam-bam. Bam. More gunfire erupted.

A stray bullet suddenly ripped through the wall and lodged itself in the headboard of the bed Bobby-Leigh had been sitting on only minutes ago. Both girls flinched.

The adrenaline floodgates opened, and Jen felt the demon inside her stir, its crazed, bloodthirsty eyes fluttering and half-open. Effortlessly she switched that inner lens of her experience to autofocus and adjusted the depth of field, muting the world around her. As the now familiar detachment spread out from her mind, she felt the demon's eyes close as the beast within once again settled into oblivious slumber.

Bobby-Leigh looked at her sister, dreading what she might see looking back at her, but she had nothing to fear. Somehow in the craziness of the day, Jen had tamed the beast inside her. She smiled, and even though bullets were flying all around them, she felt safe for the first time in as long as she could remember.

Tears of relief filled her eyes.

Jennifer misinterpreted them. "I'm okay, dude."

"I know," Bobby-Leigh said and smiled, wiping tears from her eyes.

The two sisters shared a look and suddenly transcended time and space, transcended the very fabric of the universe itself. Their look connected them together beyond their shared hereditary biology, beyond their mutual familial love, even beyond the glimpses of pure and absolute consciousness they'd occasionally felt during meditation. For a single ephemeral moment, they experienced the fundamental truth at the core of all existence. Reflected in the other's eyes, Jennifer and

Bobby-Leigh saw how all things are one and nothing at the same time.

But the human mind is simply incapable of reconciling the ramifications inherent in that true singularity, and so as quickly and profoundly as it had come to them, the moment broke apart. Reality came crashing back in, and the universe was broken into an infinite number of individual pieces again. Folks experience moments of enlightenment like this all the time, but rarely remember them beyond the warm, confident afterglow they leave in their wake. The Kessler sisters were no different. Within fractions of a millisecond from the time their shared transcendental experience began, thoughts surfaced again and broke it apart.

Jimmy was dead.

Brennachecke was after them.

Beverly had saved them.

The Raj was being torn apart by gunfire.

They needed to get out.

They needed to get out now.

They needed to get out right now.

Jen put one of her hands on the doorknob. Then, thinking for a second before pulling it open, she popped the karambit knife from its hiding place against the small of her back and tossed it to her sister. There was no back and forth about who should have the knife.

"One . . . two . . ." Jen said, as Bobby-Leigh flicked the blade open and gritted her teeth in a determined snarl.

"Three!"

Jen whipped the door open.

* * *

Beverly didn't have any idea why Dan had just shot Brennachecke with an arrow. She'd thought they were on the same team. And even if they weren't, she couldn't imagine a scenario where the goody-goody old man could have done something to deserve wrath like that from a normal person.

Bam-bam-bam.

The sound of gunshots vibrated through the air as the guards opened fire with their automatic weapons. Beverly took a stray bullet in the calf and fell to her knees. She felt no pain. In fact, she didn't realize she'd been hit until she looked down and saw the blood oozing out of the wound.

"What the fuck are you shooting at!" she screamed as she watched Brennachecke, with the end of Dan's arrow sticking out of his back, turn and launch himself like a linebacker into the guard closest to him, bringing the surprised man to the ground. The old soldier came up with the man's AR-15 and the man himself didn't come up at all.

Dan stepped forward and nocked another arrow. Brennachecke shot him in the gut just as the missile was released. The arrow zipped past Brennachecke's head, taking a chunk of his ear with it.

The old soldier didn't even flinch. Beverly really wished she knew what the beef was between her ex and the old man, but being clueless didn't stop her from enjoying the face-off between the two. She looked at the MIC to see if he was enjoying this as much as she was, but the man was all glassy eyed and pale with fear. *What a disappointing sorry sack of shit,* she thought, as one of the three remaining guards turned his weapon on the fallen archer. Fractions of a second before the guard put bullets in the man who'd almost killed Brennachecke with his fucking arrows, the old soldier inexplicitly shot the pirate in the head and saved Dan's life.

What the fuck? Beverly thought, but her attention was suddenly taken by the sound of the Man-in-Charge's screaming. For a second all eyes turned to the MIC as he ripped the IV line out of his arm and fled the room like a scared little girl.

What the fuck?! Beverly thought for the second time, as bullets started to fly from the two remaining guards.

Bam-bam-bam. Bam.

Bam. Bam. Bam-bam-bam.

She dropped all the way down to the floor as the projectiles smashed into the walls all around her, but missed Brennachecke completely.

"What the fuck are you idiots shooting at!" she repeated. But before either of her men could answer, Brennachecke cut them down. For a second, Beverly thought he was going to murder her too, but he didn't.

"Take me to the Kessler girls," the old soldier with the arrow through his chest said to the Blood Queen.

Beverly smiled, but before she could respond, Dan pierced her heart with an arrow. Brennachecke turned, mechanically raised his gun on Dan, and fired a slug into the man's chest.

"Fucking . . . hypocrite . . ." were the last words Dan ever spoke. Brennachecke was sorry about that, but his grief and pity was quickly compartmentalized. Dan was a loss, but the mission continued. One glance at Beverly was all he needed to know she was dead and he'd have to find the girls himself. Wincing as he moved, really feeling the arrow in him now that the adrenaline of the gunfight was subsiding, he opened the bullet-riddled library doors and headed into the hall.

The Man-in-Charge—recovered from his cowardly instincts, armed with a combat shotgun, and backed up by a dozen men—was waiting for him. Nobody spoke. There were no demands that Brennachecke put his weapon down. There were no questions about whether or not Beverly lived.

The MIC smiled a gleeful smile.

There was no deal to be made anymore. Brennachecke would teach them to fly or he would die where he stood. Neither one of them had to say this out loud. The only real question was what would happen once he'd trained enough of the pirates as pilots.

But it really wasn't a question, was it? The old soldier laughed to himself. He was dead either way in the end, so there was no way he was going to teach these degenerates how to fly. This too went totally understood between him and the MIC without either one of them speaking a word.

The old soldier slowly brought his weapon to bear on the Man-in-Charge and mentally prepared himself for death.

"Brennachecke?" the MIC asked, stunned the man would choose death at this point in the game.

* * *

The Kessler girls opened the door to their room expecting to be confronted immediately by armed men, but instead found just over a dozen of them standing with their backs to them, completely preoccupied by whatever was happening down the hall.

Bam!

The single gunshot after such a pregnant silence made everybody, the sisters included, jump. Then suddenly somebody stumbled out of the library and into the hallway. The dozen or so men with their backs to the girls raised their weapons as though they were all arms of the same organism, but nobody fired.

The moment stretched out. The girls were not sure what to do. If nobody turned around, they could get to the emergency stairs at the end of the hall and get out without anybody being the wiser, but that was a *big* if. Still, it was a better option than just turning back to their room and trapping themselves inside. So, as the silent standoff went on behind them, they softly slinked down the hall one secretive step after another. Jen had her hand on the stairwell door when suddenly one of the men spoke. His words fell out of his mouth the way a man would say the name of a dog he knew was about to snatch food from the table, right in front of his eyes.

"Brennachecke?"

Fuck. Jen turned and looked back. *Fuck. Fuck. Fuck.*

Bobby-Leigh read her sister's mind—well, not really, not in any kind of mystical sense, but in the way all sisters who are close do—and swallowed, unable to believe that Jen was even thinking about doing what she was thinking about doing.

"No fucking way," she whispered. "Let him die."

"I can't," Jen whispered back.

"You have to," Bobby-Leigh pleaded. "There's nothing you can do."

Jen smiled.

"No," Bobby-Leigh said, the blood draining from her face as she realized what her big sister was about to do.

"Wait in the stairwell for it to be over."

"Jen!" Bobby-Leigh hissed, but it was too late. Her older sister was already turning away and running down the hall toward the small army of men who were seconds away from killing the man who had every intention of murdering her. In her head, Jen grabbed the mental image of the lens and switched off the autofocus control she had thus far so successfully used to keep the berserker inside subdued.

A heartbeat later the monster awoke.

Chapter Ten

The Old Man Staring into the Abyss

BRENNACHECKE DIDN'T HAVE mixed feelings about dying. He was tired. Too many people he loved had died. Eric was more than capable of carrying on without him. He probably should have told him more often that he was proud of the man he'd become, but he had told him, and more importantly he'd shown him. At least, he was pretty sure he had. Eric knows, he thought. He has to know. Leaving his only remaining son was pretty much the only thing that would hurt. Not the impending hail of bullets. He knew he wouldn't feel those.

Leaving Jimmy's death unavenged stung his ego a little, but in Brennachecke's mind, the universe's scales would be equally balanced with the weight of his soul in lieu of Jennifer's, maybe even more so. At the end of the day, he was responsible for his son. Jen may have been the weapon that killed him, but as far as Brennachecke was concerned he had allowed the boy to play with that weapon unsupervised. He was all too aware of the potential dangers that came with allowing the boy to spend so much time with Jen. Dangers that were significantly worse than the girl's potty mouth. A berserker could be lying in wait inside anybody. *Anybody.* Jen was just a kid, and obviously both Kessler girls had known Jen had the demon inside her, but he could hardly blame them for not wanting to tell anybody. He didn't understand the biological mechanics of how the whole berserking thing worked. He didn't know what triggered it. He didn't know what, if anything, could stop the demon or whatever it was from taking over and destroying all it touched. In light of that, it was hard to really be angry at the girl. But you didn't need to be angry to hold a person responsible for the consequences of something they did. It was complicated.

The old soldier felt his son's death was on his own shoulders as much as anybody else's. But, on some level, he knew it was all just a part of an impossibly complicated cosmic equation that for reasons he'd never understand had needed Jen to take his son's life before it could be solved. The universe wasn't malicious. Brutal and cruel at times, sure, but never malevolent, and in turn he'd never had malice in his heart for the girl. Years of violence before and after Fairfield went dark had numbed him to the point that very little emotion made it through anymore, and malice was a hard emotion to maintain. It had to be nurtured and fed regularly or it would shrivel up and die.

As his mind danced with these thoughts, the coldly efficient automation that was now a part of his body moved of its own accord. The AR-15 he'd just killed his friend Dan Patterson with swung up in his hands. That murder, which was done more or less in self-defense, Brennachecke had not had time to process yet. Its aftermath was hanging just out of reach of his consciousness like a sword on a string. And as he pulled the trigger and bullets popped out of the submachine gun, it seemed pretty unlikely that he'd ever get a chance to process it.

Bam!

The Man-in-Charge took the first bullet, but the arrow piercing Brennachecke's chest threw off the effectiveness of his aim, and the wound was only superficial.

Bam!

Bam-bam!

The two pirates to the MIC's right were not so lucky and died before their bodies hit the ground.

The others returned fire and Brennachecke instinctively dodged left, evading the shots, but the move put him on his side and he felt the arrow tear at his chest in a way that set alarm bells off somewhere deep inside. Thankfully, he was pretty sure he'd be shot to death long before whatever had just torn inside him had a chance to turn into a life-threatening development. As his body gave out and toppled to the ground, trapping his gun underneath his own weight, he knew this was it.

Bam!

The shot took a sizable chunk out of the wall. A couple inches to the right and the chunk would have been out of his head. Close, but a miss. Brennachecke was surprised to find himself more than a little frustrated by the ineptitude of the adversaries who were going to lay claim to his life. The only thing more pathetic than not being able to put a bullet in a man's head when he's prone on the floor, stuck through and through with an arrow, and less than fifteen feet away was *being* the man who was prone on the floor, stuck through with the arrow, and waiting for a bunch of brute idiots who couldn't hit the side of a barn, much less his incapacitated bulk, to finish him off.

"Do *not* kill that motherfucker!" the Man-in-Charge shrieked from where he was lying, bleeding, on the floor. "He gots work to do!"

As his pirates started to lower their weapons in compliance with his orders, the MIC caught a glimpse of Jen out of the corner of his eye just as she reached them. He almost managed to get out the word *what*, before all hell broke loose.

* * *

With each contact her feet made against the floor as she ran toward the armed men, Jennifer Kessler felt the undertow of the fugue state that blocked out all her senses, pulling her deeper and deeper into its murky blackness. She heard Brennachecke fire his weapon, but the sound was muffled and faraway. Her vision was so clouded she couldn't even make out individuals anymore; everything was just a single fuzzy shifting mass of light, colors, and dark. In her mind's eye, she reached for the lens and tried to adjust the aperture to let more information in, but the ring was stiff and hard to move. Her success at keeping the demon asleep by controlling the focus of her experience didn't seem to work nearly as well when her and the monster's roles were in reverse.

Bobby-Leigh was out of sight, and thus out of Jen's berserker mind (or what mind existed in the berserk state anyway). *So . . . my sister . . . is . . . safe*, she thought, feeling the fugue digging its fingernails into her and dragging her further and further down. She tried to grasp the mental image of the lens for one last desperate attempt at making an adjustment, but it was too late. As she saw herself reaching for it, it was suddenly just gone. Then, a split second later, so was she.

* * *

The pirates had a lot of experience with berserkers, but their experience almost universally came from situations where they were in control. Like duck and deer hunters of old, they'd sit in their blinds and reap the advantages of surprise and superior technology, only picking their prey off when circumstances were most favorable to them. A loose berserker catching them by surprise was outside of their realm of expertise. Armed and used to dictating the terms of engagement, the pirates attempted to fight back, but failed spectacularly.

Jen tore into them. Grabbing the first body she came into contact with—a seasoned felon who had earned his vicious and violent death many times over—she twisted and yanked so savagely at his arm that she tore it off at the shoulder. As he screamed in shock and sprayed blood all over the walls, she used the dismembered arm as a flesh-and-blood club to beat the two men standing nearest to her to death. Her impossible strength and savagery was only surpassed by her speed and agility.

Bam!

One of the pirates got a shot off, but true to Brennachecke's assessment of the blood pirates in general, his aim was wild. His AR-15 was shoved through his eye for his trouble, splitting his head in half.

The Man-in-Charge's cowardly true nature is what saved him in the end. He squeezed his eyes shut and lay frozen in fear, pressed so tightly against the floor and the adjoining wall that berserker Jen didn't even know he was there. The rest of his men were not so predisposed to playing dead, which was really the only effective strategy for dealing with a berserker under the circumstances, so they continued to die for real.

The demon wearing Jennifier Kessler's skin leaped onto one man's back and kicked off of him, sending him stumbling down and allowing her to launch herself into the air. She landed on the head of another man who was trying to get up, her knee crushing his face and breaking his jaw. Reaching down between her legs and into the mess that used to be his mouth and nose, she grabbed his head and twisted, snapping his neck.

A heartbeat later, she bit into a new adversary's forearm as she absorbed the punch he'd tried to land. She tore a chunk out of it before grabbing his other arm and leaping over him, catapulting his body like a rag doll into the wall.

Jen moved so fast that blood sprayed off her like water off a wet dog. A head was snapped back so hard it was almost torn completely off. Two skulls were crushed against each other, sending brains and viscera all over the scrambling remaining men.

Bam! Bam-bam-bam!
Bam! Bam-bam!

As effective a weapon as an AR-15 was, in close quarters it was easier to use it as a club than as a machine gun. As two more men were torn apart and not a single bullet found its way into the intended target, this fact became painfully apparent, but the two remaining pirates didn't bother trying to use the guns that way—they just turned and ran as fast as they could for the main stairs, almost tripping over Brennachecke as they fled.

Berserker Jen didn't pursue the runners. Her attention was drawn to the man with the arrow stuck through him as he desperately tried to drag himself out of harm's way. Panting heavily and quickly losing steam now that nobody was actively trying to hurt her, she dropped to a squat and snarled at Brennachecke, then grabbed him, whipped him up like he was made of paper, and pinned him to the wall.

The old soldier didn't move, he just met her eyes and looked deep into the abyss behind her green-rimmed, extremely dilated pupils. He saw the reflection of his own face staring back, but nothing more. No recognition. No consciousness. Not even rage. And certainly not Jen. Just emptiness.

A second passed.

Then another.

Jen's breathing was now becoming painfully labored. Her whole body was heaving. Her muscles, taunt with overexertion, twitched and spasmed, the way a horse's skin does when it's trying to shake off flies. She took one last deep breath in and used it to scream. Then she dropped to her knees, leaving the old soldier to half slide, half fall off the wall and land beside her. In a last burst of violence, berserker Jen put two holes in the wall with her fists where Brennachecke had been only moments ago, and then tore angrily at the drywall until she collapsed from exhaustion in the blood-soaked hall of horrors.

Movement at the far end of the hall caught Brennachecke's attention out of the corner of his eye, and he looked up from Jen's blood-covered unconscious form to see a little girl slowly approaching.

"Six one-thousand. Seven one-thousand. Eight one-thousand . . ."

Suddenly, he realized the little girl was Bobby-Leigh, just without her usual makeup and costume—though he did notice, to his dismay, that she still had the dog collars on. It'd been so long since he'd seen her look like a little girl that it somehow now felt inappropriate, like watching her shower or undress herself.

"Eleven one-thousand."

"Why are you counting?" he asked.

Bobby-Leigh put her finger to her lips to tell him to shut the fuck up.

He got the message.

Once she'd gotten through the requisite count to sixty, she dropped to her knees beside her sister and started trying to bring her around. Brennachecke watched and bled in silence on the floor as patiently as he could.

"Why the counting?"

"They're not always really out when they first collapse in exhaustion. You want to make sure they're really down and the person inside is coming back before you . . . get too close."

The old soldier nodded.

"She's going to be really hungry when she wakes up. Any ideas on a safe place we can find some serious calories?"

"There's a kitchen downstairs, but I wouldn't call it a safe place."

"Fuck."

"Language, missy."

"Are you being serious?"

Brennachecke smiled. He *was* being serious, but he'd let it go for once, at least for a while. Jen's eyes opened and she quickly took in the damage she'd caused and that Brennachecke had survived. Tears welled up almost instantly as she met his tired old gaze. She opened her mouth to say something, but ended up coughing instead. Jen hacked and hacked until two of her back teeth came up from where they'd slipped down her throat. She spit them into her hands and looked at them, disgusted, then back to the father figure who had spent the last three days hell-bent on killing her. The teeth dropped out of her hands as she raised them to cover her face as she sobbed.

"I'm sorry," she managed to get out between her tears. "I didn't . . ." She tried to continue, but there wasn't really anything she could say. She was exhausted. Her whole body ached from extreme exertion. Her stomach growled long and loud. She met Brennachecke's eyes again and smiled the most pathetic, humiliated, and miserable smile the old man had ever seen.

Then suddenly, to everybody's surprise, Jen's hands wrapped around one of the blood-covered AR-15s strewn about with the bodies, and she tossed it to Brennachecke.

"I can't bring him back, so . . . I know you need to balance the scales, or whatever."

Brennachecke picked up the assault weapon she'd tossed to him and used it as a crutch to get himself painfully up onto his feet. Bobby-Leigh's eyes widened, but before she could protest, the old man spoke.

"You just balanced the scales, sweetheart. That monster inside you that took . . . Jimmy away . . ." It was hard for him to speak, but he knew she needed to hear the absolution in its entirety, so he choked on. "You saved my life. You didn't have to, but you did. My life for my son's balances things just as well as yours would."

"Really?"

"Yeah."

"Plus there is the fact that I'd have to fucking kill you—with my bare hands, if it came to that—if you ever actually tried to hurt her," Bobby-Leigh said. She was not joking, but all three of them laughed just the same.

"What can we do for you?" Jen asked.

"Nothing, until we get to a safe place."

Jen's stomach growled again even louder than it had before. She closed her eyes and looked like she might faint.

"I need to eat. I'm sorry . . ."

"Restaurant is on the lower level."

"This place is going to be crawling with dudes any minute. I don't think we're going to have time to get—"

"I'll go. You stay here and play dead if anybody comes," Bobby-Leigh said.

"That's never going to—" Jen started to say, but then changed her mind. They didn't have much of a viable alternative.

"You'd be surprised how effective a survival strategy playing dead is," the little girl said quietly, the fact that she knew this from personal experience painfully evident in her tone. Then before anybody could say or do anything else, she jumped to her feet, grabbed an AR-15 in each hand, and ran for the stairwell.

Neither Jen nor Brennachecke could have stopped her if they wanted to.

* * *

The Raj was eerily quiet now that the majority of the people in it were dead. The lights were off downstairs to conserve what power they had, which was fine by her, but it slowed her down. The distance between the second-floor hall and the lower-floor dining area, which would have taken thirty seconds during the day under normal conditions to traverse, took her almost two minutes to get through. As she moved through the darkness as quickly as she dared, she realized she wasn't even sure if she knew how to fire the guns in her hands. Was it as simple as just pointing the barrel and pulling the trigger? Or was there a safety or something she had to switch off first?

Fuck.

As she arrived at the dining area of the restaurant, she was grateful for the light coming through rows of windows all along the outer walls. The snow, it seemed, had stopped. The moon was out, and it was full, or close to it. But when she pushed through the swinging doors to the kitchen, which had no windows, that wonderfully soft blue light was simply gone. She couldn't see six inches in front of her face. She groped along the wall for a light switch, but found nothing.

Double fuck.

She thought about firing one of the guns to see if the muzzle flash would reveal anything (and just to make sure they were really that easy to use) but that would surely draw attention to herself. Groaning softly, she turned around toward the dining room to see if she could find matches or something at a host station, but a sound froze her in place.

Clank!

Her mind raced to place the familiar sound in context. The results came in fast: Metal. Lightweight. A can. Being set down. Quietly. Somebody was in the kitchen with her.

Fuckity-fuck fuck.

But whoever was in there with her didn't seem to want to be discovered, so maybe that meant they weren't a threat. Or maybe that meant they were even more of one. *Double fuckity-fuck fuck.* She just didn't know.

Again she groped for the light switch.

Again she came up empty-handed.

Pitter-pat. Pitter-pat.

Feet. Small. Maybe barefoot. A child. It had to be a child. Relief flooded through her, as she felt the adrenaline drain away—no part of her ever considering that she too was a child, that she had killed more than once in her life, and that she was more than prepared to do it again.

"I'm not going to hurt you," she said quietly, still feeling for the light switch.

Squeak. Thump! Pitter-patter.

Pitter-patter.

She wondered, trying to place the sounds in the totally black and unfamiliar environment with little success, if maybe there was more than one child with her in the dark kitchen space. The hairs on the back of her neck slowly stood up as a chill found its way up her spine.

Why are there kids in the kitchen in the dark?

Why are there kids (free ones, anyway) in Vedic City at all?

Thump! Tee-he-he!

The childish giggle sounded wet against the tiled kitchen, and worse, it didn't sound like it was coming from the same place as the other sounds were.

"I'm not going to hurt you!" Bobby-Leigh repeated, this time plenty loud enough to be heard. "I just need to get food for my sister."

"I not gonna 'urt ya!" a high voice answered her from the dark, followed by a round of laughter that was picked up first by one, then another, then another, and then another voice.

"Na' gonna 'urt ya!" the children in the dark chanted. Bobby-Leigh wasn't sure they understood what they were saying, much less what she was. Then all of a sudden, the chanting just stopped. It was so abruptly cut off that it almost seemed like a switch had been thrown.

Where the fuck is that light switch!

No sooner than she had thought the question did she find the answer. It was right where it should have been the whole time. *How did I miss it?* she wondered as her fingers closed over the protruding plastic nub and flipped it up.

Blinding white light filled the space instantly. Bobby-Leigh winced and squeezed her eyes shut against it, but she wasn't the only one. Eight kids between the ages of four and twelve responded the same way, and then scurried like cockroaches for cover. They were dirty and all seemed to have never had a haircut in their lives. Bobby-Leigh couldn't tell if they were boys or girls. Several of them had sores from what she thought must be malnourishment, judging by how sickly thin they all were. Cuts and bruises and other signs of physical abuse also covered their bodies. But their eyes were huge and bright. Mongrel, almost feral, children born of rape and sexual assault, but still loved by their mothers and kept alive (if barely) in secret.

One raised its hand and waved. It was a girl, probably, but no one would be able to tell for sure without checking, and Bobby-Leigh wasn't about to do that. She was smaller than most of the others. Not more innocent, but somehow softer. More fragile.

"I'm not going to hurt you," Bobby-Leigh repeated for a third time as she returned the wave.

"Na' gonna 'urt ya!" the children chanted back as one.

She moved forward deeper into the kitchen, and the secret children shrank back like the abused animals they were. Moving slowly, looking them in the eye one at a time as she did so, Bobby-Leigh gave each of them a smile. She saw the metal can she'd heard in the dark. It was on the floor, next to a prep station. Enchilada sauce, licked clean. Bobby-Leigh couldn't imagine that anybody at the Raj had ever made enchiladas while it was still operating as an Ayurveda health spa, which was a good sign. It meant the pirates were keeping the place stocked. She spotted the boy who must have been eating the sauce. She knew it was a boy because he held his penis in his hand like a security blanket through his pants, and she knew he was the one who had been eating the sauce because it ringed his mouth and covered one of his hands.

"Good?" she asked him with a smile.

He didn't answer.

She wondered if these kids even knew what they were eating, but guessed they probably didn't because they'd bashed open and eaten a can of enchilada sauce instead of one of the four family-sized jars of Jif peanut butter that were in plain sight on a shelf behind them, which would have been a significantly better food choice both on a nutritional level and just a plain taste level. Moving fast, she grabbed two of the jars of peanut butter, opened one, and tossed it to the biggest of the kids. He was probably a boy, she thought, but she really couldn't tell. The boy caught the jar with surprisingly quick and steady hands. He looked at it, then looked at her, then set it on the table next to him with a frown.

"It's good," Bobby-Leigh said encouragingly.

"No!" the kid yelled.

Whatever, Bobby-Leigh thought. She didn't have time for this shit. Tucking the other big jar under her arm, she turned to go.

"NO!" the big kid yelled again.

She felt a small hand close around her wrist and looked down to see the little girl who had waved at her.

"No," she whimpered.

"No what?" Bobby-Leigh asked as she pulled her hand free. Instinctive alarm bells had started ringing in her head.

"No!" another kid said sharply.

"No!" said another. Then another.

A boy's hand closed on her arm. "No," he told her, like she was a dog that had just tried to snatch a hot dog off the table at a family picnic. Suddenly, another hand from another kid reached in and actually tried to pull the jar of Jif from her hands. *Fuck, these little kids are strong,* she thought as she twisted and wrenched herself away from them for a second time. Not berserker strong, but significantly stronger than their pint-sized, emaciated bodies suggested.

"No," the big one scolded her again.

The pack of feral kids was slowly moving in and surrounding her, but Bobby-Leigh couldn't understand why. *What's the big deal about the stupid peanut butter anyway?* she almost had time to wonder, before one of the feral kids hit the light switch and plunged the whole room back into darkness.

"Motherfucker," Bobby-Leigh said mostly to herself as she felt a dozen small hands grabbing at her, trying to wrestle the peanut butter out of her arms. One of the AR-15s she'd slung over her shoulder was pulled off. She heard it clatter heavily to the ground, just as she felt a set of tiny teeth sink into her arm. She kicked and twisted and punched. She got a hold of the other AR-15 she had slung over the other shoulder and swung it wildly like a club, cringing at the hollow smack it made as it connected with the tiny bodies of her attackers.

Then suddenly one of the kids wrapped himself around her legs, and Bobby-Leigh went down. As she fell, the peanut butter flew from her hands and rolled toward the kitchen door that led to the restaurant. There was a mad scramble to get it, but Bobby-Leigh wasn't playing around anymore. As the little girl who had waved got her hands on the jar and stood up with it, triumphantly silhouetted by the light in the small window of the swinging door, Bobby-Leigh turned to face her. With her back to the rest of the brood, the little fuckers continued trying to drag her down, though with less zeal and ferocity now that the prize was back in their collective possession.

"Get the fuck off me!"

She managed to shake herself loose from their little grips. Without another thought, Bobby-Leigh pointed the AR-15 toward the little girl holding the jar of Jif and pulled the trigger. Her miss was intentional, but only she knew that.

The magnitude of the muzzle flash and boom from the single exploded shell caught everybody, including Bobby-Leigh, completely off guard. Nobody moved for several seconds. The ringing in their ears felt like it might be the only sound they'd ever hear again, but that fear was short-lived and quickly replaced by more realistic ones as the deafening roar of silence jingle-jangled its way out of their heads.

The little feral girl still held the peanut butter, but her cohorts had backed off into the shadowy pitch of the dark kitchen.

"That's mine," Bobby-Leigh said.

The little feral girl started to sob, but she put the jar of Jif down and took a step away from it.

"No. Peas. No ache," a voice said from the darkness behind her.

Bobby-Leigh thought it probably belonged to the biggest of the kids, the one who had instigated this whole ridiculous battle over a jar of peanut butter *that he didn't even seem to want*. But she couldn't be sure. She didn't understand what he meant, but she didn't care. Picking up the jar of high-calorie fuel, Bobby-Leigh turned and left.

The feral kids didn't follow her out.

They knew the master of the kitchen would notice the peanut butter was missing—it was one of the foods he kept track of, unlike the enchilada sauce. They knew he'd blame them for taking it. They knew punishment was coming. They knew they better hide.

* * *

"Are you sure we shouldn't just pull it out?" Jen asked, still starving even after eating the entire sixty-four ounces of peanut butter (nearly eleven thousand calories' worth) Bobby-Leigh had brought her. She'd not been this hungry last time. Or felt this exhausted. The idea of dragging a wounded dude God knows how many miles to wherever they ended up going made her want to puke. She never thought she'd experience two berserker episodes so close together—it was just over seventy-two hours ago that she'd murdered Jimmy—and she was a little afraid of what she might have done to her body.

"I'm sure. This is fine for now," Brennachecke said.

Bobby-Leigh had wrapped the protruding sides of the arrow with towels to stem the bleeding while her sister had shoveled peanut butter into her mouth. For now it was all that could be done. Pulling the arrow out would open the wound, and opening a wound like his was like opening Pandora's box. It would have to be done eventually, but Brennachecke hoped to be in a safe, preferably sterile, place and in the company of some kind of medical professional when they did it, though he'd settle for any one of the three.

The Kessler girls gathered as many blankets as they could and the threesome moved downstairs expecting to see reinforcements arriving any second, but there didn't seem to be any movement anywhere in the Raj or outside it. The sun would be rising soon, but for now the sandman ruled the white land.

Brennachecke had hoped they'd be able to get their hands on a vehicle of some kind, but as soon as he saw how much snow had fallen during the night he scrapped that idea. Their whole world was buried under nearly a foot and a half of heavy snow. They didn't have the kind of time it would take to find a four-wheel-drive vehicle that would be able to drive through it, though he was sure the pirates had at least one or two trucks, plus tractors, that would be able to traverse it. And that meant they were not going to be pursued by men on foot. They needed to get a solid head start before the place woke up and somebody decided to come after them.

At least they can't fly yet, Brennachecke thought to himself with a dry laugh that turned into a hacking cough, drawing a concerned look from both of the Kessler girls.

"Where do we go?" Jen asked, a little disturbed by how much relief she felt not being the one in charge anymore.

"To your uncle's."

"Good fucking luck. That's been our plan this whole time." Bobby-Leigh laughed.

"Language, missy."

"Sorry," Bobby-Leigh too was glad to have Brennachecke back in charge. Even though the man was severely wounded and pretty much useless in a fight at the moment, she still felt protected just being around him. It was a feeling she hadn't thought she'd feel again, and the weight of her relief was almost crushing. Fighting back tears, she helped her sister bundle their surrogate father up in stolen blankets and do what they could to keep him warm.

"Why is nobody coming after us?" Bobby-Leigh whispered to her sister. She could have asked Brennachecke, but she didn't really want to know what the answer was, and something told her the old man might actually know.

"I don't know," Jen said. "I'm sure they will be soon enough."

Meanwhile, Brennachecke was using all his strength to appear better off than he felt, and fighting the pain was so distracting that he didn't hear the question or the answer. But if he had, he wouldn't have had anything better to say that Jen did, though he might have added something along the lines of it being a wise idea not to look a gift horse in the mouth.

With a girl under each arm to shoulder his weight, the trio took their first steps through the deep snow toward a lightening sky in the east.

* * *

They only had a little over five miles to go, but the going was slow. It took them almost an hour just to get out of sight of the Raj. In that hour the sun had risen and suddenly seemed to have remembered that it wasn't supposed to be winter. The temperature quickly rose from below freezing into the fifties, but that good news was a double-edged sword. The melting snow had started soaking them from the bottom up and running them through with cold. The girls were wrapped in blankets, just like Brennachecke, but all of their shoes were totally inadequate for this kind of adventure. To make matters worse, the old man seemed to be getting heavier and heavier with each step. He was clearly more hurt than he was letting on.

"My feet are fucking freezing off, dude," Jen said to Bobby-Leigh. "I think I'm getting frostbite."

"Me too."

Brennachecke said nothing. It was all the man could do to put one foot in front of the other at this point. He barely even heard the girls talking, but if he had been able to focus on anything outside of the burning in his chest, he'd have only agreed with them. His feet were numb with cold too.

The temperature hung in the sixties like a vulture once it got there—still cool for a July morning in Iowa by any kind of normal standards, but nonetheless a significant improvement over the day before when the freak snowstorm had begun. They didn't really need the blankets they were all wrapped in, except that somehow being too hot up top seemed to balance out their feet being so cold below. Jen and Bobby-Leigh were both annoyed by the fact that the melting snow didn't actually make things any easier for them. Had the weather stayed cold, the snow would have just fallen off their feet like dust without turning instantly to ice water against their skin. The idea of getting frostbite on their feet while they sweat through their shirts was so utterly ridiculous that the only thing that kept them from howling with laughter was that it was a real possibility, and that nothing really felt funny carrying Brennachecke through the snow like they were.

"We need to stop, get our feet dry," Jen said, gesturing toward an abandoned decrepit farmhouse off to the right with a tired-looking wooden swing hanging off an ancient white oak.

"Okay."

The door was already broken in when they got there. A half-eaten long-dead body, the sex of which could no longer be easily determined, lay nearly mummified in the kitchen. The house had been ransacked at least once, but even at first glance seemed like it may not have been cleaned out completely. It was a good place to stop and catch their breath and warm their feet.

The girls put Brennachecke in the living room on a torn old love seat and stripped off their wet shoes and socks. Barefoot they set about searching the house for food and better things to wear. Bobby-Leigh found a hatchet in the kitchen, where somebody had been chopping the cabinetry up for firewood. She picked it up with a nostalgic smile. Then she went upstairs, where she discovered the family that had ounce lived there had had a girl her age. When she saw what was in the girl's closet, she burst out in a laugh that carried all the way down the stairs to Brennachecke, who, even in the fog of his pain and discomfort, couldn't help but smile.

Jen for her part found a box of winter clothes in the basement that had a plethora of snow boots, wool socks, pants, and jackets. The boots were all either too big or too small to fit her comfortably, but given a choice between blisters and frostbite, she'd go for blisters every day of the week and twice on Sunday. She was about to drag the box upstairs when her eye fell on something in the shadows in the back of the damp room. A sled.

"Motherfucking jackpot, dude!" she said quietly to herself, thinking they could drag Brennachecke and maybe even some supplies in it. That was going to make things so much easier! She hauled her load upstairs with a smile and continued on with the search. There were some cans of garbanzo beans and pumpkin pie filling still in the back of one of the cupboards in the kitchen. She even found a can opener.

"Gun!" Bobby-Leigh screamed, excited. They still had one of the pirate AR-15s with them, of course, but more firepower was always a good thing. Jen smiled at Brennachecke, who tried to smile back but only ended up snarling.

"How you doing?" she asked him, painfully aware of how stupid the question was.

"Still . . . alive," he croaked.

"Let's go! Bobby-Leigh!" she yelled up the stairs.

Bobby-Leigh came down a changed girl. In the ten minutes she'd been upstairs, she'd found a Maharishi School of the Age of Enlightenment (the primary and secondary school attached to MUM) plaid uniform skirt. She'd folded it up at the top, making it scandalously short. She'd then added a girl's dress shirt that was too small in a perfect way and a plaid tie, which she wore just under her ever-present dog collars. Then she'd gone to the bathroom and rimmed her eyes with heavy eyeliner and thick mascara. Blood-red lipstick now lined her mouth. Her red-streaked raven-black hair was now up in pigtails, Pippi Longstocking style. Her legs were clad in knee-high stockings, and her feet were blessed with the pièce de résistance—a pair of neon-blue Doc Martins. Her Lolita-goth image was restored and her confidence had clearly been restored with it. As she pranced down the stairs, she held a huge nickel-plated Colt .45 in one hand and carried three boxes of ammo and her new ax pressed against her chest with the other.

"Holy shit, dude!" Jen squealed.

"I know, right?"

"Brennachecke is fading pretty fast. We better go. I found a sled, though, so we should have a fucking easier time of it."

"Can I try the swing before we go?"

"What?"

"I want to try the swing." This was the first time, since Walmart at least, that Bobby-Leigh had ever expressed a desire to do a normal kid thing. Jen smiled. Dog collars notwithstanding, maybe her little sister wasn't a lost cause after all.

"Sorry, dude." The words broke her heart to say, but they just didn't have time to waste. By now the blood pirates would be up, and the three of them would be pretty easy to track through the snow. Plus Brennachecke was, like, fucking dying.

"Just five minutes."

Jen shook her head, no.

Bobby-Leigh nodded, her bright smile dampening into a disappointed one. She knew the pirates would probably be coming after them. She knew Brennachecke was literally dying in front of them. This just wasn't a good time to catch up on her childhood innocence. She understood.

Brennachecke grunted and cleared his throat, trying to speak but failing at first. Jen and Bobby-Leigh moved to his side so all he would have to do was whisper if he did manage to get the words out.

"Let her . . . swing," he croaked at last. "Give me . . . the AR-15. Stand . . . watch with the . . . Colt."

"But—" Jen began, then changed her mind and simply nodded to her sister to go ahead. "Five minutes!" she said, and as the next couple hundred seconds passed, Jen stood watch in the snow, Brennachecke bled on the couch, and Bobby-Leigh pumped her legs and transcended it all on the swing.

Chapter Eleven
The Army Marching through the Snow

FROM THE BROKEN balcony doors of the library on the second floor of the Raj, the Man-in-Charge watched the two Kessler twats support his flight instructor as the three of them struggled out through the snow. He stood there in silence, favoring the leg that did not have a bullet in it. The regenerative power of the berserker blood in his system was already working its magic, but he'd need to find the doc anyway just to be safe, because even through the intoxicating fog of berserker blood, he knew the pain from the wound would be intense when he finally felt it. As he stood there alone, the cold morning air rubbing up against him like an annoying cat he'd forgotten to feed, he smiled.

All the kidnapping, rape, and murder, while certainly entertaining to him and the pirates he ruled over, just didn't have any real purpose behind it. Sure, they were harvesting blood, but milking monsters was actually pretty fucking boring once you got them penned. The constant blood high for the most part distracted him from the transient pointlessness of his army's endeavors, but like the missing dull, steady ache that should have been in his leg, he was still aware there was something absent from his experience. Something important.

But now he had a game afoot. A hunt. A mission of reprisal. A reason to get out of bed in the morning. He looked at Beverly's body lying almost naked and grotesquely exposed on the library floor. He looked at the arrow sticking out of her like a flagpole staking Brennachecke's claim on her. He didn't really care that she was dead. But he did care that the old soldier had had the audacity to think he could get away with killing her. It would have made no difference to him at all that Dan had actually been the one who put the arrow into his whore's heart. To the MIC, that man was just an extension of Brennachecke. Likewise, it didn't matter to him that it had been the older of the two bitches who'd slaughtered his men in the hallway. The little cunt was just an extension of the soldier as well. His only interest in Jen was for her blood, and maybe for her body if he was feeling adventurous. He'd fucked a couple of berserkers since he'd taken control of Vedic City, but the amount of preparation and manpower needed to not be hurt in the process took most of the fun out of it. Bragging rights had motivated him, but he'd earned those rights already, so he'd just bleed the bitch, and if he wanted to fuck something he'd just take her little sister instead. He'd be sure to make Brennachecke watch it too, he thought, his cruel smile widening as he finally shut the door against the cold.

He really needed to put a stop to the running and hiding his men did whenever there was a shooting. He'd been alone now for almost an hour, maybe even longer.

He'd have thought the jackals would have been all over the place. Not to help, of course—he knew it wasn't loyalty that kept them here, only fear and greed—but he'd have thought his men would have been aching to confirm his death and begin the infighting over who would take control. Beverly would have already had the whole lot of them under her thumb by now if it had been his body lying on the ground with an arrow to the chest and her with just the superficial bullet wound to the leg. With that thought, he came as close as he'd ever come to mourning her death. Her treacherousness was part of what had made her so attractive to him in the first place. Unpredictable, cruel, vicious, and utterly driven by her desire for power—she'd been like that from day one. It had been seriously fucking hot.

Not that it mattered now.

Not that he really cared about her.

The Man-in-Charge had cowered with his eyes closed under the oozing, dripping, twitching corpses of his men, trying not to make a sound or even breathe, the entire time Jen had tended to Brennachecke's arrow wound and waited for Bobby-Leigh to return with food. He'd heard every word of their reconciliation, their planning—that bitch berserker's pathetic little tears. Stuck there playing dead, not daring for one second to reveal himself until the coast was indisputably clear, he had just waited, willing himself not to move. The lengths he'd have gone to to avoid losing his precious flight instructor were endless in his mind, but actually putting himself in danger was always where he drew the line. So, as he listened to Jennifer's lips smacking as she crammed peanut butter down her cunt throat, he'd made a plan B.

The plan was simple. As soon as they were gone, he'd find Beverly, who was undoubtedly dead—she'd been a fighter, not a pragmatist like him, which had certainly sealed her fate—then he would take her to the doc, run blood lines to her veins, hook her up to a battery, cut her chest open, and manually stimulate her heart until enough of the curative berserker blood circulated through her brain to wake her up. He'd seen the procedure done a number of times while he was still in the army, before he'd gone AWOL and come to Fairfield. His platoon leader used it for *intelligence extraction*. It was super messy, but it had always gotten the interrogator almost five extra minutes with the man in question after he'd been pushed too far and died on them.

But it'd turned out he didn't need to resurrect the whore after all. It didn't matter that she knew where the Kessler farm was. God was smiling on him today. The storm had passed. The snow had stopped. The sky was blue. And Brennachecke's stupid treasonous threesome was now leaving enough tracks behind them in the snow for a blind man to follow.

* * *

Tiny looked at the video screen and wondered how far down he could get the drone before the folks with the sled noticed it. In broad daylight he liked to fly at least eight hundred feet above the ground. The angry wasp-like hum of the little electric motors was almost imperceptible at that altitude. Although, most people these days wouldn't be able to recognize a drone for what it was if they saw one. It'd been years and years since they'd been used commercially or recreationally. The military factions still had some, of course, but those were mostly old Predators and Blackjacks, which were so far beyond what his little JPLs could do specs wise that he always made the distinction of calling them UAVs (unmanned aerial vehicles) and not drones. But just because folks didn't really know they were out there anymore wouldn't stop them from taking a shot at one if they saw it hovering above them. Folks who wasted the time it took to wonder what something was before blowing it to hell had died out pretty fast in the US. Tiny couldn't speak for the rest of the world, but he was pretty sure that nugget was just as true wherever you were.

So why the hell do we always have to risk identifying folks before we do anything? he wondered with his usual level of internal frustration at everything he wasn't directly involved in. With a flick of his finger, he sent the imagery to Anoona and Hamm's glasses.

"I think it's the Kessler girls," he added, and though he spoke the words, the message was sent as text superimposed over the video feed.

"What's the ETA?"

"I can't get close enough to do facial rec, but just look at it. It's got to be them."

"ETA, Tiny."

"I don't know. Whatever's in the sled is heavy and slowing them down. I'd say we have at least thirty before they hit the perimeter. Want me to take it down and confirm?"

"No. Let the perimeter cams do that. Let's bring everybody in and get a welcome party ready."

Tiny took a bite of his Star Crunch patty and sent the alert out over the network. Across the farm, various devices buzzed and chimed. It only took a few minutes for everybody to wrap up what they were doing and gather around Tiny's control station. Eric imagined this was more or less exactly what Anoona's people had done when Tiny's drones had spotted them coming up Mahogany Avenue in the middle of the night, except that then there had been an entire discussion about whether or not Hamm and Rodney should just put bullets in each of their heads. A serious discussion. Eric secretly wished he'd been able to listen in on it.

Anoona's people were nothing but gracious to his people's faces. In fact they'd gone out of their way to make them feel at home, but nothing they could ever say or do would ever change the fact that they'd all stood here, just like he was right now, and made a choice to let them all live. He had no idea why, but it bothered him—a lot. If he could just hear what they'd said and how they'd said it, if he were just able to watch them make the decision, he thought he'd be able to put it behind him. He wasn't sure why he needed to know so badly, but he did have an idea of how he might be able to be the fly on the wall he so wished to be.

"They made it," Eric said.

"It's not confirmed," Tiny responded.

"That's them. Who's in the sled?"

"I think it's your dad."

"Are you recording these video feeds?" Eric asked.

"Yeah, but the archives get recorded over as they fill up the drive," Tiny said, not at all thrown by the non sequitur. Any chance to show off what his tech could do made him happy. Plus he was really excited about being Eric's friend. The kid was spunky and made him laugh.

"How hard is it to get access to the archives?" Eric asked, but before Tiny had a chance to tell him the answer, Anoona and the rest of the folks showed up.

* * *

Jen was so hungry she was shaking, or maybe she was just shaking from fatigue, she couldn't tell anymore. She couldn't understand why each time, the aftermath of berserking out got exponentially harder to physically deal with than the last time. The rapid and massive increase in muscle mass from all the hormone-enhanced exertion that accompanied tearing into people and smashing things apart had seemed like a blessing when it had left her more and more beautifully toned and allowed her to eat anything she ever wanted, twice over. But after this last episode, she was pretty sure she didn't just have a ripped physique anymore. The fact was she was now probably past the point of making an eighties East German Olympic swimmer look scrawny. If the demon got out again, she was pretty sure she'd have to relocate to the land of the freaks, if there was such a place. Plus, there was that little detail of her teeth starting to fall out, which was just fucking creepy.

Can you even get dentures anymore? she wondered absently, as she pulled the sled side by side with her sister, consumed by the arbitrary vain and self-indulgent thoughts of an American teenager that even the end of the world couldn't stop.

The sun reflected off the snow in a blinding glare. An odd, very subtle vaguely mechanical buzzing sound seemed to be drifting down from somewhere above them, but Jennifer wasn't completely sure that the buzz wasn't just in her head. She should have meditated when they'd stopped at that house. Her mind was bouncing all over the place, making her feel crazy.

How long have we been pulling the sled? she wondered without really caring what the answer was because it didn't matter anyway. *Jimmy would have known how long it's been, though,* she thought, but before the now familiar sadness could fill her heart up, she realized Brennachecke had been awfully quiet back there for an awfully long time.

Fuck, she thought. *Did the dude die on us? What the hell should we do if he has? Stop and bury him? No, we're too exposed out here for that. So, what? We just keep pulling a corpse? That's just stupid. Leave him? That's just cruel. Fuck . . . Maybe the blood pirates aren't even coming after us.* But she knew better. Her intuition was screaming at her to keep moving.

"You still alive back there, dude?" she yelled over her shoulder.

Brennachecke didn't answer. Jen and Bobby-Leigh shared a look and waited a second longer for a response, but the only sound was the slushy groan of the snow under the sled and the girls' laboring breath—and that damn mechanical buzzing coming from above.

"I'll check on him," Bobby-Leigh said. Her sister nodded and stopped pulling.

Bobby-Leigh jogged around to the sled and looked at Brennachecke. The man smiled at her but didn't say anything. His smile was sad, as was the one she smiled back with.

"Hang in there, sir," she whispered and, without realizing she'd done it until it was done, kissed him on his cheek.

Brennachecke closed his eyes, so overwhelmed by the amount of emotion the little girl's simple act of affection stirred in him that he just couldn't look at her and keep it together—and he *had* to keep it together, at least for a little while longer, because he simply refused to die without seeing Eric's face one last time and telling him at least some of the things he should have been telling him all along. He took a deep, painful, shuddering breath and opened his eyes again.

Thank you, he mouthed.

Bobby-Leigh winked at him and then looked at her sister, struck by the amount of exhaustion she saw on the young woman's face, and worse, the emotions she could feel behind Jen's absinthe-green eyes.

"He's alive, but he's—"

Bobby-Leigh abruptly stopped talking, her attention suddenly drawn to something in the distance. Jen turned to see what had taken the words from her sister's mouth. When she saw Eric and a bunch of Brennachecke's group emerging onto the road from the snow-covered graveyard of corn with a hairless black woman and two especially well-armed commando types, her knees gave out and she collapsed in the snow.

"Help us!" Bobby-Leigh yelled to them, as she rushed to her sister's side. Jen was okay, at least relatively; it was just exhaustion that had knocked her off her feet.

"Get the Colt," Jen whispered as she sat heavily up in the snow.

"It's Eric and Ace," Bobby-Leigh whispered back as if to say Jen didn't need to worry. "And JP and Cooperman . . ." But it quickly became obvious that Jen was fully aware of who was now rushing toward them and that she still did not find any comfort from it.

"I know who it is." She panted.

Last time she'd seen Eric he'd tried to burn them both to a crisp with a flamethrower, so even if she was ninety percent sure they were not coming to kill her, she was not going to let her guard down. Plus, who knew who the fuck this new black chick was? Her guys seemed to be even better equipped than the blood pirates she was sure were hot on their heels, which could be a blessing, or it could be trouble. She was just too exhausted to think straight anymore, and that meant it was going to be up to Bobby-Leigh to defend them if it did turn out Eric had more of a mind for vengeance than assistance, or if this new set of characters in *The Tragedy of Jennifer Kessler* turned out to be more foe than friend. She had to keep a reserve of strength tucked away for the demon inside her, and that little bit of strength was all she had left. Jen thrust the big handgun into Bobby-Leigh's hands and passed out face-first in the snow.

Even though she knew in her gut that nobody coming out of the corn was going to hurt them, the little girl took the gun from her sister, checked that a round was chambered, and clicked the safety off just the same.

* * *

"I wasn't sure if you'd still be here," Brennachecke croaked. It was not what he wanted to say, but it was what came out of his mouth. He was lying on a twin bed in a make-shift operating theater in one of the back bedrooms of the Kessler house.

Eric nodded but said nothing. Tentatively, the boy reached out and took his father's hand. Physical affection was not a very common occurrence between Brennachecke and either of his sons. When they were young (and still alive, in the case of Jimmy), the old man had never bounced either of the boys on his knee, nor had he read stories with them on his lap. He had never kissed them good night.

There may have been a mechanical awkward hug here and there, but that was about as far as affection went with him. As their hands touched now, Eric was afraid his dad would pull away from him. But Brennachecke didn't pull away. Instead, the father's hand clamped down on his son's with such emotional ferocity that it was Eric who, just as a reflex, almost jerked his hand back. His heart pounding, the boy quickly matched the strength of his father's grip and the last two men of the Brennachecke line found themselves clinging on to each other. It was time to get the arrow out of the old man's chest, and neither of them had any illusions about how dangerous a procedure it was going to be.

Several doctors were on Anoona's recruitment list, but none of them had actually been recruited yet. Tiny had a medical app loaded up on Hamm's glasses that would visually guide him through the procedure, but even with the tech assist, there was no getting around the fact that this was going to be amateur surgery.

To make matters worse, Eric could tell that Hamm was nervous, and the man's anxiety grabbed at both father and son like a desperate, starving child seeking out its mother's breast. And yet, it was obvious even to their untrained eyes that Brennachecke would not survive another day if the wound couldn't be treated. Even then, the old man's odds were probably about the equivalent of catching a king in an ace-high straight at the river, which even beginner poker players knew better than to bet on.

"So, I think we're going to have to restrain you for this, Sergeant," Hamm said as he came in and shut the door behind him carrying a handful of belts. "The only real anesthetic we have at the moment is lidocaine, and while I am certainly going to give you a shot of it on both sides of the wound, this is not the kind of procedure the drug was meant for, so it's still going to hurt like a motherfucker."

"There's no need for that kind of language, Hamm," Eric said, smiling as encouragingly as he could at his father. "My dad kind of has a thing with swearing."

"What'd I say?"

"Never mind." *It was the gesture anyway,* Eric thought. Hopefully his old man would at least appreciate the effort.

"Anoona's bringing in hot water and towels. Rachel, Cooperman, JP, and Ace are all going to assist. Everybody is just washing up and getting the last of the stuff we think we need. We're going to cut the arrow first. It's fiberglass, so we've got to keep it from splintering—I'm going to try to tape the cut point before we do the sawing, which should do the trick. You're going to feel the vibrations of the saw going through the shaft, though, and it'll probably not be particularly pleasant."

Brennachecke nodded. He was ready. This whole walk-through of what they were going to do was a waste of time, as far as he was concerned. He'd never understood why doctors—and reasonable facsimiles of them such as Hamm—did these kinds of procedural step-by-steps in the first place, but in this particular case, it did seem to help with Hamm's own nervousness. So he just let the man talk and tried not to die.

"Tiny is going to be monitoring your vitals from upstairs and he's got me patched into a surgery assistant app that'll be guiding me," Hamm continued.

The words *surgery assistant app* were just about the most terrifying thing Brennachecke had ever heard, but he said nothing. Hamm droned on about the procedure he was about to do and who would be doing what as the room slowly filled up with everybody who had a role to play. JP and Ace carefully strapped their commander down. Rachel stuck him on both sides with the lidocaine. Cooperman taped off the shaft just below the arrowhead with masking tape. Everybody in the room took a collective deep breath.

"You might not want to be here for this," Anoona told Eric gently, but the boy's grip on his father's hand only tightened. "Suit yourself," she said and nodded to Hamm.

Brennachecke didn't scream out once. He barely even struggled against the pain. Years of battle wounds in deserts and mountains on the other side of the world had taught him that the best way to manage pain was not to hold on to it, not to fight it, but to simply allow it to exist. It came in waves, just like his thoughts would back when he was still practicing Transcendental Meditation. As the arrow was pulled from his body, he found his old TM mantra coming to him and, for the first time in what felt like a hundred years, he embraced it.

As Brennachecke was operated on, Jennifer slept soundly in the room next door to him. On the floor above them, Bobby-Leigh sat eating microwave popcorn and feeling like a kid again as she watched one of the last Pixar movies with Anoona's daughter, Mari. At his control center, Tiny monitored the operation now underway downstairs with one eye and the live drone footage with the other. Above them, in the steeple-like kalash that they'd converted into a sniper's crow's nest, Rodney read an old Stephen King paperback and waited. His weapon of choice—a .300 Win Mag sniper rifle outfitted with a tracking point-precision guidance system that broadcast the scope's feed to both his glasses and to one of Tiny's monitors—was leaning against the wall next to him.

This was the calm before the storm. Everybody in the house felt it. Somewhere between them and Vedic City, getting closer every minute, violent winds were blowing toward them.

It was only a matter of time.

Before Jennifer woke up; before the credits rolled on the film Bobby-Leigh and Mari were watching; before Hamm, Anoona, and the makeshift surgical team had patched Brennachecke up enough to risk hoping he'd survive; before Eric was ready to let go of his father's hand; before Rodney finished his chapter, something on one of the drone video feeds caught Tiny's eye.

"That's not good," the fat man said, quickly redirecting all the JLP drones to converge and monitor what had grabbed his attention. As the feeds came in, the bleakness of the situation became clear.

Silhouetted by the lowering sun to the west and steadily rolling over the tracks Jen and Bobby-Leigh had left as they'd dragged their surrogate father on the sled through the snow, the blood pirates were coming.

They marched on foot. They advanced in trucks. They drove enormous tractors retrofitted with crude weapons and dragging trailers of berserkers tied down with chains, chomping at their very real bits to be unleashed. Nearly a thousand strong, an army was descending on the Kessler farm like a plague.

"Fuck me," Tiny whispered to himself. He wasn't sure if Brennachecke would survive an interruption to the operation going on downstairs or not, but he was sure that if he didn't stop it and get everybody battle ready, the rest of them were all going to die.

* * *

Jen's eyes sprang open, but the scream in her throat never made it out. Even before she realized she was awake, the terrible visions that had roused her faded away into the nothing from whence they came. The sun was setting outside the window. The afternoon light was beautiful on the snow, but she wouldn't remember it that way. What she would remember was that the house had been quiet, like it was lying in wait for something, and that no matter how much she tried, she simply hadn't been able to shake the anxiety that had followed her out of the abyss.

The nightmare is over, she would remember thinking as she took a deep breath and smiled, but she'd also remember that it hadn't been a very convincing smile. Nobody had told her yet what was coming, but she hadn't needed anybody to. Even in the void of existence she'd just pulled herself out off, she'd known the truth: all the horrors they'd survived up to now were just the idle daydreams of spoiled children compared to the flesh-and-blood nightmares that were about to come knocking on their door.

Not that most folks would care about what was about to happen on a little farm in a once eccentric little town in the middle of what, once upon a time, was called America. Most folks would find it hard to believe that such a seemingly inconsequential event in the grand scheme of things could matter much at all. But most folks are idiots, which is probably why the world ended in the first place.

Before you go...

PLEASE TAKE THE TIME TO REVIEW THIS BOOK.

Independant authors, such as myself, depend on honest reviews to get the word out about our work. And, opinions from readers like yourself are often some of the most valuable feedback we get. So take five minutes and review this book online. It really does make a difference.

Thank you!

Acknowledgments

This book wouldn't have been possible without the love and support of my family—especially my wife, Josephine, who has graciously listened to me bounce the details around ad nauseam on a daily basis for years now, and my father, Mark, who helped me get the facts about the history of the TM movement in Fairfield and in general right; any mistakes are on me, not him. I also want to acknowledge my mother, Wendy, who steadfastly called me a writer from the beginning, even though it took nearly forty years for me to actually claim the title. A special thank-you goes out to Natan for his insights in flying small planes. Since he actually knows how to fly and I don't, I can assure you any mistakes in this book regarding flying are mine and mine alone. And it goes without saying that this book wouldn't be as good without the hard work of this book's official editor, Jessica, and it's unofficial one, my stepmom, JoAnne. The list of family and friends who have encouraged this endeavor and supported it in one way or another is long.

Thank you all.

I want to take an opportunity to give a shout-out to the Transcendental Meditation movement. My dad taught me TM when I was five years old and while there have been periods in my life when I haven't always been inspired to keep up with the practice, I have always respected it and held on to it, like an ace up my sleeve in the twisted poker game of life.

Now, this is obviously a work of fiction—or at least it should be obvious—and while I've taken care to depict the real places (such as the Raj), public figures (such as Elon Musk), and products (such as Twinkies) with a careful eye for accuracy, there is no getting around the fact that at the end of the day I am making all this up. Nothing written in these pages should be construed as true. No harm, offense, disparagement, or endorsement of anything is intended.

Finally, I'll leave you all with a reminder that if you sign up for my mailing list to be notified when I release new books, you'll get the second book in the long apocalypse for your trouble.

You can sign up at:

http://www.benjaminwilkins.com/list_signup2

Lastly, I want to acknowledge you, readers of this book—fans and haters alike. I am an independent author and your support, interest, and willingness to go on this journey with me and these characters I've created is truly an honor.

See you in the next installment.

About the Author

Benjamin Wilkins worked in the film and television industry in Los Angeles for over a decade and even managed to write, direct, and produce a little no-budget indie feature film entitled Pretty Dead, hailed by Dread Central as "The movie Paranormal Activity should have been: Intelligent, unique and completely enthralling." Then he had a kid and more or less turned his back on the Hollywood scene.

This is his first published novel.

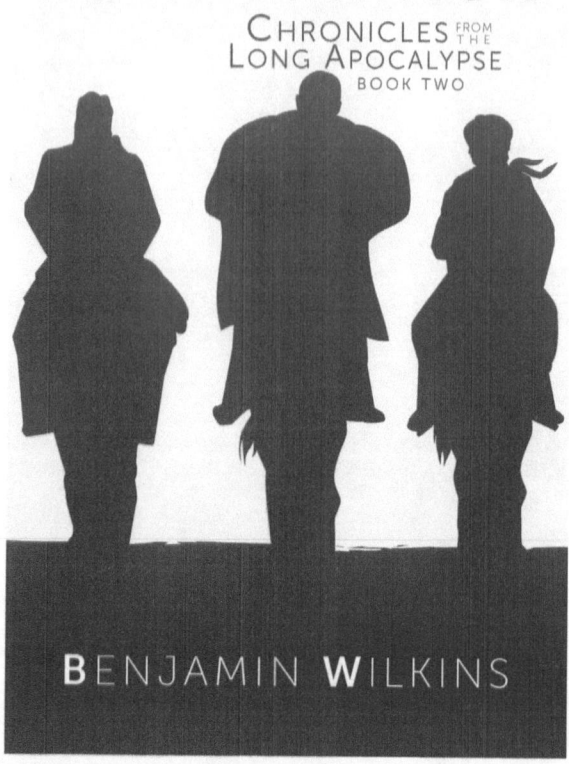

REINCARNATION

CHRONICLES FROM THE
LONG APOCALYPSE
BOOK TWO

BENJAMIN WILKINS

Free Download

Sign up for the author's New Releases mailing list and get a free copy of the second book in the Chronicles from the Long Apocalypse series for your trouble.

Follow the link below to get started:

http://www.benjaminwilkins.com/list_signup2